Nick's Tender Rogue

Naughty Book One

Christine Young

Published by Rogue Phoenix Press, LLP
Copyright © 2022

ISBN: 978-1-62420-708-2

Cover Artist: Designs by Ms G

Editor: Sherry Derr-Wille

Chapter One

London 1837

Bored to tears, Collin McInnis watched his mistress of two months stretch one long leg into the air as she slowly rolled her silk stocking to her thigh. Sabrina Anderson was vain about her legs. Whenever possible, without creating an unsalvageable scandal, she showed them off, a bit of ankle here and there sometimes a *wee* bit higher just for affect. She took this moment to don her second stocking seductively securing the garter. She wanted to induce him to stay the rest of the night. Short of an earthquake, there was nothing she could do to keep him in her bedroom. The need to move on to a different woman clamored in every male part he possessed. The blunt truth, Sabrina wearied him to the brink of tears. She was everything in a woman he loathed. Why he took her as his mistress he would never understand.

Once, this sight would have been enticing, might have kept him for another round of lovemaking. Now, he simply didn't care what she did. Her female body was much the same as any other woman's. She could undress in front of him. Hell, at this moment, she was practically naked. Time to find another beguiling lady was his first and second thoughts. He rarely kept a woman this long. With Sabrina, he didn't understand why he continued to torture himself. Well, a man did need relief, a means to soothe himself after a day's hard work. Fact of the matter was, he had yet to find a replacement for her. Once he did...no, he couldn't stand one more encounter with her.

"You promised to take me to the Montgomerie ball tomorrow night, darling."

She sat back, turned her lips into a thin line, which was her attempt to pout while she pushed out her rather enormous assets. His next mistress would need to have smaller breasts. A man didn't need more than a mouthful to suck and lave with his tongue. Her dark lashes fluttered across alabaster cheeks making a decided contrast. Even a hardened rake like Collin could appreciate a beautiful woman. Sabrina was beautiful. He would give her that. If she had anything except air in her head, he would be surprised. Perhaps his next ladylove would have a brain. He could always hope. He did appreciate intelligence. Until now he never thought about that particular trait in a woman.

He found that odd. A woman's intelligence had never been important to him before, just the ability to give and receive pleasure. Bloody hell, it wasn't now. So, why did he care? Why did the notion of a woman with a smattering of intelligence cross his overtaxed brain?

"Never said I would take you. That was a week ago. Don't know if I've an inclination to attend even with you. Could get yourself there by yourself. The ball is meant to bring out debutantes. Don't have use for beginners. You are the farthest woman from a debutante I've ever known."

A ball was the last place he wanted to be seen or to attend. However, in the midst of the most influential and wealthy patrons of London's upper crust, the fete might be the best place to end this relationship that had lasted too long as it was. Sabrina would be hard pressed to make a scene in front of the discerning eyes of the ton. He wouldn't have to put up with the wretched sobbing along with the wealth of tears he knew would be running down her cheeks if he chose tonight to put a stop to the union that was leaving him drained of energy, exhausted to his very core as well as jaded to his soul. He would have to think of a suitable gift, one that would start the appeasement in lieu of his departure. A diamond necklace might do the trick.

"You're horrible, Collin," she said as she fluttered her dark lashes.

Provocatively, she strode to him. After she knelt beside the couch where he was stretched out, she ran a slender fingertip across his jaw then his lips. Slowly, she formed a path directed toward his male parts. Parts he had no intention of allowing her the use of again tonight or ever.

He held her wrist, tightened his fingers when she continued her journey. "Stop!"

"You're hurting me," she whined pretentiously.

Collin dropped her wrist knowing full well he didn't give her an iota of pain. "I'm not in the mood."

Dropping her hands so they were in front of him, she stared hard at him. "You didn't change your mind," she told him indignantly. "You can't do that. I've made plans. The gown is to be delivered tomorrow morning. I can't possibly go alone. What would people think if you abandoned me?"

Her anger shimmered in her eyes. Once her eyes attracted him, along with her voluptuous body. At this given time, he didn't know what he once saw in her. The affair between them was over. He wished he had the balls to tell her so this instant.

"A promise is a promise. However, when work is involved, I can't be held to higher standards."

He let a loud sigh escape, hoping to signal to her the conversation was over. Sabrina never caught on to not so subtle suggestions. Perhaps she chose to ignore them.

"So, you will take me." She tossed a pillow at him, a grin forming on her delicately pink lips. "Collin, you never listen to me. Even when there is no one else in the room your mind is somewhere else."

Her eagerness appalled him. Well, the devil, she didn't listen to what he told her either. What did he expect? He knew her well enough now to realize she would continue on until she wore him down. Her demands would grow with each of his concessions. He heaved in a long breath of air preparing himself to leave.

No, he wasn't going to take her to the gala. Escorting her would just take too much time and energy. Doing something so stupid would make him obligated to bring her home even if he cried off when they were at the ball. He didn't want another night with her. If she went alone, she would have her carriage at her disposal.

"Didn't promise to take you. Told you I would attend, nothing more."

He lay back, his hands behind his head, staring at the ceiling. If there was something to count, flowers or nicks in the plaster, anything at all, he might be able to keep his temper in check. As it was now, emotions began to ascend to an inferno. The need to remove himself assailed him, posthaste would not be soon enough.

"Collin, darling."

She placed her hands on her long legs, smoothing her fingers along her flesh to the tops of her thighs. She fluttered her sooty lashes several times. Her words strained to a whisper thin tone. "What are you telling me? I now know I will not be pleased with the outcome. You will have to make it up to me. You do understand that. Perhaps a diamond necklace would suffice."

He grinned at her proposal. That was exactly what he had in mind for a parting gift. "Suppose I'll meet you there. Business, you know. Can't neglect building the family fortune now, can I?"

If he got lucky, he might find a widow who was willing or a divorcee for his next mistress. He needed a woman who wouldn't make demands on his time or his patience, who wouldn't expect anything he wasn't willing to give. After he watched Sabrina's hysterics because of her newfound and unwanted freedom, he would need to bury himself in a warm body.

"You cad."

She tossed back her hair, her eyes hardening.

Colin thought the look she shot him to be something close to hatred. Hatred might be the best way to end this fiasco between them. "It's simple, Sabrina. I don't wish to be the first there or the last to leave. You will have to get yourself to the Montgomerie estate all by yourself. I'm sure you can manage to do so with that outlandish carriage of yours. You will also need to find a way to return home without me. My suggestion is that you take that transport of yours. Everyone will know you have arrived. You can be the first as well as the last. That should suit your humors."

By the set of her shoulders along with the way she helped herself to brandy, he could tell her emotions were running the gamut. He also knew she expected a proposal of marriage soon. That wouldn't happen. She should have understood by now he wasn't the marrying kind. He had years before that would be necessary.

"My what?" She rounded on him, a few drops of brandy slipping out of the glass to land on her chemise. She flicked the drops off with the wicked tip of her pointed fingernail. "At least you could look at me when you tell me you're about to break a promise. In any case, I know you well enough. When we are at the ball, you won't pay attention to me, will you? You'll go off, gamble until you've won more than the family fortune you're trying to build. Promise me one dance, Colly. I'll be satisfied with that."

The use of her pet-name for him sent him over the edge. Quickly, he did sit up. Buck-naked. He began to drag his trousers over his hips. He didn't mean to spend any more precious seconds with this female than he was obligated to do. Was surprised he spent the last fifteen minutes with the lady. "I will see you there, Sabrina, not one second before. Might even dance with you once. Wouldn't want tongues to start wagging if we danced more." He slipped his arms into his crisp, white lawn shirt. If he stayed longer, she would continue to nag until he conceded to take her.

As he stood at the door, his back to her, the scent of mint and warm woman assailed his nostrils. The heat of her body pressed softly against his back. She ran her hands along his stomach, lower to find their way between his unfastened pants and bare skin. Sabrina understood what she was about. Stopping her he grasped her hand with his. A month ago, he would have appreciated the gesture. Now, he loathed what she was doing. Escape was the only solution.

"No, Sabrina. I'm not in the mood." The sooner he left the better he would feel. "Going to see what other entertainments I can find this evening. Thought I'd meet up with Percy and Drew. Haven't spent enough time with the lads."

"Jeremy and Black?" she questioned, her voice taking on an indignant air. "If you stayed, we could have more fun," she purred moving her lush rounded globes across his back.

"Not tonight!" He was bone-weary of playing the games she invented. Fresh air would help. Seeing his friends would be even better.

When she stepped back, she appeared different. It was almost as if she began to understand he meant to leave her. "You always spend most of the night with me. Why not now?"

She seemed to question everything.

"I can make your body sing. I'll dance to whatever tune you wish to set."

It was none of her damn business what he did or did not do. Tonight, or any night for that matter. "Yes. Not tonight, Sabrina."

He finished dressing. A few minutes later he stepped out the front door, heard the crash against the wood. He wondered what she pitched at his back. He hoped it wasn't the costly crystal-vase he purchased for her a few weeks ago.

Didn't matter. He was free of her for now. Collin whistled as he strode to his carriage. Having made the decision to retire her from his protection, he felt lighthearted, ready to take on a new adventure. He would find someone else infinitely more suitable than the lovely yet irritating Sabrina.

"The Hound and the Boar's Head Inn," he told his driver.

Sitting back, he closed his eyes for a few minutes while he soaked up all the good feelings rushing through him. It was his favorite dockside tavern. His favorite friends along with his favorite drinks. There were a few women he enjoyed who worked at the inn. What more could a man want? Now, in the mood to talk with male friends who he knew would be drinking a pint or two. Thought maybe he'd find a willing lass who would want a night of pleasure, nothing more. At the moment he was tired of the game he played.

Bored.

Jaded.

Weary of this life. Thought he would return to the highlands. Perhaps he should make arrangements tomorrow before the fete. Going home would be pleasant. A new environment that might suffuse energy into his work-weary body.

It all came back to a healthy dose of tediousness that would send him scurrying for adventure or a good fight. His life was too much the same. One day after the other with no exciting entertainments. A diversion would be nice. The distraction would have to be something more than another woman who was just like all the other women in London.

Did a different type of woman exist? He was hard pressed to

believe so.

Admittedly, he was a good catch. Though he needed to sire an heir, that was years away. Good God, he was only eight and twenty. Plenty of time before he would have to shackle himself to a single woman. What he needed now was a ladybird who would please him, a woman who didn't want his title or his wealth. A woman who wouldn't be expecting a marriage proposal. One who liked adventure would also be nice. A lady who was honest in every way, including her passion. Of course, she still must be beautiful, even ravishing, an intelligent woman if he was building the perfect woman in his mind. Perhaps one who would care more for him than she did for herself. No, a woman such as that would be more than nice. Up to now, he'd never met a woman like he described in his imagination.

To Collin's jaded heart, he didn't believe for a single moment a woman such as that existed. When he stepped inside the tavern, he spotted Jeremy and Percy. Drew should be somewhere about. So should the stuffy Earl of Blackmore, Black they called him. Everyone he met tried to call him Blacky. After the first try when the man's dark blue eyes turned to the darkest navy, no one tried again. Of all of them, Black was the most efficient with weapons, knife, pistol even the bow and arrow. How he learned that was everyone's guess. He showed up in London with his grandfather about fifteen years ago. All kinds of rumors surrounded his name. Some of the buzz suggested he was part Lakota Sioux. Wherever he came from his grandfather, the late Earl of Blackmore, squelched the gossip before the innuendos could take root.

Black wasn't forthcoming. His heritage was anyone's guess. Secrets about him were abundant. The more secretive he was the more rumors flourished.

Percy waved a hand at him, motioning him to join them. He grinned, pleased the men were in attendance. Quickly, he ordered a glass of ale, a basket of cheeses, bread along with different meats. He sat back, hands behind his head, legs stretched out in front of him, as he searched the room. Relaxed, amongst his friends he could be himself. In truth, he wished to find a woman who was more like his friends.

"Thought you were spending time with Sabrina tonight," Jeremy said as he lifted his glass to his lips. "Change your mind about that lady?"

Collin grunted. Jeremy warned him many a time about that woman, as he would call her. Unfortunately, Jeremy was right in his assessment of Sabrina. "For some reason I needed to leave. Didn't want to spend the night with her. Will have to be with the lady too many minutes tomorrow if I can't figure a way out of attending the ball at the Montgomerie's home."

He pulled one of the serving girls toward him. She landed on his lap. His hands circled her waist as he was able to see quite a bit beneath her bodice. Collin wasn't going to air his grievances with anyone, even his best friends. Tonight, he had simple plans, a bit of pleasure, a little bit of willing woman in his arms. He meant to enjoy this evening while he left Sabrina behind. She was no longer anything to him.

"Why, g*ov'nor…*"

Flirtatiously, the girl pushed against him. Her lips were moist, reddened slightly from some form of rouge. She swept the tip of her hot pink tongue across them while she placed her hand on his chest. "Never saw a gent so big and handsome." She wrapped her fingers around his bicep. "Oooo…you're so big. Is all of you…?" The little flirt stared at his crotch when she asked the question. "…so big?"

"Tonight? Upstairs? After work?" Collin asked as he squeezed his hands that circled her waist.

She wasn't refined nor did she put on airs. Her eyes were pretty, her bubbies more than a handful. She would do. The best part…this little gel wasn't going to want anything from him except a good tumble along with a bit of extra coin he'd freely give. She was exactly what he needed as well as wished for tonight. Something to bridge the gap now between his ex and finding a new woman. If she pleased him, he'd come back another time.

"Didn't take you long to find a willing woman," Black said laughing as he sipped his ale. "You do realize, she passed the rest of us by. Guess she didn't think we were big enough." Black looked to Collin's crotch.

"At least certain parts of us," Drew's laughter combined with the other two men.

"Speak for yourself," Percy said, laughter in his words as well. "Mines got to be just as big. If we're all talking about the same part."

"Bite your tongue. She just came downstairs a few seconds ago. I'd be careful with that one," Drew put his opinion into the mix. "She might be looking for more than you're willing to give. Believe she's a new one here. Might be searching for a protector."

"Enough doom and gloom. We all know it never takes him long. One would think with that dark brooding look in those eyes, the ladies would run away from him not to him."

"That's what they find attractive. It's that ever-present scowl. Every woman thinks she can put a smile on his lips," Drew said as he seemed to look over the room.

"I'm sure all of you have a place to go before the night is over. You've your mistresses to visit, I assume," Collin said with a quick chuckle.

He was more than willing to wager all of them had ladies at their beck and call. He was also willing to gamble on that because of his actions just now, they all knew he was about to call it off with Sabrina. Or, he already had.

"Will I see you all at the Montgomerie ball tomorrow night?"

He could hope at least one of his closest friends would attend. It was truly too much to be at the debutante affair by himself. Why he ever agreed to meet Sabrina he couldn't for the life of him fathom. Word had it that Lady Montgomerie agreed to chaperone two of the ladies who would be in attendance.

"God's teeth no," Black said just before the others joined him in their denials. "It's the last place I'd turn up. A debutante ball, you've got to be joking."

"Why would you go there? All the debutantes in attendance merely make a man want to run in the opposite direction. If the debutantes aren't bad enough, there are the mothers to contend with. Bloody eyes, but they can be more aggressive than anyone I've ever encountered."

Collin's shrug was nonchalant even though he didn't feel that way. "Promised Sabrina. What's a poor fellow to do? Did tell her she would have to get there and back on her own. Told me the Duke of

Richmond's ball was where everyone who was anyone would be seen. Don't actually care if I'm seen, however this last time..."

"Well, hells bells," Jeremy said seeming to understand more than he said. "You're going to use the gala to cry off. I see that look in your eyes. Not a bit of guilt, I hope. We're all surprised you lasted this long, old fella. Sabrina is not a lady who is easy on the pocketbook though I've heard she is fairly good in bed."

"Genius," Percy said rubbing his jaw as if he thought about what Collin planned. "If I've ever a need for something like that, I'll have to remember your tactic. The little lady can hardly put up a scene in front of all those people. You will be scot free of her without having to live through her tears along with the hysterics. Can't abide either. Much easier to send them a letter along with a gift."

"No, she wouldn't be showing her true colors at the ball. Gossip would run rampant throughout London. A new protector would be hard to find if she did so. No man wishes to put up with that nonsense when the time is over," Collin said languidly while he sported a huge grin. He didn't have to be told the approach was unmatchable. "Couldn't have found a better time or place, don't you think? I'm bored to tears with her. Shouldn't have kept her so long. Seems I didn't have the energy to fight. Need to be a free man again."

"No prospects on the horizon for the next lady love?" Black asked blandly as he toyed with a piece of bread.

"Tonight I'm not going to worry over what will happen after the ball. This evening I'm going to enjoy the little miss along with her bountiful curves. The one who was nestled against me a few minutes ago. What about the rest of you?"

"Same as you," Percy and Jeremy agreed.

"Got a rendezvous planned with a gal," Percy went on to say. "So does Jeremy."

As his friends left to go their separate ways, Collin sat back, relaxed for the first time since he took on Sabrina as his mistress. His friends warned him about her. At the time, however, he'd been enamored of her long white legs. Before he actually made love to her, all he could think about was the length wrapped around his flanks. One thought about her personality never crossed his mind. Nor did the fact she was a demanding puss. It seemed to Collin nothing he did was ever good enough for her.

Sabrina was a widow. Her first marriage was to a man much older, ended quickly with his death. The lady could not have been happy with an old man for a lover. After the obligatory mourning time, she set off to make use of the wasted years she spent in not so blissful wedlock. He'd been her second conquest. The first protector lasted less than two weeks. Black, along with the others, warned him he should take stock of all the facts before he set about supporting another mistress.

After his first sexual encounter with the spicy lady, he wasn't ready to let go of what she had to offer. Sabrina knew how to do things other women did not. In the beginning, her aggressiveness pleased him, until she took the aggression too far. Collin wasn't about to be controlled by anyone, let alone a woman. Too many times, she took it upon herself to dictate the terms of their relationship.

"I'm through with work."

The young lady stood in front of him her hands clasped beneath her chin, her breasts so lush they spilled from her gown to a point where he could almost see the rouged tips. When he looked into her eyes, he read the passion, the desire she made no effort to hide from him.

She wanted him.

Collin jumped, startled as the lady sat on his lap, slipping her hands around his neck, pushing herself against him as if she had to do so. He'd been lost in thought. God's teeth he was strung tight. She purred, touched his earlobe with the tip of her tongue. She laughed heartily when her hand rubbed against his erection. Bloody hell, he wasn't sure he wanted someone who pursued him so hotly. He just got rid of one such lady.

"See you're ready," she purred as she rubbed the tops of her rounded breasts across his mouth. He scented hot willingness a woman who would hold nothing back. Earlier, he thought that was exactly what he needed.

"Are you?" she squeezed.

"If I'm not now, I will be in the next second."

Slipping her hand inside his trousers, "Oooh, lovey, I think you're ready now."

~ * ~

Nickie Gray sat on the outside patio at the Duke of Richmond's stylish country residence. Ella, the duke's wife, along with several of her other London aunties were visiting. The husbands were due back soon. They'd been out riding. The children were off somewhere with their nanny. Nickie wasn't exactly sure where. Certainly, she would rather play with the children than try to assume a role she didn't want to be part of.

"This is so exciting," Piper, the daughter of 'The' notorious 'Duchess' who ruled the London aristocracy with knowledge of their secrets until her death two years prior said.

Piper was kidnapped by her uncle when she was a wee thing. Spent her life in the bowels of London, St James Parish to be exact, learning how to pick pockets. The Duchess didn't discover her daughter until late in her life.

"For you. Not for me," Nickie Gray said dejectedly.

Her heart just wasn't in this. All she wanted was to go home, back to McClellan lands where she could be free again. "The ball is the last place I want to be tomorrow night. Being presented in front of a bunch of simpering court dandies does not please me. If I wanted to marry, which I don't, I'd want a real man, one who doesn't need to pad his shoulders or leg muscles with sawdust to appear bigger than they are."

She did have an image of the perfect man in her head. The image sent little thrills of delight through her. If only she could find him.

"I understand," Ella, Drake Montgomerie's wife, bent forward patting her on the hand. "Felt the same way when I was forced to my first ball. The first dance—I found the man of my fondest imaginations when he asked to dance with me. Was sure Aunty Charlotte was going to make me tell him no. I think she knew then he was a rake with every intention of compromising me. Everyone here knows the end to that story. He wasn't the least bit remorseful when he did so. The fact is neither was I. We both got exactly what we wanted."

"You got lucky," Nickie shot back quickly understanding that wasn't true in every case. "You only had to attend one gala affair. Who's to say I have your luck. In any case it doesn't matter. Not getting married to anyone."

Would rather take a lover. *Wouldn't be saddled with the man for the rest of my life if I made a bad choice.* Nickie crossed her arms over her chest in defiance. She wasn't about to cooperate. She also didn't understand where the rebelliousness came from. Her parents were exhaustingly happy. They sent her to London to find a man she could love for the rest of her life.

No one would want her. She would end up sitting in a corner throughout the hours until the ball ended. It was her intention to slip away as soon as she could so she could go riding. If she had her preference, she would stay behind any potted palm she could find. The sunrise was gorgeous over the lake near the estate. In any case, her appearance was not fashionable as her body didn't possess the requisite curves. She was reed thin, too thin, taller than all her friends. Her brother, Colby, never failed to tease her about her figure said she had no bubbies to speak of then he would taunt her that when she got older, she might have something a man could appreciate. Bloody eyes, she was twenty. How old did she have to get to possess bubbies a man would want to hold and to taste? All the young ladies she met since coming to London were filled out in all the right places. Everyone except for her.

"Your gown is beautiful, Nickie." Ella smiled at her as she poured tea for everyone. "Cream or lemon?"

"Both. If your seamstress doesn't take the corsage in, anyone looking will be able to see all the way to my navel," Nickie said wishing for a different gown one that didn't reveal so much of her. She didn't understand how the seamstress got her measurements so wrong.

Actually, she wished for a pair of trousers along with a nice white shirt that laced in front. She recalled so vividly all the days she ran through the forest surrounding her home. Remembered how every once in a blue moon she could sneak to the island close to the castle. Most of the time one of her father's men would be close behind guarding her. When they were newlywed, Hunter Gray, her father, made his wife promise she would never go to the island without him. That was when her mother was younger. Seemed she almost drowned rescuing a kitten. If not for Hunter realizing what she was up to, Allura might have died that night.

Needless to say, she never promised such an outlandish thing to her father. A vow would have made her feel guilty about her exploits. To her way of thinking, it didn't seem her father meant to make his girls promise not to go to the island. Making them promise something so ludicrous was far too difficult when her brother got to do whatever he pleased. She wasn't about to make assurances to any man, especially the one to obey. She was her own woman. She would do exactly as she pleased with her life with no man's interference.

"Relax, dear. Your dress will be perfect. My seamstress, although new to me, has credentials that surpass anyone else in town," Ella tried to reassure while sipping her tea. "You know you will have fun when you actually get to dance with a nice young man. There will be too many to choose from. What you have to do is make sure you don't dance with any gentleman more than once. It is far too early in the season to make a commitment to one fellow. Remember, dear, I'll be there with my cane just in case a young man is taking unwanted liberties."

All in this room recalled what the original duchess did with that cane. She would wrap them on the back if they took wanted or unwanted liberties. Ella's husband received more than one tap to remind him he was not acting the gentleman where Ella was concerned. Drake never did act in that manner. He always did as he pleased. Although he did make a few concessions where Ella was concerned.

"Have two left feet as you well know. No man is going to ask me to dance let alone take liberties, wanted or unwanted when they know I'll be stepping on their feet all night and you'll be whacking them with that blasted cane of yours," Nickie muttered with the hint of a tiny smile. After all, Aunt Ella's cane was exactly what she needed to keep unwanted suitors at bay. "Rather go riding than dance; rather fish than play parlor games with the dandies. If I were to want a man, he would be dashing and strong. Would be taller than my father as well as stronger. He would like adventures. Gambling along with drinking would be a rare occurrence. Also," she paused in thought while she toyed with more characteristics she sought in a man. "This is the most important. He wouldn't take a mistress. Would want only me. Doesn't matter anyway. I'm not the marrying kind. I won't be tied down to a male, subject to his whims or anything else a man might think up."

"That's quite a wish list of prerequisites for the man in your dreams," Piper put in her thoughts before she questioned further. "What about love? Isn't that important enough to be part of your list?" With a gesture around the room encompassing all the ladies sitting on the patio. "We've all found love, our hearts desire. You can too. When you least expect to see that man you described, he'll be there all smiles waiting for you."

"You must keep an open mind, dear. If you don't, this trip to London will be wasted," Ella said, her voice soft. "Your mother and father might send you back for a second season. That would certainly be appalling. They want to see you happy. I know your mother wants you to find your own true love."

A second season?

Impossible.

Never! I would do everything in my power to avoid something so awful. I don't care what it would take.

Nickie didn't know how to respond. She would keep an open mind the best she could. An open mind wouldn't change her feelings about wedded bliss. Truth was she shouldn't need to feel that way. Didn't understand why she did. Her parents along with all her uncles and aunts were happy. It was just there was no one she'd ever met that interested her in any way, no one she wanted to kiss her. For so long she felt different, too different to fit in. She wasn't like her cousins or the other girls of her acquaintance.

The young men in the village teased her, just as her brother did. At one time, she hoped Colby would understand, would put a stop to the jests. In his defense this last year, he did try. Now the boys only taunted her about her skinny body and only when Colby was nowhere to be found.

"Is anyone else coming?" Cat waltzed into the room, her violin case in hand. Cat had wed Roc the son of 'The' notorious 'Duchess'. She was a duchess in her own right. Roc was the duke of Ravenswood.

From all she heard, Ella Montgomerie was taking over the role of The Duchess including the tap, tap, tapping of the cane even though Ella didn't need a cane to walk, along with serving the traditional lemon bars Aunty Charlotte was known for. With her husband's connections, she had details on almost every aristocrat in London as well as the surrounding cities. In many ways because of her husband's connection, she was more powerful than the original duchess.

"You're going to play and dance for us?" Ella laughed, clapping her hands together. "It's always so enjoyable when you do. A lively tune always lifts one's spirits. I've never actually understood how you are so very talented."

"All of you know I can't go anywhere without my fiddle. It seems to be as much a part of me as my arms and legs." Cat pulled out the instrument before setting it atop the case. "Don't know I'll perform. Ella asked me to play a tune or two at the ball. Roc would rather I save all that entertainment for him. He agreed though grudgingly. My husband can be a real spoil sport when he sets his mind to it. If he had his way, I would never leave the bed or the house." With that said, she smiled dreamily.

"Roc's always been the jealous type," Piper laughed, her eyes shining with merriment, as it seemed she thought about her brother. "You must play. It will be so much fun. It's just so amazing the way you can actually play that thing, let alone dance with the fiddle atop your shoulder. I'll never forget the first time I watched you. Found myself mesmerized."

"Inherited the ability from my mum although I never saw her, never met her. She died when I was born."

Momentarily Piper's lips turned down.

"I wish I could have known her. I look just like her. At least that's what everyone who knew her says."

Cat never knew her mother. Roc found her in a pub in Ireland, immediately falling in love with her. He always told her it was love at first sight. For herself Nickie didn't believe in such fairytales. In her life there would never be love at first sight. She didn't expect a man to ever have those sentiments concerning her. Her mother never understood why she was so insecure. That insecurity was part of the reason Allura and Hunter sent her to London to have a season. Bottom line, she didn't want to be a debutante. There was nothing new about her.

They believed the experience would be good for her.

Ha!

Two years ago, her heart changed when she was cornered by a visiting dignitary. A man who thought any woman he chose was his for the taking. Colby found them before he could take anything from her that she wasn't willing to give. Nickie realized that day she didn't like the way it felt for a man to put his lips on hers. Never wanted to chance another kiss. Time and again her brother assured her the right man's mouth on hers would not be like that revulsion she felt. She wasn't sure she believed him even though she wanted to.

Perhaps if she met the right man as he said the caress would be different.

See, I do have an open mind. Her gaze turned to Ella as if the woman might be able to read her thoughts.

"Your head is in the clouds, Nickie Gray. Are you having a change of heart? Thinking about dancing the night away? Of discovering a handsome beau to give your love to? I absolutely hope you are doing just that."

Piper's eyes went all dreamy as if she was remembering the time she met her beloved Scottish highlander, Brett MacLachlan.

With this conversation, it seemed to Nickie all her auntie's eyes were dreamy.

"No, no change of heart. I *dinna* want to find a beau who's a dandy with no muscles, only padding. Does any other type of man attend the galas? I think not. From what I've heard all the best men stay away. They can't abide the simpering debutantes along with their adoring mamas."

"Rakes as well as the bounders rarely show their faces," Ella told her as once again her eyes turned dreamy.

Rakes and bounders were probably the only men who weren't dandies with no backbone. Numerous times she heard Colby referred to as a bounder. She knew he loved women...all of them. Didn't think he ever took advantage of a woman. Knew for certain, he kept away from innocent *lasses*.

Thinking once more about the ball, Nickie wasn't about to tell them how she would sneak away as soon as she could find an opening. She would do so the moment Ella wasn't watching. She yearned to watch the sunrise over the lake near the country estate. The sight reminded her of home. Most likely as soon as Ella and Drake retired for the evening, she could slip from the house. So far Ella was not an imposing chaperone. She talked a great deal about how strict she would be along with the rules she would enforce. That fact remained to be seen. Nickie often wondered if she would wrap a man on the back to stop him from kissing one of her charges. She knew that task would not be necessary for her. No man would attempt to steal a kiss from her. They would never find her attractive.

Ella told her kissing was fine. It was the other places a man's hands roamed that she would have to be careful about. Told her also it would be difficult once she allowed any intimacy at all. If it was the right man for her, she might not have the will to tell him no.

Alma, Ella's lady's maid, brought out a tray of lemon bars along with more tea. Ella rescued Alma from a brothel. That night Alma helped her escape evil men who hated her husband and wanted revenge meant to sell her into slavery. Instead of waiting to be rescued, Ella with the help of Alma, saved herself. It was a tale she heard numerous times.

"All our men are the jealous type. You should see the way Drake's eyes narrow if he sees me speaking with another man. Why, if looks could kill…"

Ella rearranged her skirts, her lashes lowered momentarily.

"We are talking about possessiveness?" Addie stepped onto the patio with a wink coupled with a grin. "No man is as bad as my Hamilton."

Addie was an aunt simply because she became part of the family when she along with her husband, Hamilton, rescued another aunt, Tavia, one of the twins. A rejected suitor of Tavia's dumped Tavia, with her husband James, into the Tames with the intention of murder.

"Don't know one man who isn't possessive of their lady," Piper spoke softly. "My Brett seemed to be domineering from the first moment he realized I wasn't a boy but a young lady. I attacked him with a butcher knife to keep him from watching me undress. Of course he thought I was a lad. Believed also I was being a bit foolish with the missish airs."

Cat agreed as she nodded her head. "Think Roc is the worst of all of our husbands. Even with a bodyguard he won't allow me to play and dance unless he has time to make room in his busy schedule to attend the event. The tavern where I play is in a fairly good part of town. Roc certainly has enough men at his disposal to keep me secure as well as safe when I perform. Nothing will happen. He understands that. Still, he refuses to give in to my wishes."

Ella looked to the doorway, "Oh, my, there he is now."

Ella stood, her hands stretched out to welcome her husband. He kissed her. Even in front of all the other ladies, his kiss was far from chaste.

Nickie watched as her aunty melted in the man's arms. It was obvious how her knees seemed to grow weak. Heard a soft moan that was recognizable pleasure. His big hands drifted to a spot that was far from appropriate amidst company. Ella tugged them to her waist before she pushed away, her cheeks flaming.

"Stop that, Drake Montgomerie!" She poked him on the chest. "You know better than to do be so brazen. As you well know, we've company. There is a young woman present. You need to set an example," After a short pause when she heard him chuckle. "A good example, not a bad one."

He bobbed his head, grinning wickedly. "I'm sure she has seen her mother and father kissing before this. Probably other things too, if I know Hunter Gray. If you haven't forgotten, we all know the man. Besides..." It appeared he meant to defend his actions. "There was nothing wrong with my actions, a loving husband greeting his wife after a long hard day of work," he said blandly as he smiled at her his eyes alight with humor, "is entitled to a kiss or more if he so chooses."

Blatantly, Nickie grinned back at the two of them. Her mother always blushed when caught in such a pose with Hunter. "True enough. It was the hand though…"

"Ah, so you noticed. Something else I'm sure you've seen before," Drake said, his soft chuckle turning into a hoot of full-blown laughter. He ran his knuckles down his wife's heated cheeks, kissed her nose.

Ella looked as if she wanted to poke her husband in the chest again or perhaps toss something hard at him. "That's just what I'm talking about. Our young charge is going to believe it's acceptable for her beau to touch her like that. You don't want her acting…"

It seemed he realized the truth of Ella's words. Before he spoke, Drake let out a loud woosh of air. "Bloody hell! Don't think I'm cut out to be a chaperone."

"Most likely that is true," Piper laughed out right. "That's why your wife is going to assume the major duties. You both realize Lyssa Andrews will arrive in less than two weeks. You've got to be ready for her as well. Two charges will obviously be twice the responsibility. We will all have to be on our toes."

Drake groaned softly. His look of chagrin sent a sparkle of amusement Ella's way. "Tell me again why you volunteered for this duty?"

"The girls need someone older and wiser as well as experienced to guide them," Ella told her husband, sweetly smiling, seeming to wait for his comment.

"You, my love, are still an innocent. You've no idea about the wicked ways of this world along with the scope of lecherous men inhabiting the streets of London." He brought her hand to his lips, kissed the back. "I've protected you from the worst," Drake said, his smug expression telling Nickie a tale that would sound pretty much like the one her father would tell her mother.

"True," Cat said agreeing with Ella and Drake, "Just as Roc could never chaperone a young woman." Cat picked up her fiddle and began tuning the instrument before placing the instrument on her shoulder. The jingle she played was lively as she danced, twirling around the room.

Nickie had never watched her perform before. What she did was certainly a presentation to remember, entertainment at its finest. She heard stories of her playing in a pub here in London. Once a month Roc would allow her to play. The patrons loved her. Tickets were sold days before. Cat was so popular she drew packed crowds. Many waited in lines for their turn to watch the nimble lady.

The scene between Ella and Drake reminded her of her mother and father whenever Hunter could steal a kiss from Allura. Thoughts that something like what she saw in front of her could ever be hers seemed irrational at times. Still, that first contact with a man wasn't something she wanted to experience again.

At that idea shuffling through her brain, she decided she would open herself to a kiss or two if the man attracted her. If he was handsome and *braw*, she would give over to his teachings. Marriage was still out of the question for more than one reason, one being that she didn't want to be controlled or dictated to by a man. Nickie toyed with idea of taking a lover. Oh, she wouldn't be like her brother who dallied with just about any willing skirt he found. No, one man was enough for her. He would be her lover for as long as she wanted him. After that she would look to someone different. If a man could do so, why couldn't she?

Seemed logical to her.

She understood just how vehemently her entire family would protest, didn't believe they could force her to wed. The thought made her blanch. Could they?

After all, it was the nineteenth century. The man involved, well, they would both have to agree to such foolishness. She would never do such a thing. Never say "I do" unless that was what she wished.

Nickie supposed it wasn't a concept she should indulge to anyone in this room. No, even her brother shouldn't hear what she was thinking. He would protest, try to talk her out of the scheme.

Drake poured a brandy for himself. When he saw Roc saunter into the room, he filled another glass. Roc's gaze remained on Cat until she danced too close to him. When she found herself in arm's reach, his hand snaked out, grabbing her around the waist, his grin self-satisfied and wolfish.

"Roc, stop!" Cat laughed, her protest landing on deaf ears. She had to let her fiddle fall to her side.

"Bloody hell! Stop? Never. I want you, Cat. When I see you, can't keep my hands to myself. Don't want to bother with the strain of resisting your sweet charms. It's too exhausting to do so."

He pulled her close for a long lingering kiss, a deep heated kiss that seemed to Nickie too intimate for this setting.

At Cat's look of chagrin when he finally let go of her, Nickie laughed. Her uncles were all irredeemable rakes as well as hopeless when it came to their respective wives. They did as they pleased, when they wished. All were larger than most men both physically as well as in the way they managed their lives, confidence exuded through every pore. All had soft spots for their wives. She realized, suddenly, this was what true love was about. These men would lay down their lives if necessary for the women they loved.

If she found someone like that…the notion left her breathless, her blood pulsing heatedly through her body.

The only husband missing now was Brett MacLachlan, Piper's husband. Nickie supposed he would be here later. With his appearance she would be treated to another round of kissing. The idea she would never experience something so earth-shattering and poignant left her desolate, wishing for a man who would be hers.

With Ella secured on Drake's lap, his hand running the length of her arm, he asked. "Any of those bounders going to show up at the ball?"

"You speaking of Percy and Drew?" Cat asked sweetly.

To Nickie it seemed she knew something about the pair.

"They are regulars the nights I play at the pub. One time only, Percy thought to seduce me. Once only, Roc punched him. The poor man hit the floor hard, rubbing his jaw. The man never tried again."

"They declined the invitation I sent," Ella told him, directing her attention toward Nickie. "That doesn't mean something might provoke them to turn up. They are two of the most notorious rakes in the town along with Collin McInnis as well as with the stuffy earl who goes by the name of Black."

"He has the blackest hair and the darkest blue eyes I've ever seen. Is a loner, rarely comes to the balls and fetes. Keeps to himself with the exception of his closest friends. He's extremely tall, not as broad as McInnis," Piper mused thoughtfully to receive a sour look from Brett who just joined them. Smiling thoughtfully, her gaze riveted on her husband. "He's not nearly so handsome as you darling."

"Those are the words I was looking for," Brett grinned before

Christine Young

pulling Piper into his arms for another kiss, much like the other uncles who arrived before him.

Drake shot her a look, a scowl telling her she should listen to well-meaning advice. The look wasn't too far from the ones her father sent her when he tried to make a point. "Stay away from those four. They are nothing but trouble."

Her uncle didn't know it yet. Without realizing what he did, he sent her a challenge she intended to meet head-on. There was something about the way he said the words, not so much what he said that had her wanting to find out what had her uncle warning her away from the men. If she got the chance, she would discover why these particular males were taboo. All her uncles were considered rakes at one time. She once heard that reformed rakes make the best husbands. Ah, but she didn't intend to wed.

Shortly after midnight she retired, bent on rising early enough to watch the sunrise. When she woke the next morning, the day of the ball, the time was well past sunrise. She would have to try tomorrow.

In fact, the hustle and bustle surrounding her unnerved her, stripped her nerves raw. Preparations for the party were already blossoming. Maids chattered. Bathwater was brought to her room. She heard the maids discussing several guests. More debutantes undoubtedly would arrive today. Some would stay the night.

Her stomach coiled. The need to run assailed her. In order to ward off the chills, she closed her eyes. Nothing helped the nervous tension ricocheting through her entire body before settling in her belly. It seemed from the top of her head to the very tips of her toes, she shook.

Nickie had to see Colby. He was the only person who would understand how she felt. Last night he rode to the townhouse in the city he purchased on their arrival. By carriage the journey would only take thirty minutes. If she hurried up, she might have time before this ridiculous coming out to reach him. The need to convince him, to take her home shuffled through her.

Ella was in her room, the dress she was to wear over her arm. "It's lovely. Suits your coloring. Undoubtedly, you will be the most beautiful debutant at the gala."

She'd asked for something dark and somber to suit the occasion along with her mood. This gown was eggshell blue with delicate lace trimming. The bodice was cut lower than anything she owned before. Ella assured her the corsage was in the height of fashion. Guaranteed her too that it was not too low for a debutante. Blast all things debutante. At twenty she could hardly be considered a beginner at anything.

Except love.

She had no experience with love or the carnal delights she heard Colby talking about when he didn't know she could hear. He would have fits if he ever discovered that truth. With an older brother, she didn't suppose she could possibly be that innocent.

Nickie meant to remedy her inexperience with the first man who attracted her, the first man who could make her heart dance and speed faster than lightening. Once she was no longer innocent, she would also no longer be an eligible catch to the wealthy aristocrats who frequented these traditions. No one would allow her to be part of the ritual that the wealthy seemed to need in order for their young ladies to find husbands.

She had to remind herself she didn't want to find a husband.

Unless that husband was like her father and her uncles.

When she finished with everything, she sought out Ella, her breath held hoping her aunt would allow her this one concession.

"Aunty…"

The way her voice wavered annoyed her. Confidence here was the key to achieving her goals. If she acted as if she wasn't sure of herself or her intentions, Ella was certain to tell her no.

"My, you're beautiful tonight." Ella seemed to be staring at her bodice, frowning. Her forehead creased with concern, "We have to fix that before we do anything else. It seems the dress maker didn't receive the note I sent her."

"Oh," Nickie followed her gaze. She'd been in such a rush. She didn't notice the way the top gaped open. "I can't be seen like this. How on earth can we fix it now? Don't know about you. I can't sew a straight stitch to save my soul."

If she couldn't go to the ball, that would suit her just fine. If Ella wouldn't allow her to see her brother, that was bad. Tears stung her eyes, dotted her lashes.

"What is it, Nickie? Nothing to cry over. I can fix this with a few strategically placed scarves. We might even use a couple to fill out the bodice. No one will notice. You will look more curvaceous. The sight should please you."

That would be a lie. She didn't want to advertise something she didn't have. Fact of the matter was she was pancake flat. Pretending she wasn't didn't suit. Nor did she care that men liked women with large breasts, all the better for her.

When Ella finished her new creation, Nickie actually looked as if she possessed breasts. She turned sideways to examine her new shape more thoroughly. "What if they slip out? The scarves..." That was a disaster she didn't want to contemplate.

"Be careful when you dance. Don't move too fast. They won't slip, I promise you. They wouldn't dare," Ella grinned as she stepped back to survey her seemingly from head to toe. "Now, what brings you here a few hours before the ball dressed and ready? It wasn't the gown since you didn't know anything was wrong with the bodice." Ella tapped her fingers on the armrest of the chair where she sat.

Suddenly, Nickie found herself breathless, her heart chattering nonstop beneath her ribs, terrified Ella would say no, "I have to see Colby. Have to talk to him tonight. It can't wait."

After going through the preparations for this evening she realized more pointedly than before that she didn't belong. She had to go home.

"Whatever for? The ball is only a few hours away."

"Just know I have to talk to him. I'll come right back. You'll see. I won't miss anything important."

"So, the reason is too personal for you to tell me?" One eyebrow rose a fraction as Ella studied her fingernails. Then with a long swish of air as if she didn't want to give permission, she studied her one more time. "We don't have an available carriage. If seeing your brother is that important to you, I'll see if Sabrina Anderson's coach is accessible for you. It's an outlandish sight. I wouldn't wish my worst enemy be caught dead in it. However, I will ask. If she is agreeable, you can go speak with Colby. I do, though, want a promise you will return in a timely fashion."

"Oh!" Nickie grabbed Ella's hands. "I will, I will, I will." She was thrilled her quest went off without a hitch.

A few minutes later, Nickie was happily ensconced in Sabrina's carriage on her way to her brother's townhouse in London. She closed her eyes listening to the rolling wheels. With each passing mile, she realized she would be able to go home soon. It was what she wanted.

Wasn't it?"

~ * ~

"God's teeth, she's moved on already. Whose townhouse is she at? Don't recognize it." Collin laughed hard, relieved there would be no scene after all. He now held irrefutable proof of Sabrina's infidelity in his hands. The advantage was his. There would be no diamond necklace for Sabina. He savored the moment. There was no mistaking that carriage. Only one of its kind existed in the world. No one save Sabrina would dare be seen in that monstrosity. The main body had been painted bright pink, the trim green. Ornate flecks of gold occurred haphazardly along the main body. The coach was pulled by two perfectly matched horses. The cattle were the only part of the scenario that wasn't garish.

When Collin drew abreast of the transport, he saw a young man still in his dressing gown and trousers holding Sabrina's hands. He was smiling besotted at Sabrina. Her back was to him, dressed in a long cape, the hood pulled over her head. A few seconds later the man hugged her. Stepping back, he shook his head then kissed her on the cheek. The man turned striding into the home. Sabrina stared at his back unmoving. It didn't seem to Collin she was in any hurry to climb inside the vehicle.

This was exactly what he needed. The plan formed unexpectedly in his head. He chortled, pleased with himself.

"Don't like what you're thinking," Drew said blandly as his horse sidestepped. "Should have found a willing *lass* somewhere like I said. You can't just haul her off as if she's a sack of grain. Though she might deserve something like that. You'll miss the perfect opportunity to toss her faithlessness in her small yet beguiling face."

Drew's thoughts were too close to his own. Collin didn't want to admit to anything, even to his friend. "You don't know what I'm thinking. However, I do guarantee that you won't like what I've planned for the little lady, treacherous that she is. Doesn't matter to me. If she's going to cry off before me, I'll have my fun with her now."

He knew exactly what he meant to do. He would get his pound of flesh, maybe more before this little dance she was playing was over.

"Don't want to be a part of this," Drew said even while he was laughing. "Don't want to know what you have planned. See you later at the tavern if you can manage to escape her clutches."

"Oh, I'll be there. You can count on that."

His scheme was now coming together one little detail at a time. What Drew didn't know was that his words were the beginning of his strategy.

Collin turned his horse around before waiting until the young man left the scene. He then spurred his horse forward. He drew up next to her cloaked form, nodded at the coach driver who he knew very well. I'll make sure she gets to the ball. He would, too, though not when she wanted to be there. With expertise honed over the years in the highlands, he swooped Sabrina onto the horse, undid his pristine cravat, then wrapped the fabric around her mouth so she couldn't yell then settled her stomach side down across his lap.

"I will see her home," Collin told the man as he grinned, delighted so far with this adventure. He was well pleased.

"She's planning to stay the night at the Montgomerie's estate," her driver told him.

That was information he needed. "You should plan on getting her in the morning as scheduled then."

Having known the woman intimately for two months, he settled his hand on her rear, squeezed, grinned at her gasp of seeming outrage coupled with the bucking of her hips. Sabrina was never outraged at sexual contact. This was a new side to her as she wiggled tying to dislodge herself. He did enjoy a good tussle. Before this night ended, they would have their last argument as he would make sure she found her way to the ball when the last notes were heard. For all he cared, she could stay the week as long as she understood the status of their relationship.

"Hold still," he chuckled while she strained to rear up trying to see. "Don't want you to fall off, now do we?" He slipped his hand along the outside of her naked leg. Heard the gasp as he found silken flesh. She was making noises. He imagined the screams of outrage when she discovered what he intended. Ah, well, he wouldn't stay around to hear them.

He needed to confront her even if it was just a few pointed words. "So, my sweet disloyal mistress, you thought to cry off. Another protector so soon, Sabrina? That was not well done of you or did you read my mind? Did you think to find a new protector as well as receive a diamond necklace from me?"

He cocked one eyebrow thinking of the young pup he saw her with. Collin wondered if the young'un had any whiskers yet. His chuckle reverberated all the way to his belly. "You're picking them younger and younger these days. Does he expect you to teach him a thing or two about the finer art of making love? You are experienced. Perhaps you are teaching the boy."

Again, she wiggled her bottom across his hand, reared up as if she meant to search for something. Her cloak as well as her hood covered her head. All she'd be able to see would be the cobblestones below. This scenario was just too good to be true. He'd done her in. The task so easy it was child's play.

He grinned. Sabrina was exactly where he wanted her. It seemed she failed to accept her plight. She struggled so hard that she moved downward. Her path could result in an injury. That wasn't what he wanted. "Hold still. You might slip off if you keep squirming. Don't want you hurt."

No, all he wished was for her to miss the ball. Wanted her to understand he would no longer be her protector. After all, she found her next paramour. He had no more obligations or responsibilities where she was concerned. This was a good day, a very good day in deed.

Feeling better than he had in a long time, he spurred his horse toward his townhouse going over in his head exactly how he would handle this delicate situation. The few miles sped by while his mind did the same. By the second his grin grew larger. Pulling up, he flipped his reigns over the post, tossed Sabrina across his shoulder then two stepped it to the third floor.

His butler, Charley, stood behind him. He was grizzled with age, his nose bulbous, his cheeks red. Collin found him in the streets of Inverness about ten years ago. The man had been shanghaied several years before. Now, all he needed was a job that would secure a roof over his head along with a full belly. The man escaped his captivity somehow. Charley didn't want to talk about what happened. Since that fateful night, Charley never disappointed him. He was true-blue loyal. He wouldn't question or judge him about this. No, his butler would accept whatever he chose to do.

Collin meant to lock her in the room until he returned for her. "Let her yell her head off. I want her right where I put her when I get home. She'll try to finagle a way out of the room. Don't let her. Don't feel sorry for her. The two of us have a myriad of things to talk about. She'll be madder than a hornet. Just leave her be no matter what she yells or tries to tell you."

"Sir, I…"

He lifted an eyebrow surprised at the man's questioning glance. It was the first ever. "Sabrina will yell, you can count on it. No matter what she tells you, don't let her out," Collin repeated himself.

Without a second look, Collin tossed her onto the bed in the third story room, her hood still over her face. He locked the door. Whistling, he set off for the Montgomerie ball. He found this night was becoming more enjoyable with each passing moment. He could hardly wait to visit with her again.

He wanted to see the look on her face when he returned well after the hour. Confronting her with her new love, first on his list in about five hours from now. Pleased, he wouldn't feel obliged to give her parting gifts. She managed to burn her bridges quite effortlessly. Even if she begged, he now had the ammunition to do whatever pleased him.

When he entered the ball, he nodded to Ella then spoke a moment with Drake. He made his way toward one of the tables laid out with food. There were two large ballrooms. With his hands clasped behind his back he went in search of dance partners. One of his earlier mistresses willingly obliged.

"Miriam," he nodded, "how have you been?"

She laughed softly tapping him on his shoulder with her fan. "Small talk, Collin. Do you care how I've been? I doubt it."

"Of course, I care, sweet. We spent some enjoyable nights together. I would never wish you ill. Have only your happiness at heart."

She was correct though. Sincerely, he didn't have one reason to care how she was doing. Heard she wed a while back.

"I married or did you not hear?" she told him nicely. "You don't have to pretend, Collin. You never did have any concerns for me except for the pleasure we gave and received. You were a good lover. For the weeks it lasted, I appreciated you."

He whirled around while he thought on Sabrina locked in the third floor. He spied another acquaintance, intending to dance with the woman when this tune ended. "How jaded you've become, my dear."

"You think?" One of her finely sculpted eyebrows arched with sarcasm.

"Not pretending, Miriam. Hope you are happy. Is the man rich as Midas? Did you acquire a title along with the marriage?"

"Both," she laughed softly again. "It's exactly what a woman of my status would wish to happen. For the rest of my life, I've nothing to worry about. When he passes on, I'll be left with a small fortune even though his children contest the will. The earl won't budge simply because I will continue to give him whatever he asks for. I please him."

"Bloody hell!"

Collin didn't believe what was right in front of him. He stopped, Miriam running into him. Under his breath, he cursed, continued to swear as he watched the apparition directly across the room.

Sabrina whirled around the dance floor. She was smiling. Her head tilted sideways in what Collin knew first hand was her seductive ploy. He watched as she slowly lowered her lashes to lift them a second later as she flirted with her dance partner. His gut rolled. Who the hell did he have locked in the third-floor bedroom? Who would be in Sabrina's carriage besides the lady herself?

Sabrina is here.

At the ball.

Who did I toss in his third-floor bedroom?

His gut curdled.

"What's wrong?" Miriam asked thoughtfully as it seemed she noticed who he was blatantly staring at. "You didn't expect your mistress to dance with someone else? How possessive of you, darling. Didn't think you had that particular quality inside you especially where it concerns that lady."

"Hells bells, she can dance with anyone she chooses."

He didn't care. Who the devil did he have locked away in his house? Who?

Now, immediately, he needed to extricate himself from Mariam then make his apologies to the hostess. Anticipation surged hot in his blood. Excited at the prospect of seeing the little lady he abducted, he could imagine his reception. A good fight with the female might be exhilarating. He wasn't about to apologize. Her abduction was as much her fault as his. She was using that damn carriage; the one proclaiming Sabrina Anderson was inside. Chuckling, he found the duchess, said his goodbyes then with eagerness in his step, he collected his mount. Staying long at the ball had never been his intention. Now, he had the best reason to depart.

Collin wondered why the lady didn't put up more of a fight. Wondered about a lot of things while knowing he did manage to gag her quickly. She did squirm enough to almost fall onto the bricks below. Not much later, he stood in his house.

"Did she make a ruckus?" Collin asked as he slipped off his cloak and riding gloves.

"One hell of one," Charley told him laughing. "Truth be told if you're wanting honesty, didn't hear a peep from that door, dead silent for the hour you've been gone. Thought you would have stayed at the ball a mite longer."

"Truly?"

He would have thought any lady would have screamed her head

off in order to get out. This put the abduction into a new light.

"She must have heard you tell me not to open the door for any reason," his butler said still seeming to find this situation amusing.

Chapter Two

In front of the third-floor bedroom, Collin debated the merits of the next confrontation with the sweet lady he mistook for his mistress. Well, he prayed she was sweet. What he did comprehend was if he'd been locked in a room for a couple of hours, he'd come out swinging. He wiped his sweaty hands on his trousers, ran his arm across his forehead to cover up the nervous fear he was displaying. He wasn't a man given to nerves as he was known for his calm, cold control.

Tonight was different. Walking into this bedroom stretched his nerves until he thought for certain each would snap. Once more he paused with his hand outstretched to turn the doorknob.

He didn't know yet what exactly he meant to tell this little lady. All the way from the Montgomerie estate he'd thought on the words. He damn well didn't intend to apologize. Told himself she needed to explain why she was in his mistress' carriage. A one-of-a-kind carriage. What to say…

Nothing came to mind when he was riding home.

Still didn't.

"Better sooner than later," he mumbled the words while his hand twisted the knob.

Before he pushed the door open, he sucked in a deep breath of air.

When he stepped inside, her slim back was presented to him. What he saw of her was a narrow waist flaring gently to slightly curved hips. She was looking out the window, her forehead pressed against the pane of glass. She would be seeing the back gardens. They were immaculately groomed. At the end of a brick walk, there was a gazebo. On hot summer days, he enjoyed a drink in the shadowed confines. He wondered if this woman would be open to a tryst there.

Well, hell, it seemed he jumped ahead of himself. That was not his usual style as he didn't even know who she was.

Slowly, the woman turned.

Startled, his body tightened with need. The lady was ravishing. Stunning. Magnificent.

Collin's breath caught in his throat, hung inside for the longest time before he managed to exhale a thin stream of air. When she smiled, his heart overlooked the fact it needed to beat. A few seconds later, he gained control of his body, emotions ceasing to quiver. He bade his body to stop reacting to her. Never in his adult life could he remember having this response to a woman. So far this evening he encountered a lot of 'nevers'. What exactly was in store for him in the ensuing minutes?

Her hands were clasped in front of her. She swayed as if she was dancing to an imaginary tune. Perhaps she was pretending she was at the ball. There wasn't a doubt in his mind the Montgomerie estate was where she was supposed to be.

While he was gone, she had removed the cloak that disguised her identity. Her wheat-blond hair fell in stunning confusion around a heart-shaped face. The aqua-blue of her eyes shimmered with what appeared to be amusement. Her lips were full, moist, meant for a man's lips to mold to them. An urgent need to taste her sweetness enveloped him. She was tall, taller than most women, thinner too.

While he watched transfixed, unable to put together a coherent thought let alone speak, she moved her tiny pink tongue across her bottom lip. The gesture left even more moisture glimmering in the muted candlelight of the room. When she inhaled a deep breath of air, her modest but deliciously charming bosom rose a fraction. His gut coiled then twisted as his body jumped to the occasion.

He caught himself staring at the slope of her neck, thinking he would like to explore the length with his lips and teeth, sightsee other parts of her too. She tilted her head for a moment as if she read his blatantly sexual thoughts. All his deliberations toward this woman were carnal. When she righted her head, he found she stared unashamedly at his mouth then if he wasn't mistaken, her gaze dropped to his crotch. At that point she left another dewy trail of wetness across her mouth.

Desperate to maintain control, he stifled the groan rumbling up from his loins. She would be his, tonight, he hoped.

She spoke. Lowered her sooty lashes before she looked to him again.

"Not who you expected to see? Hmm…" She tapped a long slender finger on her temple. Her voice was a soft-sultry purr. He fantasized pillow-talk with her lying naked, her head resting on his chest. "Perhaps you wanted to secure Miss Sabrina Andrews instead? I hope I don't disappoint you. It would have been interesting though to see the expression on your face when you saw her dancing at the ball. That is where you took off to in such a hurry you didn't even introduce yourself."

For too many seconds to count, he found himself devoid of words. This lady was turning out to be a brazen piece of baggage. "Mind telling me who you are? After all, I did abscond with your person thinking you were someone else. The carriage belongs to Miss Anderson. Why were you using it? You will come to realize the fault of your kidnapping lay on you." He understood there could be several very convincing explanations to his question. He didn't like any of them.

"Mayhap you should tell me your name, the absconder of innocents. I could, after all, have you arrested. Tossed in the slammer. In these parts kidnapping is a crime."

This time she tapped her chin. Used her sweet tongue to tempt and lure as she slowly drew him into her web said the spider to the fly.

If she continued in this vein, he would not be responsible for his actions. "An innocent? You? Not by the way you are acting. You have more feminine wiles than all my mistresses combined." He chuckled, stepping forward to put action to some of his imaginings.

"I assure you my experience is nil. However strangely, I find you intriguing. You are too handsome for your own good. You are so big. When I look at your massive forearms and legs, I would equate you with a brick wall. Believe I long for something I've never thought would be possible. You could turn my life into an adventure. Always did like new concepts, new experiences. You realize, I've never been kidnapped. For me this is a first, one I'll most likely remember when I'm old and gray."

Brick wall?
Old and gray?

The innuendos she spouted caught him off guard. Pushing too fast for something that with patience would be his was reckless. Past the time he decided to be on first name basis. "Collin McInnis, now yours?"

When he held out his hand, he hoped she would reciprocate, so he could tug her quickly into his arms, massive arms.

Her lavish smile caught him at his bootstraps then as if a lightning bolt was attached struck directly at his groin.

"So, you're one of the bounders my uncle told me to stay away from? At the time, I took his order as a challenge to be defied. Never did like a man telling me what I could or could not do. I also didn't expect to meet one of the bounders I was supposed to avoid in quite this fashion. Actually, didn't think I would meet you at all even though I had every intention of doing so."

"Why is that?"

Nerves vanishing as her true colors became more apparent, he stepped closer. It pleased him she didn't move back. Stood her ground. He could wait for her name, dance to her tune for the time being. Soon she would be dancing to his.

"My aunty said the rakes don't attend debutante balls. They don't like the end result, marriages to simpering debutantes. Guess she was wrong since that's where you went after you dumped me on the bed. Did you find a debutante? Not that I'm applying for the position, I've never simpered in my entire life." She looked to the bed then back to him. "I want other things."

As an invitation? Not yet. The gesture meant to let him know he should understand his actions along with the implications. No, perhaps it was an invite. If it was, he had no trouble accepting the request blatant as it appeared.

"Your...aunty is correct in most circumstances. Days ago, I promised to attend and dance with Sabrina."

Why the hell was he telling this provocative young lady his life story? He felt no need to incorporate any of his mistresses in his story.

"You thought I was Sabrina? How drole."

She adjusted her corsage. To his delight and what seemed to be her chagrin the bodice appeared to be falling. A filmy blue something poked up where her cleavage should be. She looked where his gaze rested. Quickly, she pushed the fabric back where it supposedly belonged.

Fascinating little white lie.

Exploring the truth now looked to be an objective worth pursuing.

The lady was pretending something she wasn't. He didn't have one doubt her bodice was filled with something other than her breasts. Over his jaded life, he'd seen more than one woman entice a man with something she didn't possess. Somehow, with this beguiling lady, he didn't believe that was her intent.

The woman was clearly uncomfortable with his perusal or quite possibly the fact she embellished her lack of endowments, which made her situation amusing. Her face flamed with color. He grinned, knowing the affect to be wolfish. For the moment, he enjoyed the upper hand. He doubted if that sought for place on top would last long. What would she do next to confuse his opinion of her?

With the base of his thumb, he touched the slickness of her full bottom lips, relished the slight tremble, startled when she jumped back, her eyes wide with some emotion he'd like to discover.

Pausing a moment as he studied her before speaking, "Skittish?" he asked while he settled the palm of his hand on her delicate shoulder, drinking in the satin texture of her soft white flesh. The scent of her wafted through his nostrils, saucy-sweetness coupled with hot woman made for his pleasures.

"Didn't expect you to…"

She stared at his lips. Her hand rose then retreated.

It seemed to him she thought to reciprocate his caress on her mouth. More than anything now he wanted her name. "We haven't finished the introduction. Want your name before I kiss you." His message of intent was sent clearly to her.

"Kiss me…?" she murmured softly, her eyes absorbing a dreamy hue.

"What did you expect after you spent several hours in my bedroom? A man would presume something in return. A kiss is not much to ask." He almost laughed at her look of indignation.

"Not by choice," she seemed to grit out before her voice softened.

"If you would apologize, I might consider staying. Might consider a kiss. Well, no, I can't stay. Promised Aunty I would return to the ball at an appropriate hour. Suppose it's long past proper or even suitable. She will send out my uncles to search for me."

This time, he stroked her cheek with the back of his hand. "A search party? Hmm…where do you think they might start? With the young man I saw you with a few hours ago. He appeared to have come from the bedroom?" Collin didn't like the idea she'd been in bed with a young pup earlier in the evening. "That boy is too young for you. You do know that don't you?"

She placed her hand on his chest. Her laughter sent a jolt of apprehension through him. To Collin, that single action didn't seem she meant to push him away. By the darkening of her eyes, it was his inclination to think she wanted to touch him. That suited him fine.

"Two years older he is." Her hand settled on his shoulder, dipped along his arm before she suddenly withdrew.

He savored the sensations her caress sent through his body. If he didn't miss his guess, she was exploring. Meant to discover more of what she could do to his person. "That old, is he? How old are you?" With his hand once more beneath her chin, his thumb roamed across her lip tugging slightly luring her to open for him. She either didn't know what he wanted or she played coy.

"*Och, 'Tis no* your business *laddie*."

One more thing he learned about her. When he unnerved her, a Scottish brogue became apparent. The sound lilting, seductive while challenging every ounce of patience he possessed.

"If our relationship progresses as I've planned, love, I intend to make everything about you my business."

Pleased by her reaction as he watched her swallow then straighten her shoulders, he enjoyed the way her body moved provocatively while she seemed unaware. "Still don't *ken* your name."

"Nickie," she sipped air.

One fingertip traced the length of her neck before following the delicate line of Belgian lace atop her corsage. "Nick," he corrected. "Does this please you?"

"Nickie," she gasped for breath as his roving finger dipped beneath the fabric to caress gently the valley between her breasts.

"Nick," he insisted as he slowly pulled scarves from her bodice. One, two, three, four more. "It…it wasn't mine…was my cousins…" Her fingers tightened on his shoulders. "You touched me!"

The tips of her breasts hardened exquisitely when his fingers lightly brushed across them, "Can discern that fact for myself, Nick. Clearly someone else owns this gown. How?" This could categorically be a thought-provoking tale. "Where is yours? I emphatically hope your cousin is not adorned in the one meant for you. The sight would leave nothing to one's imagination. Although without the delicate little scarves filling out your bodice." He rubbed his chin while he stared, "Don't believe there is anything left to my imagination either." He was a man well pleased.

More delightfully heated color washed across her cheeks before settling lower to adorn the tops of the small, perfectly curved spheres of pleasure he wished to explore more thoroughly. The pouting globes were exquisite. He'd enjoy cupping them in his hands, tasting the tips that were hardening even more as he watched.

"Y-you shouldn't stare."

"Why is that? You lured me into your web. Did you know that you could have me anytime you wished? If you crooked your little finger, I would come to you panting with my male parts eagerly waiting."

She laughed, the sound filling his senses. Hers was a deep throaty laughter. One he didn't contemplate he'd ever grow used to hearing. "How old are you?"

"We return to the earlier topic. Seems it took forever for me to coax your name from your saucy mouth, love. Now we're dwelling on age. Let's just say I'm old enough for you, unlike the young pup I saw you with."

"None of this should be happening. I'm supposed to stay away from you. You are a *verra* dangerous man for a girl such as me." She pointed a slim finger at him.

"Eight and twenty. Don't think I can allow that. At least not until I know you better, every part of you better. Your parts are just as intriguing to me as I'm assuming my parts are to you. I mean to see you often as well as thoroughly."

"You should take me back to the ball."

"Who is the young'un that was kissing you."

With his words it seemed she bristled. Her light brows narrowed in a perfect scowl. "Thought I told you…"

"Who? I won't let this go until I understand what you see in the boy. Because of the unique circumstances of our meeting, I would learn as much as I can about you."

She let out a woosh of air that seemed to say, if I must. "Colby."

"Colby. You tell the pup you're mine. Let him know that he doesn't need to give you parting gifts of conciliation. I'll take care of you from now on. Does the boy have a last name in case I have to tell him myself?" He would make sure the lad cried off. There would be no claim on Nick from another man.

She shoved him. Taken unaware and slightly off balance, he stumbled toward the bed. Quick thinking, he snaked his hand around her waist pulling her with him. Well, it was what he wanted from the moment he looked at her long slim back slowly disrobing her in his imagination.

"I *no be tellin'* him anything like that! Neither will you. You'll be *stayin'* out of my affairs."

She was yelling at him. His enjoyment blossomed while her eyes sparked fire. He chuckled before he set his lips on her pert nose then her hot cheeks. "You will, love, or I will. The choice of who says the words is up to you."

"*Nay!*"

"As I said a moment ago, if you won't, I will," he reiterated his earlier intentions.

"There is no need to *be tellin'* the pup anything. He's my brother."

She pushed on his chest. His hands tightened around her waist as his laughter as well as relief roared from deep in his chest.

"Might do more harm than good to tell the boy. In any case, considering who you are, would he care?"

"I'm not what *ye be thinkin'*. Arrogant bastard!" She punched his shoulder.

Indeed he was arrogant, a bastard, no, at least not in parentage. He had the distinct feeling that wasn't what she was thinking.

She managed to struggle off him. Perhaps because he let her go. If he didn't, they would never reach the ball. Personally, he didn't give a damn about the fete. For some reason he couldn't figure, she did though. She promised. As she told him, if he didn't return her, he might meet her brother. Supposed that wasn't something he wanted at the moment. He would do the meeting as well as greeting of relatives in due time.

"What am I thinking?" He smirked as he pondered the question.

"That I'm available to be a mistress. I'm not. I would take you as a lover since I'm attracted to you. I won't be a kept woman."

She appeared indignant which amused him more than he ever thought possible.

Lover?

Nick could be his lover. That notion pleased him immensely. "You wouldn't mind interviewing for the position?"

"I would be *doin'* the interviewing."

Several times, she poked him in the chest to give emphasis to her words.

Grinning devilishly, he let his hands fall to his sides, satisfied he was at least one step in front of her on this assumption. "Interview on…"

He couldn't stop the grin that seemed to be increasing despite his best efforts to the contrary. She looked so lost. Forlorn also seemed a creditable likelihood, "Well…?"

"I don't know what to ask." She lifted her shoulders slightly as she shifted beneath him. He knew firsthand the flesh there was silken, so soft to the touch he could spend the night reveling in the sensations.

Collin knew what his requirements would be for a lover. "Believe you need to discover this without asking my opinion about myself. Suppose I could lie about my male prowess. You would never discern the truth until I was your lover. By then it would be too late to change your mind. You would be mine, Nick."

"Nickie. Don't understand what you're getting at, Collin." Her brows drew together. "Your male prowess? Does that have something to do with kissing?"

She was trying to decipher his words. That was a good sign for the negotiations. He held his hoot of laughter in the back of his throat. He felt certain she was more innocent than he originally believed.

"So, if it was me doing the interviewing, I would want to know if I appreciated and," he paused in thought, "adored the lady's kisses. If the touch of her lips upon mine left me panting for more. Would have to sample to know for certain. We could try. You could find out if you love the way I would kiss my lover."

"Panting?"

"Yes."

He settled one hand around her waist, drawing her close then one beneath her chin lifting her face to his. Her eyes were deep pools of simmering blue he could drown in. "Shall I kiss you, love? Shall we give this interview a try?"

The tip of her tongue rested between her lips.

Innocent?

Experienced?

Damned if he cared. He intended to discover the truth about this high-spirited minx soon enough. Lightly, he brushed his mouth across hers, a teasing caress that promised so much more. Her lips were slick with moisture. Her tongue touched his mouth so very hesitantly. She had not moved it. He tugged on the bottom lip suggesting she open to him. She didn't. Pushing his way through her mouth to the dark inner recesses, he swept his tongue along her teeth.

"Open for me, love. You want to taste me. Want to know what it feels like when you enter me just as I want the same." His breath was hard and fast while he waited for her response.

As she did what he suggested, her fingers tightened on his shoulders. He kissed her again and again, showing her his talents. Yes, his male prowess as well. He was well-versed in kissing. Encouraged her to reciprocate move for move. If his Nick was experienced, she was one hell of an actress. It seemed to him, she had no idea what he was about or what he expected from her.

Though she was a brazen little piece of sweet sauciness.

Seconds turned to minutes as he investigated all she offered.

When he finally pulled away, her lips were puffed-up from his fervent devotion. He complained low in the back of his throat before he nipped at the pulse point on her neck. He nipped then sucked once, twice then more until a small red spot blossomed. With gentle persuasion, he sipped one more time while he listened to the tender purr flooding her throat.

She would have some explaining to do when whoever she answered to noticed the mark. "Did I pass inspection?" he queried softly as he touched upon the small flower of his attentiveness at the base of her neck where her pulse still beat a rapid staccato seeming to ask for more tender care.

For an instant her eyes crossed. Her small bosom rose and fell with each stuttered breath she inhaled. "Seems I need more information if you're going to proceed as my lover. One kiss isn't enough to make such an important decision," her voice hummed softly into his chest as she seemed to melt into him. The sensation delicious. He pulled her to her feet, understanding he couldn't keep her in the attic room.

His hands fell lower to her delectable bottom. He squeezed remembering the way she felt against his thighs when she lay across them. Should have known the girl he absconded with wasn't Sabrina. Nick's arse was small and tightly muscled, nothing like Sabrina's. He'd been so sure of himself he failed to notice what a delightful creature he escaped with.

His new lady rose on the tips of her toes to wind her fingers around his neck then through his hair, her long slender body pressed flush against his. Delightful. Delicious as well. Her sweetly unique scent swamped him. He couldn't say no to such a request as a second kiss. Several minutes passed before he finally drew away.

"We've got to get you to the ball before it's over," he murmured against the delicate shell of her ear sending more tremors along her frame. It was not what he wished to do with her.

"Why? I've found what I wanted here."

"Search parties, love."

When she moved away from him, he felt her displeasure. It appeared she wanted what he did. "Don't know what my uncles would do if they ever discovered where I've been or who I've been with. They've no right to make demands or judge my actions. I'm of age."

He found that aroused as he was, a good fight might alleviate some or most of his discomfort. He felt sure her uncles would demand restitution for appearances sake even though they did nothing save kiss. The devil but he wanted to bury himself in her woman's hot, moist core. Instead, he turned from her to gather her cloak.

"Do you want to ride or take the carriage?"

She looked at her gown then back to him. When she lifted her shoulders in a resigned shrug. "Ride. Nothing will help my hair. It seems you've demolished the coif. My dress might be the worse for wear, however…"

"As long as your strategically placed fabric remains in place you've nothing to worry over."

He was laughing. Couldn't help himself. She was such a complex package of scrumptiousness. His mistake tonight was an unexpected enchantment to him. Expertly he placed the scarves where they belonged.

If nothing else, Nick would be his lover. For how long, he didn't know. She told him she didn't want to wed. He would hold her to that fact since marriage for him was out of the question for at least a decade. Search parties and uncles be damned. They would weather any storm coming their way.

When they reached the Montgomerie stables, she dismounted. "Thank you. Will I see you inside?"

Collin realized he was a besotted fool. She thanked him for kidnapping her. The devil, that was unique about her. "Still have to tell Sabrina I no longer want her as my mistress. So, yes."

"Will you dance with me once?"

Being over eager was not part of his make-up. With Nick he was different. She touched something deep inside he didn't want to escape. "I would be honored."

All he wished for was to hold her in his arms until he stuck his spoon in the wall. He shook his head to clear his mucked up brain.

Until he stuck his spoon in the wall? Where the devil did that notion come from?

Her sheepish grin had him wondering what she would tell him

next, had him waiting impatiently for any possible surprise that might come his way. "Have to tell you when it comes to dancing, I've two left feet. You will have to guard your toes, your very male toes." Her laughter was infectious deep and throaty, sexy as hell. "I'll sneak up the back steps to fix my hair along with," she looked at her bodice, "other things."

Nick was his delight.

"I'll meet you in the ballroom. Don't take too long. Make sure you get all those scarves back exactly where they belong. Don't want anyone else seeing your precious jewels."

His makeshift job wasn't the best. At that time it had been all he could do to keep from exploring her further.

He watched her adorable fanny as she dashed to the house to disappear the backway her skirts swaying as they revealed trim ankles. Once she vanished, his long strides took him to the ballroom. At the entrance he stood for several seconds surveying the scene.

"I see you're back," Ella said as it seemed she watched him with a thoughtful gaze.

The decided feeling he should have asked Nick who her uncles were when he had a chance flooded him. Thoughts of where she was staying brought unpleasant images to mind. He flexed his hands as if readying himself for someone's wrath.

"Had a bit of business to take care of before I could return."

Before he found the chance to search for Sabrina, the woman he was about to disappoint grasped his arm dragging him to a secluded spot on the terrace. He supposed since he snatched the wrong lady he would have to pay with a few gifts along with extended time in the townhouse before he could demand that she vacate the rooms.

"Where have you been?" she gritted out her displeasure obvious to anyone who dared listen. "I've been waiting. Not so patiently for that matter."

"As I told the duchess, I had business to attend to. I came as quickly as I could. Please sit down." His voice must have been harsher than his intention. "We need to talk."

Sabrina's face drained of color. "What is it? Don't leave me hanging."

She sounded resigned to the inevitable. After their last night together along with his very noticeable absence from the ball, she must be expecting his dismissal.

It was quite possible she guessed his intentions. "I wish to give you leave to seek another man to keep you. I…"

"Knew it!" She marched away without turning back.

Thank God, she acted as he expected. Didn't want her to have histrionics tonight in front of half the London aristocrats. Now he would find Nick, dance then go home after arranging an assignation for the following day. His ultimate plans for Nick began to take form.

"There you are. You are so tall as well as large, it is easy to pick you out of a crowd," Nick stood beside him smiling sweetly, one delicate hand on his arm. Her hair was a delight, her jewels hidden from anyone's sight. "Is this my dance?"

She was stunning, especially when she smiled at him, for his pleasure. Now, it seemed she adeptly avoided her chaperone, whoever that might be. Ah, the aunt who didn't have a name yet. He had the decided feeling it would be beneficial to learn their identities sooner than later. They danced more than once, more times than he cared to count. There would be rumors. More rumors would abound when the well-meaning ton learned they were lovers. That she stayed in a bedroom inside his townhouse for more than an hour.

"I'm going now." She stood on the tips of her toes to whisper in his ear, touching the lobe with the tip of her tongue. "Have to leave. I've a promise to myself I intend to keep."

Brazen piece of baggage.

"To bed?"

He couldn't will his disappointment away. Thought he had a bit more time with her before she took her leave. He would have to work quickly to secure a rendezvous tomorrow.

"No, not to bed." She looked down then back to him her eyes twinkling with mischief. "If you like you can come with me. I'm going to the lake to watch the sun show itself from behind the hills. Should be a glorious sight. Love to see the beginning of each new day, a day that will hold whatever promise a person wants."

The sunrise, "Hmm…would love to watch the sun with you. Among other things," he said as his gaze shifted to her bodice along with the scarves that appeared to be sliding downward revealing more than they concealed. He couldn't hold back his grin of delight.

~ * ~

Nickie dodged Aunty Ella several times in her attempt to leave the ball before she rushed up the stairs to change her clothing. Collin, she would meet in the stables. To her delight, he was going with her. The devil but she was a shameless hussy. Never in her wildest imagination would she have thought to behave that way. The devil, she asked a man to meet her to watch the sun show itself hoping there would be more kisses.

The man was handsome as sin, large with all the muscles in the right places. He was hard as a brick wall. Tall and broad, his physique fit all her perquisites for her lover. As much as told her, he liked adventure, enjoyed the surprise of new things. His green eyes enchanted her, twinkled merrily when he tried to hold back a grin. They were such a vivid green. His mahogany-colored hair touched with subtle shades of red was cut rakishly long. Why, it nearly touched his shoulders. When she ran her fingers through the length, the strands were silken. His jaw, chiseled. A dimple graced one cheek. Oh my, when he arched an eyebrow while he looked at her, she almost swooned. She was not a lady given over to vapors. Never laced her corset so tight she couldn't breathe. He touched her rear, squeezed, more than once. Thinking about the way his long slender finger created heated sensation until she wanted to twist and coil before she asked for him to do it again then one more time for satisfaction.

She was tall for a woman. When he pulled her into his arms, she didn't reach his chin. Nickie closed her eyes as she recalled the rigid length of him pressed against her. She wanted to see all of him, all of him with nothing on. Naughty, wicked thoughts swamped her. She wished to feel his flesh with her fingertips, explore his chest perhaps squeeze his backside as he did hers. When her brother didn't know she was listening, she heard sinfully delicious things that happened between a man and a woman. Heat flooded her, took over her body when her thoughts drifted to the erotic.

Husband material, he wasn't. Neither was she in the market for a man to dictate her life, control her in any way. Determined to make her way in this life, she refused to be told how to behave. She would never swear to obey. Her girlish laughter filled her with more happiness than she believed possible. Collin was everything she'd ever fantasized in a man. For this morning while they watched the sun peak its head over the horizon, he was hers.

When she touched her mouth, she recalled the sweet taste of his lips upon hers, the sensations so different from her first hated encounter. She understood the heady sent of man and spice. Her aunties told her if the man didn't make her feel as if liquid heat flooded her veins, he wasn't the man for her. Was told she should feel all that when the man meant for her arrived in her life. They told her not to settle.

Fortunate for her, Collin McInnis' kisses did all that and more. They heated her from the tips of her toes to the top of her head. Spilled uncertain emotions into her mind as her body danced to the tune he expertly played. She didn't mind his expertise in lovemaking since she knew nothing. She harbored no delusions that the man didn't know what he was about. He was indeed proficient in the art of love.

Nicole supposed he passed the interview to be her lover with high marks. What else would she ever need to know? Understanding what she proposed was wickedly naughty.

Did she care? Hell no.

As soon as possible she meant to discover what all the to do was about when it came to sexual relations. What her brother shared with the women he bedded was certainly more than a kiss or two. She heard the sensual information from the source. Didn't understand why something was right for a man yet taboo for a *lass*. Hurriedly, she tossed off the ballgown as well as all her underthings before she tugged on her trousers and shirt over bare skin.

Sticking her head out the door to make sure no one would see her racing to the stable, she was in luck. Nickie stuck to the backway as well as shadows on the way to the horses and her clandestine meeting with her new lover. When she stepped inside, she spotted Collin with both horses. The sight of his long well-muscled legs and broad chest sent her heart pounding. The devil but did he have the same notions about tonight that she had?

"Need a leg up?" he asked his broad grin seemed to stretch across his face.

"Yes."

She didn't. Decided to let him help simply because she liked the way he felt along with the manly scent of him when his expansive frame was so very close to her. She wasn't disappointed. Once mounted, they started toward the lake. He rode slightly to the side and behind her.

"No one saw you?" he asked sounding genuinely concerned. "Was waiting for a few uncles or aunts to appear bent on fisticuffs. Perhaps you should enumerate on your uncles as to how many so we can best avoid them."

She nodded. "Seems there were no search parties sent out for me before or after the ball."

She wasn't sure how exactly she felt about that little tid bit of information. The way she was carrying on, it was likely she needed a chaperone. Still, she didn't like the notion no one missed her for several hours.

"That might be lucky. What's your chaperone going to say when she finds you missing again? Seems you're taking a risk."

He must not care about the risk since he was riding beside her. "She won't. Aunty doesn't come around to wake me. She'll let me sleep, especially tonight since the ball is just now winding down. Besides, I've spoken about getting up early to watch the sun start a new day. She wouldn't be surprised. If she did look in on me, I left a note by my bed."

The devil take her. She tugged in a huge lump of air as she began to think about tonight or more appropriately this morning. What was she doing running off with a man she barely knew?

"So, tell me about your uncles. They must have names."

"*Dinna fash* yourself."

Breathing hard, waving a hand in the air, thinking if she told him too soon, he would leave her. Before he abandoned her, she wanted another kiss, more if the man was willing. "Later, *dinna* want to ruin the sunrise."

"Would it be that bad if you told me who these inattentive guardians are? Seems they should be held accountable. With that said, I'm heartily glad they've shirked their duties where you are concerned."

"In that case," she paused as she tossed him a cheeky grin, "They are debutants at this particular notion. While they are very, very good at what they do best, watching over a young woman goes beyond the pale if you get my drift. None of them have the slightest idea how to go about keeping a *lass* safe from a rake since they were all once rakes themselves."

He surprised her with a hoot of laughter. "Perfectly. I'm especially pleased your uncles are beginners. I'm the lucky recipient of all their bumbling. Certain in time they will get better if the need arises. Are you their only niece?"

"Oh, the need will arise. As I told you earlier the gown I wore was meant for my cousin, Lyssa. She was supposed to be here two days ago. Suppose her ship was delayed. One of my uncles builds the best vessels as well as the fastest. Satisfaction, Lyssa's ship, was intended to set sail three months ago from Baltimore. The ship should have made it to London by now. Uncle Jamie brags his ships can make the voyage in one hundred days instead of the usual time which is about two extra weeks."

"Summer squalls can come up in a moment's notice. I hold to my heart one of your uncles' names. Nevertheless, will need a surname if I'm to put a face to the man. Your cousins, Nick and Lyssa, hmm...I hope she figures out a different name to use. Perhaps her intended will. Is she the only other cousin to be chaperoned by these doting uncles of yours?"

"No, you will positively swoon when you hear the great number I'm not certain of. I would have to count up all the children. Would surely miss at least one of the females. Don't suppose the boys will be in need of a chaperone. They are all most likely to show up here sometime, with the possible exception of my American male cousins."

"Out with it then, love. How many? A guess will suffice. I will leave room in my head for minus or a plus." He was laughing, grinning at her as they rode. He acted as if he enjoyed the tête-à-tête.

"My best estimate is fifteen debutantes."

She watched for a reaction, saw the drawing together of his brows as the number began to register in his oh so manly brain. She was afraid he was thinking in totals, girls including the boys. He would be wrong. Seriously wrong.

"Fifteen, you say." His brows drew together while he looked at her. He stroked his chin. "Half then would be of the female persuasion in need of guidance."

"Guidance! You arrogant man." She wanted to slap the smug grin off his face. "Women don't need guidance!" While she was yelling at him, he was laughing, his eyes alight with amusement.

"Suppose that was the wrong choice of words, sweetheart." He tried to take back his assumptive thinking. "Of course, love, you are in no need of manly leadership. You have your life mapped, out at least where sexual encounters are concerned. I doubt if your uncles will agree to your plans when they discover what exactly you are plotting."

"After our banter this evening, how do you dare spout such nonsense. My female cousins are in no more need of direction than I am. If you want to know the truth of all this, there are approximately fifteen females who will eventually arrive in London for their season. I've a strong feeling they will, with slight variations to account for temperament, advance in much the same fashion as I have."

"Fifteen young debutantes to chaperone will prove intriguing as well as exhausting to any male worth his salt. They all think as you? London will be taken by storm, turned topsy-turvy."

She nodded, feeling as if he finally understood the dilemma, "Much the same fashion. Nevertheless, the age differences are quite daunting."

At his look of chagrin, she wanted to burst out in laughter. "The women we are speaking of will not all descend in mass. The youngest is at least ten years my junior. Can't tell you exactly as I'm not sure. Guess I should be though. She's the daughter of my mother's littlest sister. Just for you, I'll make a point of asking next time I'm in the highlands."

"Another highlander," he mused, stroking the back of his neck.

"Would I know the man?"

"Anything is possible." Telling him the names of said uncles should be delayed more, definitely delayed. It wasn't time to put such a damper on the morning.

Oh, she understood giving the names over to him might eventually have to be done. Now was not the right time. "I do think my aunty and uncle will have this chaperone business down to perfection by the time the littlest one arrives. However, if she is anything like her mother…"

Purposely she allowed the end of the sentence to be finished by Collin. When he grimaced, although the expression suggested thoughtfulness not agitation, she felt a tug at her heart.

"Fifteen females," he mused, "Perhaps it is time to move on with our conversation. My feeble man's brain is muddled at all the possibilities. Thankfully happy, I won't have the duty of chaperone."

They rode in silence for only a few seconds before he asked, "Are there as many boys?"

"Approximately." She chuckled softly. "Were you're concerned there were too many females in the mix?"

"Bite your tongue, no, I'd rather bite it gently for you. No, I don't prefer the company of either sex. Have reasons to love a female while the reasons to be in male company varies greatly. Men are much more entertaining as drinking buddies than a woman."

Her body quivered. Butterflies danced. She swallowed as her breath rushed into her lungs. "You would bite my tongue?"

"Yes."

"Would it hurt?" Nickie didn't understand why. She wanted him to do that. Wondered how she would respond. His kisses were exquisite. "Is biting of the tongue part of kissing?" Almost, almost she regretted the question.

Rather than laughing at her, he appeared to drink in the inquiry. With a solemn face that surprised her he replied, "If the kisser knows what he is doing, why then yes. Biting gently, tenderly is part of the process. We will have to experiment. See if you like the activity. I will be more than pleased to teach."

"Will you do that? Bite my tongue?"

Thinking about the process her body tightened, parts of her moved she didn't know could move. Deep in the most secret parts of her, her body squeezed tightly.

"I'll bite you anywhere you would like," he told her, his words whiskey-smooth.

"As you did my neck. There is a red mark where you did so." She arched her back, tried to adjust herself in the saddle as she thought about his teeth upon her. "Can I bite you?"

Damn and blast, that wasn't something she should ask a man. He laughed softly as he leaned toward her. "You, my love, can bite me anywhere you would like. Your small white teeth upon my body turns parts of me to steel. My sword is waiting and ready for whatever you wish."

"Your sword?" She didn't have a clue as to what he spoke of. While she didn't wish to show her ignorance, she did need an explanation. Her curiosity peeked, "Care to explain?"

He roared with laughter. "Later when you are ready for me, I'll show you. Look," he pointed toward the lake. "We are almost there. The sky is growing lighter, the colors more vivid."

Nickie spurred her horse forward, setting her sights on the large boulder near the lake. When she reached the spot she dismounted, letting the reins fall to the ground. Collin did the same, catching up to her as she reached the stone. When she visited the lake, she always came to the same place. Occasionally, she watched the sun go down.

"There are a few clouds. We should have color. The sky will be exquisite," she murmured.

"Not so fast. I want to hold you in my arms as we observe the colors this morning."

Leaning against the boulder, he encased her in his embrace, her back against his chest. His fingers spread wide were settled on her waist. The tender squeeze on her belly surprised her. When his heated fingers rested on the curve of her hips, she exhaled softly. Her head rested against his chest. More than anything she wanted to hang onto this moment forever. When he discovered the truth about her uncles, he would leave. A lover for one night? That would be better than nothing. She would savor this moment for the rest of her life.

His lips touched upon the back of her neck. Found their way to the tender spot where he took on more intimate flesh.

"It's beautiful," her words squeaked out as he ran his large hands up her sides, teasing, elusive, so very sensitive places. Spaces where a man's hands didn't belong.

"Ravishing."

He tugged on her shirt. The fabric fell away from her trousers. "The…" she swallowed the words.

"The?" he queried, the slight sound of amusement rumbled from his chest. "Like to know what you're thinking."

"Sunset."

"Yes. Lift your arms, Love."

"Why?"

"Because you'll like what I'm going to do." The sound of his voice ruffled warmly, seductively across her ear. Shivers beat a path down her spine.

"Oh…"

She liked everything he did. Nickie did as he said. Her shirt fell to the ground. The soft morning breeze caressed her bared skin. The tips of her breasts tightened. His nimble fingers worked at the lacings of her trousers.

Oh my…oh my…oh…

He turned her. "My goodness…"

Her breasts brushed against the bared skin of his chest. The tender caress burned, enflamed. She didn't know when he unfastened his shirt.

"Do you like this?" he asked as his hands found their way beneath her trousers. He squeezed her rear. "Your bottom is adorable, so firm and tight."

She pushed against him, felt his body, the steel of his length against her. "Wonderful," the single word whispered against his chest. Nickie ran her fingers along his back, her nails scratching lightly.

"I thought so. Wrap your legs around me."

She did.

He fixed his mouth upon hers. The tip of his tongue investigated inside. This time she grasped what he wanted. When his tongue was inside her, she played and fenced, dueled for supremacy then brought her teeth down on the exploring tongue. His rumble of pleasure sent heated chills seething to sensitive, erotic spots. He reciprocated the bite when she found her way inside him.

"Oh, love…" Squeezing again, he moved lower, tenderly attended her neck with lips, teeth and tongue. She moved closer, her heart accelerating with each exquisite glided caress.

When his lips closed over the crest of one breast then his teeth closed upon the tip, she lurched. Her fingers tightened on his shoulders, pulling him closer, her silent way of encouraging.

Nickie couldn't get enough of him. The warmth of the sun embraced her back. Birds sang welcoming the morning while her body hummed to the tune he set in motion. A squirrel sat on the boulder staring at her then chatting harshly as if lecturing. She felt as if there were other eyes upon her, critical eyes, judging eyes. He switched his focus to the opposite side, charming her, luring her to become his. It was what she wanted.

"Collin…" she whispered his name. the sound floated in the early morning mist. "You make me feel so…"

"So?" he queried with a tender chuckle as one hand cupped her breast, his thumb flicking across the hardened crests. He guided her hand to the juncture of his thighs. "My sword, do you feel it? Whenever you say the word, it's yours to command."

"That hard part of you that is so different from me?" She did feel the rigid length against her. "Can I see you."

"Not now but soon," he murmured softly. "Later."

The truth, he coaxed her, charmed his way into her life. She wanted to savor this before they moved on to something that could never be taken back. Unable to stop herself, she ran her hands along the wall of his chest, touching upon the tips of his tiny nipples. He groaned then flexed the muscles her hands rested upon.

"What comes next?" she asked, moistening her lips leaving them slick while begging for his kiss again.

He didn't answer with words. His next kiss was deep and

formidable, biting then soothing, licking then biting again, teaching her all she liked, exquisitely tempting. In time what she would beg for. His fingers squeezed her breasts before dipping lower to settle on her rear again.

"So much more than I'm going to gift you with now."

He lifted his head, his nostrils flaring as if he scented something on the wind. His eyes darkened to molten green.

"Why?" Why would he enchant her with all these new and wondrous sensations to stop, leaving her in need of something she didn't understand.

"Company coming," he paused as he looked over her shoulder. "We've got company. Don't move, love. Let me handle this. I should have never taken this so far here where anyone might come along. I thought the spot more private."

Quickly, he turned her so whoever was approaching couldn't see her face. She buried her head against his chest. "Company?" she wheezed.

Whoever it was cleared his throat. "What have we here? A little love tryst in the early morning. What are you doing on the duke's land?"

Colby?

She stiffened. Hell was about to break lose. If he wanted to avoid her uncles, this was not the way to go about it. All her brother would have to do is see her horse. He would know who was trysting with Collin McInnis.

"I'd request you move on. Give us a bit of privacy," Collin said with a snarl.

While he spoke, his hands gripped her tightly then gentled. He gave support. He didn't understand half the story.

"Just checking to see if the *lass* needed help." Colby laughed. "Can see she's enjoying herself as are you. Since I just came from a similar encounter, believe I will be moving on just as you asked."

Thank all the saints above. Small miracles can happen.

"Good to hear," Collin said, his voice rumbling against her chest.

He stroked her back, his intent clearly to calm her rattled nerves.

Nickie could not be calm until she heard the sound of Colby's hoofbeats vanishing into the early morning mist.

"You should truly take more care when you plan your little dalliances." Colby's laughter grated on her nerves. "What the hell!"

Colby knew. He knew. Oh God! Unable to help herself, she clung tighter to Collin as she closed her eyes waiting for what she wasn't certain. She was going to be sick.

"Nickie!"

"Who the hell are you, pup?"

"The lady's brother. Nickie, you're coming with me."

Never having heard her brother command so, she held tighter to the only man she wanted to see her with very nearly nothing on. "Collin, do something, please," she whispered, her voice shaking, understanding now the time would be sooner than later he would meet her uncles.

"Intend to, love."

"Nickie!"

"Nick isn't going anywhere with you. Don't suppose she wants you to see her without her clothing on. When was the last time, pup? When she was toddling? Might embarrass you also."

"My sister won't stay with the likes of you," Colby grit out. "Who are you?"

"The man your little sister wants to be with," Collin replied smoothly, his fingertips touching upon each vertebra as they soothed instead of coaxed. "Now go on with you. I'll bring her home in one piece, nothing broken."

"Nothing broken?" Colby parroted, his anger seeming to grow with each word bantered between the two of them. "Good to hear. If I hadn't come along then you would have broken through."

"Not your business," Collin replied smoothly.

Peeking around his broad shoulders. "Promise me, promise not to tell anyone. At least not until I've a chance to speak with you in private."

"Hells bells, Nickie, I can't promise something so absurd." There was a slight pause. "Not unless I get a few reassurances of my own from you."

"Such as," Collin answered for her.

It appeared he tried to get Colby to back off.

"That you won't see this bounder again," he was quick to say.

"Collin is no more a bounder than you, Colby. Besides, he's special to me."

She shouldn't have to explain or promise anything to her brother. Her life was hers to live as she pleased.

"Glad to hear that, love," Collin chuckled. "Go on with you. I'll have her back to the Montgomerie estate in record time. She can speak with you then."

"Thank you," she whispered against Collin's chest.

When she did hear the hoofbeats vanish, "Is he gone?"

"Yes." He unwound her death grip from his body. His smile of encouragement sent a jolt of pleasure to her heart. "We can get you dressed now."

With practiced speed coupled with agility that spoke to more expertise in the area of lady's fashion, her trousers were laced. His hand on her shoulders, he looked from her breasts to her eyes. A few moments lingered, while she shuddered and heated from his ardent perusal. "Ravishing. I regret I have to wait to taste you again."

His soft-spoken yet throaty words sent another jolt of heat straight to her core.

Seconds later he slipped her shirt over her head then fastened his. "What are you going to say to your brother? Seems I should be there too."

"Your presence would serve to make things worse. I will argue in favor of women's rights, my rights to be exact. The men in my life can keep their tongues in the backs of their throats when it comes to me. I will do as I please when I please."

"That should get you far." His sarcasm gave her a chill. "Perhaps you should adopt a different tact."

The breath of air leaving her lungs left her wishing for something that couldn't be. "I don't know what to do."

"Agree to see me this afternoon. We can go for another ride. I *ken* just where I'd like to take you as well as what I want to speak with you about."

"If Colby tells what he saw, what we were doing here, we'll have a chaperone."

"I have faith in you, love. Don't believe your brother will give you away. If he does, much of his unsavory behavior will come to light. What you must understand about your big brother is that, he was coming home from the evening after tossing a lady's skirts. You can hold his dalliances over his head. Reassure him what happened this morning will not happen again."

"That would be a lie, or would it?" Nickie was deathly afraid he was intending on saying his goodbyes.

"Of course not. Next time we won't be sitting on a boulder with your lovely long legs wrapped around my waist. If there is a next time, you will be stark naked as will I. If there is a next time, I will also make sure no one will invade our privacy."

"Devil, I'll remember what you said. You do want to see me again?"

"As I said earlier, this afternoon, when all goes as planned, your brother will not give up our secret. He will most likely be sound asleep dreaming of his next conquest while we ride to a beautiful secluded spot I've planned for our next tryst."

~ * ~

With great reluctance, Collin left Nick at the backsteps to the estate. Too much to do in the few hours remaining, he had plans to make, details of his eminent departure from London had to be seen to. This afternoon she would commit to him, or say goodbye. Certain Drake Montgomerie was one of her uncles, he understood the danger in crossing the man. His Nick was more than worth that risk.

At one time Drake Montgomerie had been ruthless with his enemies. Collin didn't believe anything could have changed with the passage of time. Certainly, fatherhood must have tamed him in some respects. However, the ruthless nature that made him a valuable asset to the English government would not have vanished, especially when the emotion would concern one of his nieces.

He needed to take great care. Biding his time with Nick was necessary while also impossible. Trouble was he didn't have time to convince her he was not intending to be her lover. He needed more of a commitment from her. Mistress was what he had in mind. He didn't like the idea of her coming and going as she pleased. Her dependence on him was necessary for his peace of mind.

What he wished for was to convince her to leave London with him. He meant to return to his home in the highlands. He longed for the scents and sounds that could only be found in the crags and heather covered land. He needed to look over his property, inhale the view until the scent remained part of his senses forever. Watch the elk as they grazed. At one point, he believed he'd remain in London for another few years. The bustling vice-filled city no longer enticed or enchanted him. No longer lured him with its forbidden charms. Instead, a willow slim woman stole rational thought, setting him on a different course than previously planned.

Easily finding his first mate near the docks, he charged the man to round up the crew then prepare them to sail, Promise was her name. In hopes Nick would accompany him, he stopped at Sabrina's favorite modiste where he purchased several gowns along with underthings for her to wear until he could acquire more. He would have his first mate pick them up later. The devil but he hoped they would fit.

She was so tall and slender. A strong wind might blow her over.

He closed his eyes, recalling her small breasts in his hands, imagining the rest of her, touching, kissing every intimate, sensual part of her. His heated breath caught in the back of his throat. Where a woman was concerned, he'd never become a besotted fool. He had though. Nick touched every bored, fed-up part of him giving his life more meaning than he'd ever known.

Before he rode to the estate to meet Nick, he visited his ship. His crew was boarding. The first mate was grinning appearing ready to sail at a moment's notice. Collin hoped Nick was able to convince Colby not to give up their secret, wished too there would be no chaperones when she met him in the glade. He needed time to speak with her in private.

Dornoch called to him. Home, the wild churning North Sea crashing on the rocks, the scent of salt stinging his nostrils and face. Sharing the highlands with Nick…ah…the sharing would be pleasant indeed. He wouldn't be able to sail straight to Dornoch. Once the

Montgomerie figured out who he was, the task of locating his home would be simple work.

Nick was Scottish. She'd not shared enough about herself for him to know what part she came from, highlander or lowlander. Where she hailed from made no difference. For the time being, Nick was his. As he remembered her now, he didn't believe he'd ever grow tired of her. Even in old age, he was sure he would want her.

When he reached the Montgomerie estate, she was waiting for him, dressed this time in a blue velvet riding habit, a fashionable hat perched daringly on her head. Riding astride, the clothing seemed to be out of place. He almost laughed, the sight was such a contrast to this morning. It seemed she wore armor. Well, indeed, perhaps she sought to impress. A good sign, if he didn't think so himself.

"Ready?" he asked while still surveying the precocious lady.

She nodded grinning. "Where too?"

Her eagerness appealed to his senses; uprooted his normal calm circumspect when it came to the opposite sex. He pointed in the direction of the Thames and the spot where his ship was moored, ready to set sail. They would stop in a place where he had much needed privacy for the ensuing conversation. He couldn't be interrupted.

"No chaperones? he queried as he looked around them. "Your talk with Colby was a success I assume."

"None. Haven't spoken to anyone except for a few minutes to Colby. You were right in your assessments of my brother. Didn't have trouble convincing him his silence was necessary if he hoped to continue with his midnight pursuits. We don't know the Montgomeries enough to *ken* how they would react to his activities. At one time Drake might have been just like him, a true bounder. Colby didn't wish to take the chance he might have reformed."

"I've heard tales of that very thing, at least until he met the duchess. Seems it's time for you to tell me more about your family other than the fact your aunts and uncles have a great deal of children between them."

"Did put it off, didn't I? Self-preservation. I didn't want the morning to end before it began. I was terrified you would leave without kissing me a second time."

She slanted him the smile that never failed to grab his heart.

"Witch," he mumbled laughingly. "Let's start with how many aunts and uncles you have, shall we?"

"A good place to start. I've eleven aunts. They are all either sisters of my mother or cousins. You see, four sisters wed to men who either lived in the highlands or the lowlands. Each of the sisters bore four daughters."

"Good God, no sons between all of them?" He was appalled at the thought of raising all girls. "A man should have at least one son, shouldn't they?"

"Not a one among them. Afraid choosing isn't possible. If I had children, I believe I'd like one of each. What would you like?"

"Never thought of anything except gaining an heir. Thinking farther ahead than that isn't in my nature. Do go on with your family tree."

"Well, should I start from the beginning?"

"Always a good place," he snorted as he once again thought of siring only girls.

The devil, if they were anything like Nick, he'd have to put a twenty-four-hour guard on them when they came of age. "However, I'm more concerned about the uncles who might come after me demanding blood. Hopefully the aunts are more easy-going. Won't have to be dodging any fist where the women are concerned."

"Fists?"

"Yes, when they seek retribution for the deflowering of their favorite niece, or daughter if your father comes after me, fists will undoubtedly fly."

"I'm not deflowered yet…does that mean the loss of my virginity? I want to get everything straight for future reference."

"I'll be certain you understand everything."

"In that case should we speak of the ones residing in London? Think you should be worried about all of them. When they join forces, nothing can hold them back."

"Well then, who's in the city I need to concern myself with?" Other than the notorious Montgomerie, he didn't have any ideas.

"You most likely guessed by now that one of my uncles, the one who agreed to chaperone this adventure of mine, is Drake Montgomerie, the Duke of Richmond and Ella, his wife, who has become The Duchess following in the footsteps of the woman who made a reputation during her reign of power."

"I'm intrigued, you can tell me more about that reign of power later. Who else? Seems we're here."

Before she could dismount, he was beside her, his hands on her waist. He wasn't positive the best way to proceed. As he told her, the beginning was usually the best. A small pool created from one of the streams pouring into the Thames created the beauty of the secluded place. Finding a small flat stone, he skipped it across the water.

Nick did the same.

A plan formed.

"Who else?"

He turned to watch her endeavors, smiled broadly when she puffed the ostrich feather decorating her hat away from her nose.

She skipped another stone watching as it bounced along the surface of the water. "Roc Leighton is one of my uncles, a second or third, perhaps a great uncle. Could never keep track of such things. He's the Duke of Ravenswood, his mother being the original duchess. Also, Brett MacLachlan, a highlander such as yourself. Again, he's a second or third cousin as he wed Roc's sister, Piper."

With those identities revealed, he groaned understanding he should rethink his plans for Nick. No, he would take his chances. The devil, he'd never been so struck by a woman he'd risk his life to have her. Have her he would.

"A little wager?" he asked as he skipped another stone, thinking he might not have to encourage her to travel with him. "Let's see who can bounce the rock the farthest, shall we?"

"'Tis not fair. You're stronger. We'll see who can skip the most times. I've equal chance in that."

"What will you wager?" he asked, his grin widening as he thought of his request when she lost. He had no doubt about his prowess. He would win. "The best two out of three to give you the greatest chance."

"Arrogant man. It's a deal. I'll wager a kiss given to me by you."

He looked down a moment. With a hearty breath of air filling his lungs, he put forth his offer. "I'm leaving town, Nick. If I win, I want you to go with me to my home in Dornoch, though I intend to take the longest route possible. Even if I lose, I want you travel with me."

Chapter Three

The Promise slowly sailed past the city, heading down the Thames toward the ocean, the weather perfect for sailing with fair winds and sunny skies. A few billowy white clouds dotted the sky. Seagulls soared catching the winds. Nick stood beside Collin at the steering. She was tucked in front of him between his chest and the wheel. When she leaned against him, he wanted to pull her tight. His large hands were spread across her belly. Could not believe his good fortune when she so easily agreed to this venture.

When he made the outrageous suggestion, he expected a denial. Instead, she told him the night he kidnapped her, she visited Colby to plead with her brother to convince the duke and duchess she should return to the highlands. With all her heart she wanted to leave London. Knew she didn't belong in the city. Could not manage the necessary smiles to be presented as a debutante to the smirking young dandies who searched for a wife. In this position she saw herself as a bargaining chip. She didn't want to become a man's meal ticket to either wealth or a title. She had little to give a man except herself along with love. So be it.

They didn't need to wager, though she allowed him to play the game as he chose to do so. He laughed when he discovered her ruse. Her abilities in the rock-skipping category were good. For a few breathless throws, he thought she might win the wager. His last toss sent him ahead as the obvious winner. After that, she had the unmitigated audacity to flutter her lashes before telling him she lost on purpose.

Indeed, she did try to tell him she gave him the win. Not for one instance did he believe her.

"Where is it exactly we are going?"

Her adorable bottom pushed against his straining arousal. He taught her well as of this moment, he hadn't even made love to her. She knew what she was doing to him, the little minx.

"You're eager. I like that." He pulled her tighter against him trying to give back a measure of the temptation she heaped on him. If she was half as stimulated by this ploy she was wreaking on him, she'd be hot and slick when they finally reached the cabin. "Planning to take my time as we move up the Irish Sea then into the Hebrides. We'll stop as often as you like. Do you get seasick, love?"

"Only sailed between the land and our small island. Don't know. Suppose whether or not I have that malady remains to be seen."

She snuggled closer, the chill of the wind seeming to seep through the lightweight cloak she wore.

His body heated. She tempted and lured, enticed every nerve he possessed. She would need little coaxing once they were in the cabin with privacy to do as they pleased. "You cold? I can have my first mate, Hayes, take the wheel for me. Go to my cabin. Warm up a bit before we move on to more exciting entertainments."

"A bit? Rousing distractions?" She shivered as if meaning to make her point. "So, your home is on the western side of the island?"

Reasonable guess for the direction were headed. His hand settled more evocatively on her belly, splaying his fingers to measure the width, "*Nay* it's simply a ploy to put your uncles off our scent long enough for us to enjoy each other's company. I have this unexplainable need to get to know you better, all of you. They will discover easily enough the location of my home. It's not a secret. I'm wondering how long it will take them to figure out you've come with me instead of taking a carriage to the McLellan castle."

At her startled gasp, he squeezed her waist. His fingers tightened then massaged. "You know my family? Who they are, where they live? You should have told me. I've a right to know what you know about me."

He chuckled, his laughter floating in a whisp of air past her ear creating a fine trembling. He felt the sensation she experienced travel from her into him. Satisfied with the results of his tender coaxing, he meant to continue until they reached the English Channel then headed for open water.

"Started putting things together early this morning. Remembered some of our conversation from last night. Asked a few questions here and there on the waterfront while I was tending to my ship. Your mother's maiden name is McClellan, yours is Gray. Everyone in the highlands knows the tale of how your parents met. How Hunter Gray persevered until he discovered the secret of your mother's nighttime wanderings. How she pretended to be ugly."

"Truthfully? What else do you know about me?"

She turned her head, her hand resting on his cheek, her eyes huge pools of crystal-blue laughter. Her tongue found a way across her bottom lip leaving a trail of dewy moisture he wanted for a pre-dinner snack.

As he brushed his lips across hers, he tasted salt from the sea spray, caught the scent of her silken flesh along with her unique woman's scent. Felt an urgent need to discover more of her secrets. What he knew of her was only the foundation, beginning of more to come.

"Not nearly enough. You will be telling this man more about your aunts, especially your uncles. Need to know what I'll be dealing with when they come to collect you. What restitution the lot of them will demand in exchange. They will, you do understand that fact. While, I do *ken* you've one obnoxious brother. Any more of them to look out for?"

She was laughing, the sound infectious. As he joined her, his crew stared at them, grins etched on their weathered faces. They understood what they'd be doin' in the captain's cabin later on.

"No more," she told him. "Colby has been a thorn in my side since I was old enough to walk. He's always taunted me with his age. It's more than a girl should have to bear. If I had two unruly brothers, I'd like do away with one of them."

"Probably true. I'm sure not an expert in ways to handle the lad." He pointed south. "See, we are sailing into the estuary then on to the English Channel. As I told you earlier, we won't go left to the North Sea but travel right to the Irish Sea." He pointed to ocean swells, rising and falling. Seagulls swooped then dove to the water in search of food. The wind picked up. The sails filled. She pulled her cloak close around her.

"I thought…" she began only to stop herself. "I should truly cease thinking. It is only keeping me from remembering what you've told me."

"You did forget so soon. We will not stay on the North Sea.

Instead, I'll turn the ship to cut through the channel then on to the Irish Sea. I would not be such an easy catch for your uncles if I were to do the predictable. Do any of your uncles have a ship on hand?" He wondered as he plotted the next few months with his mouthwatering lover.

"I did remember." Her breathless voice gave him reason to continue his journeyings beneath her cloak, finding ripe plush skin for the sampling. "It's just that…you are making me forget. Yes, a couple do, most do if not all. Drake along with Roc can snap their fingers to receive the gift of a vessel along with a crew. As I told you before, my cousin Lyssa will arrive in Jamie Lundin's ship any day now, one of his newly built clippers."

"The one who builds the best as well as the fastest clipper ships ever to sail the seven seas?" He lifted an eyebrow as he gazed at her a smirk on his face. He loved the way she coiled and twisted wherever he caressed tender sensitive female parts.

"The very one, then there is my other uncle James who buys ships."

She squirmed when his hand settled higher. Moved against him as she tried to keep talking. "Collin…" His name was a shaking whisper of a breath. "He owns a fleet now of at least ten vessels. If he has any on hand, I'm sure all of my uncles could put together a crew within a day's time."

His ensuing groan surprised him. While he understood there would be repercussions when he decided to ask Nick to sail with him, he never realized her uncles could launch an armada against him. He didn't stand a chance in hell of living once her male relatives caught up with them, simply because he had every intention of making love to her every moment he got the chance.

Putting thoughts of his doom aside, his nip on her earlobe gifted him with a tiny gasp then a mewl of delight. With his tongue he soothed the tiny hurt. "Are you ready to go to my cabin? Dinner will be served soon. What would you like to enjoy while we wait? Perhaps my man's body? You can explore all you like as long as I get to do the same with your beautiful form." He was famished; not for food, for Nick.

To his groin, he felt her soft shudder rip through her then into him as he delighted in her passion. The back of her head rested on his chest. He allowed a fingertip to run the length of the delicate ivory column she exposed for him.

"It seems you're doing the enjoying of my body. If you're to be my lover, I should have more say in what we do."

Ah, she was breathless. It seemed his zealous persuading was working to his advantage.

"Correct, can't it be a bit of both?"

With great care paired with a great deal of work, he unfastened the top of her riding habit. Sneaking his hand inside, he discovered she wore nothing else. "Witch, you mean to seduce me," he murmured as he found the pulse at the base of her neck, sucked and nipped while he cupped her delightful breast in one of his hands while he attended to her pleasure.

"Is it working," she sighed a long breath of air.

"Yes."

His thumb danced with one hard tip, playing and teasing.

"Seems the two of you should be takin' this to your cabin," Hayes said with a hearty laugh when he stepped up to take the wheel. "Can't have the ship faltering because you're payin' no attention to the steering. If this continues, we could end up in France. I'll take over now, unless the two of you are having too much fun to be seekin' the privacy of the cabin."

"Fine with me. Thought she might want to feel the fresh air for a while. What do you say? Should we take our discussion along with the activities Hayes has alluded to, to the captain's cabin?"

He pulled her cloak tight. With a hand on her back, he guided the way to the cabin not giving her a chance to reply. He was in too much of a hurry to wait.

Inside it was warm. Nevertheless, his gaze focused on the trembling of her shoulders. Soon he would claim her as his. First, they would eat, enjoy a few glasses of wine. All the while he thought about the hasty actions that led her to his cabin on his ship. He meant to be at sea several months. By the time they reached the hunting lodge in the highlands, she would be well and truly on the way to becoming his mistress. When the timing was impeccable, he would ask.

Any regrets?

If she had regrets, despite the peril for him, he'd turn the ship around. He understood it was only time before the confrontation with her family. His motives in this situation were beyond his ability to define. All he could reiterate to himself was that he wanted her so badly he was willing to chance any and all altercations coming his way.

"You thinking of my uncles?" she asked, a silly grin on her face. "They are all pussycats. I'm sure if I plead my case, they will not hurt you."

"Dream on. If you plead your case, well, they will most assuredly lock you away until you're forty."

He found this to be rather amusing as he looked forward to the quarrel. He couldn't say why though.

"They are reasonable men, all of them."

It seemed she tried to defend them. She couldn't. In this instance they would be far from evenhanded.

His thoughts wandered. If I had a daughter or a niece…I'd make sure she remained a virgin until she was wed. They've not done their job by you. You were supposed to have a chaperone. Still, you managed to be alone with me not only the one time when I abducted you but twice more. That was not the way of a proper chaperone. They will have to hold themselves accountable to you as well as what they have not done for you."

"I'm only going to tell you this one more time because I don't feel the need to dispel all your arrogant assumptions. I am a virgin despite the duke and duchesses' slip ups."

She sounded indignant. He wanted to laugh. She was his virgin, his first virgin.

Time would tell the truth of her declaration. He wondered why she would make such a statement such as that when she must know he meant to bed her. Tonight, he would discover the reality of her words. What the devil would he do if she spoke true? There would be certain commitments expected. This was a major reason why he kept his dalliances to widows or divorcées.

She didn't want to wed any more than he did. Between them there would be no obligations or expectations except to themselves. For her uncles, they would envisage a proposal of marriage. The devil, he needed to think on other more pleasurable topics.

When they entered his cabin, dinner was served. Lanterns were lit as well as turned down. Hayes, he mused, must have ordered this. He pulled out a chair for her. As she started to fasten her bodice, he had other ideas. Wanted to look at her sweet curves while he thought about what they would do together on his bunk. He reached out a hand to stop her.

"Leave it, love," he told her his voice gruff with building desire he couldn't keep in check. "Took me a long time to get the damn gown where I want it."

Well, almost where he wanted the bodice. What he truly wanted was for the fabric to vanish.

Half open, he watched the rise and fall of her breasts. Saw the tight hard buds waiting for him to finish this meal before he began the next phase of this evening's escapade. "Drink up, there is lots of wine," he bade her. "At the moment the sea is calm. One never knows what will happen in the next instant."

Over the rim of her glass, she watched him, seeming to study his lips until she set the crystal on the table. "You've never spoken of your family," she said between bites of fresh salmon and the crisp greens that were served along with potatoes and bacon baked in a cream sauce.

"No," he paused thoughtfully. "Seems they are not so entertaining or dangerous as yours. I've four brothers. They will come together to defend me if need be. Before we left, I sent a man overland to apprise them of my guessed-at situation which seems more dire now than it was when I relayed the message."

She leaned forward, her elbows resting on the table her hands clasped beneath her chin. "Four brothers? Are they all bounders like you?"

He needed to ignore her question in lieu of more important information. "Told them to meet me at our family's hunting lodge. Intend to take the better part of the month perhaps two to get there. If the crew is willing, two months would be best."

Her brows drew together. "We're going to be aboard this ship for two months? We could almost reach the states in that time. Not certain I want to be confined to this cabin for that long. Why?"

"Need time to gather the clan, not just my brothers. We don't know how long it will take your well-meaning relatives to figure out that you travel with me instead of returning to your home. I believe from everything you've told me along with what I've guessed, proceeding without a show of force would be foolhardy. As to the other part, there are places up north we can stay on land."

"Doesn't that also give my uncles time to gather their armada as you put it?"

"Good question, however, they already have a wealth of resources at their immediate disposal. I've still a great deal to think on. Not too sure about anything. What I do need to understand is if you're willing."

"You know I am." She breathed out the words stiffly.

He heard urgency to the words almost as if she thought he changed his mind.

Collin almost laughed she sounded so indignant. "I'm speaking as your lover if you still want me. Do you, *lassie?*"

Her smile was precocious, eyes alight, glimmering as if she knew something he didn't. "If I don't want you any longer? Would you turn the ship around?"

"*Nay,* love, I would endeavor to persuade you to the point that you can't live without me."

The smirk rose from his loins before it centered in his belly his body rapidly becoming steel. For a moment he realized he didn't want to live without her. Bloody hell, bloody, bloody hell!

Nick would be his mistress, that was all there was to it. Damn her interfering uncles for assuming something more. They didn't have a say in what was going to happen here. Their wishes were not hers or his.

Nick reached out, took his hands into hers. Her fingers stroked him before she kissed the back of his hand. When she looked to meet his gaze, he saw a wealth of desire shining through the brilliant blue depths. "I wish to stay here with you. For you to finish what we began last night then into this morning, that is what I want."

"Me inside you? Loving you as you deserve to be loved. Nick, I *dinna* care if you've had a dozen lovers or none." *I mean to be your last.* The notion he didn't want another woman ever, startled him.

Her brows drew together fiercely in that line he was coming to understand she was displeased with him. Abruptly, she let go of his hands. Her eyes flashed ominously.

"You are the most stubborn, *unlistening* man I've ever met. At times you are worse than my brother!" she yelled at him. She rose, her little fists clenched tightly at her sides as she stomped the length of the cabin and back. She pointed a finger at him, appeared to be saying more before she fell silent.

Grinning, he sat back crossing his arms. He stretched out his legs, relaxed while he enjoyed the show she put on for him. Her bared breasts, small as they were, were swaying sweetly beneath the open fabric of her bodice. His body tightened further. If possible, his need for this adorable and very furious woman sprouted by leaps and bounds. All the while, his rod grew in anticipation of the rest of the night. If he wasn't needed on deck, he would spend the night loving her, teaching her the ways of the flesh. As things stood now, he would love her well and truly before going about his duties.

"What are you grinning about?"

She was so loud he was sure Hayes would hear her while he stood at the wheel. Tomorrow the first mate would have plenty to say. Hayes would tease as he was sure his first mate would find this amusing.

"You, the way you look so delectable when you're angry. The way your soft blue eyes darken while they seem to cross with every furious word. Will you be that passionate when you lay beneath me, or when you straddle me? Perhaps the passion will build more if I take you on the table. We could test this out. I'll call for Hayes. He can take the dishes away so we can analyze the theory. See what position you like best. Wouldn't be doing my job as your lover if we didn't pursue all possible avenues, now would I?"

To his delight, her mouth gaped open. "You're serious?" She plopped down on her chair before she looked at the table. All her previous anger seemed to be knocked from her. "How would you make love to me on the table? Seems to me the hard wood might be uncomfortable."

"You'd forget the discomfort. So, how would we do it?" he paused thoughtfully, "Should I tell or show? Suppose tell for now. With your long legs wound tightly around my flanks. No, perhaps you would prefer them over my shoulders. Yes, I'd plunge deep inside. You'd cry out my name when you reached the ecstasy I mean to give you. Inside your sweet sheathe your body will kiss my rod with the spasms I create for you, Love, just for you."

Her face flushed with color deep pink on ivory. She drank the last of her wine while she stared everywhere except at him. He'd like her to focus on his lips. Obligingly, he topped the glass off. Again, she didn't sip but drank long and deep.

"What else aren't you telling me?"

"Suspicious are we."

"Only because I *dinna ken* of what you are speaking."

"Soon you will. Perhaps we should move from the telling stage to the doing stage. Hmm…what do you think? Shall we begin? The first time we won't do anything different or unique."

"What I think is that you've made me hot from the inside out. That I want you to do all those things you spoke of nonetheless thinking of your doing those things to me terrifies."

"Terrifies?" The sound of that word horrified him. She shouldn't be afraid of making love or him. After all the innuendos, all that was implied she should…well hell, she should be playing with him.

"Yes, terrifies. We should drink more wine. Take a walk on the deck. See if the stars are as beautiful over the ocean as they are in the highlands. Maybe the moon will be looking down on us. You could kiss me on the deck. I believe I'd like that."

"We could do all that. I don't want to though. I would rather kiss you in the privacy of my cabin where others can't see where my hands are exploring. Since I'm your lover, you are going to have to direct me in all things. Tell me what you like as well as what you don't."

"Don't think that will work," she mumbled softly. "Don't know what to tell you to do. After what you just said, I've come to realize…"

He picked up her hand, turned it over. "Well, you could direct me to kiss the palm of your hand, here and again here."

He did so. The smile deep in his belly grew as he felt the shudder slowly sneak through her. Continuing in this vein seemed ultimately pleasant. "Or you could tell me to suck the tip of each of your fingers deep into my mouth." He did so. "You're delicious. Have I told you that before? No, well, yes, I believe I might have. Every part of you I've tasted is delightful."

"You're a devil incarnate, Collin McInnis." Her breaths were tiny short breaths of air that enchanted him.

"Tell me, Nick. I want to do your bidding. What next? Do I taste delectably delicious to you?"

She moaned softly. "I…"

He wasn't sure if she breathed. "I…?"

"You've already done those things. Don't know what I would do next. Just think, breathing would be nice at the moment."

"Ah, so you want me to do something else though you don't *ken* what to ask of me. Sincerely, you should be more versed in the art of love when you take a lover."

Inside he shook with amusement. Tried to keep the grin behind his teeth. The act was very nearly impossible.

"Told you…"

"Hush, I have listened to every sweet word uttered from your lips. What you say doesn't matter, it's the fact you're a true innocent. A bounder like myself recognizes innocents. Most times, stays away from women such as yourself. You're wrong in your assumptions, however, I still would have left with you aboard my ship if I'd known the truth about your intact maidenhead."

"You wouldn't have turned to run in the opposite direction?" She appeared shocked by the revelation. "I find I'm havin' a hard time believin' the fact."

He kissed the fingers on her other hand before he began speaking, "You are unique. I've never met a woman that stirs my blood to its boiling point so quickly or as intensely as you do, has me breathing hard while my heart pounds out of control when you smile. The first time I saw your face I knew you would be mine."

"I do that? You did?" she sounded incredulous at his statement.

"*Nay*, if I told you that was my reaction when I'm around you, it would give too much control over to you. Of course, every word I've uttered is true. Now, shall we proceed with the wheedling? If I were the leader in this affair, which I'm not. I would ask me to sit on your lap where I could more easily reach all the tender erotic spots I possess. Well, I suppose there are more than a few tender spots on my person. However, there are places that will get me more than ready to possess you. Do you think you can find them?"

She giggled. The sound touched his heart. He snaked out his hand as he brought her easily to sit upon him. "In our case, you must do the sitting on my lap. I'm far too big to sit atop you."

"What would I do next?" she asked as she gazed longingly at his lips. "Now that I'm taking your place."

It was too soon to kiss. He brushed away silken strands of hair, touched the lobe of her ear with a fingertip then his lips. He nipped at the spot on her neck that still blossomed a wonderous shade from his attentiveness. "Your turn," his lips parted as he waited for the innocent touch to send him soaring to new heights.

When she leaned forward to do his bidding, her softness caressed him, pushed against him. She was his delight. When her teeth bit endearingly on the lobe of his ear, he shuddered. She swirled her tongue inside his ear while her fanny squirmed against him. It seemed she was taking some initiative. He had not done that particular piece of gentle luring.

"Should you do that to me now?"

She sat back, her delicate hands resting on his shoulders while they fiddled with the fastenings on his shirt. "Should I proceed to something new?"

He winked at her as he parted the fabric of her bodice, traced the outline of her aureole. "Only if you ask."

He concentrated on the pink crest while he waited for her next audacious words.

"Will you touch me as I did you?"

"Don't be so shy. Say the words, love, or I won't be able to give you the pleasure you want. My poor man's brain doesn't know how to proceed in matters of the heart. You must be blindingly explicit."

She laughed, laughed so hard her breasts moved more tantalizingly than ever. He unfastened all the buttons.

"Can you please be serious? I want you to make love to me now. I want to understand what all the to do is about."

"Ask me to swirl my tongue inside your ear."

His voice was husky, waiting this long was his undoing. He needed to take care with this tender luring or he might embarrass himself.

"Stubborn man. Suppose you will do this your way or not at all."

She ran her fingers through his hair. Touched her lips upon his briefly. Swept her tongue across his mouth.

"Need I remind you? You're the leader, the boss, the captain of this affair. You must be the serious one or nothing here will be accomplished."

She let out a long whoosh of air he knew now meant she was resigned to what he asked. "Very well then, will you swirl your tongue in my ear." She giggled again. "Faithfully, Collin you are exasperating. Need I yell at you again so you will take over this process? So, we can finish before morning."

"We will finish more than before morning. So, you want me to be the head in this affair? You willingly hand over the reins to me? A mere man?"

She punched him on the shoulder. "Yes, yes, yes…or nothing will happen. I want to lose my maidenhead tonight. I'm gifting you with it you know. You should not make this so difficult for me, a mere debutante who knows nothing of carnal delights."

With her words all humor vanished. He sucked in a bite of air then another. This was more than a bounder could ever hope for. She shouldn't be doing this. He shouldn't be taking what she was offering.

It was all wrong.

He was in over his head with no regrets.

The devil, but he wasn't going to stop now. There was no way in hell another man would have what she wanted to give him.

"We are through role playing? You want me to proceed with your deflowering?"

The devil, why did he feel even a twinge of guilt.

She wanted him.

He wanted her, more than he'd ever wanted another woman.

Gently, he picked her up. He carried her to the bed, setting her upon it with the greatest of care. This would be a first for both of them. He didn't want to hurt her. Knew there was no alternative except to leave her alone.

That wasn't going to happen.

"I do," her voice was soft, whisper thin in the dim light of the room.

The vessel rocked gently, rose and fell with the waves.

"I'm glad of that, love."

Slowly, he slipped her shoes and stocking off, tracing his fingertips along the inside of her thighs, across the bottom of her feet to tender spots behind her knees. He changed tactics now, following the path of his fingertip with his mouth and tongue. An occasional nip caused her hips to rise. She moaned the sound coming from deep in the back of her throat. The pressure to make this right, fell tensely in his gut. Never before had he sweet-talked a virgin to his bed. Never before did his actions mean so much.

Her lacy and very frilly undergarments were next to fall onto the floor. Beneath the skirts she wore nothing at all. His imagination buzzed in many directions. If this wasn't her first time, he'd taste her in the most intimate part of her. She told him she was terrified. He supposed that was normal.

"Are you going to take anything off? I'd like to see you naked," her voice purred sweetness in breathy little puffs when she asked. The sounds endeared her even more to his world-weary soul.

"When I've got you completely naked before me. When I've seen my fill. After that I'll disrobe slowly so you can ogle every part of me to your heart's desire."

Once again at her expression, he wanted to laugh. Angry or teasing, she was so precious, his treasure.

Though he did slip from his shirt. As it joined her clothing on the floor, he stretched out beside her. The length of him pressed against her side.

"Not fair," she told him as her hands rose to touch his chest, to smooth a path across then lower to his waist. Her fingertips glided slowly, erotically. He was sure she didn't understand what she did to him.

He sucked air at the unashamed contact. His belly contracted. The sensations entranced him. "Witch," he murmured while he enjoyed everything about her. "Touch me again if you want. If you do though, I won't be responsible for what comes next. You do know you are playing with fire, tempting while luring me to take over this sensual dance."

"What will that be, Collin McInnis. You will not just plunge inside me now, will you? No, you will take your time, make certain I feel everything you wish to gift me with all the way to the tips of my toes," she purred softly, a low hum emanating from the back of her throat.

Even her voice created sexual havoc.

"Minx, you have no idea what I'll do. Where do those words come from," he spoke before she could, "You overheard your brother with his friends, didn't you? Now fess up. A young lass shouldn't be ease-dropping on her big brother and friends. She might learn more than she should." Lord almighty, he hoped when the time came, he sired only sons. He wouldn't know what to do with a girl. Blasphemy, if the good Lord heard him now, he would undoubtedly have only daughters.

Soon the bodice along with her skirt lay on the floor, scattered between the door and the bed. He moved back to look his fill. He'd not seen her from head to toe wearing nothing at all. She was the most beautiful, ravishing woman he'd ever seen. He'd seen his share. Of all things she was smiling at him, her arms outstretched to bring him closer. The way she seemed to always want him, excited him beyond anything he'd experienced before. While women wanted him, the light in their eyes never shone quite so brilliantly, their expression never one of such deep passion.

~ * ~

The way Collin regarded her sent an inferno of liquefied heat blasting through her flooding her senses, her body, her mind. Her heart caught, held still for several seconds while she tried to grab air into her lungs. She heard the soft moan seeming to come from somewhere inside. Reached out to him. He was her heart. He didn't know it. She wouldn't tell him. If he asked, she would do anything for him. Anything with the single exclusion of marriage.

"Please..." she sighed, not understanding what she was pleading for.

Though he knew. This was the sweetest torture. With each passing second, her body became more sensitive to his touch more aflame. She squirmed and coiled, reaching for some intangible point she didn't understand yet instinctively knew existed.

"Please what, love? Tell me. Speak to me candidly." Amusement colored his voice. He was a devil to tease her so.

Before she could answer, he flipped her onto her stomach. It happened so fast she couldn't protest or struggle against him. Not that she wanted to deny him his devilish way with her. *Nay,* he had free reign as far as she was concerned. He could do whatever pleased him as she was sure it would please her also.

"I *dinnae ken*...that's why I have you," she moaned into the pillow at her head. Her body twisted with need. Her hips lurched upward.

He laughed softly. His fingertips teasing and taunting tender flesh. "Indeed, you do have me. I would not leave you."

He straddled her, his hands resting on her back for a moment only before they started traveling down her spine, stopping at her bottom. Her muscles twitched beneath the slight pressure of his fingers.

"You have the most lovable bottom I've ever seen. All smooth and round, well-muscled, which is surprising for a woman."

His hand traveled lower, between her legs, touching places that made her jump then sigh with the strange feelings coursing through her.

"You make wonderful sounds."

"Wh-what are you doing? You're touching me...I didn't know you would..." she swallowed hard when he found more pleasure points.

"Making sure you find as much gratification tonight as I do. I'll indulge you in every way I can think of. If you have some thoughts on that, you must tell me."

He spoke softly, his voice tender while his hand caressed and parted slick folds between her thighs.

Once more she jumped when he nipped her buttocks, licked and soothed each place his teeth found purchase. Inside the deepest darkest part of her she throbbed, pulsed and twinged with the greatest need. His lips discovered more of her, stopping often to kiss as he journeyed up her spine then down again.

"You've the most beautiful back. Just like the rest of you," he murmured while he brushed hair away from her neck nibbled and sipped sensitive flesh.

"I want to see you too. I'm naked. You told me… Oh…."

Her hips jerked upward again. She possessed no control.

The room was hot, the air so very quiet around her while the ship dipped into waves. Water sprayed across the small window. She held her breath in the back of her throat dying from anticipation of what he might do next.

"Do you still want to walk upon the deck? See the stars. I can assure you they are quite beautiful even though you outshine them. We would have to delay this if you say yes. If you choose to walk tonight, I'll remind you of how you be feelin' at this moment while we are gazing heavenward."

"You are torturing me, Collin. Why don't you just get this done with. I want you now." She breathed in the scent of the man as his body rested against hers. She felt him. His long-hardened body against hers, so different from hers.

"There is no just getting it done with. Loving a woman takes time and patience. A man needs a slow hand. Do you *ken*? Needs to see to her delight before his. A man will always reach his climax. Not so a woman. This is my responsibility to see it done right."

"Stupid question from a stubborn man. You know I don't *ken* anything about love making except what I've overheard." She groaned as his hands slid down her sides then her legs only to return in more intimate places. A tempest brewed around her. She ached for him in too many different ways.

"That knowledge coming in tiny bits and pieces. One should never listen in on other's conversations. One can come out of the ordeal quite confused about some very important topics."

He turned her over then sat on the bed next to her. He didn't touch her but handed her a full glass of wine. She had no idea when he poured wine. "Are we done? If we are, then I'm well and truly disappointed."

"Tired, you've worn this poor man out. I've need of subsentence before I can continue coaxing you to the greatest ecstasy known to mankind."

"If my mouth wasn't so parched, I do believe I'd toss the wine in your face. I'm hot and pulsing in places I never knew existed like this. You want to drink wine."

He roared with laughter. "Now, my lovely one, why would you do that? Wine is much more enjoyable when it travels down one's throat. Although...if you tossed the liquid, you could sip it from my body."

"I swear," she was yelling at him again and no longer cared. She punched his shoulder hard. "You know why...I could lick it from you..."

"Impatient, are we? Should we try it? We could begin with a drop or two." He grinned. "I want this night to last as long as possible."

She downed her glass, unwilling to test her stamina against all he suggested. It was too much, just too much. "No wine. I want to see you. Want to drink my fill of your muscles. Want to discover for myself if you're truly the brick wall I think you are."

"Brick wall?"

"You are so hard, unyielding as well. Big." She ran her hands along his chest, testing the hard wall of muscles she found there.

"You are so soft. We are a good compliment for each other, don't you think? I would not want to bed a woman who wasn't soft in all the right places."

"I wouldn't know about this compliment thing. Haven't seen enough of you to make a decision. I never truthfully thought of myself as soft." She was indignant, angry.

"Curvaceous," he smiled. "I do hope you're pleased. Not sure what I'd do if you don't like the way I look."

"I will like your body, know I will." With anticipation she held

Christine Young

her breath as he slowly removed his clothing. It was what she wanted.

Silence seemed to stop the seconds from passing. He was everything she ever imagined. His shoulders broad narrowed to slim hips. His belly was hardly a belly, there was nothing soft or moving. His core reminded her of the washboards in the scullery. She sucked air when she saw the part of him that was so different from her. He dazzled her female senses.

She stared.

Watched as it grew in size.

"Can I touch you?" she asked softly as she reached trembling fingers toward him. Toward that part of him she sought to know more about.

"If you want me to explode outside of you instead of where we both want me to be, go ahead. Suppose, I could recover."

"Explode? Will that hurt?" She ran her tongue along her lips then tucked the bottom one beneath her teeth as she thought over his words. "I want to taste you. Is that something I can do?"

"Drink."

He sat next to her, his shoulder against hers. He chuckled softly as he poured more wine.

She needed to understand why he laughed. "I don't want any more wine. Why are you stalling? Teasing me? Are you having second thoughts? You don't want me."

Beside herself, she felt helpless. Moisture brimmed in her eyes.

"Good God, no! I want you desperately." He let his head settle against the backboard. "Sorry, love, I've never done this with an innocent. Guess I am stalling. Want your first time to be perfect for you even though I understand pain will be involved." His voice shook as he spoke. "Not looking forward to your pain. Don't like to know I'm going to hurt you."

She set her glass on the table. "Don't put this off any longer. You are making me more afraid than before. Make love to me, please. Love me as I know you can. Don't think about something you know will subside."

Suddenly, she found herself beneath him, his weight delightfully covering her. His chest pushed against her breasts even while he tried to

83

hold himself above her. His lips discovered hers again. He tasted of the sweet wine they'd been drinking. He explored her with his lips. She delighted in the exquisite sensations. Her hips jerked and twisted, searching for fulfillment.

His long slender fingers caressed her intimately, parted her. Found a place that sent vibrations she'd never felt before course through her. His fingers were suddenly inside her, moving within her, teaching her a rhythm she couldn't ignore. Didn't want to in any case.

"I'm going to come inside you, love. I touched the membrane. It's intact." His growl rumbled from the back of his throat.

She whimpered, moved her hips upward as if she knew what she was doing. He eased his way inside. Stopped.

"No, don't...please..."

He pushed inside, broke through so she sheathed him completely.

Collin swallowed her cry of pain with his mouth. It was done. Nothing would change. She gave her virginity to the man she chose.

"Regrets?" he asked as his body began to move slowly inside her.

"No. You?"

Her question was cut off as once more she was brought higher and higher, the pinnacle a dizzying blur. He was over her, inside her, his tongue deep inside her mouth playing with hers, fencing and dueling. She sizzled, heated. Tempest and storm raged inside her body. Her nails bit into his shoulders, ran them down his spine then back. She moved with him then against him. Spiraling, whirling, lightheaded with need, she clung unable to do nothing else. It seemed even the ship rocked with them.

"Collin..." her cry of delight was once more cut off when he absorbed the pleasure into him. He thrust harder and faster until he roared his ecstasy.

For a moment, his body rested atop hers, slick with the sheen of moisture. She heard his rasp of air, felt his body part from hers. She wanted to hold him against her. When he finally entered into her, it all happened so quickly. Her breath was stolen while her heart still thundered. She reached that sought after pinnacle so quickly. Now it was done. She was no longer a virgin.

He rolled to her side, his finger trailing along her arm. "Thank you," he murmured as he brushed his lips across hers. His smile so very endearing. "Can't tell you what that meant to me. Profound, I suppose. Did I give you pleasure?"

"You know you did," she whispered as she turned into him, her fingertip caressing his mouth. "I…"

"Yes?" he queried, a slow chuckle following.

"Oh, I don't know."

"We should eat. Drink more wine."

Do it again?

"Yes, love, make love again and again until we are both sated."

"Would like that."

She watched as he rose, striding to the counter where a basin and a pitcher of water was kept.

His buttocks were solid muscle. His shoulders broad. He strode with easy confidence, a manly swagger to his stride. She admired so much about him. He dipped a rag into the water he poured into the basin. When he turned, she saw the blood on him.

Her blood.

As he turned, he must have seen her shocked expression. Her eyes were wide. "What are you doing?" she felt sure she squeaked.

"Well." He stepped closer, "Plan on cleaning us up. What did you think I mean to do?"

"That's my blood."

She pointed at him, her hand shaking.

His eyes narrowed, a crease on his forehead grew, "Is there still pain?" He sat beside her. His expression tender. His eyes shining with emotion.

"No, just for a few seconds then…then it was," she swallowed the lump that seemed to grow in her throat. "You played my body. It was magical. Can't think of anything else to describe what I felt. That's why you're a bounder, a rake. You know what to do when you're with a woman." She reached out to him, drew back. "Did I give you pleasure? Do the other women you bed give you pleasure?"

It seemed she couldn't stop the questions. Her curiosity was getting the better of her. She didn't want him to know how hurt she would be if he saw another woman after being with her.

He ran his knuckles along her cheek. "To begin with, perhaps that's why I like to be with a willing woman. The pleasure is always amazing, as you say magical. There is nothing else in the world like the ecstasy that comes when a man or a woman climax. Secondly, I never bed a different woman when I'm with another. I'm your lover. That makes you mine just as I'm yours. There will be no others while we are together." He held up the wet rag. "Spread your legs, love. Open for me again so I can rid you of the evidence claiming your virginity."

"What?" She pushed at his hands, as it appeared he meant to do it for her.

Embarrassment wilted her, seethed within. Felt heat rise quickly. "You'll see me."

His chuckle was soft yet the sound unnerved her. "That's what I intend. Actually, my dear, I've seen all of you, touched you, played you intimately with my lips and tongue. Now, where I'm going to clean you, I will taste. The sweet scent of you gives more pleasure to me. We will enjoy each other thoroughly, you and me."

"Truthfully, Collin, It's not the same…" She couldn't speak when the soft rag touched upon her.

"No, you're right. This is much more clinical." He swept the cloth against her until the blood was gone then he cleaned himself. "Was that so bad?"

"Not exactly bad; embarrassing, disturbing."

The moment he touched her, looking at her intimately, heat flooded her.

"Wine? Food?" He handed her a full glass of wine.

She started to pull the quilt over her. He stopped her, shaking his head. His grin stretched across his chiseled face. The hard lines softened. There were no coherent thoughts in her head. A few moments before she blurted her curiosity. Now…now she drank. The wine was delicious. She looked at him. He was still grinning.

"What are you thinking?" She didn't have one single misgiving about what she did here in the cabin with Collin. If a woman chose to do so, she did believe with all her heart a woman should be able to love a man without benefit of marriage. Why should a man have all the benefits as well as freedoms to do as he pleased?

"I was wondering the same about you. Worried you were having second or even third thoughts about what we just did. It can't be taken back. You should know I consider myself a *verra* lucky *mon*."

"If you're not intending to remain on the ship for two months, what do you have in mind."

She knew she would grow claustrophobic if expected to stay in this small room for such an extended period of time.

"You change the subject quite handily. A friend." Held up a finger to stop more questions. "All my friends are considered rakes and bounders. Black is his name. He likes seclusion. Times when he wants to be absolutely alone, he travels to the Hebrides to get away from the city. He bought the land several years ago. The lodge is rustic, however comfortable. He's part Lakota Sioux. Actually, I think the man would return to the plains if he could avoid the commitment he made to his grandfather when the man brought him home ten years ago."

"A rustic hunting lodge owned by a man who is part Sioux? My mind is boggled trying to conceive what that might look like. We will stay there?"

"Until you wish to move on. I'll leave that up to you. He won't intrude on our privacy," Collin assured her. "Before we reach his second home, we will stay a few nights in some favorite ports. Many of my crew have agreeable women who are ready and eager to see them when we sail into port."

"Privacy, that's what you want. Just like now?"

Asking him to make love to her again was out of the question. Hadn't she heard her brother talking about the very real impossibilities of doing so twice in one night? Colby told her the woman had to be an extraordinary lover for something like that to occur. She wasn't knowledgeable, a debutante newly introduced to *amour*. Truly, she couldn't be astonishing in her ability as a lover.

He downed the wine in his glass, took hers from her hands. "Would you like to try something different?" His lips brushed hers softly, tenderly as the palm of one of his large hands swept against the tip of her breast. She gasped startled by the contact. He laughed, seeming pleased with her.

"Different?" Her voice warbled. "What do you mean, different?"

"One of the ways we spoke of earlier. You can straddle me. I'll show you how it's done?"

One perfectly formed dark eyebrow rose. His grin unnerved her, sent her suspicious nerves shivering.

She tucked her bottom lip beneath her teeth. "You want to…to…to do, it, again? I thought men couldn't unless the woman was exceptionally good at…it."

His roar of laughter had the decided effect to rattle every nerve that wasn't already shivering with anticipation of the unknown. "Now where did you get an absurd notion such as that? While the statement probably has some truth to it, applying the fanciful statement to us, it is not worth a second thought." He paused then tapping his long well-shaped finger on his chin, "Your brother. You *ken* he's just a young pup. Of course, he wouldn't have the stamina."

One more time embarrassment drowned her in heat. She covered her face with her hands before she looked at him to answer, "Well, if you must know then yes. I heard it when he was talking to a couple of his buddies."

"As you told me earlier, the act was magical. I have a great manly need to feel that enchantment again with you. You are enchanting, more enticing than anyone I've ever known. Truth be told, I don't intend to wait for another night before I enjoy your considerable charms a second then possibly a third time."

She stiffened, her back straight not understanding totally why she took umbrage at his words. "I don't like to be compared to other women," she blurted hearing only the words that told her he equated her to his previous bedmates.

"Because you don't have a man to compare me with? Can't say that I'm disappointed with that fact. Shall we? Are you willing to please this man again? There are so many fascinating avenues to survey. We can explore to your heart's content."

He didn't give her the opportunity to answer. In any case she would have told him yes. The tiny bit of coaxing he'd been tempting her with when they spoke had her panting with need for something she now understood better.

Suddenly, while she was thinking on all the things he told her, she was straddling him. His rod was thick and growing between her legs. Once again, she quivered, her voice trembling. "How does this work?"

Her curiosity leapt high.

"Thought you'd never ask. When you're ready you can lower yourself on me. That would be nice for you, me as well. Don't want to overlook how the penetration will give my heart a bounce."

She couldn't help the widening of her eyes. Her skepticism, she was sure, shone through. "Impale myself?"

She looked at his swollen member then his laughing eyes. Behind his grin, his teeth were as white as newly fallen snow.

"I don't believe so. No, it won't work. It's absurd. Truly, Collin what makes you think?" Unable to help herself, she was shaking her head, her heart pounding double time.

"You're babbling is endearing. I promise you this position will work. Will also make a solemn vow that you will find the process quite enjoyable. I'm handing over the captain's command to you. Do you trust me to have your best interest at heart? Need for you to be a bricky lass in this new endeavor."

She wasn't sure what he was getting at just now. Where this was concerned, she didn't understand how courage or the lack of the commodity had a place. "I don't want to disappoint you."

"Never, Love. You could never disappoint me even if you told me no. You aren't going to do that are you? I feel the dewy moisture between your legs. Your woman's petals are soft and hot, more than ready for my sex to enter into you. Say the word and I'll show you how you can control our loving. You like that, control. I know you do. I give it all over to you now that you're experienced."

His hands roamed expertly, tempted her as he did before. She squirmed and twisted against him as she tried to get closer. The newly found sensations built inside while he continued to sightsee sensual spots. "Collin…" The pulsing spasms started again, built and built until she was certain she would explode.

"Do you want me to help? I can if you ask me. Tell me the words. Say that you want my great rod inside you so I can grace you with exquisite pleasure. Tell me, Nick."

She couldn't swallow, could barely breathe the words he wanted to hear.

"Tell me, Nick. Do you need a drink of your wine first?"

She nodded then drank deep after he handed the glass to her. She inhaled a huge lung full of air. "Show me, please. Help me. I want you so much. Desperate for you."

She felt sure he knew how much she needed him. Didn't understand why she had to say the words to get what she so frantically needed.

"Tell me you want my member inside your hot tight sheath. I want the spasms I generate to kiss my shaft over and over again. Want to send you to newfound heights."

"Show me. Put your rod inside me so I can feel the that dizzying pinnacle of rapture again."

Nickie couldn't believe she spoke those words to a man. What would her brother think if he knew? Her uncles would be beside themselves if they discovered their charge was so very brazen. Her father would lock her in the tower until she was forty.

"Thought you'd never ask."

Suddenly, the heat and length of him filled her exquisitely. He was so deep. She was certain he touched her womb. When she looked down, she saw how they were joined. As she caught his gaze, he nodded, understanding what she was thinking.

"You've the power. Make love to me as if I'm your very own lover meant to please you. Move fast or slow. I'll make sure you feel all you expect, enjoy the magic. This tiny jewel of delight," he caressed and massaged a place that left her soaring higher. "Will bring you there quickly."

~ * ~

"How long has Nicole been missing?" Addie asked the assembly of uncles along with aunts gathered together.

She was pacing the room, tapping her slender finger against her chin.

As the less biased of all the relatives simply because they were only aunt and uncle because they were friends of the immediate family, they were given the task of snooping for answers. She and Hamilton were sent by Drake to gather information. This meeting was the culmination of all their ease dropping and meddling. Years ago, the two worked for Drake. When Hamilton and Addie retired, the two of them agreed to go on missions that weren't life threatening.

"It's been two weeks tomorrow," Ella said looking guilty as hell. "Two long weeks while we waited for Colby to go home then return with the unwanted information that she wasn't safely ensconced in her home."

Well, in Addie's estimation the two of them had a great deal to account for when it came to taking care of their charge. Why, if they failed this miserably with the rest of the girls who would arrive on this very doorstep over the years, none of the doting parents would trust either of the pair. They were novices at chaperoning. Their own story of love and courtship was not one to be told to the young women who would come their way for advice. The telling of it would make a horrific impression. Drake did exactly as he pleased where Ella was concerned. To Addie, it seemed Collin was following in the duke's footsteps. She hoped the couple was in love. If they were, that fact would soothe all the angry feelings.

Drake cleared his throat, his long fingers tapping on his thigh. "Are the two of you going to prevaricate as usual or will you get to the point? We've some plans to make if we are going to retrieve my niece."

Addie smiled fondly as she looked to her husband. Drake was right. The two of them did enjoy the banter, especially when it served to offset the duke. To Addie, nothing delighted her more than seeing the frown lines form on Drake's forehead. "Do you wish to tell them the information we worked our fingers to the bone to discover? Or...do you want me to do the explaining. You are so much better at it though."

"Pshaw," Ella waved her hand in the air before wrapping the cane on the floor three times. "Get on with it. Don't have time for all the theatrics we know the two of you are capable of. You both are equally as good at explaining."

"You can give her the good news," Hamilton said shooting her a pleasant smile, one he honed to excellence over the years. "Or, perhaps it's bad news. Depends on one's prospective now, doesn't it?"

"Well, you do tend to get off the topic if I recall. You love to make everyone wait on the edge of their seats while they hold their breath in anticipation of the words to come. It's been so long since we've been called on to spy. I simply don't know what kind of news good or bad will sprout from your manly lips."

She slanted him what could only be described as a precocious grin before she winked.

"We weren't spying, my love. We were asking questions, delving into Nicole's whereabouts," Hamilton bit out with a chuckle. "You must get your facts straight."

"In all the right places it seems," Addie said while she graced her husband with another broad smile tilting her head slightly to one side before sending him another flirtatious wink.

"One of you needs to get on with the topic at hand. At this rate we will never catch up to her wherever that might be!" Ella shouted as if that would bring Addie around. Not while she enjoyed this so much. Seemed the duchess was just as impatient as the duke.

Addie wasn't about to take the fun out of this interview. What difference did a few minutes make in locating the long-lost niece? Nickie was a woman who wasn't lost. Nonetheless, she was in the hands of one of London's most notorious womanizers. By now she was compromised, no doubt about that little fact. What these men would do when they caught up to the pair of lovers was still up in the air? Addie hoped no one would die. From what she understood about the duke, she wouldn't hold her breath.

"My, my, losing patience so soon?" Addie chuckled softly. "Nicole did not go home. We finally heard from Colby about the lack of her presence at McClellan castle. She has not been seen by anyone at home since before she left for London."

"Where the devil is she?" Roc asked not appearing to have any more patience than the other duke. "You need to tell us!" His hands were fisted, his jaw ticking. "We need to retrieve her before anything happens to her that cannot be undone."

"Do you suppose dukes are born with no patience?" Hamilton asked blandly while he stared hard at the two men. "Seems our dukes have none and neither does the duchess. We should strive to teach them that patience is a virtue that should be courted."

"Truly, Hamilton, you should never provoke these important aristocrats. You might end up in the brig or London Tower. Yes," she tapped a flawlessly manicured nail on her chin, "I'm sure the location would be the Tower."

Hamilton gestured in the air with his hand seeming to believe these people suffered long enough. "There is no proof as to where she is at the moment. We compiled a list of guesses from all the people she knew here in London."

"Because of what her brother told us about her behavior the morning after the ball, we have good reason to believe your niece is with the bounder Collin McInnis."

Addie took pity on the uncles whose fists were now clenched and the lines of their faces livid with anger.

"As to their whereabouts, we haven't a clue. Could be anywhere. No one at the docks is talking. His best friends are devoid of speech. Seems the other notorious reprobates are loyal to a fault. Either that or they know nothing." Addie lifted her shoulders a bit. "Who's to say?" She turned to Hamilton before pointedly casting her glance Drake's direction. "Does their loyalty remind you of certain rogues from a by gone day?"

Hamilton shot his wife a look at to say she shouldn't keep up this verbal exchange of theirs while she knew he didn't intend to abide by his own wishes.

"As Addie said outright, seems the earl has a bevy of men who are loyal to him. We heard he took sail on his way to wherever. We can assume he's headed home via whatever route suits his fancy," Hamilton handed over the news. "If he's a smart man, he won't make this easy for us. Collin McInnis will know we will come for Nicole."

"Although we don't pretend to assume that if he has Nicole with him, he isn't taking divertive measures. He won't have a death wish," Hamilton said quietly. "This ship of his could be a ploy. They could be traveling overland. Also, there is a wealth of directions by sea the man could take. Believe I heard he owned land in Bermuda. They might have headed west."

"I ran into his butler, Charley, who told me they traveled overland via his carriage to Dornoch. Although the man told me he does possess several townhouses in various cities. He could be going to any one of those places. Also implied he needed to visit his estate on the island."

"Perhaps," Drake paused in thought, "we should divide our resources. Jamie, your ship is still birthed on the Thames. You should head to Dornoch, invade his household with your crew. If you can find a way to do so, take over the home. If he is there, lock him in somewhere until I can come for Nickie."

"Do you forget he will be two weeks ahead of me?" Jamie asked pleasantly. "I'm willing to help although I don't appreciate being sent on a wild goose chase. He will gather his clansmen, as he would understand we would go after our niece. Don't want a single man on my crew to get hurt, not in this adventure to encounter bloodshed."

"Only if she's told him who she is," Ella said. "I've the feeling Nicki is enamored of the man. She has fallen for him as I did you." Sweetly, she looked at her husband with starry eyes just as she'd done years ago. "You will not find her willing to leave the man, bounder or not. You cannot force her to return with you. If you do so, or try, she will rebel. I would have, if anyone forced me to leave you. Our Nickie is a strong-minded woman, bent on having her way in all things."

"I'm sure the man will go to Dornoch. What I have heard is that it is his favorite home, the family home. The route he takes is up in the air. The condition of your niece is something else to consider. As Ella said, Nickie is enamored of the man. Colby told me the morning before she is rumored to have left with him, he saw her half naked straddling him. Colby thinks if he hadn't come along at that time, she would have found herself compromised that very morning," Ella said, once again sending her husband starry-eyed looks.

"The lot of you need to be realistic, there isn't a chance in hell by the time we find her she won't have given herself to the bounder," Hamilton told the assembly pointedly. "As we speak, she is no longer a maiden."

"He'll wed her on the spot. Won't take no for an answer. After that we'll take Nickie home. The bounder can't have everything his way. Nickie won't be allowed to see him ever again."

"I'm sure you believe that now. What will you do when Nicole runs off again? Will you go after her then drag her home again? Will you lock her in a tower, keeping her prisoner in her home? What if she is carrying his child? That is a very good possibility. What does her father and mother want?"

Drake fisted his hands. "We will have to drive home the point then. If she is with child, I'm sure Hunter along with the rest of us will insist he marry her. If he still refuses, he might find himself in the dungeon of the McClellan castle for an extended stay. That would knock some modicum of sense into his addled brain."

"Ah, fisticuffs a very good way to reason with a grown man. Heard he's one hell of a fighter. Well versed in different arts besides boxing. You would all do well to remember you're twenty years his senior," Addie's final remark seemed to sink home. "He's also one of the largest men I've ever encountered."

"We will deal with all this when we find her," Ella said softly. "All of you bristling males will listen to Nickie's wishes as well. We cannot and will not run roughshod over Nicole."

"You're not going with us," Drake shot furious words her way, his eyes sparking dangerously.

She seemed the epitome of calm serenity despite the bristling and posturing of her husband, the duke. "I am. Don't think to stop me, Drake. If things go horribly awry as I'm beginning to think they will, Nickie will need a woman to console her. You don't possess one consoling bone in your lovely body."

Chapter Four

With each day passing, Collin found he became increasingly under Nick's enchantment. If he believed in the dark arts, he would say she bewitched him, cast a spell over him. In his experiences with his many women, no female ever touched him this deeply. Her singular beauty was the light of every day as well as each night. Thoughts of her spilled into everything he did, all that he saw. If she was near, her scent filled him. If she was the length of the ship, the sight of her drew him.

His hands were ever upon her as keeping to himself was nearly unbearable. Now, from the steering wheel, he watched her slight form sway with the dance of the vessel. She stood at the bow of the ship, her hands resting lightly on the wood railing. Wind filled the white sails. The Promise rose on the crest of a wave before sliding downward. The ensuing breeze snatched her glorious wheat-blond hair from the pins that were supposed to be keeping the strands in place. Undoing her pins was one less thing he needed to do in the privacy of his cabin before he made love to her, before he wove the silken strands through his fingers. They would have privacy in minutes.

Collin nodded to Hayes to take the wheel.

Hayes looked to Nick then back to him. "Storms brewin' to the east of us. Should be upon us before we can blink," Hayes said as he replaced Collin at the steering. "Better apprise your lady friend she best stays in the cabin. Tell her why. Don't take any chances that her curiosity or fear will bring her on deck."

Nick did not take to orders. She preferred to make decisions on her own, not be told what she could or couldn't do. "You're right. We'll both be needed out here most of the night if those dark clouds are an indication of the storm's ferocity." Collin's gaze focused on Nick, the slenderness of her back, the fragility of her. His heart lurched to his throat as he thought about what could happen to her in a storm this size if she disobeyed, if she didn't heed his warnings. He would make certain she understood what could happen if she ventured from the safety of the cabin.

No orders would be issued. He would hand her the information. She would know what was right. Collin had every confidence in Nick's intelligence as well as common sense.

"Go get her now. Do your little love dance then get back up here," Hayes said grinning, understanding he shouldn't be ordering the captain. His cackle swept away by the increasing wind. "Seems you've about one hour before this one hits. Is that enough time?"

"Good thing I'm in the best of moods," Collin said wryly thinking on the audacity of his first mate. Bloody eyes, they'd been together more years than he could count. "That sounded a great deal like insubordination, Hayes. I'll see you when the storm hits the ship. Could be a long night ahead."

Hayes wiped his forehead with the back of his hand as he eyed the dark clouds that were growing closer. "It's a doozy coming our way. Not usual that a storm can overtake this ship. You might want to strap her to the bed," Hayes followed with a loud chortle. "Just to keep her safe for the duration, mind you."

During the trip he'd taken some ribbing from his crew about Nick's presence in his cabin. Though he made sure they stopped in a port almost every night. The time he spent with Nick was well worth every moment as well as the shore leave he gave his men. The crew was happily content. They didn't resent him keeping his woman with him or the hours he spent in his cabin. Time was no issue for him. He had his reasons to make the journey as long as possible.

When he walked to the bow, she turned. Her smile never ceased to make his heart race while his breath would catch in his throat. He held out his hand. She accepted it. Her fingers were cold. He brought her hand to his lips to kiss her fingers. When he looked up, her eyes sparkled with the passion he so easily created with his zealous devotion to certain parts of her. He was thinking of those special female parts just now and how he would savor her charms.

"You should be inside where it's warm," he murmured as he brought her arm around his waist, pulling her close to shelter her from the strong gust of wind. "It's getting cold. We're in for a storm this evening. Won't stop at a warm inn tonight."

"Wanted to watch you as you captained your ship." She lifted her shoulders, her hand resting on his chest. Slowly, her lashes lowered flirtatiously. "Can't seem to get enough of you. So, you say we're not stopping?"

Her words twisted his heart coiled with longing in other parts. He understood better than she did what the consequences of their constant mating would be. They'd been at sea over a month now. He had every intention of staying in Black's hunting lodge for at least another month, perhaps longer. He ushered her to the cabin.

What would be would be. He would deal with everything that happened his way. He was certain the moment he saw her, grinning besotted at him after he kidnapped her, he would never let her go. Women, all women, he was certain, would have acted quite differently if placed in a similar situation.

His Nick seemed to enjoy the abduction.

"We've things to talk about, important things," he told her while they walked to the cabin. On the table cook left food and wine. He heard her stomach rumble. "We can talk while we eat." There wouldn't be another time for him to share the possible dangers until the storm blew itself out. If she didn't understand, he would have to impress certain facts.

"You're worrying me," she spoke softly, her words trembling. For a moment it seemed to Collin she stared at her feet. While he watched, she tugged in a deep breath of air. "What is it that has your handsome face filled with worry lines? Is it something I said or did?"

Dishing up the plates and pouring the wine he thought on the words to be said, the right words. He didn't want to terrify her, just make her aware. "Nothing you did or said." He tried to reassure. "It's what we are about to encounter." When he noticed the color drain from her face, he held up a hand. "It's not what you're thinking. Your uncles are not catching up to us. We haven't seen one sign of another ship for weeks. My guess is that they are waiting for us in Dornoch. I'm positive they'll be there ahead of us. We will deal with your uncles as well as your father when the time comes."

"What then has you so serious? You're scaring me."

Her voice strained against the stillness in the room. Winds outside moaned around the ship as it plunged slightly into a trough. She steadied herself, her hands on the table.

"Don't mean to frighten you, just instill a *wee* bit of prudence in that beautiful head of yours. While there are times I want you more courageous in the sexual games I play with you, tonight is not one of them. Tonight, you must heed my words. They are not meant as an order but as prudence for a woman I care deeply about."

Her hands were in his. He brought them to his lips to kiss softly. His gaze lingered on hers, assessing.

"You best get on with the telling then." She skipped from terrified to indignant in a flash. Her face regained some of the lost color. "I'm not a mind reader, you *ken*. The longer this takes the more terrified you be havin' me."

Certain she was blustering. He wasn't all that pleased with the way he brokered this conversation. Telling her of the dangers didn't have to be difficult. Nor did his warnings need to be blurted out. "While we eat." Courteously, he pulled out a chair for her. "I'll tell you all that's on my mind."

He sat across from her. "Here's to us," he lifted his glass pressing on her what he hoped was a reassuring smile on his face.

Her eyes crossed. "To us, now..."

She seemed to understand nothing was going to be said until she ate. First, she drank. The wine as usual was delicious. The food on her plate would have appealed to her another time. Not seeming to taste the meal, she ate quickly, shooting lingering glances at him. Seeming to ask when the talking would begin.

He set his fork on his plate. Sat back, crossing his arms over his chest, his gaze focused on her. To him the meal wasn't as appetizing as usual. He was worried about her. Feared during the storm she'd want to see him, to check on his condition. He was discovering she was a worrier at least where he was concerned. If she did so, she would find herself in a position and place she was ill suited to encounter. When pitted against the wrath of the storm gods, Nick would not fare well.

"We are in for a tempest...a devil of a storm."

He waited several seconds for a reaction. Her face was blank. "It's going to be a wild night. You will have to take precautions."

He thought of other precautions to her wellbeing he intentionally ignored.

She waved her hand in the air. "Is that all? Thought you were going to tell me you were tired of me. Set me aside in the next port." She heaved in a huge breath of air before letting the wind from her lungs explode out in a rush.

"Love, what I've told you is not all. This squall we're about to encounter is a big one, nothing to laugh at. I won't be inside the cabin to ease your nerves or fears. You are going to have to weather this one on your own, by yourself. You have to trust me in this scenario. I'm the captain. I have to stay on deck. The ship, along with all the men as well as you, my love, are my responsibility. There will be times when the waves wash over the deck. They could take a person with them when they roam back to the ocean."

Collin wasn't sure why he added the last bit that sounded ridiculous to him. He was afraid it would make what he was going to tell her into an order instead of her decision. Nick didn't like or appreciate commands.

"Why?" Her fork fell to the floor, her eyes widened. "Why won't you stay with me? There is no reason for you to go topside and risk your life."

While he picked up the utensil, he spoke, "As I just said, I'm the captain of this ship. It's my responsibility to be in command. I'll be outside making certain the ship survives the gusty wind and rain. We don't want to end up on the bottom of the ocean, fish food, now do we? You don't want to find yourself washed over the side of the ship by a huge wave."

There was so much more to be said as he watched her reaction, inhaled the scent of her fear. Her fingers wound into the fabric of her gown, tightening.

"Bottom...fish food?" Her voice floated through the damp, chilly air was whisper thin. "I'd like to be outside with you. Where I can see you. I won't get in the way. Don't want to be where I don't know what is happening."

At her words terror coursed through him while his body prickled and the hair on the back of his neck stood on end. She could not think to stand on the deck during the storm. "No!" His voice boomed in the small room.

She cringed back into the chair, her eyes wide. A moment later, she drew in a ragged breath, then, "No? Why ever not? You!" The single word of disobedience exploded.

Her eyes glittered. She jabbed a finger at him, hitting his chest once, twice. "You cannot order me around. I'm not part of your crew." She prodded him again.

His anger along with fear for her blossomed into rage then fear again. He caught her hand in his larger one before he drew in a deep breath. "I can and will direct you to do certain things so you won't end up at the bottom of the ocean...fish food."

He was standing in front of her. His relaxed pose vanished with the spoken words. After he let go of her hands, he stuffed his hands in his pockets. He inhaled several quick breaths of air.

She stood while she glowered at him. Seeing the glitter of her eyes, his fury eased. He loved the way she fought, the way her eyes shimmered when she thought an injustice was being served up. Pulling her into his arms, open mouthed, he kissed her deep and hard, his tongue reaching deep. His hands cupped her adorable fanny as he dragged her to him. Hayes told him to play with her. Time was running out.

Nick wrapped her arms around his neck as she responded to his zealous devotions to her mouth. The devil take him, he lifted her skirt, dragging her underwear down her long slender legs. "Wrap them around me."

It seemed she understood what he wanted. With one fast thrust he was inside her. She was pinned against the door, climaxing as he moved within the sweltering heat of her sheathe. Her body enveloped his, seemed to control his raging desire.

"Collin...!"

His name on her lips sent him over the edge. His seed emptied inside. She rested her head against his chest, her breasts still heaving. "I'm still angry with you."

He chuckled softly, enjoying the way she spent her anger. "I'm sorry, love. That was not well done of me. I did not mean to give commands. Shall we talk some more?"

"Don't like what you've been trying to tell me. I..." She played him as she left a dewy trail of moisture across her lips. "I don't want to be fish food. Need to understand what you're telling me."

"You don't like orders much either. What would you do if you stepped out that door just when a wave washes over the ship?"

He meant to drive his point home even if it meant her displeasure.

"That happens?"

Her eyes were wide pools of blue, the sound of her voice incredulous.

"In a storm, yes. You might get washed over the side of the ship before I can get to you."

He was pushing damp strands of hair from her face. The devil, she responded so quickly and so passionately to him. He didn't want to leave her, to go topside. No, he wanted to make love to her again.

"What about you? You're bigger than me but does that make it impossible for a wave to wash you over the side? If you leave me in your cabin, I'll worry."

Nick understood so much more about his big body that she labeled a brick wall than she did a few weeks ago. She touched his lips, pressed her breasts against his chest. She meant to seduce him, to convince him with sensual games to do her bidding.

"Yes, I could catch a wave also. However, I can also read the ship as well as the way it moves, how it responds. I understand when it is more likely a wave will rise over the bow to wash across the deck. And," he paused while his hand closed over one small breast, lightly testing the shape and texture, "and, I will be outside before the worst hits. I'll tie myself to the steering wheel. The crew will also take precautions."

"Oh..."

Her breath rushed from her lungs in a defeated puff of air. It seemed to him, she wilted against him, resigned, hopefully to do his bidding.

"We will take safeguards. We know what we are doing. You do not." Collin was relieved to realize she understood.

"I...still...Collin, I don't want to be in here alone, worried, anxious about your well-being. What if the worst happens and you don't survive? What will I do then?"

"You care about me?"

He grinned at her, squeezing the breast he cupped, slipping his hand inside her bodice to sweep his thumb over a hardened crest. He kissed her nose, feathered kisses across her cheeks then the width of her mouth. He framed her face in his hands, gazing at her.

She swept her small pink tongue across her bottom lip. "*Dinna fash* yourself. I'm just afraid of...I do care! Don't you dare go to the bottom of the ocean, Collin McInnis. Don't you dare become fish food. If you do, I'll murder you with my own hands!"

She prodded him with the tip of one of her slender fingers.

He roared with laughter erupting from the wealth of feelings he had for this *lass*. He held her hands in his. Brought them to his lips, "I won't."

"Promise me."

"I vow that nothing will happen to me. I won't sink to the bottom of the ocean to feed the fish. Now kiss me."

The kiss was short as well as bittersweet. He did wish he could take her with him, bind her to him, so he would also know she would survive. Even that was risky. Staying in the cabin was the only solution. He left after giving her instructions to try to stay on the bed throughout. She might be tossed around the room.

As he stood at the door, he couldn't help himself from giving one final order. "Under no circumstances are you to leave the cabin even if you think the ship is sinking. If that is to happen, which it won't, either I or Hayes will be here to help you."

"I promise," were her last words as he stepped into the pouring rain and pulled his slicker tight around him.

The black clouds were almost upon them. A gust of wind clouted him on the side. He braced his feet to steady himself.

"It's a god-awful night," he muttered to no one's ears save his while rain plummeted his face. He strode toward the wheel.

Sails were hauled in at his orders, Hayes barking the commands to the crew. Most of the crew was sent below deck. Without the sails furled they would weather the waves along with the wind until it passed them by. After that, they would bask in the sunshine, catch up on much needed sleep before they ate their fill. In two days, they would arrive at the hunting lodge. The storm would push them a bit faster to their destination even without all sails go.

At times, he felt the cad. Nick was a true innocent, one who appealed to him more than he ever wanted to admit. Once he needed her for a one-night-dalliance. He was a fool to ever believe one night of pleasure with this woman would be enough to last a lifetime. After he knew her intimately, he was certain she would become his next mistress.

The devil take him, he was too young to wed. If he didn't change her mind, in the process convince her she should become his mistress, he'd never forgive himself. A man ought to know when the best woman that ever happened to him came into his life. A man ought to comprehend how to go about persuading her she wanted to remain with him. He couldn't let her get away. Nick told him she never wanted to marry. She only wanted him for her lover. Damn the new breed of independent, pig-headed women.

His means of persuasion was underhanded. It was all he could think about.

He was sure his method of encouragement would work to his benefit if she didn't resent him for something he could have dodged. Bloody hell, he sidestepped siring children his entire adult life. As far as he knew, there were no bastards of his in this world. Perhaps she should marry him instead of becoming his mistress. That brought on more thought, more confusion, more muddle to his brain.

If she didn't agree to marriage, there most assuredly would be one bastard in his life. Did she understand what they did every day would cause her to increase? He didn't comprehend the answer to his question.

Her father, her uncles, they would see that he did the right thing by her. He smiled as the ship hit the first big trough. He would manage this situation to his advantage making sure her relatives understood she was well and truly compromised. For her there would be no going back.

Bracing his feet apart, he spent his energy keeping the vessel afloat. Waves rushed across the deck, spilled from one side to the other. The fight was man against nature, the challenging test invigorating. This battle was exactly what he needed to clear his mind while cementing his intentions. No guilt, no regrets, he would have his heart's desire. The night passed slowly. His muscles ached from the strain of extreme use. Far out on the eastern sky, beams of light began to break through thinning clouds.

The wind was still brisk as the tempest began to blow itself out. Rain sluiced from the few clouds that were left above them. Giving silent thanks, a short prayer, Collin rested his head on the wheel. He enjoyed storms, delighted in casting his strength along with that of his ship to the test against the elements of nature.

Not this time.

Not with Nick on board, sequestered in his cabin. He grinned thoughtfully. She did his bidding, stayed safe and secure inside the room they shared. He hoped she would not have too many bruises to show for her indoor stay. He understood she would have been bounced around quite thoroughly.

Hayes arrived at the wheel, ready to take over. His grin broad. "Well, we weathered it with no problems. Ordered a hot bath for you along with food. Go get some sleep. Hope your little miss survived the night with minimal damage."

The devil, he did too. At this very instant, all he wanted was to hold her in his arms, touch every part of her just to makes sure she endured the tempest safely. When he was positive all was good, then, well, then he wanted to make love to her.

He entered the cabin. Searched the spaces where he expected to see her. Panic imploded within. "Nick! Nick, where are you? Don't do this." He was afraid she was making a point he wouldn't like. After all, he did utter one last order. She might have resented his departing words even though they were legitimate coming from the captain.

Bloody, bloody hell but she couldn't have gone outside. He would have seen her. *Not if she got washed away the moment she stepped outside.* The cabin lay in disaster as he expected after the storm. What wasn't tied down was distributed across the room, littering the surface. He strode through the debris-strewn floor, lifting things as he made his way toward the bed.

She wasn't on the bed. Not beneath the covers.

For that matter she didn't appear to be in his cabin. "Nick! Where are you?" His heart lodged in his throat. His breath flashed from his lungs. It seemed his life sped in front of him.

His gut somersaulted while his mind whirled with all the possible scenarios. None of them good. She promised. Vowed she would remain here where she would be safe. She wasn't in the room. Once again, his breath tore through him. Perhaps he should see if Hayes knew where she was. He turned to the door.

"Collin?"

Her voice was weak, nearly nonexistent. With a breathless sultry quality, the sound whispered through the cabin.

He whirled on a heel, viewing the interior of his cabin once more. Her name whistled from his lips. "Nick...?"

His knees weakened when he caught his first glimpse of her. His heart began to beat. What he saw gave new meaning to joy. Between the wall and his bed, he could see her beautiful face poking just above the mattress, her sleepy blue eyes wide and peering at him.

While he watched, she pulled herself higher. She rose from behind the bed, her hair a tangled mess, her clothes falling around her lopsidedly. He grinned, his smile reaching all the way to his toes. She was safe. He drew in air, his lungs inflating as he cautiously watched her.

Nick's eyes flashed dangerously. He was beginning to recognize the warning signs signaling the onslaught of her anger. If he didn't miss his guess, she was angry, furiously so. The question for him was why. He didn't have the tiniest speck of an idea in his muddled brain. Indeed, by the looks of her, Nick was furious with him. Now that she stood, her *wee* hands were fisted on her hips. She didn't seem to know how to get across the bed. Though she seemed hell bent to do just that. Her forehead creased with frown lines. She eyed the bed then began to crawl. He held his indrawn breath in anticipation waiting for the passion that would inevitably break free when she vented her wrath on him.

Her skirt caught beneath her knees. She looked up as she pulled fabric away so she could continue. The bodice of her gown dipped provocatively. The fabric caught beneath her knees again, bringing her face down on the bed. She pushed up, glaring at him, her lovely eyebrows furrowed together. She waved a hand in the air, her lips thinned, "Don't you dare laugh at me, Collin McInnis. Don't you dare! I will have your head if you do!"

He held his hands in front of him, the smile he tried to hide tugging at his lips. "I wouldn't dream of such a dastardly thing. You're unquestionably delectable, a masterpiece for this man's sore, tired eyes. Beside the bed and next to the wall was an intelligent choice of places to weather the storm," he said unable to keep the ensuing chortle behind his teeth.

She was alive. Nick weathered the storm. Now he would withstand whatever had her seething mad. He would enjoy the encounter too. He always did. Her passion would explode. The raw hunger in her would erupt to his benefit, *nay* to their benefit.

"You are too. You're laughing at me. I don't..."

She stood in front of him, all of her in charming disarray. Poking him with her finger. He backed up a step. She followed. Her eyes blazing, "Don't you ever terrify me like that ever again. I nearly died of fright every time this blasted ship dipped. I want off this...this... You were gone all night. I thought you were at the bottom of the sea feeding the fish as you so eloquently put what might happen. You could have sent someone to tell me you were fine..."

She gasped for air. Her small provocative bosom heaved upward. He caught the site of minute pert breasts between the gaping fabric of her gown.

Roughly, he pulled her into his arms. "You're rambling, love. We can put the time to better use even though I do enjoy listening to your words tumble from your exquisitely kissable lips."

His mouth closed over hers. In this case kissing her thoroughly and most soundly was the only way he could think of to silence her anger. In the process, end the accusations she hurtled his direction. He was thrilled she worried about him even while he didn't like the notion she was put in that position.

In seconds, she was naked as was he. They were on the bed. She was beneath him. The lovemaking wasn't tender. It was primal and raw giving notice that life was pure. It existed from one moment to the next. There was nothing that was granted without diligent work. On top of her, he lay sated.

I love you, Nick.

I'll never let you go. Never. You can fight the marriage with all the strength you have. You won't win. I will make sure your uncles find a way to see this relationship to its proper conclusion. Eventually, you will be pleased with me as your husband.

The sudden thoughts didn't surprise him. Everything he did, all that happened since that fated abduction pointed in this direction. Well, hell, all his carefully laid plans were going to be blasted from the scenarios he judiciously developed for his life. Collin found he didn't care. *Nay*, he looked forward to his future with Nick.

She pushed him aside. Naked, her small breasts begging for him, she prodded him in the chest again. "Don't think you can always win me over with sex. You *ken* I can't resist your blatant charm. It's not well done of you. You have not managed to change my feelings about your abhorrent behavior."

He grinned. "Win you over with sex? I do like the sound of that. The thought delights me. Should I try again?" His lips brushed across hers.

"Water and food coming."

The knock on the door coupled with the warning gave him just enough time before the entry to cover Nick. She would be furious with him again. He adored her anger. Cherished everything about her; the passion, the honesty, maybe even her uncles. He had yet to hear much about her father. Ah, he would also come for her. Perhaps even the mother. When the anger died, the most glorious passion overcame her.

He could live a lifetime soaking up that magnificent hunger when it was just for him.

Naked, he rose from his position atop her, wrapped a quilt around his hips. The men bringing in the water seemed to understand what they interrupted as they kept their gaze focused on the tub. Beyond the opening he heard Hayes's chuckle. "Knew I would need to give you a moment."

"That was barely a moment," Collin shot back.

He should have remembered Hayes would bring in the water and food sooner than later.

Crewmembers brought food. Hayes poked his head in the door again. "Hope we didn't interrupt something important. Enjoy the meal. Suppose the two of you are appreciating other things as well."

With the last of the men leaving the door shut, he heaved a great sigh relieved that nothing of Nick was seen.

Collin knelt beside the bed, tugging at the covers, eager to reveal her face. "Are you alright?"

Finally, he pulled the covers back from her face, smiling. He hoped to see the smile from her that always sent his heart into a frenzy.

She punched him hard on the shoulder. "You planned that."

Once again, her eyes blazed with intensity.

"No, I would never want another man to see what is mine. Nick, you know that you are mine, don't you?"

He prayed she would acknowledge his words even though he understood it was too soon to be more explicit.

Her eyes crossed. He knew he was in for another argument. "We are lovers, that is all. When we are done with each other that will be that. We will move on. No commitment. No regrets. No belonging to one or the other. Nothing to…"

"Tiring of you will take one hell of a long time," he gritted out through clenched teeth.

The devil, he hoped she didn't actually believe that spout of nonsense she gifted him with. Never would he move on. At the moment, he didn't have a valid argument for her. In the beginning they agreed marriage was not an acceptable institution for either of them. Now, he had other ideas. At least not a notion he could tell her. Lord, but she was innocent to think she could make love with him several times a day and not come out of this unscathed, her virtue demolished, torn asunder.

He would never move on.

"The bath water will get cold."

The tub was big. He'd never bathed with a woman before. Never wanted to do so. Until now.

Without a second thought, Collin scooped Nick into his arms. In the next second they were in the tub. "Collin. What are you doing?"

She pounded on his chest. Easily, he flipped her around.

"Taking a bath with my lover."

She was in front of him. Her back rested against his chest. His legs were spread wide. She fit there quite nicely. His fingers and lips played and danced with her body. When she panted, her body coiling and squirming against him, he turned her again. She straddled him, his rod deep inside. Moments ticked by turning into minutes. She cried out his name. One more time he detonated inside her hot sheathe.

They stayed in the water until it turned tepid. Wrapped in towels they ate the breakfast that was brought to them.

"We'll be at the lodge soon. I'm looking forward to a few weeks on solid ground. Do you still want to be with me, love?"

He had to always ask. If she had a change of heart, he would...no he would never send her home. She was his. He would have to work on his persuasive skills if she told him no to his marriage proposal.

~ * ~

Nickie watched as the land drew near, her eyes filled with moisture. She understood she would not be with him much longer. Her father and uncles would find her. Would demand certain things that would not happen. That morning after the tempest, he told her two days until they would land. For some reason three days passed before they reached the little spit of land at the northern tip of Scotland. They sailed through several islands, finally stopping at a place called Scapa. The village was quaint and small. There was one inn for the crew to use. All had permission to catch another vessel home, if that was what they wanted.

She had no idea where they were. No idea how to find her way home, if it ever proved necessary. Somehow, she didn't think it would. No, she had the decided opinion Collin made plans for them. He just didn't think it necessary to apprise her of them.

Behind her she heard his soft footfalls. Caught the spicy scent of him as his lips touched lightly upon her neck. Anticipation crowded her body with heat. He stood beside her, tugging her into his arms for a quick kiss.

"Are you eager to step onto firm land? I know I am. Need some time to figure out how to proceed when we return to our families."

Around her waist his fingers squeezed before moving lower to rest on her belly. He pulled her against him. She felt his long hard length pressed along her back.

"The unmoving land will feel strange. Don't know how I'll feel if it's not swaying and dipping beneath my feet."

She turned in his arms, smiled at him. Wished for him to set his lips on hers, to give her reason to hum with the pleasure he could elicit so easily. Lightly, she touched his chin with her finger.

He sucked in a deep breath of air. His eyes preyed upon her, settled on her mouth just as she hoped. "You won't get land sick now, will you?" There was an abundance of amusement in his words. "I hope you will not be losing your meals once we touch our feet down."

Nickie bristled as her lips thinned in protest. He implied something she wasn't at all sure about. "I didn't get seasick. Doubt if I'll be plagued now by land sickness or any other kind. I'm as healthy as a stoat."

She leaned back, gazing into the vivid green eyes that seemed to question all she said. By looking at him, the strange expression on his face, she decided Collin knew something he wasn't telling her. The fact clouded her head with unanswered questions. She didn't understand him.

"I'm sure you won't."

He bent toward her, nuzzled softly behind her ear. Touched the lobe with his tongue then teeth. Her hands pressed on his chest in a feeble attempt to push him away. She didn't want to push him away. No, she would never grow tired of him. If she moved on, it would be because he wanted to leave her or refused the invitation her family would try to insist upon. Indeed, this was the nineteenth century. A marriage could never be forced. At least she didn't believe one could.

"If you continue in this vein, your men will see what you do."

Her breath caught as he nipped at her ear. She squirmed against him. Her body coiled in expectation of what she knew was sure to come. "Do you want that?"

"My men *ken* what we are about inside my cabin. Not one man aboard is an innocent boy."

"I *dinna* want you to toss my skirts outside with all to look upon us."

Her breath rasped out softly when his lips sucked on the heatedly beating pulse at the base of her neck. The mark he left her with that first night was still there yelling out she was his. It seemed he claimed her in too many ways. Marked her as his. She wasn't sure she understood all the intricate meanings.

"Would never do that, Love. My men will no' get a look at you. I'll make sure of that. It is the teasing I'm enjoying at the moment."

He stepped back, his hands still on her waist. He made no more moves to lure her into submitting to him. All he did was watch, a strange expression in his vivid green eyes. His focus seemed to burn into her sending a myriad of different emotions bursting within.

She turned in his arms, her back now against him. Pressed as close as she could. Wind caressed her face. His hand warmed her hips then her belly. She squirmed against him as the hand rose. "Where will we go from the port? How long do you think we will stay?"

She wished they could remain here forever. Knew that to be wistful thinking. Returning to a place where her family would barrage her with questions terrified her.

"The lodge is about five miles inland. We'll ride there as soon as the ship docks. Our belongings will be sent tomorrow morning."

His breath whispered against her neck. He seduced as well as cajoled responses from her. The task was an easy one simply because she loved him so very much.

In his own way, he still lured her, coaxed her to respond to whatever he had in mind. She understood what he wanted now. It was the future that concerned her. Over the months that passed at sea, their relationship changed. At least her feelings for him did. How he felt now might still be the same as when they first met.

"Actually, as well you know, I've only what I'm wearing now along with another gown."

In order to wash what little she possessed, there were times she wore only Collin's shirt. He seemed to enjoy watching her in the oversized garment.

His hands roamed her sides, pulled her tight again. "I'm sorry for that. We had to leave so quickly there was not enough time to purchase a wardrobe for you. I tried but it was never delivered. I'll take care of that when we reach Dornoch. For now, I suppose we will have to continue as we did on board. I rather like watching your long legs beneath my shirt while you waltz around the cabin."

She punched him on the arm, knowing it would do little to affect him. He would carry on as usual, as he pleased. "Isn't as if I need a lot of clothing. All I've done for the weeks we've been on board is entertain you inside the cabin and walk on deck."

Nickie felt no regrets at what they did together. The distress came as she thought about her mother. Allura would be devastated by the actions of her daughter. She had not been raised to act so brazenly. *Nay,* never that, however, she'd also been taught to think independently. When she met Collin, all rational thought fled her brain. She reacted to him to how he made her feel.

She understood there might well be efforts to force her to wed Collin. When she began this journey, she thought only of herself. He didn't want marriage. Neither did she. She'd come to London for the season with the express purpose of doing everything in her power to avoid a marriage.

"I won't let them force you to wed me," she blurted without a thought. "They cannot make us do something so unwanted."

Now, for her, marriage was not unwanted. She'd never thought to meet a man such as Collin McInnis. Never believed she could fall in love. *Nay,* what she felt could not be love. The emotions simmering so deep and rampant inside was lust, nothing more. Neither could keep their hands to themselves when they were in the privacy of his cabin sometimes on deck as well.

Behind her, she heard him clear his throat. She felt the waft of air as his breath left his lungs resulting in a huge sigh, "No one can make me do something I *dinna* want to do, love."

His voice was husky, throaty, didn't sound at all like himself. If she didn't understand the man so well, she would likely believe there was hidden meaning in what he said.

Her breath whispered softly from her lungs. She snuggled against him, a buffer for the moment from the gusting breezes. "That would be my only regret. My father can be *verra* persuasive if he wants."

"What?" he queried, this time his voice was harsh unbending. "You regret this journey we've undertaken, the adventure we've shared together. Why didn't you tell me you weren't willing?"

"You misunderstand," she murmured softly as she stared into the distance. The land in front of them was beautiful, harsh in some ways. "I don't regret anything we've done together. My guilt is for the possible consequence of this time we shared and what you will feel when all is said and done, when we part ways. My father and uncles will insist we wed. Don't know what they will do when I refuse to say the words. They cannot force me to do something I don't want either."

"You don't want to wed me?"

He sounded petulant, almost as if he was a small boy being denied a sweet.

She laughed softly, her smile growing. Lying to him was not what she wanted though she had to do so, "No more than you want to wed me. We made a pact before I stepped foot on the Promise. We both agreed, we both wanted to be just lovers. Have you changed your mind?"

"I remember."

He sounded hesitant as well as quite irritated she reminded him. He didn't answer her question.

"As do I. We both agreed we would be lovers. I wouldn't marry you nor would I be your mistress." She sucked in a draft of air wondering how she could have been so very naïve. "What will we do when they catch up to us? My father will not stand by and allow me to sleep with you. We will not be allowed to continue as we've been doing. I don't feel as if I want this all to end just yet."

"Need I remind you that you are an adult? You can make decisions without their help. They cannot tell you what you can and cannot do. It is not as if you are seventeen. Come, let's not worry about possible problems in our future. The ship is about to land. We will be on our way to the lodge. We will have more time to discover more about each other."

"You need to learn more about me?" she laughed softly.

There wasn't one spot on her entire body he didn't know intimately. Perhaps there was something else he needed to learn about her.

"Always."

"Where you'll have me all to yourself. You can be as wicked as you please."

"Anywhere I please. The crew will be staying in the village, even Hayes. Unless a ship is sighted, we will be by ourselves."

"I'd like that."

"*Aye*, for a month perhaps, unless you grow bored with long walks and nightly pleasures. Unless you want to explore more thoroughly the world, we could sail wherever pleases you." Once more he nipped her ear, soothed the spot then explored more sweetly feminine territory. "We could explore the Bahamas."

She jerked, her body continuing to heat with each gentle, intimate caress. It seemed to her throughout their conversations he never stopped roaming or exploring tender evocative spots. He was a wicked devil. She loved the way he frolicked with her body. She danced to the music he played.

Once the gangplank was down, they found the nearest stable. Collin purchased two horses. His steed was a chestnut stallion with white marking on his head and forelegs. Hers was a gray mare. During the ride to the lodge, they didn't speak. She soaked in the ambiance of the beautiful land. Unable to help herself, her thoughts continued to meander to the reunion she was sure to have with her family. The meeting was impossible for her to foresee. What would occur unimaginable to predict.

Her actions had been impulsive, so unlike her usual behavior. She was hesitant to explain what she did.

The lodge was nestled in a valley with rocky crags jutting upward. A lazy river found its way nearby, tempting a swim or a fishing expedition. The river pooled in a glen spanned by large rocks. At their arrival the sun sat low on the horizon. A few gauzy clouds whispered across the sky. She was reminded of the small wager before all this started. A few skipped rocks, a hope he'd kiss her if she won. The bet for him if he won was her presence on board his ship.

Forcing herself back to the present, "This is beautiful." She breathed deeply of the summer fragrances surrounding her. All around her was fresh and clear, nothing like the scents and sounds of the city. "A delightful Eden."

"'Tis a wondrous place to spend time before we return to the real world. Come..." Collin held out his hand. "Let's explore. I've been here once before a few years ago. Black invited me along with a few of our friends. It was a bachelor's paradise until we all felt the need for a willing woman. The village *lasses*, except for a few, were out-of-bounds for us. None of us wanted to dally with anyone other than widows and agreeable barmaids."

"Then...there was me."

"Nick, you didn't fit the bill. I wanted you any way I could get you. Didn't want to live without sampling your lovely charms."

She soaked in his statements. Wasn't sure about his choice of words. Still, she understood he experimented with her. Would let her go eventually. Moisture rushed to her eyes at the thought of living without him. She bit her lip while she attempted to keep dampness from overflowing her eyes. She wouldn't want to explain herself to Collin. If he saw tears, he would insist she enlighten him as to their appearance.

They made their way to the stable where a man took the reins of their horses. Again, he held out his hand to her. Hand in hand they walked the remaining way to the home. Climbed the steps on the porch. Why did she have the feeling she would meet her doom here. Perhaps she realized this place might determine the rest of her life. She swallowed the apprehension clogging her throat.

Charley, his butler opened the door. His chortle of delight surprised her. "Took the two of you long enough to get here. My grandmother could have traveled faster. Been here three weeks waiting for the two of you. Before you ask, no one has come looking for the *wee lassie*. Not a whispered hint that there might be others searching for the lodge. The two of you are safe for the time being."

Collin laughed as he stepped inside. He seemed pleased. "Everything and everyone get here in good condition?"

"They did," Charley said. "We had no trouble as we were away from London before anyone missed the little one, strange that they all believed she left for Scotland. I've a trunk of clothes for her, the ones you ordered at the modiste before you left."

"You did what?" She punched his arm, a tiny bit of anger rising only to be tamped down when he touched her softly on her cheek. "Why didn't you tell me? I told you…"

"Purchased clothing for you when you agreed to come with me. Knew you would be needing something when we arrived here." He held up his hands as if to silence her. "If you wish, you can pay me back. Otherwise, I'd appreciate this gift to be taken as a simple gesture of goodwill, a gift between friends. Don't deny the fact you are in need of something other than the riding habit you showed up wearing that afternoon, in addition a pair of trousers and shirt I forget where they came from and my shirts while you tend to your other clothing. It would please me to no end if you accepted my generosity without complaint." Quickly, he kissed her forehead.

"You *dinna* like me wearing your shirts!"

For some reason she felt insulted she shouted poking him on his broad chest. She'd thought...well, she'd thought he liked watching her wearing almost nothing. The anger turned to fury. Inside she raged. This was all too much for her. The last few weeks she'd been such a seething jumble of emotions, happy then sad. She didn't normally vacillate so easily. "I'm no' your mistress. You can't just be buyin' me things. I won't accept them."

It seemed Charley disappeared before the squall between them escalated to a fever pitch.

117

"Suit yourself."

He grinned before he hauled her into his arms, his lips hard upon hers, his tongue sweeping across her lips urging her to either turn to liquid sunshine for him or to open herself completely.

She wasn't about to do either while she attempted to resist the instant lust. When he tore himself away, "Just trying to do something nice for you," he said softly before he kissed her nose then her forehead once more. Brushed his mouth across her lips. "I adore you in my shirts. Want to fondle the curvaceous backside of yours when you are wearing one. When you bend over there are other things that come to mind, as you well know...as we've experienced together."

The lump of outrage blocking her throat slipped to her stomach. Shame at her anger speared her deeply. She didn't want to lose precious time with him by being angry even though when she showed her temper, they ended up making love. Those times were always volatile raw passion exuding from both parties. "I'm sorry. We did have an agreement. I wasn't going to accept gifts from you. I don't understand why I keep getting angry with you over nothing."

"Nor do I, friends gift each other with things of importance. As I said, I'll not be offended if you decide not to accept the presents or decide to pay me for them. I'm sure there are *lasses* in town who would love to have a few new articles of clothing straight from London. Ones that are in the highest fashion."

"Don't you dare!" She hit his arm with her fist. This anger was different. "I'll take them."

The wave of jealousy that seemed to drown her at his suggestion of giving away the clothing wasn't something she'd ever known before. She discovered she wanted everything he would gift her with so she could savor the moments when they weren't together. When she wore the new gowns, she would always think of Collin removing each article, kissing her bared skin as he did so.

He eyed her skeptically, one dark brow arched perfectly. When he smiled, his eyes twinkled in merriment as if he knew she would give in to her own needs and wants.

"I believe this is where we make love," he outright laughed.

"However, I'd like to give you the grand tour first. Perhaps we can test out the furnishings in each room. See how they suit. Hmm...would you enjoy a few dalliances during the tour? I know I would."

"If you must know, I'm exhausted. Too tired to succumb to your advances. Hungry too."

Inside she was laughing knowing full well she would never say no to him. Thinking about his hands on her created a burn in the most private parts of her she'd come to understand over the past weeks. Denying Collin was indeed out of the realm of possibilities.

"Little minx, you're a terrible liar."

He chucked her under the chin. As he took hold of her hand, he led her through the entry into the main room. A charming staircase made its way to the second floor. Instead of heading for the bedroom, he led her into the dining room. For a moment he stopped to stare at the table then her, his meaning implicit.

"You've wicked plans for that table?" she whispered as her body responded to the unsaid suggestion.

Perhaps it wasn't Collin suggesting not so subtly that he'd make love to her here in this room. Maybe it was her expectations coupled with what he knew so well. The moment she held dear to her heart.

"Of course, I'm one of the most lecherous rakes known to London. What other scenario would I be thinking of having with you? If I wasn't thinking about the table in addition to your charming body atop the wood with your legs wrapped around my flanks, I would not be living up to my reputation, now, would I?"

During the remaining minutes of the tour, Nickie sunk deeper and deeper into a dark depression she couldn't seem to fight even though Collin kept a banter that should have her giggling. Everything she ever wanted was within reaching distance. She couldn't have it.

Collin didn't want her that way.

Didn't want a wife.

Probably not a family either.

As he told her more often than not, he was a bounder, a man who would not wed until he found himself absolutely desperate for an heir. Nickie understood from the beginning of their escapade he was her lover and she his. In this relationship there would be nothing more between them. She initiated the concept. Put it in front of him. She'd even been proud of herself for avoiding the debutante scene.

~ * ~

During the days on the island, Nickie began to realize she made a grave mistake agreeing with Collin, following her instincts. She should have listened to the advice of the elders. Now, she didn't have the vaguest clue as to how to right the wrong she created with her unwitting and selfish endeavor. Owing Collin had never been her intent. The unraveling of her deeds would not be possible. There were too many avenues, too many tales surrounding them. Nothing that happened between them could ever be undone.

Ach, she didn't care if no other man would want her simply because the only man she would ever desire was the man she held close to her for as long as he decided to stay away from Dornoch. The moment to leave this magical sanctuary would come soon. He was an attentive lover. It seemed the deeper in despair she sank the more thoughtful he became asking her over then over again what was wrong.

What could he do for her?

How could he help?

She was sitting at her favorite place on the island, her back resting against a large moss-covered boulder overlooking the pond wondering what the rest of her life would look like. Every scenario her imagination created, she tossed aside. There were things she knew along with things she didn't. Mentally, she thought to make a list. For starters she understood Collin would not be part of her life much longer. Her father would come for her. Of course, those thoughts were in the wrong order. She needed to decide how she wanted to spend her life after Collin. The only thought coming to mind was in seclusion. After knowing Collin so very intimately, she couldn't see sharing herself with any other man.

For her, life after the man she loved wasn't tenable. Soon, they would go their separate way. She sensed his presence before she looked up to see him standing beside her. Wistfully, he was gazing at her. Her smile did ease some of the tension she read on his face. Nickie didn't know what to say to him. There was nothing she could tell him that would ease his mind. When they made love, the act now seemed bittersweet. Always amazing, he was tender and sweet, a gentle lover. In truth, he was the sweetest man she'd ever known except for her father. The reputation he coveted didn't describe the true person at all. She often wondered why he hid behind the labels presumed of him.

"We have company."

His voice harsh, he watched her with tender-sweet longing. His gaze swept the length of her as if he tried to memorize.

Her heart lurched. By the expression on his dear face, she didn't have to ask to know who it was. "My father?"

For a moment she didn't think she could breathe. What little air she inhaled stuck in her throat.

"Your father, I'm sure of the fact. Had a message from Hayes. A ship has been spotted in the harbor. We have to get back to the lodge before they are actually here, in the process pray that Hayes beats the relatives." He sounded sure of himself, confident. "We both knew this would eventually happen."

"Where are they?" She thought her relatives were at the home or looking in other parts of Scotland.

"They landed about an hour ago. My crew is headed here. They've been on the lookout for a ship. They don't have any intention of leaving us alone to fend for ourselves. The crew means to help me. They are loyal to both of us."

His words were calm, resigned as if he understood what was about to happen to his life.

"What are you going to do?"

She thought she would have more time with Collin. Now, she understood both their lives would change drastically.

"Whatever is necessary. What I have to do." The acceptance of his fate she heard in his voice terrified her. "I still want you, Nick. Don't ever forget that fact."

"What are you talking about? What do you have to do?" she was worried.

His temper had never been put to the test. "You're frightening me. I don't like it when you say things like that." She remembered how she felt after the storm. How urgent her response to him had been. "I wouldn't be able to live with myself if my father and uncles hurt you."

Without further words they walked quickly. Once inside, he sat down with her. Taking her hands in his, he massaged gentle circles on the underside of her wrists. She understood he hoped to encourage as well as give comfort. Didn't believe that possible. "Don't worry. All will be fine. I'll make sure nothing happens to hurt you."

A long slow breath of air escaped her lungs. She didn't think he could do what he said. "I'm not worried about me. It's you that terrifies me. They are going to make you…"

She swallowed the words, moistened her lips as she tried desperately to think about what was going to happen when the men she recently admired the most stepped back into her life hell bent on protecting her. She didn't need protection. She understood quite well what she did.

"I will promise you this. I won't do anything I don't want to do." He smiled as he fingered a strand of hair, brought it to his face, inhaled. "Also understand this, even if you give into their ploys and agree to marriage, I'll say no. Won't let you down. You don't have to worry that I'll do something that will give you no recourse."

She prayed it wouldn't come to that. It seemed he was glib tongued. He could convince them nothing happened between them. Even then all could change in a few months when it became obvious she was with child. When that happened, they would be after him again. There would be no place he could hide.

How would he feel if he knew she might carry his heir within her? Of course the child would be a bastard, not a legitimate heir. Until she was certain she was increasing, she never thought on that happening. As she was waiting for the right time to tell him, their tiny world imploded. She considered herself an intelligent woman. She should have put all the facts together sooner. He must not even guess as to her condition. At one time, she thought he did from something he said.

An imminent baby would make a huge difference in her encounter with her father. This child she carried, despite Collin's dislike of marriage, was not going to be a bastard. She would do everything in her power to make sure of the child's heritage. How could she do that if she refused to marry him?

Unable to face the man she fell in love with, she looked away. The deception she meant to play on him was not something she was proud of. He would hate her for the lie. At this point there was nothing to do about the facts facing her head on. She must think of the baby before herself or Collin. Right now, she didn't like herself. What she was about to do was something she despised.

"What are you thinking? It seems your mind is going off in too many different directions to keep up with you. One second, you're pensive. After that your lips thin as if you are making a decision you don't like. The next you look at me with such tender yearning, I want to solve all your problems. Tell me, love."

"It's just this came too soon. Thought we'd have more time to ourselves. There is so much I wanted to learn about you. How did they find us? You didn't believe they would ever think to look here."

She truly did trust they would be at his home in Dornoch before her father caught up to her. He would have his clan along with his brothers standing beside him. Now, well, he had his crew. Naught more.

"The Duke of Richmond can be persuasive. He has so many retainers to employ to seek out information. I'm actually surprised he didn't discover this island sooner. The Earl of Blackmore is a friend to the duchess. He might have caved under pressure, although I rather doubt that fact. He is so stoic and secretive. There are other means. They might have just made an educated guess. The duchess knows I'm good friends with Black. She might know of this place. She would always place her niece's welfare in front of everything else."

"Do you think one of your other friends told him?"

She watched him for any sign or thought. His brows didn't narrow.

"It's possible. The duke has something on almost every member of the London aristocracy. Don't think he has anything on Black, at least not something the earl would allow the man to blackmail him with. You see, Black doesn't care what others think about him. There is Drew as well as Jeremy. They might have confided this place inadvertently to one of the duke's retainers. Neither one is good at keeping secrets when they are foxed."

Nervous energy consuming her, she moistened her lips. "I...will you kiss me? Do we have time to make love one more time before they haul me away from you? After tonight, I'm afraid I'll never see you again."

There was that small fact. They could take her from him. Make sure she never laid eyes on Collin McInnis again. She understood how they disapproved of his lifestyle. He was a notorious bounder. She was an innocent *lass. Not so much anymore.* She paused as she thought on all her uncles. They were all, each and every one of them, notorious for something in their day. Drake was the worst of the lot. He had no right to judge either of them after his actions with Ella. Of course, though, he wed her.

Collin didn't want anything to do with that particular institution.

Without answering he swept her into his arms, two stepping the stairs to the second-floor and the master bedroom. By the time they reached the room, he was half dressed. His shirt was off and lay somewhere between the room and the first floor. Her gown gaped open, giving him sensitive places to explore. All her clothing soon joined his.

The coupling was urgent, intense. She was frantic to feel everything, to remember how all this was between them. It seemed they both feared what was about to come their way. They gambled with fate. They lost the game as the two of them understood it would eventually come to this.

When the first pounding on the door ricocheted up to the room, they were sated, sweat sheened from the loving. She closed her eyes, willing the sound to vanish. The tempo along with the intensity increased.

He groaned deep in the back of his throat, kissing her quickly on the lips. "It's got to be Hayes along with my crew. At least I hope they've beaten your family here. If not, we best prepare for the worst possible scenario. Do you want to stay in the bedroom while I speak with them? I'm certain they won't invade this space if they have me standing in front of them.""

"No, I want to be there when you talk to my family. I want to be able to tell the uncles my part in all this, explain that I was willing. You didn't do any forcing." She would make sure that was said. "I need to tell them about my feelings about marriage. We both agreed there would be no vows exchanged when we started out. There is nothing they can do to change that fact."

Her insides churned. Recriminations bombarded her. Guilt flowed. For a moment she thought she might lose the contents of her stomach. So far, she hid the malady from Collin. Thankfully her sickness in the mornings was not bad. Most of the time something small to eat would suffice to keep her stomach calm. He usually rose before she did. That fact also helped hide her condition. Her breasts were larger as well as more sensitive. She noticed when they made love. He didn't seem to think any part of her was different. He never commented. Perhaps the change was so gradual it wouldn't come to his attention.

"Never knew a woman could be so intent on defending me along with my wishes. In the past, they wanted to walk down the aisle of matrimony instead. If faced with this situation, each and every one of them would have used the fact to get me to the alter." Quickly, he kissed her on the lips. In seconds he was dressed, heading out the door. "Come down as soon as you're ready. You should do something with your hair. Don't want you to appear to your family as if you just rose from our bed even if it is the stark-naked truth." He grinned as he perused her body clearly enjoying the view she presented.

"Don't understand how you can make light of this situation."

Her anger bristled. This time he wouldn't be able to ease the tempest inside her with his lovemaking. She clenched her fists until the nails bit into her palms. Her breath remained in her lungs, burning until she let it out.

"That isn't my intention. This is serious. The result of the interview will affect the rest of our lives. We both understand that fact. We need to present a united front, even though I understand things could go awry with little provocation. They love you after all."

He left her to wallow in her thoughts. She did think she should look her best when she met her family. Too many minutes passed before she thought she looked presentable. Still, her lips were slightly swollen, her hair a bit out of place. Talent with her hair was nonexistent. She let the length fall around her shoulders. The brushing would have to do. Hoping for instant courage, she sucked in a deep breath of air, wishing the act would help calm her rattled nerves.

When she entered the main room, all seemed peaceful. Her father, Uncle Drake and Aunt Ella were in the room, along with her other uncle's, Roc and Brett. Colby stood framed in the doorway, his legs crossed, arms over his chest. They each held a friendly glass of brandy in hand. It seemed a good sign at least until Collin strode toward her, holding out his hand. The glint in his eyes told her he was ready for a fight. He didn't stand a chance against all of them.

"Nick."

He kissed her in front of one and all. Drug her into his arms, his hand possessively set on her backside. It wasn't one of his soul-shattering kisses that turned her into heated liquid, causing her knees to go weak. The caress wasn't chaste either. Angry murmurs surrounded her. She heard words: *bounder, cad, reprobate. How could he? In front of us, does the man have no shame? He'll pay for this travesty and more. Is he trying to antagonize?*

His arm snaked around her, drew her close, too close for the situation they found themselves in. She didn't dare protest. That act would condemn him further in the eyes of her family. She toted in a shaky breath of air willing her body to calm. Nothing would give her the peace she sought so diligently.

"Nicole, you're coming with us. He's not good enough for you, the bounder. Doesn't matter what happened over the last weeks," her father told her as he reached out to take her hand to move her away from Collin.

She never heard his voice this formidable or threatening. He was always so reserved and quiet. His anger was quite new to her.

Collin would have none of that. He pulled her closer while he backed up a step then two more. She fought for the courage to defy her father while she clung to Collin's arm. Would have fallen if he wasn't there to steady her.

"No, no, I'm not. I want to stay with Collin. It's my choice. There is nothing you can do to make me leave him. Nothing!"

She found herself yelling at the man she always adored, never disobeyed. He appeared shocked at her defiance. A muscle along his jaw ticked. What? Had her father expected her to just come along? She'd been with Collin for close to three months now.

"You disobey me?"

"When you're wrong," she told him, the defiance in her tone clear. "I'm a grown woman. You cannot dictate to me."

"See, no disrespect intended here, sir. It's just as I told you, Nick doesn't want to go with you. We've enjoyed our months together. Haven't we, love?"

Tenderly, he brushed his knuckles along her jaw. The caress was feather-light, gentle to the extreme. When he switched his attention from her back to Hunter, he spoke softly, "The lass is a fine traveling companion as well as cabin mate. I would want no one else to fill her shoes or sleep in my bed. The two of us are compatible in every way, if you get my meaning."

She sucked in a startled gasp of air, turning to look into his penetrating green eyes. He knew exactly how he was provoking them. The question was why. His fists were clenched tightly, one at his side the other where it possessively rested on her waist. Her father stepped forward, his brows drawn tightly together, as it seemed he tried to hold his temper in check. To her it seemed steam was coming from his face.

Those words must have been enough for her father to lose his always-guarded control.

Unexpectedly, Hunter hit Collin solidly on the chin. He staggered back a step, his hold on her loosening slightly. Collin rubbed the spot, a slow grin forming as he kept his gaze focused on the older man.

"I'll give you that one. Nick, you need to step away. Go, sit over there by your aunt," Collin ground out as he pointed to a chair near Ella.

With one quick blow to Hunter's head, it only took a few seconds to send her father straight to the floor. One by one the others stepped up, fists flying. Collin used his feet expertly, kicking the Duke of Richmond in the stomach, incapacitating him. Roc was next in line. With a quick move, the Duke of Ravenswood landed backside down staring at the ceiling. She supposed Collin had the age advantage since her relatives failed to use their sheer numbers against him.

Uncle Brett was the last one to test his fighting skills against the man she loved, rubbed his jaw as if in thought. When he spoke, the words were directed at her would-be rescuers. "Suppose we'll have to cheat a bit in order to win this game. Probably will end up the same as the rest of you if I go it alone. Understand we're all getting on in age though I hate to admit to the fact. Not as potent as we once were."

"Perhaps, we should try negotiating instead of fisticuffs," Ella said, raising her voice to be heard over the rest of the group. Her suggestion went unheeded. She sat back with a sigh while she patted Nickie's hand. Her words now directed her way, "You truly love this man?"

Nickie didn't have time to answer with more than an affirmative nod. Her eyes widened in disbelief as her uncles attacked in mass.

At that same moment all the men ganged up on Collin. The fight lasted far too long. Collin didn't come out the winner. He was battered and bruised. Uncle Brett held him while the others took their turn pummeling him.

Slowly, he slipped to the floor.

The sight of his face, eyes blackened, blood running from his nose and mouth was the last she saw. Gradually, she also slipped to the ground.

~ * ~

"The devil take the lot of you!" Despite arms along with numerous hands attempting to hold him back, Collin was beside her, running his finger along her jaw. "Nick? Nick, wake up, it will be all right. I promise." he told her his voice soft as if he was more concerned for her possible injuries than he was for himself. "I'm not hurt. Looks worse than it is. I've felt worse after a barroom brawl. Wake up, please, love."

In that one unguarded instant, Hunter saw the love in the bounder's eyes. He grimaced. There was no getting around hard cold facts. Collin McInnis loved his daughter. To anyone who dared look at him, watch the tender expression, see the fear in his eyes, the fact was blatantly obvious. This wasn't what he expected when they encountered the earl. Actually, Hunter believed the man would graciously hand his daughter over. Would not risk offending the Duke of Richmond who held considerable sway over the ton. The detail shouldn't have surprised him. After all, the pair had been together longer than Collin's usual relationships. If they shared a cabin as well as a bed for more than two months, nearing three, Nicki was well and truly compromised. The earl should be well and truly tired of her. Instead, he appeared smitten.

"What's wrong with her?" Collin asked, sweeping hair from her face.

He checked her pulse. Much to Hunter's further dismay, ran his hands along her body almost as if he checked for broken bones. The act was sensual more than chaste in the exploration. He understood if this was Allura, he would have done the same.

"She saw your face," Ella said, her softly spoken words caught Hunter's attention. "All that is wrong with her is that she fainted. You should see yourself. You must have terrified her. Although I doubt Nickie is a woman prone to fainting. It can happen when the man one loves is beaten near to death."

Ella sent a pointed look toward her husband admonishing him. "The lot of you could have stopped sooner. This was not well done of you since you made your point early on. Now what are the lot of you planning?"

"Needed to teach a much-needed lesson," Drake mumbled as he looked a bit chagrin at his wife's chiding remarks.

"Lesson taught but not learned," Ella told him sweetly as they all watched the tender interlude between Nickie and Collin.

Collin touched his swollen lips, licked the blood. He looked at her again. His eyes deepened in color. He picked her up off the floor to set her tenderly on the sofa. "Can you wake her?"

"No problem," Colby seemed to appear from nowhere.

Her brother poured a pitcher of water on her face. She sat up sputtering, "What? What happened? Colby! How dare you!"

"You fainted, love." Collin spoke softly, wiping drops of water from her face, caressing her soothingly. "Why?"

Gently, she reached out and touched his face. Ran a fingertip along his swollen and bloody lip. "You're hurt. Why did you fight all of them?" A long pause followed while the tender expression on her face changed. "You terrified me!"

It seemed her anger surfaced unexpectedly. She pushed at him. "How dare you do something so foolish?"

Collin caught her hands in his. "Now, love, I only did what was necessary. We can't solve this problem you have right now in our usual manner."

Hunter found himself caught off guard by that sudden altercation. Nickie had a temper. Most often, all who were near disappeared as quickly as possible when she sported the look she did now. It would be a testimonial to the man as to how he handled her rage.

"Collin, I swear..."

He grinned then chuckled softly brushing one finger tenderly down her nose. "Hush…love, we can't do anything about that anger of yours, at least not until your family leaves. We both understand the only way to get your lovely, blossoming temper under control is for me to have my wicked way with you. We can't do that here with everyone watching. I doubt if your father will allow me to carry you off to the bedroom."

He kissed her on the lips, ran his tongue lightly across them. She sighed softly as if her father as well as uncles, aunt and her brother weren't witness to the blatant display of affection between the pair.

Sputters of outrage rose around the room again. Hunter understood what the man was doing. He might have done the same when he was courting Allura if confronted with this unique scenario. Collin wanted to wed his daughter. The only problem in the events occurring was that the man didn't want to admit to the fact. If he were forced, he would have an excuse when provoked by his friends. As with most bounders, Hunter was quite positive Collin had touted he wouldn't marry until he had no other recourse in order to gain an heir. The trouble for Collin McInnis lay in the noticeable fact he fell in love.

This was rich.

"You're going to marry Nickie," Drake said as he stepped toward them, a slight limp from the past fight slowing him down. His voice calm, holding the ducal authority he was used to, he said, "I'll send someone for the minister."

"No!" Nickie blurted. "You can't..."

At her defiance, Hunter slanted his eyebrows upward. "I'm your father. I can and I will see the two of you wed if it is necessary."

Hunter knew the pair was in love. He would have to figure this out though he didn't mean to make anything easy for the McInnis. A marriage tonight, as far as he was concerned, wasn't going to happen. First, the young pup would have to prove himself. Needed to show just how much he loved Nickie before Hunter would feel secure in allowing her to be with the man.

One glance at Collin, the relief written clearly on his face, told Hunter a wealth of things. All confirmed his original diagnosis of the young couple.

The man was besotted with his daughter.

He wasn't going to have her, at least not without demonstrating to him just how much he loved her. Not without a fight.

Chapter Five

"I want to speak with, Nick. Alone."

Collin knew these men would never allow such a thing to happen. He had to try, for her sake, as he needed to reassure Nick. How to do that, well, he wasn't at all sure. He'd said some outrageous things. Knew the words hurt her deeply.

Drake left the room. Was gone only a few minutes. Collin knew the minister in the small village. The man would welcome the extra coin he was certain Drake would give to have the wedding performed, posthaste. It was what he wanted. Needed to secure this woman to him. Wanted his son to hold his name along with the title. Born a bastard, he would have to have him legally declared his heir. He would do anything.

"What harm can come of that?" Ella asked sweetly. "I'm sure this couple have a great deal to talk over now that all their dirty laundry has been aired publicly. After all they weren't expecting to be wed today."

"The man doesn't deserve concessions. He kidnapped her, ran off with her. If he'd chosen, he could be half way around the world. We would never find them," Hunter said, as he seemed to stare at his daughter then him.

"I didn't. Planned on sending her home unscathed. Of course, that didn't happen. Perhaps..." Collin said watching as her brows knit together fine-tuning her anger.

With his words, he sealed their fate. He prayed they would be allowed to remain together after the marriage. His crew would come for them. Would fight tooth and nail to get him back.

Roc cleared his throat as he pointed at him, his scowl slowly darkening. "You best keep your words behind your teeth youngun'. There won't be anyone rescuing you today. Your crew, I'm sure that's who you are waiting for are in the hold of our ship. You along with your crew are guilty of kidnapping."

"It's a hanging offense," Brett reminded him blandly.

"You don't mean to include my crew in this offense. They had nothing to do with this. Besides..."

"He didn't kidnap me," Nickie blurted. "I came with him quite willingly. I chose to leave London and the horrible debutante balls you all were forcing on me. I hated it."

"After the marriage, we'll see to the hanging," Drake walked back into the room. "I've passed sentence."

"No!" Nickie cried out while she scrambled to reach Collin. Roc held her back. She pounded on his chest. "You cannot! He's guilty of nothing. You can't hang him! He'll die. I'll never see him again." Her voice trailed off into nothingness as tears slipping down her face turned to gut wrenching sobs.

Burning rage swept through him. While Collin knew this meeting wouldn't be pleasant...hanging? When he suggested she travel with him, he understood in part the consequences. Now she was sobbing her heart out. He couldn't reach her.

Hanging?

His crew too?

How dare they?

A few moments later he found himself trussed up quite handily. Drake stepped back admiring their handiwork. "Not so smug now are you, pup? Don't have all the cards in hand any longer, not even one."

It seemed he'd be hog-tied for his wedding.

"Are the lot of you going to tie me as well?"

Nick stepped forward, her tiny hands fisted on her hips. His lady never ceased to amaze him. She was pointing at her relatives, her finger shaking. "You *dinna* dare. I'll never speak to any of you again if you carry through with this travesty of justice. Doesn't my word mean anything? You can brow beat him, black his eyes time and again. Force this wedding. You cannot hang him or his crew for something he *dinna* do!"

Hunter stood, his look solemn as he proceeded to say quite calmly. "Come away from the bounder, dear. He's not right for you."

"This is vigilante justice."

"True," Drake spoke softly, smirking as he did so. "If you're inclined, you could call it ducal justice."

"You're meaning to wed me to him. Why? No sense, no earthly sense. The lot of you are making no earthly sense. I won't let you hang him. You'll have to do the same to me. I'll never..."

Ella touched her hand, pulled her back to the couch. "They are all bluster right now. They are just angry, also a bit put in their places because he beat each one of them in a fair fight. They don't like the minor detail that they had to gang up on him to win. The fight wasn't at all fair. Goes against their manly pride. Sincerely, the men won't go through with the hanging. If it does happen, I'll never speak to Drake again. I'll divorce the man."

She turned to Ella. "You don't know my father. If he says he'll do something, why then he will. You have to do something to stop them. You're the only one who can shake some sense into those men."

~ * ~

Collin thought for a moment his life flashed before his eyes. That was just a moment in time. Now, he plotted how to get out of this situation he stumbled into with his life. He needed more help than Nick could provide. She would do what she could. The only possibility in this herd of men was Nick's brother. If she could speak with him, beseech his help in some way; he might stand a chance against the uncles. A chance until he could reach home in the process rally his clan.

Mayhap provoking them had not been such a credible idea. He intended the exchange of words to help him get what he wanted, a wedding. She still told him she didn't want to marry. He could think of no other way to have his wishes fulfilled. Now, now he faced the noose. If he wasn't tied, hands behind his back, he would have run his fingers along his neck.

At least he knew where his men were located because of their faux pas. All he had to do was reach his knife, cut the ropes. He needed privacy for that to succeed. Needed to render her uncles so boiling mad they wouldn't want to see him until the preacher arrived.

Collin had the sinking feeling as soon as the words were exchanged, he was a dead man. His gut clenched. Dying tonight with Nick looking on was not part of his planned agenda for his life with Nick. "I thought you told me your uncles and father were reasonable men. Was I wrong about that, Nick?"

"Until today I always believed that notion to be true. What do you want me to say?" Tears slipped from her eyes. "It's as if I don't know them, never knew them. I remember when they bounced me on their knee."

Bloody, bloody hell, he didn't want her to cry, didn't want to see her tears. Also didn't want to learn of their tender side. "Want you to give me your sweet body one more time."

"You fool!"

She stood, hands on her hips appearing angrier than he'd ever seen her. "Maybe I'll murder you myself. Why are you doing everything in your power to make them angrier?"

Good question, he grinned at the men surrounding him. "Telling of the truth is what I need to do if I'm going to meet my maker today. If they hadn't ganged up on me, I wouldn't be in this predicament. They don't fight fair, you know."

"Put him in another room," Hunter said, disgustedly waving a hand in the air while he shot him a look. "Don't want to hear any more of this nonsense. Don't want to hear what he's done or wants to do with my daughter. He's a dead *mon* soon."

Collin didn't understand that look. Though he was glad his words had the desired effect. All he had to do as soon as he was no longer trussed up like a hog for the slaughter was figure out how to get Nick away from the lodge as well as his crew out of the hold of the ship.

Shouldn't be a problem.

Cutting the ropes proved more difficult than he anticipated simply because it took him longer than expected to reach his knife. Through the door he heard Hunter grumble that the minister was away from the village seeing to his parishioners' needs and would be unable to wed them until the morning if that.

That bit of information fell into his plans smoothly, giving him more time than he thought he had to live. He waited until the men went to bed. If these men were as intelligent as he believed them to be, a guard would be placed at his door as well as Nick's. He would have to find a way around that disturbing fact.

He had his knife along with the element of surprise working on his side. He was also certain Nick wanted to be with him. When the door to the room he'd been placed in opened, he was shocked to see Colby, Nick behind him.

"Hush..." She placed a finger over her soft lips. In hushed tones, she whispered. "We've come to rescue you though it appears you don't need that particular commodity. Colby is also here to help. We need him to get on board Drake's ship."

Collin would believe those words when they proved true, not a moment before. "How are you planning to get out of the house?" His whisper was met with another hush from Nick. "I'm sure it's..."

"Colby is our guard. Come..."

Against his better judgment, he decided to follow behind Colby, Nick striding behind him. They kept to the shadows as they made their way to the stable. Three horses were saddled, ready for them. The other mounts had seemingly vanished. He looked to Colby then Nick. She smiled at him. Her grin was wide; holding a sense of humor at the fact her family would be left to walk when they decided to follow. When she lifted tiny shoulders then looked toward the crags, he wanted to laugh.

"You got rid of them..."

"They are all most likely now ensconced in the stable in the village where they were rented. My family will be afoot when they discover you've escaped with me in tow. They will not like the fact you have bested them yet again. They will be seething."

Colby still leading the way, they rode slowly trying to keep all noise at a minimum. It would not do to be discovered too soon. By the time they were a good mile down the road, they kicked their horses into a gallop. Collin wasn't sure how they were going to get his crew from the hold. He figured Colby had a plan for that too, smart young pup.

It seemed Nick's brother did a bit of quick talking to convince the two men left on board that the Duke of Richmond as well as the Duke of

Ravenswood ordered the release of Collin's men. He told them it was simply a joke, a test of sorts as to the loyalty of my men. Nick confirmed that her father wanted the same, as part of the crew came from the McClellan castle. Before another hour passed, they'd set sail and were winding their way between the islands to the ocean.

Nick refused to go below. She stood at the bow of the Promise watching the land disappear behind them while open ocean greeted them. He couldn't help but wonder if she would have said I do. Now, it was up to him to persuade her he changed his mind. If he had his way, she would come around to his way of thinking. Somehow, he would also have to figure out the words to explain to his friends that he was reformed, had seen a new life, one he wanted more than anything.

Once they reached the ocean all the sails were unfurled. The ship lurched forward picking up speed as the wind filled the sheets. Hayes had the steering wheel in hand. They would be home by late evening tomorrow as long as the wind held. When he wrapped his arms around her, he felt her stiffen before she relaxed a bit. If he didn't miss his guess, there was another tempest brewing.

He pointed to the north. Colorful lights danced on the horizon reaching all the way to uppermost part of the sky. The northern lights were a sight he could never get enough of. They rivaled all sunsets and sunrises. When she realized what he pointed to, she did sink against his chest. He nibbled her ear, hoping for the shuddering of her desire to pass from her into him.

These feelings between them were all good and right. From all that happened and didn't happen as well, she was tightly strung. Sex would release that tension. He planned on that in just a few minutes.

"What will happen if some more of my uncles are at Dornoch when we arrive? Couldn't we just go on to France, in the process thumb our noses at the well-meaning relatives who are tormenting my life? We could be lovers for as long as we both want. Wouldn't have to answer to anyone."

"We could..." his hand brushed against the tip of her breast then the other. "What if I want more? Would you refuse me?"

Her body trembled, shuddered as he felt her hips push against him.

"You understand if you keep that up, you're going to remind me how angry I am at you."

She held her hand over his as if the pressure could stop him from exploring.

"How angry are you?"

He kissed and nipped at the pulse at the base of her throat, remembered that small pink mark he gifted her with that first evening they met.

Her low purr of contentment, sifted through her. She wriggled against him. Her adorable backside pressed against the hardest part of him.

Soft against steel.

"I'd just as soon relieve that temper of yours then move on to more pleasant conversation. We've only a few hours to come to terms with the fact your uncles mean business. They won't stop until you're wed and I'm dangling from a noose. As soon as they wake, they will be after us. You can count on that fact."

"No, not after what you said about us. You must have been daft to come across so outrageously. You're right of course. It's time to take this to your cabin."

Once inside, just as he expected, she turned on him. "Why did you tell him I was your cabin mate among other things?"

Her shoulders squared, her hands fisted, she had that look he loved. Her eyes flashed fire. They would end this in their usual way.

One eyebrow arched suggestively as he studied her, ran his gaze hotly along her body while stopping at strategic spots that he knew would inflame her further. "Truth? Why did I tell them the truth?"

"You provoked them. Purposefully." She punched his chest before she reverted to jabbing him in the same place. "You gave them every reason to suggest a hanging. They might have backed off with the marriage and been satisfied."

"There is no law that says I cannot bed a willing woman. Since I didn't kidnap you, why then they had no reason to mention my swinging from the yardarm or a tree. Don't know which they perceived for me. They got to me when they included my crew. That was low."

"It was. Still, Collin McInnis, I *dinna* like what you told them about what we did together. What we do is private only to be between the two of us."

He sighed realizing as much as he wanted to tap into the fire and passion blazing from her, he needed to begin the gentle persuasion. While he felt sure she would make him sweat, he was also certain she would eventually see things his way.

"Well..."

She was tapping her foot, her hand resting on his chest.

"I thought to have them force me to wed. Was hoping."

His words were weak as was his courage. He didn't want to go back on his word to her when they embarked on this trip months ago in London. Quite a lot changed between them during this time.

I fell in love.

Then...why don't you have the courage to tell her so? Ask her to marry you. Get down on one knee. If you're a lucky chap and until now you've been that way, she'll say yes.

Because I'm terrified she'll tell me no. Hasn't she told me more than once she doesn't ever want to marry? She wanted a lover not a husband.

"You wanted what?" she gasped clearly stupefied.

"The devil woman, I want you for my wife. Didn't know how to ask in lieu of our agreement." He held out his hands in supplication. "Was terrified."

"So, you provoked my father with something that should have been kept between us?" Her eyes flashed fire.

"Your father knew what we'd been doing. All I did was confirm his thoughts."

He meant to defend himself. By the blazing inferno in her eyes his ploy didn't work.

She found a pen sitting on his desk, threw it at him, then a pillow from the bed, after that a book. She cursed and swore. He wanted this conversation out of the way before he made love to her. It wasn't going to happen that way. Her temper at such an explosive level only sex would calm her.

Her hair fell around her shoulders. Her shirt came unbuttoned showing tender white skin as well as the rounded curves of the beautiful white jewels he delighted fondling. Temptingly, her rapid breaths from the exertion caused her breasts to rise and fall, swaying beneath her shirt. Her lips formed a thin line. The ship dipped. She lost her balance. Her arms waved in circles while she tried desperately to keep on her feet.

He took wicked advantage as he tackled her onto the bed. "This is where you want to be, love. Admit it."

She punched his chin. He grinned while he brushed his lips across hers once, twice. His hand slipped beneath her shirt to explore her charming body more thoroughly. The mating was fast, intense as it always was after an argument. She lay on his bed naked, sweat sheened beneath him. Lightly, he kissed her lips understanding this time he would do the majority of the talking.

"I fail to understand why provoking them to the point of forcing a marriage was your intent," she sighed softly as he continued his sightseeing expedition along her neck sent her body throbbing once more. "This isn't accomplishing an explanation."

"No, suppose it's not. The fact of the matter is I've changed my mind about you and me."

"About what?" She tried to sit up.

He wouldn't allow her to do so. "About marriage. You see, Nick, I want to marry you. The only way I can see to accomplish that fact with you so dead set against the notion is by getting your father and uncles to force the marriage."

"You did? You do?"

She appeared stunned, her eyes crossing with his sudden revelation.

"Didn't expect this hanging thing to come up since you came willing as well as of your own accord." He rose over her, his forearms braced to either side. "You're just too tempting for me to ever leave behind. I'll never grow tired of you or the tempest that rises so quickly within you."

"It was your fault." She punched him again. This time, however, she smiled back at him. "And...I don't mind pointing this out. We aren't wed. They will be mad as hornets when they discover us missing."

"I'm hoping Colby won't receive the brunt of their anger," he said softly as he thought on her brother. Her brother seemed to have her back. "In any case, I'm going to try my best to convince you that's what you want too."

"What do I want?" She ran a finger down his chest then back up. "What I believe I want is to make love again. All your wheedling is making me squirm against you. If you want to talk, you'd better stop that examination that has you caressing parts of me that burn with need."

"You want to marry me."

"*Dinna* you recall I told you I want to wed no one?" She placed kisses along his chest where her hand had been a few seconds earlier.

"Bloody hell, bloody, bloody hell!"

He flipped her so she sat astride him. This conversation was going to take forever. The next moment he was encased deep inside her tight sheathe kissing his rod, sucking him deeper and deeper still.

The tempest was milder, the speed of their coupling not so frantic. She climaxed. He emptied his seed. She fell upon him, her head against his chest. Her lashes fluttered across his muscles. He drank in a long draught of air.

"Willing or not, you're going to have to wed me."

He braced himself for the upcoming detonation. The rise of her temper once again. Neither his suggestions nor reasons were having the desired effect.

"Why is that?"

She rolled off him, his arm still wrapped possessively around her, his fingers resting on top of her breast.

"You are going to bear my child. I won't have a bastard."

When she lifted herself to see his eyes, he understood his careless words hurt her. Her eyes darkened with moisture.

Well, hell, I should have told her I love her.

"That is the only reason?" she asked, her voice so soft he could barely hear the words.

He bristled even though he knew he should have tempered his answer with less careless words. "Does there have to be another reason?"

She pulled away from him. He saw no anger. Temper he could deal with. Her shoulders were slumped, her body quivering. She pulled on the clothing that he dumped on the floor. He thought for a moment she might leave. Instead, she leaned against his desk, her arms crossed beneath her breast, enticingly pushing them up. Suddenly, sensual thoughts vanished.

"When did you know?" she asked as her gaze remained fixed on him.

"Know what?" he asked feigning ignorance over the fact he blurted a few moments ago.

"That I'm carrying your child."

He lifted his shoulders to shrug. He didn't want to put any more emphasis on her pregnancy. "I suppose I guessed about five or six weeks ago. Was pretty certain after another month came and went. When did you know?"

"About a month...I thought well, I didn't have...you know, maybe you don't."

Keeping his laughter inside his mouth would be the wise and prudent thing to do for now. She looked so adorable in the shade of pink she wore, "I do know what you're speaking of. Men do know about women's bodies as well as the changes that occur every month. It's helpful to a bounder who doesn't want a child to *ken* such things."

"I want my child to have a father, a last name that he can be proud of. I wouldn't have said no if asked to say my vows to you. When I saw what you were doing, I was shocked. Even without your blatant words, they would have insisted on a marriage. I'd been alone with you far too long for anything else to happen."

He let out a rush of air, relieved in the extreme to hear her words. "Knowing you has changed my jaded heart as well as my mind about a lot of different things."

"Such as..."

"Well to start, with marriage. Nick, it isn't just the child you carry that has me wanting other things besides my old ways. I've come to care about you. Can't see life without you by my side."

Tell her it's more than care. I'm sure she would be rewarding you in so many splendid ways if you did.

"I care about you too." Slowly she removed the clothing she hastily donned.

The discussion ended.

~ * ~

When Nickie woke the next morning, she wasn't certain if the conversation the night before had been real or a dream. They didn't actually decide anything about their future. Her father would keep coming after her. Nothing would stop. Collin would have to find a means to avoid her relative's wrath, marriage being the only long-term solution.

To avoid all that, they should stop at the next port. An elopement was perfect to suit her purpose. If he wanted or if her family insisted, they could wed with all the grandeur later. Truthfully, she didn't know how far along she was. He would most likely have a better idea than she had. The ship dipped as he sat down on the bed.

He was still naked.

Still so very handsome.

"You're awake. You can sleep as long as you wish, you know. Last night was trying." He trailed a finger along her jaw his smile disarming her one nerve at a time. "You still want to wed?"

To her ears, he sounded insecure the notion so very strange. She'd never believed Collin McInnis could be apprehensive about a woman, anything for that matter. "Yes. I..."

She reached up to touch him. He caught her hand in his. Pressed a kiss to her palm.

"I gave orders to stop at Lybster. I've a friend from my school days who lives there. He's a minister. I'm sure he'll be happy to wed us. I want to be officially married before we meet any more uncles. Who do you think will be at Dornoch when we arrive?"

She laughed pleased with his thoughts of marriage while taking care of the small issues as quickly as possible. "Yes, I thought along the same lines a few moments ago. As to who will be waiting for us? Uncle Jamie, since it wasn't his ship the others sailed to meet us. Ryder will most likely be there."

"The McLaren? I've heard tell he's wicked with his hands and feet. I can feel more bruises multiplying as I'm sure they will all want to vent their displeasure with their fists. However." He touched a finger to her nose, "I won't be tryin' to rile your uncles. Anyone else?"

"There is Logan Maxwell, unless he's at one of his wineries. Perhaps, Jarret Kingsley. Uncle Jarret lives near my mother and father. The uncle you should be worried most about is Blade, Blade MacPherson. He lives the closest to Dornoch. Although, if Uncle Jamie's ship is in use, well, then there is also uncle James...as well uncle Gavin. Have I managed all twelve? Well, no, Lyssa's father won't be here, Aric Lakeland. He stayed at his place outside Baltimore."

He groaned. "I don't believe I can handle any more bad news. With Brett and Roc included as uncles I believe that is thirteen. Unlucky thirteen," he groaned again even as he kissed the tip of her nose.

"You're not worried about any of them, are you?" She didn't want to see any more bruises and cut lips.

"Not as long as they come at me one at a time."

"Perhaps our luck is changing, I forgot about uncle Damian, Amorica's husband. He won't be here either."

"That still makes thirteen uncles."

~ * ~

Just before the noon hour they sailed into the harbor in Lybster. The church sat near the center of town. Once the gangplank was lowered only a few minutes passed before Collin and Nick, Hayes serving as a witness, walked into the small parish church. The interior was dim. Few of the lanterns had been lit since it was the middle of the week. Candles burned near the altar. Silence seemed overwhelming. Tiny hairs on the back of her neck stood on end. Cold shivers trembled down her spine. Something felt wrong.

Afraid, Nickie clasped his hand tightly. For some reason, she had multiple misgivings about this. They should have sailed on to Dornoch. Should have evaded land. She pulled in a tight breath of air. She was sure there was a minister near Dornoch that could have seen to the marriage.

"Daniel?" Collin asked sounding unsure at the moment. "Perhaps we should try his home. It's around back. No reason for him to spend his days in the church."

"No need of that, lad." A giant figure rose from a corner chair. The man had been sitting in the shadows. His plaid was wrapped around him although he didn't wear a kilt, appeared at the moment to be wearing buckskins. "Daniel won't be here to help with a travesty of justice. Bounders don't get the prize. Don't you know? Everyone has to pay the price for their crimes."

"Uncle Blade!" Her hand flew to cover her mouth. She turned her attention to Collin, who was quickly turning to leave the church.

"We need to get out of here." Collin tugged on her hand. He scooped her beneath his arm, carrying her like a sack of grain from the church.

"No, Collin. Stop this now. Put me down. You big brick wall. Stop acting like that."

"Not on your life. He's going to have to come after me." He kept walking. "If I set you on your feet, you might do something stupid."

"Collin!"

She wanted to talk to Blade. Hadn't seen him in the longest time. How the devil did he know to come here? It would have been nice to understand.

Hayes led the way from the church then down the lane toward the ship. It couldn't be this easy. Surely, Blade would not let them just walk away.

It wasn't.

"Can't let the two of you go back to your ship without a little tête-à-tête about what the two of you have been up to. Besides, Aidan wants to see you. She doesn't think there is all that to worry about considering the solid head she thinks sits on Nickie's shoulders. I'm inclined to disagree after what I've heard. However, if I want a place in my bed, I will go along with my wife's wishes. The two of you are invited to dinner this evening. Nothing more. We won't hold you overnight. I won't try to beat sense into your head. If Nickie has had her way, you don't have any sense left."

Collin looked distrustful. She was suspicious. Collin set her on her feet. "Do we have the right to refuse the invitation?"

"No, no you don't. I like my wife to be happy. If I let the two of you go now, she'll be displeased. As I said before, if that happens, well, I'll be relegated to the cold stone floor." Blade said while he ran his hands through his hair. "You can go back to your ship when the meal is over. I'll send an escort with you just to make sure the two of you arrive safe and sound."

"Your home is at least a half day ride from here, isn't it?" Nickie said, searching for some of Blade's men, men who she was certain would force them to his bidding.

"It is not so far as that. A couple hours is all if one knows the shortcut."

"We will be returning to the ship tonight," Collin said, as he seemed to be contemplating a refusal to Blade's invitation. "Where is Daniel?"

"At my home," Blade spoke softly while he rocked on the balls of his feet. The color of his face heated.

"To see us wed?" Collin asked.

By the look on her uncle's face, she was certain that wasn't the case. "To see that we aren't wed."

"You've got the gist of the matter now, Nickie. Always was a smart girl. Got that memo months ago. Been waiting here ever since for your possible arrival. Unless things have changed and I hear about it from your father, I'm duty bound to carry out the missive I received."

"Which was what?" Nickie asked.

"To keep the two of you from tying the knot. Figure if the only minister in the area is resting comfortably at my home, the two of you can't do something you'll regret."

That was months ago. Blade wouldn't have heard about what happened last night. Wouldn't know anything about her uncles wanting to hang Collin. Aidan wanted to see her. Possibly to make sure she was untouched. Nickie looked to Collin to see if he was going to put his head on the chopping block again. By the way he used his hands and feet against her family, she was positive he could fight his way back to the ship.

It seemed Blade was thinking along the same lines, as was Collin. "Don't want to ride a half day to your place. If we do, we'll be making our way to the ship as soon as the meal is finished. Don't care whether or not you lose the right to your bed. Nick and I have been through more than we should have to endure because of her doting uncles. Her father as well, as I see it though, he's the only one who has rights here. All we wanted was to marry. It seems you are hell bent on keeping us from that."

Blade held up his hands. "Shouldn't you allow Nickie to decide how and when this wedding is going to happen? Allura is my wife's older sister. Aidan understands that Nickie's mother would want her to be married at home. A wedding fit her status as the laird's daughter. Would you be denying her mother that small joy? That would not be well done of either of you."

Guilt swept through Nickie. She didn't want to make anyone unhappy, least of all her mother. "This has all gotten out of hand. Why would you have Daniel at your place if you wanted to keep us from tying the knot? You know we can handfast, forget a marriage all together. Who's to say we haven't done that? After all you and Aidan did the same thing not too many years ago."

"I cannot pretend to know anything that has been going on with the two of you. If you have handfasted, there is no reason you can't have the wedding Allura has planned for you. If I left Daniel here, Collin might have found a way to coerce the man to help you with your vows. At my place, we can make sure a meal is enjoyed, nothing more."

"Handfasting never occurred to me," Collin said seeming to mull over the thought, "Or it might have been done." He turned to her a wry smile on his lips. "Should we?"

She couldn't help gifting him with a hesitant grin. At least not now that she knew there would be no more fights. "If you think it's better than nothing," she tossed back flirtatiously.

The smile would be what he termed impish. If they were alone, he might have blessed her with the other name he used often, little minx.

It didn't take half the day to arrive at the MacPherson castle.

Actually, the ride there was accomplished in less than three hours. Aidan ran out to meet them. Her arms open wide.

"I've missed you, Nickie. What has kept you away besides getting ready for the season." She linked her arm in hers as they started for the main hall. "Instead of a season you found this strapping Scotsman to run away with. Just don't know what all the to do is about. Blade acted much worse as I informed him, as did all of your uncles. I would have run away with him, long before he decided I was old enough for him."

"You're not going to force a marriage then? One both of us wants?" Nickie asked as they arrived where the most splendid meal was set out. Her stomach grumbled.

"Forcing a marriage is not my plan nor my business. It's up to the two of you to decide what is best. However," Aidan did pause to push a wealth of her thick red hair from her face, "that particular job is up to your *dah*. The forcing part, not your doting aunt. I would do most anything to see you happy except go against your father's wishes."

At the mention of her father, Nickie blanched. "Well, he tried last night to force us. After that he informed us he was going to hang Collin. We had to leave before either he or Drake could accomplish the feat. Drake said he had ducal authority to do so." She continued with the story, leaving nothing out.

"Allura will be furious with the man. He won't see her bed for weeks when she discovers what Hunter was up to. Just as I'm teaching my girl to be independent, in the process think for herself. I know that's how Allura brought you up."

"I'm glad I've at least one friend among my relatives," Nickie murmured softly as her gaze swept the room, stopping fondly on Collin.

"You do love the man?" Aidan queried. "I waited so long for Blade. Never thought he would believe me old enough for him. He always thought I was a little girl. Treated me that way until he finally didn't."

"Love and want him, yes. Even though he says he wants to wed me, it's only because..." Nickie didn't know how much to tell. It wasn't as if her condition would be a secret much longer. Collin believed her to be almost three months along. She would be showing soon.

"He compromised you, didn't he?"

"It's been almost three months since we set sail from London. I couldn't resist him. In any case, didn't want to do so. He didn't seem to be able to keep his hands to himself. That was just fine by me."

"That's a good sign for a lasting marriage, you *ken*. Never could resist Blade. Once when I was visiting Christel, I stripped naked in his chamber and waited for him."

"Oh! You didn't?"

"*Aye*, I did."

"What did he do?"

"Not what I planned and hoped. He wrapped me up in one of the blankets on his bed then carried me to my room. Told me I was still a little girl. Men didn't make love to little girls. I think I must have been seventeen or eighteen. Knew girls who were married at that age with children."

"The two of you finally found each other though. I wouldn't be at all hesitant to marry Collin if he loved me. He did tell me he cared for me."

Perhaps she shouldn't confide in Aidan. This was, after all, their private life she shared. Collin would have every right to be furious with her.

"Guess that's a start. You do have to give the child a name. Keep that fact in mind. Nonetheless, the way that man looks at you, I believe he feels more than care. Have you ventured to tell him your feelings or are you waiting for him?"

"I understand all that. Understand too, that on some level I must have known what would happen if I sailed away with him. My curiosity got the best of me. When he offered the use of his ship then also agreed to be my lover, I couldn't refuse. Bottom line I wanted to know what would happen after the kisses. Told him I wouldn't be his mistress though. He didn't seem to care."

"Just as I'm talking to my girls, I suppose Allura spoke of things between a man and a woman before you left for your season."

Aidan patted her on the hand. It seemed she understood the conversation would not have been explicit.

Nickie laughed softly while she remembered the tepid

conversations she had with her mother. Discussion that did not prepare her at all for what was to come her way when Collin sweet-talked and charmed her stockings off. Well, it was more than just her stockings that were charmed off her. Willingly as well as most eagerly, she gave into the man. "She did. What she failed to tell me was that his kisses...well that when he touched me in certain ways, I would never be able to or want to tell the man to stop. Whenever he kissed me, I wanted more of the same, needed to discover everything he offered."

The two shared conversation along with wine and a delicious meal. Two hours later, Collin stood next to her chair, his hands resting lightly on her shoulders. She touched his hand with one of her own, understanding it was time to leave. If nothing else, Aidan was able to convince her a hasty wedding was not appropriate despite the situation she created for herself. Now that she made the decision, she wanted more than Hayes as a witness and a quick I do in some out of the way church. Even though Nickie was certain Collin wouldn't agree, this unannounced stop to speak with Aidan revealed her feelings.

By the time a wedding could be planned and relatives summoned she would be showing one-and-all that she'd been well and truly compromised during her months with the McInnis. As they rode back to the ship, she wondered if she cared. What she did understand was that once her child was born, no one would remember the incident or that Collin had his wicked way with her before the vows were said.

"What is it you want, Collin? I would know."

The look in his eyes surprised her. She wasn't positive at the moment he wanted to leave. It seemed there was something he wasn't saying.

His gruff voice filled with delicious passion surprised her. For a moment took her off guard. "I think you *ken* what it is I want."

"For the child's sake you wish to marry me. You don't want a bastard any more than I," she murmured softly wishing he would tell her he loved her.

Nickie didn't know why she felt used suddenly. Didn't understand why now she wanted much, much more from Collin than the word care. When she met him, she'd thought she was honest about her feelings.

When they first made love, she'd felt as if she found heaven. At the time, didn't believe for a second, she could possibly want more.

She did.

Talk of a real wedding with Aidan left her with convoluted thoughts she couldn't vanquish from her head. This was all too much for her to sort through. Life was so much easier when it was just she and Collin. When she could wake up in his arms, without having to think of anyone except him.

"If you recall, I told you I cared about you." His voice sounded indignant.

"Care not love," she was too quick to say. She regretted the words as soon as they were said. Wished she could take them back.

She heard his loud snort, sounded a bit contemptuous. He inhaled loudly as if he still needed to make a point. "I will take care of you along with our child. We do well together. I know I won't grow tired of you. Don't know what else to tell you. I want to be married to you as soon as possible."

If he felt indignant as well as contemptuous, well, so did she. "Of my body? You won't grow tired of my body? Is that what you're saying?"

His callous words gave new meaning to refusing him. With his insensitivity, he put her back against the wall. She didn't need him to take care of her. What did she care about his heir? Her mother and father would see the boy wasn't ostracized as a bastard.

Her rage flared.

He laughed as he rode alongside her, sweeping her from her horse then into his arms. His mouth slanted across hers. The kiss was wild, intoxicating. Left her breathless as well as in need of more. More that couldn't appease her until they found the privacy of his cabin. She should learn to control her anger. Should learn not to melt.

"Of your temper also. I'll never grow tired of your wild Scottish temper. You please me thoroughly."

She shoved him, "That's my body too. You have to ask to have it. Quit acting like the brick wall that you are and put me back on my horse." To no avail she shoved at him again.

Over the months she knew this man, she couldn't stay angry with him. Perhaps that was because he soothed her annoyance and irritability with magical sex, the culmination earth shattering. He loved her anger. Loved the way she responded to him when he did make her angry.

"Do you try to provoke me so you can seduce me?" she asked watching the twinkle of merriment in his green eyes suddenly darkening with passion. His desire for her, she never questioned.

He picked up the pace. "Seems I'd like to be on board in my cabin this instant. If we can't wait that long, we'll embarrass Hayes."

She would too. "Hope there aren't any more surprises. You do realize this delay we encountered might give my father and uncles a chance to catch up to us. If they do, they might blast you out of the water."

"I checked. They aren't carrying many guns. I could probably blast them to wherever they deserve to go."

After he pulled her onto his horse, Hayes rode ahead. When they reached the Promise, the gangplank was down. The ship appeared ready to sail. Hayes waved them forward. She found she'd been holding her breath and praying her father wasn't on board waiting with a rope to wrap around Collin's neck. Their escape last night wouldn't make the next reunion more pleasant. At least Collin would still be alive to speak his peace if they gave him the chance. She was terrified in their rage they would do just that.

On board, she watched the land disappear. They headed out to sea again. Collin didn't want to sail close to land, didn't want to be spotted from shore. The sun set hours ago. She couldn't sleep. Instead, she waited for Collin to return to the cabin. A conversation would be in order.

When he entered, he leaned against the closed door. He grinned. "We should handfast. It would make what we've been doing legal."

"You *ken* that is antiquated. No one in my family will call it legal although Aidan and Blade did just that before they were married." She smiled at his weak attempt to make this right for her. "Even in the highlands."

"Thought if we did so, it would make things easier for you with your parents. I don't give a damn about your uncles. What did you and Aidan talk about? Your heads were bent together nearly the two hours we were at the castle." He settled his arms across his chest. He appeared relaxed, totally masculine.

"Weddings," she mumbled uneasy with the subject. Everything between them, all the promises they made to each other were different now.

"Would you like a real one? Blade alluded to the fact that if we sailed for the McClellan castle right now, the act would go a long way in proving my devotion to you. What do you think? Should we avoid Dornoch all together?"

"No!" Her heart leapt to her throat. She heaved in a deep drought of air. "No."

The change in plans was done too quickly. Bad things always seemed to happen when completed in the spur of the moment.

He lifted an eyebrow seeming to speculate her sudden vehemence. The answer didn't seem to come to him. "Need I ask why?"

The air stuck in her throat until she coughed then coughed again dragging in more air. "The idea has merit. However," she walked to him, holding out her hands. "Don't want to go to McClellan land alone without more of your people behind you. Don't want you to be so vulnerable to my uncle's whims."

"Your father?"

"If we are at the castle, mother will keep *dah* in check. He won't do anything so foolish again, at least not with his wife so close. If mother had been with him, there would have been no threats of hanging. He was under the influence of Lord Montgomerie."

"Should we sail to Dornoch? Gather the clan? After that make our way to your home. The confrontation is inevitable. We need to be in agreement as to what we want." He pulled her into his arms. His lips settled atop hers.

When she came up for air, pushing at his great chest to let her talk, "Only if we know the other uncles are not already gathered at your home. Sailing into a nest of hornets would be foolish, especially after we encountered them first hand. They will be madder now."

"What would you do then? There are no guarantees they aren't waiting inside my house although I'm sure my brothers will be able to handle whoever might be camping on my doorstep."

"You don't have any way to communicate with your family, do you? Send them a message when we land."

She felt as if she grasped at straws. Felt as though walls closed in around them.

"Your uncles along with their men are not stupid. They'll be watching the port for certain."

Slowly, he peeled her clothing away. His lips explored, sipping everywhere that inflamed her the most. He knew every erogenous spot she possessed. Left none untouched. He was a devil, her devil.

She moaned, the purr reverberating from the back of her throat as her mind as well as her body melted under the tender onslaught of his kisses. Pushing against him her hands fumbled with his clothing. Soon he was just as naked. He thrust inside. Held still as he rose above her.

"How then?"

She twisted. Her body coiled with deep need for what he was withholding. Still deep inside her, he remained motionless. She tried to move. His greater weight kept them immobile.

He kissed her, kissed her again deeper and longer, pulling every passion filled emotion from her. His teeth tugged on her lip, his tongue leaving moisture where it passed over places that caused the heat to rise higher then higher. Her nails bit into his shoulders, scraping down his back. His groan of pleasure delighted her.

"Please..." The sounds coming from the back of her throat seemed to delight him as well. Still, he didn't move within her.

"Do you want me, love? How much do you want me?" he asked as he gradually began to thrust. His swollen hard member filled her, left her breathless until she clung to him desperate for release. Until he brought her to the pinnacle she sought.

At the height of her pleasure, "Forever, Collin...!"

He rolled off her, bringing her along so she lay atop, straddling him. She closed her eyes, absorbing the tender yet intoxicating moments. Minute after minute ticked by while they both tried to gather their breaths, stop their hearts from racing.

"How? You ask? Why, we'll sail right into the cove by my house. I always have men stationed below to apprise me of the occurrences since

I left. Nothing will be different. While I can't be positive my home is secure, this scheme is the best chance we have. Unless you change your mind and think sailing to your home is the most productive notion. I'll abide by your wishes."

"It is not. Besides, if we are to have a true wedding, your brothers along with your clan should attend. I don't understand how something so simple as wanting a lover could change my life so drastically."

She was angry again. Her parents were attempting to direct her life, mold what she wanted into their desires.

"Do you want to marry me? If you weren't increasing, would you want to wed me?" He sounded anxious for an answer, once more the tiniest bit insecure.

His was the same question she held for him. "You? If I didn't carry your child, would you be so agreeable to a marriage?"

The cry of sail ho cut off his answer.

"The uncles?" Her heart sped. They might not have the chance to set any plans into motion.

~ * ~

"Bloody, bloody hell, the two of them aren't in the rooms where we put them." Hunter swore as he raced from the house to the stables. The uncles ran behind him. "Where the hell are the horses? My daughter? The bastard has run off with her again. Forget the noose, I'll kill him with my bare hands!"

"For that matter where is your son?" Drake asked, a curious expression on his ducal countenance. "He seems to also be missing. Do you think he helped the pair escape?"

The question managed to enrage Hunter even more. Why did the boy's actions surprise him? They shouldn't. Resigned to the truth as it appeared now, "Colby helped them. I should have seen it coming. Should not have allowed him guard duty, especially when he offered his services. Colby always has a protective way with his sister. In his eyes, she could do no wrong. This situation should have been different. Why he isn't in the same place we are regarding Collin's actions is beyond my wildest imagination."

Hunter knew though. If he saw the blistering looks the two of them shared last night, someone else would have seen the fire shooting between them too. Colby and Nickie were always close. Shared so much, often he'd find them confiding in each other. He would defend her even if he knew she was wrong. Sometimes he even took the blame for naughty things she did. If she so easily twisted her brother around her finger, she most likely had Collin coiled in the same manner.

"Colby knows those two love each other. Understands they need to be granted the time to figure out their feelings, sort out the type of life they want." Ella stood beside her husband; her hand rested on Drake's arm as they all stared at the empty stable. "Also, Colby might have believed the lot of you actually met to hang the man. From what I overheard, he saw the two of them together before they left on this ill-fated journey. Nickie pleaded with him to keep the secret."

"Misguided child that he is, he kept the damning facts behind his smirk," Hunter muttered while he rubbed the back of his neck in an obvious attempt to ease the tension. "If we'd known the plan, we could have intercepted them before they left the Thames. Caught them before they hit open water and we had no idea which way they would travel."

"Do you suppose Colby went with them this time?" Ella asked, her voice soft, almost hopeful if Hunter didn't miss the emotion.

"He's probably waiting for his punishment on board our ship. He would want to explain himself, his reasons to me. Doesn't have to though. I admire the love he has for his sister even if at the moment that love is misguided."

Hunter held the same love for the only friend he had in his youth, while he pursued enough funds to purchase land. Hunter's true brother, well stepbrother, was pure evil, almost as evil as his stepmother. The pair of them were cut from the same cloth. Blade on the other hand, was his dearest friend. Stood by him.

"Best we get on our way. It's about five miles from the village," Ella grimaced seeming to realize she would have to walk. Drake swept her into his arms. "You can't carry me five miles."

"Can do my best," Drake said as he set out matching the others strides.

"You know you can't make it all the way."

"I see that as a challenge that can't be refused." He kissed her forehead.

By the time they reached the ship, some of Hunter's anger was diffused. Some, not all, Colby didn't receive the blistering he would have gotten if he'd returned to the hunting lodge. Perhaps Colby thought about that when he made his decision to remain on the ship.

Another hour passed and they were on the way. "We won't catch up to them, will we?" Hunter asked as Drake leaned against the nearby railing."

"Wouldn't worry about that. I've other plans in motion. Pulled out all my resources to secure the coastline as well as some distance from land."

"What would that be?"

Hunter almost chuckled, couldn't though. Thought of his daughter in the bounder's arm as well as his bed. "Just don't understand why she was so quick to jump to his bidding?"

"You're going to keep denying the fact your daughter is in love with the man?" Again, one ducal eyebrow rose in question. "It would be best of you to give up on the lost cause, accept the man into the family even if it's begrudgingly. Can't imagine what your wife will say when she discovers your threats."

"Just wait until your daughter is compromised by a bounder," Hunter shot out. "What will you be telling me then?"

"Point made. Now, as to your earlier question before we took a circuitous route, I've had a goodly amount of correspondence. Before we left, Addie and Hamilton did a remarkable job finding all the ins and outs of the McInnis' life."

"Such as..." Hunter felt a surge of interest. Possibly hope to go along with it. The cause to secure his daughter might not be entirely lost.

"First off, I've two of her majesty's finest sailing vessels scouring the coast line between the tip of Scotland as well as just south of McClellan land. One is hugging the coast, the other a bit farther out to sea. I've the distinct feeling one will intercept the McInnis vessel. If everything goes as planned, we will be boarding the Promise sometime tomorrow afternoon."

"I shouldn't have underestimated you. Thought you'd given up all the spy stuff many years ago," Hunter was quick to say. "Guess that was pure rumor or speculation."

"Just because I don't go out on missions doesn't mean my resources have disappeared," he spoke unemotionally as he talked.

Hunter guessed, as did the rest of the family though they never asked that Lord Montgomerie participated directly in the keeping of the nation's secrets. "What else do you know about the lad?"

"Oh, that he has a friend from his school days who lives in Lybster," Drake paused while Hunter decided to wait for him to finish the tale. "He's a minister. I've a hunch they might stop there to get married."

"I'm sure that's not all." Hunter knew Blade lived near the small village on the coast. He was beginning to see a clear picture.

"No, there is much more that my two retired spies have ferreted out. In this situation, you know the rest. Blade lives a few hours away. His mission in all this was to capture the minister. Keep him from tying these two together through perpetuity. If Collin and Nickie do show up, his mission is to slow them down. Don't want them to reach Dornoch before my ships can catch up to them." With that said, Drake laughed seeming well and truly pleased with himself.

"I've misjudged you. Aidan would love to see her niece. If Collin chose to stop for a wedding, Aidan and Nickie would visit. They would be slowed."

"Ah, and I've even a contingent of men waiting on his doorstep if he finds a path around my men."

"He's caught. Collin McInnis will be ours to do with as we please, compliments of her majesty's navy. No Englishman...or Scotsman would dare try to evade one of her majesty's vessels."

"Best you figure out what it is you want? Your daughter's happiness or McInnis swinging from the yardarm. Time is running out to change course. Don't do something you will come to regret with all your heart."

Chapter Six

"It's the royal navy," Hayes said when Collin stepped on deck. "They want us to stop? What do you want?"

"What the devil have we done?"

Collin knew though. He displeased a very wealthy and influential duke. A man who had more resources than anyone could possibly know about. If Montgomerie could commandeer the navy...the devil, he had no more strategies.

The roar of cannon startled him. When Nickie suddenly stood beside him terrified, he cursed to himself. Would this never end? He should hand her over, negotiate his ships release then high tail it to Dornoch. Problem was, if he did that, he would have to forget about Nick. A feat at this point in their relationship that was impossible. He wasn't going to give her up. Her father, damn his soul, was going to have to come to terms with that fact if he survived the duke's wrath. The man wanted him to hang.

She clung to his arm, watching the approaching ship. Her face paled. "This is Uncle Drake's doing, isn't it?"

Instead of terror she now sounded annoyed. Her fingers tightened around his arm. "He's gone too far if he thinks to have you detained."

"Or hung for kidnapping." Hayes said with a chuckle. "Don't believe for a minute he would do that. Perhaps the two of you should have stayed put. You'd be wed now."

"There is that," he said dryly. "Never would I have ever thought our little adventure would come to this. But then," he paused as he watched the ship close the distance. "It seems I keep making that observation."

Their sails were unfurled, the Promise gliding slowly to a stop. Grappling hooks attached to the ship, the captain of the English vessel along with a couple of officers boarded.

Collin and Hayes stood together as they waited. Nickie stood slightly behind Collin, holding his arm so tightly he thought sure she would cut off the blood supply.

"To what do I owe this visit?" he asked trying to be courteous even though he understood the reasons. All the captain would know would be his orders, which he wouldn't dare disobey. "We've done nothing wrong. Indeed, I'm headed for Dornoch. This has been a spur of the moment voyage."

"I have orders to board your ship and to take you as a captive to wait interrogation. I'm also to see your vessel reaches McClellan land."

"No!" Nickie cried out. "Uncle Drake has gone too far this time. I'm going with you. Won't ever forgive that man. Don't want to go home. They'll all be sorry they tried any of this."

"Can't do that ma'am," the captain said with an obvious tinge of regret marring his voice. "Have orders to see you home to McClellan land. That's what I intend to do. In any case, I don't have a choice in this matter. Neither do you."

Nickie was slowly backing away, shaking her head as if she sought some place to flee. There was nowhere except the bottom of the ocean.

"Don't fight them, Nick. You can't win this game your uncle is playing. I will convince him of whatever it is he wants to know. Go home, plan a wedding with your mother. If all goes well, we will be married soon."

He didn't have a great deal of hope concerning this matter. Montgomerie was a wild card. He might end up in the Tower of London or Newgate Prison...deportation was also a possibility.

Collin had a pretty good idea he would have to grovel before Hunter or Drake would let him go to Nick. Whether or not he'd ever see his Nick again, depended on the words he spoke. He was certain they would want to hear the word love bandied about.

He sucked air.

Love.

Love wasn't the problem. He meant to tell her. Never actually found the right time. Thought it would have been nice to speak his feelings to Nick first, not her father or uncle. This went against the grain. He didn't like what he was being forced to do. Went against all rules of polite society.

What the devil did he know about polite society?

Nothing, absolutely nothing.

He shunned those same rules his entire adult life. Indeed, he flaunted them in the eyes of the ton. Taunted the rules, throwing them away in his pursuit of flagrant defiance along with his personal pleasures. By his actions, he spoke loudly that he didn't give a damn.

Paying for his deeds now, he hoped it would be with a marriage and not his life. With a heavy heart, he followed the captain to his ship. At this instant nothing could be changed. Looking over his shoulder he caught a glimpse of Nick. Helpless was not how he'd ever felt before. Now, he was simply Montgomerie's pawn.

He stood at the bow as he watched the Promise sail south with Nick on board. His gut churned and twisted. The loss he felt as he watched the ship vanish from sight nearly sent him to his knees. After a few minutes, he realized they were headed toward land. That they were sailing to what must be a prearranged meeting spot. An anchor was set just off the village of Lybster. Lybster and Blade did him in. He realized it must have been Blade's job to detain him. How the devil did Montgomerie find out about his friend Daniel?

Bloody hell, Drake undoubtedly knew more about him than he did himself. How the devil did he discover so much and so quickly? It seemed the bloody lord was constantly one step ahead. Lord Montgomerie's talons must be long, must reach everywhere. He, Collin McInnis, had the audacity to battle the man, to defy him in every way. He ran off with his niece, defiled her, without impunity displayed that fact in his face in hopes of a forced marriage because he wasn't man enough to get down on one knee.

He deserved whatever came his way.

"Suppose we are waiting for Lord Montgomerie," Collin spoke to the captain. "Couldn't be anyone else who could reach this far, could it?"

"We are, can wait in my cabin, enjoy a brandy or two until Lord

Montgomerie shows up here. Don't know how long it will be. Want you to understand I'm following orders. Right now, the commands were to detain then make comfortable. Have to be curious though. What did you do to get on the wrong side of the duke?"

"Wouldn't mind a drink. As to the rest," Collin sucked in a deep breath of air. "Nothing I'd repeat."

Lord Montgomerie could arrive anytime. They tarried with Blade too long. He should have trusted his instincts. Should not have gone with the man even though Nick wanted to see her aunt. The breath he held for a few seconds while he thought about his actions this day, he let out slowly. "Don't guess anything I did would have made a difference. Maybe I should have traveled overland instead of taking to the sea route."

"Don't know about any of that. Asking again, even though it's none of my business, what did you do to bring down the duke's wrath so thoroughly? Have something to do with the girl you left behind? By the way, while you're waiting you can call me Shawn. I wasn't told to toss you in the hold, just to see to your immediate needs."

"You've guessed correctly. Plan to marry her. Seems they want that too. After the marriage though, the man intends to hang me. At this point, looks as if it's your yardarm that will be doing the trick."

"Wants to give a child if there is one a good Scottish name before he rids himself of the father?" Shawn chuckled softly. "That would be yours now, wouldn't it? You compromised her. He took exception. Would have thought you smarter."

"Don't see any humor in that," Collin tossed back the brandy. Foxed, he might not feel the rope when it tightened around his neck. Drunk, he might say something stupid that would make this situation grimmer than it already was. How much worse could it get?

One hell of a lot worse, he could find himself tarred and feathered before he found himself hung…or…keelhauled.

"Don't suppose you would. Didn't anyone ever tell you not to go up against the Duke of Richmond?"

"Only after it was too late to do anything about it."

The not telling of her chaperone's identity lay on Nick's shoulders. The not asking until it was too late to change his feelings about her was on his. If he'd known, he would have tarried in London to get to know her better. Bloody hell, it would have ended the same. "Seems she didn't want to say and I didn't intend to ask. Never thought it could be as bad as this."

"That bad, so you thought your little gal didn't have protectors. Family who cared about you seducing their loved one?"

"Used to having it my way. Never did give a moment of thought to the fact she was a debutante in London for the season."

He was a blind fool, refusing to see what was in front of his face. Now, he paid the price.

He grimaced as he recalled his arrogance that first night he met her. "Didn't think that far past the bedding of the girl. She was more than willing. She was eager. I was eager. She has this way of smiling that leaves me without rational thought, my body in control or maybe not in control."

"Worse than I thought," Shawn chuckled as he tipped his glass to his lips. "Can't say I've ever met a girl who could rob me of thought."

"Hope you never do. It's a precarious position to find oneself in."

"I'm sure."

Food was brought into the cabin. Shawn didn't mean to starve him. Perhaps this was his last meal. He could do worse than the delicious roasted salmon coupled with beans and bacon cooked in a wine sauce. The sun drifted lower. The setting of the sun was beautiful. He wondered if Nick saw the same view. A sliver of a moon hung low on the horizon, the shadow of a cloud ghosting the crescent. Stars began to twinkle. He'd like to wrap his arms around her, pull her back against his chest, the scent and feel of her strong in his memory.

Tonight would be beautiful. He wouldn't be able to see it with her. Only a few hours ago he thought to share the evening along with his bed in Dornoch with Nick. He might die tonight. This moonlit evening was a beautiful night to die. Black would have told him, 'Today was a good day to die.' The stodgy earl's Lakota Sioux heritage always gave him a different slant on life. Collin didn't think it was a good time to die, night or day.

Actually, he wanted to believe it was a good night to live. If he died tonight, his child would be born never knowing his father. This duke was stretching his royal rights too far. The sound of grappling hooks startled him out of his musing. A half hour ago, the captain left him. During that time, he sipped more of the expensive French brandy. While he was a bit tipsy, he didn't think his mind was muddled enough to slip up in his dilemma, say something offensive.

"Where is he?"

The Duke of Richmond. He would recognize that arrogant, threatening voice anywhere. The sound of it was seared into his brain. The confrontation was about to begin. Collin steeled himself to behave despite the need to put the duke in his place.

"You took care of him?"

Booted steps entered the cabin. Drake and Hunter stood inside the room.

"Just as you ordered. He's been given whatever he wanted. Didn't ask for anything though," Shawn chuckled as his look swayed from the men to him. "Says you mean to hang him. Any truth to that?"

"If he doesn't answer my questions to my satisfaction, we might do that very thing. Could have him keelhauled. Might have the same outcome."

This time he heard Hunter speaking. He was certain he had more to be concerned with Hunter than Lord Montgomerie as he suspected that Nick's father would have more to say about his future than the duke. The duke would back off if Hunter told him to do so. After all that had passed knowing he should be respectful to Nick's father and doing so was a difficult if not nearly impossible feat.

When the cabin door shut behind the men, he stood, saluted them with glass of brandy. He didn't like the expression on either man's face. "Welcome to my prison," he said while he knew the courtesy he wasn't showing would work against him. Somehow, he couldn't change the tone of his voice.

"Arrogant bastard," Drake mumbled his brows drawing tightly together. "Escort him to my ship. We'll see what he has to say in explanation of the last few months."

He turned to grin at Shawn, "It's your lucky day, Captain. Won't be your yardarm I dance from. Won't have to clean up the dead body either."

"Best you think on what you want to say to these men," Shawn warned as Hunter yanked him out of the cabin. "Don't want to hear about your death."

This time he wasn't treated civilly at all. He didn't deserve civil after the way he spoke to his hopefully soon-to-be future father-in-law. Shawn was absolutely correct. He did need to curb his glib tongue. A bit of reflection was needed right now. The cold air helped. His nerves, however, didn't settle on the short trip to board Montgomerie's ship.

When he was shoved through the next cabin door then onto a chair, he was surprised to see Ella. He didn't know why. She was with them before. Perhaps she would be the calm voice of reason he needed.

"I made sure, for your sake, I was present at this interrogation. I know Nickie cares a great deal for you or she would have never agreed to your bargain in the first place. Nor would she agree to meet you all alone for the sunrise that very morning. Yes, Colby finally told me something about that meeting, though I figure not all that was noteworthy. Her acting this way around a man goes beyond everything she's been taught. Don't blow this opportunity, Collin. I understand you're angry with my husband along with her father. If you ever want to see Nickie again...well, especially mind the way you speak to her father. Respect is what is needed. Perhaps even a bit of deference if you ever want to see Nicki again. Think on it..."

Solemnly, he nodded feeling the effect of the brandy fade with the impact Ella's words had on his arrogant male ego. Understood how right the duchess was despite how difficult it would be. Ella was one of a kind. She could hold sway over her husband, perhaps Hunter as well. She could speak for her cousin, Allura. Just as Aidan seemed to be on their side, perhaps Ella was as well. His spirits brightened a tad. The aunts didn't want to see him hang.

Colby walked into the room, nodded then grinned.

He felt relieved. Colby was in one piece. Didn't sport a black eye or visible bruising for his disloyalty to his father. This was the first-time real hope sprang inside. The boy was on their side. Well, Nick's side but that meant siding with his plans also. If he could just put in a good word for the two of them, he would feel better.

When he glanced Colby's way, it was as if the young man read his mind. He shook his head, dashing Collin's hopes for help from that angle. He steeled himself to keep his condescension at bay. A bit of groveling would do no harm. At least he prayed it wouldn't. The trick, he was positive, was in the amount as well as the depth of kowtowing he should do. Wouldn't help him, if the ingratiating went over the top venturing on the unbelievable.

"What do you have to say for yourself young man?" It was Hunter's first question. "Your answer better be good."

The question along with the answer Hunter sought threw him. Couldn't the man be a little more explicit? *What did he have to say for himself?*

He swallowed hard, biting back on the sarcastic comment that almost leapt from behind his teeth. His gaze shifted from one man to the other then back. His heart jumped in his chest. They both bore grim expressions. This was no time for a jest of any sort. Still, he didn't know how to answer the question.

He cleared his throat, praying he would find the right words for this moment. "I would have liked to tell Nick this first."

It seemed only right that the woman he intended to marry hear the words of love before the father along with the uncles. While he didn't mind so much speaking to her father, after all that was the obvious as well as the correct way to proceed. Her uncles could go to hell for all he cared.

"Believe you've had lots of time to tell her any thoughts you might have for her or even explain to her how you feel about her," Hunter spoke up.

His fingers drummed on his upper thigh. To Collin, Hunter didn't seem to possess an open mind. Under the circumstances, what father would?

It wasn't the words so much that sent his mind spinning with fury. No, it was the tone they were uttered in. A slanted glare from Colby curbed the ire he felt rising from the pit of his stomach, at least for the moment. Colby, once more, appeared to have his interest at heart. Well, if not his, then Nick's.

He sucked in a deep breath of air, turning over the words in his mind the words he meant to use to begin securing his future. "It's true, Nick and I have been together for a time. At first, I wasn't aware I cared so much for your daughter."

"Nick isn't her name," Hunter waved his hand in the air, his anger tangible, his words so precise they made the hair on the back of his neck stand on end. "Call her Nickie or Nicole."

Why the devil didn't the men say something sooner? It was easy enough in their presence to call her whatever they wanted to hear. Then his mind snapped. "Or what?" His arrogance was back.

He heard Colby's sigh of dismay. Felt the noose around his neck tighten.

"You might find the yardarm the last place you encounter." Hunter's fury seemed to be rising along with his.

Perhaps starting over might be better. "A fresh start?" he inquired trying for a lighter note to his tone as he tried for supplication instead of arrogance.

Unfortunately, haughtiness was how he dealt with life. The attitude deeply ingrained within him.

"Your feelings for Nickie better rival caring by a long shot," Hunter gritted out. "Expecting to hear a few more words that might lead to a commitment her mother and I can accept."

"Let me finish," Collin held up both hands to ward off more of the lecture he thought might be forthcoming, "I love Nick...Nicole."

Quickly, he corrected himself. Bloody eyes, but she was Nick to him, always would be.

"As I said only a second ago, that's another thing I'm taking issue with here and now. Already told you once. Don't call my daughter Nick. If you do, the discussion is over. Your chance of marrying her is through. In simple words that I'm sure even a bounder such as you can understand, you're finished."

That would be blessed hard to do. Until he knew if he won these men over, he would have to try. He nodded. "I love your daughter," he told him again. "I would take care of her, treat her with all the respect she is due."

He hoped refusing to use her name would help. At this point, he didn't mean to spark any tempers. He'd already done that quite handily.

"You're going to have to prove your words. Don't think you can tell me what I want to hear and have me believe you."

Colby grinned.

Well, the boy did know his parent. Perhaps the situation wasn't quite so dire. Montgomerie along with his wife remained quiet. "Not too sure how to prove that I love her." His hands ruffled through his hair then into the pockets of his trousers. "I'll do whatever is necessary."

"If you want to marry her, you'll have to figure that out," Ella spoke softly. "Love isn't all about sex. Involves a great deal more. What you're feeling might just be lust." She slanted Drake a flirtatious grin.

Lust, ah yes, according to rumors that surfaced on occasion the duke along with his duchess had also lusted for each other. Probably would not be wise or prudent to remind them he wasn't the only one who thought with another part of his anatomy other than his head.

Drake stood, smiling at his duchess, poured all a glass of brandy. Held his up. "Glad we finished this for the time being."

"I will tell the captain to set his course for home," Hunter said as he strode to the door. "When you are at my castle, you will be chaperoned at all times. You will not be allowed to be alone with Nickie."

The door banged shut behind them. Collin had the feeling he wouldn't be seeing much of Nick in the next days. If he couldn't see her, how the devil was he going to convince anyone he loved her?

Ella reached over to pat his hand. "It won't be too hard. I've every confidence you will find some time to speak with your fiancée. However, don't think for a moment any of us will allow Colby to be one of your chaperones. Oh, Collin, by leaving you alive her father has granted you the opportunity to court her. He's already assumed she will agree to marriage."

For the rest of the night, he was left to his thoughts. If he could when they landed, he would send a message to his brother, Doughall, who would gather the clan. Hayes might have already done so as he was escorting Nick home. He wasn't sure if Hayes was in charge of the

Promise.

No, he guessed Hayes would have little to no say in anything that would happen aboard his ship. His power would come once the vessel reached Dornoch. Hayes would collect all his friends and relatives. Would then travel back to McClellan land.

In this process they were not prisoners, only guarded guests. His crew should be allowed to return to their homes if they so choose. He hoped Hayes would stay. If he was to collect his people, Hayes couldn't remain behind. Bloody eyes, he needed all the support he could find.

The ship sailed into port sometime in the middle of the night. He'd been lying on the bed, all his clothing on, waiting rather impatiently. He figured someone would come for him. As it was now, he didn't believe he could presume to walk off the ship on his own. If too much time passed, he would have to see what waited for him on the other side of the bloody door.

Slowly, the cabin grew lighter. Footsteps were heard on the deck. He was brought food and drink. Obviously, no one was escorting him to the castle. He ate the warm bread then washed it down with the hot tea laced with milk and honey. He would have preferred a strong drink.

He was eager for the situation to progress, eager to see Nick.

Waves rocked the vessel. Seagulls cried out as they caught the air currents. Pulling out his pocket watch, he looked at the time. It was nearing the noon hour. This was torture. More time ticked by.

Collin didn't believe he could wait one more second.

The door burst open. "You ready?"

"Been ready since dawn," he gritted out through clenched teeth.

Thoroughly exasperated by the long delay, which was meant to torment, if not that then to infuriate. He was being tested.

It was Colby. "Everyone has gone ashore. Thought they would leave you here as long as possible. Give you time to think, father told me. Didn't dare go against their wishes, not this time. Finally, had to take pity on Nickie though. Thought she'd start tearing her hair out if you didn't show yourself. Even though Father assured her you were unharmed, she didn't believe him. Worse, she might have defied father to come here to see for herself. She's a stubborn one."

Her brother didn't need to tell him anything he didn't already know about his *wee lass*. Collin stepped on the deck. Breathed in the clean scent of salt air. This was the promise of a new day. It was indeed a good day to live, a good day to begin the new quest, the courting of Nick. Bloody eyes, but he'd never courted a *lass* before. Didn't have any clue as to how to go about such a thing.

He floundered just thinking about the outlandish process. Despised the notion of a chaperone shadowing his every move.

He would have to seek someone out for advice. Perhaps the duchess could provide some insight as to how to go about courting, or perhaps Nick's mother. He would begin with Ella. At least he'd met her even though the meeting wasn't under the best circumstances. He felt Ella understood more than the uncles.

The hustle and bustle in the castle's courtyard surprised him. While he watched, all kinds of people came into the enclosure. He heard French along with German spoken around him. He heard English that didn't have the Scottish burr or the accent of anyone who lived on the British Isle.

Beside him Colby chuckled, "It's a working castle. We all live in the east wing now. To keep it from crumbling down around us we rent rooms to tourists. Most of our guests are from America of all places. Seem to want some Scottish ambiance along with telling people they slept in a real castle." Colby bent close to whisper to him, "The castle is haunted too. That is some of the draw."

"Haunted?" Collin laughed softly, wondering just how haunted the place was. Perhaps he could dress himself in a white sheet to find his way to her room for a short dalliance.

"Don't tell anyone I gave the truth away. The rumor is part of how we make a profit. There are tunnels behind the rooms connecting them. Most of the chambers have two doors. One that opens to the hallway along with one that opens to the tunnel. If you can find the tunnel door in your bedchamber, you can leave it unlocked. I'm sure Nick will be able to find her way to you since she knows about the passageways."

"Is this a trick?"

It wouldn't do to have her father catch him with her in his bed.

Something like that wouldn't help his pursuit...or the courting. While he didn't completely know, he was certain bedding the girl you were courting was not acceptable.

"No trick. She will most likely come to you. It's also how her aunts along with her mother snuck out of the castle at night when they were younger. It was also how Hunter won my mother. He discovered the ruse. He won her hand in marriage along with the title of laird."

"Why didn't you have it sealed?"

That seemed the obvious to Collin. The sealed passageway would prevent a great deal of shenanigans.

Colby looked to the castle, saw the window as well as Nickie leaning out. She disappeared as suddenly as she made her presence known. Colby continued with the answer Collin waited for.

"Hunter believed the sealing would result in bad luck. Believed it was prudent to have a second way out in case of an emergency among other reasons. Sometimes I think he wanted to make use of the passage to abduct mother. He was the only one allowed to take her to the island."

"Collin!"

Her voice gave him reason to grin. When he turned, he saw her running to him, her arms outstretched. He caught her up, twirled her around in tight circles. His lips found hers for a brief kiss. He wanted to deepen the caress, felt her moist tongue sweep across his as she returned the embrace.

She pulled away to look at him tenderly, to touch his cheek with a fingertip.

"I missed you," he said softly.

His thoughts turned to mush. He didn't think he'd ever told a woman he missed her before. Good Lord, she'd been out of his reach less than a day. He missed her.

The throat clearing behind him sent him reeling with fury. "Best put the little lady down before her *dah* comes out."

His first chaperone, he'd wanted to kiss her more thoroughly. Wanted to feel her pressed tightly against him. Guessed doing so might have to wait. Where Nick was concerned, he assumed there was a lot that would have to wait.

~ * ~

When Nickie watched her ship sailing away from Collin, tears slid down her cheeks. A sob caught in the back of her throat. She didn't know what would happen to Collin. She'd never seen her father so very angry. No one would tell her anything. Speaking of Collin's fate brought silence, even from Colby. The bow of the Promise was her friend until the ship stopped at the docks. If her relatives could treat her to the silent treatment, she would return that conduct twofold. As far as she felt concerned, she owed no one an explanation.

Her mother would listen to her. Would empathize; defend her actions to her father. In this moment of thoughts, Nickie hoped she would.

It was dark, only a smattering of moonlight and stars brightened the mournful scene doing nothing to alleviate her worst fears. She was cold and hungry. No one offered food, not that she could have eaten. Her stomach churned with apprehension. Her escort was severe, without manners. Probably just doing his job for the great Lord Montgomerie. She had a lot of yelling to do. If railing at Montgomerie as well as her father would help, that was exactly what she would undertake to set this right. Unfortunately, the only one who would be hearing the screaming was her mother who was now greeting her with a smile as well as open arms. Her uncles along with her father were on another ship.

"Mother," she ran to her, hugging her tightly.

After stepping back a second, her hands on her hips, her eyes flashing defiantly. "Men!" she cried out in frustration. "How dare they presume to order people around? They had no right, no right at all!"

"Your father ordered you home?"

"He gave me no choice. There is more that has me crying foul. He had no reason to presume he knew what I wanted. Hunter just assumed his wishes suited me best."

Nickie didn't intend to get over her pique anytime soon. She wanted her fury to last.

Allura's first response was to smile. "Yes, I know. They can all be quite exasperating. Men accept one mode of behavior for all the male species then something entirely different for women. Now, when it comes to their daughters...well they can be absolutely annoying and infuriating. Still, you have...I will let you explain. Never before set store in rumors, don't intend to do so now with my daughter. Also, I'll make no excuses for Hunter. Although I'm sure in the end he will need forgiveness from his daughter in order to have your love again."

"Irritating. They are all arrogant, conceited oafs!"

She needed to vent her anger before she could settle down then plead her case. Nickie understood she would have to choose her words carefully. She had, after all, given herself to a man. Her size was increasing. Her mother would notice.

"That too, and you can add maddening to the list. Now," they started for the main room then continued up the stairs. "Why don't you tell me what happened over a glass of wine and some food. Cook made those little lavender cakes you like. Would you rather have something more filling?"

"No, no, don't know if I can eat anything. My stomach is tumbling and churning. Though the wine will be nice. As to my story, you're going to be disappointed in me. What you have to understand though was that I was following my heart. You always told me to follow my heart. Did I get that wrong?"

Nickie was suddenly afraid. She wanted her mother's encouragement as well as approval that she did right. For a few seconds she held her breath while she waited. A myriad of expressions swept across Allura's face. Truly, Nickie didn't know what to think when Allura finally began to speak.

"No, dear, you didn't. Following your heart is the only way to find the man you love. However, doing so can get a woman into a wealth of trouble that she doesn't have any way to dig herself out. I believe that was what you actually accomplished."

It seemed Allura tried to reassure yet failed since Nickie was indeed in a predicament she couldn't get out from underneath.

Once inside and up the stairs they went to Nickie's chamber to talk and eat. Nickie wanted more privacy than she could get in the main hall. A fire crackled merrily in front of her, embers snapping, creating a warm glow in the otherwise somber room. Everything in the chamber was exactly as she left, all her things in place, awaiting her return. If she got her way, she wouldn't return here ever again.

Nickie drank deeply, letting the warmth of the fire heat her from the outside and the wine from the inside. The liquid was delicious. Her stomach seemed to settle. "*Dah* was so unbending when he spoke with me. He doesn't understand how I feel. Wouldn't listen to my side. I'm sure he won't consider what Collin has to say. Don't think he even cares that I love Collin."

If she could, she would forget the look on her father's face, forever vanquish his words from her mind. The devil, if she could, she would be with Collin now, wrapped in his arms. He would be deep inside her. His warmth and caring would encompass her. She rubbed her arms. A chill swept through her.

"You have to remember all the information he had came from the first missive from Drake. You were gone. Seemed to vanish into thin air. No one knew where you were. He hightailed it to London to search for you, his fear tangible. We were both terrified. You've no idea, Nickie, as to how we felt. Thankfully, Drake has the resources that enabled him to find you. After that...we discovered you were with one of the most notorious rakes in London. What were we to think?"

"Damn that man, he used the British navy to capture Collin's ship. He had no legal right to do something so nefarious. He also doesn't have the right to hang anyone without a trial. Uncle Drake called his conviction his ducal right. Bloody hell!"

Allura seemed to soothe, at least the following words sounded like her intent. "Still, sweetheart, you need to see this from our eyes too. We believed you'd been kidnapped. If you had written a note to let us know what was going on..."

"Father still would have come after me. Uncle Drake would not have changed his mind about hanging Collin. All of you have to see this from my viewpoint too. You cannot decide the course of my life. I love him."

"True on all counts, now why don't you tell me something about this man I believe you love with all your heart. Does he make you laugh?

Does he treat you with respect? Is he a friend? The man you love should also be a friend, a companion, a confident someone who you can pour your heart out to. Tell him your darkest thoughts as well as your most ardent desires."

She heaved in a long breath of air before answering. "I do love him." *Enough for both of us if it's necessary.* "Think I might have loved him from the second I saw him. He looked so chagrinned then arrogant as if he'd done nothing wrong. Even at that moment it seemed he wanted to apologize. The words wouldn't clear his throat. Collin is a man who is not used to asking forgiveness."

Vividly, she remembered the look on his face when she grinned at him. She also remembered wishing she could see the expression on his handsome face when he realized his current mistress was at a ball where she was not supposed to be. He would be wondering exactly who he had abducted and now sat in his townhouse. Nickie wanted that even before she saw his face. Watched his eyes change color while he looked her over from head to toe, his gaze lingering on several parts of her. Watched them darken with what she now knew was desire when his gaze met her eyes after his thorough perusal. She understood he showed tremendous restraint that night.

Allura sipped her wine, her eyes seeming to search her face for more than what she was volunteering, "So, tell me how the two of you met. No one seems to know the details. Although something tells me your brother *kens* more than he wants to share. The meeting along with the agreement to leave with him must be interesting. We do have as long as we want. Your father won't be here until tomorrow morning at the earliest."

"True, Colby ran across us the morning we were watching the sun rise over the hills. You know how much I love watching the sun come up over the ocean. Well, the sight is just as grand inland as it is here on McClellan land."

She loved the sunrise better than the sunset. Sunrises heralded the beginning of a new day. Gave a body reason to start anew if the day before wasn't to the liking. Today was not at all to her liking, except the part where she spent a few hours with her Aunt Aidan. That meeting had been deliberate as well as planned to delay them. How the devil did Montgomerie discover Collin's friend in Lybster? Nickie found herself shaking her head, while she wondered about the network of informants her Uncle Drake must have on hand.

Tomorrow had to be better.

"That isn't how you met," Allura prompted softly. "Is it something you *dinna* want to share? It's all right you *ken*. Some information can't be told to anyone, especially a mother."

"I'm sure Father would take umbrage with what happened that night before the ball. You have to promise me you won't tell him. While I don't mind telling you, I don't want father to have more information to condemn Collin with."

Nickie held her breath as she watched her mother's delicate features change; watched, as her eyes seemed to speak the truth. She wasn't sure her mother would refrain from telling Hunter. As far as she knew, they shared everything. This situation would prove to be no different.

"I'll be honest with you. Not certain I can do that, even for you. Not used to keeping anything from your father...I will, however, promise not to mention it until after the two of you are well and truly wed and the marriage consummated."

Her face drained of color at her mother's words. It was something Allura would notice. Nickie wasn't positive a marriage was in her future. Though, she understood the direction of her mother's thoughts when she mentioned the consummation of her marriage. Well, all her uncles along with her father knew the bedding came before the wedding. After all this time, she was sure her mother guessed the truth. Hopefully, there would be a wedding. If there wasn't...Nickie couldn't bare that thought."

"I can accept that fact. You've always been honest with him, at least as far as I know. Collin is already on father's bad side. If he heard, well, if he knew what happened that night, he might indeed take matters into his hands before he heard the explanation. It wasn't well done of Collin even though he believed me to be an acquaintance of his, an intimate acquaintance, if all the truth is told, one of his mistresses."

"What you say is too intriguing. Go on." Allura was smiling, grinning broadly while she sat back with her glass of wine. "I can't wait to hear the story in its entirety. Your man is truly the bounder your father claims he is."

She didn't answer, couldn't. To her he wasn't a cad. "So, I needed to see Colby. It was urgent. At least I thought seeing him couldn't wait until after the ball. I wanted to convince him to bring me home. I never wanted to go to London in the first place. The debutante scene wasn't for me. There was so much I wanted to tell him, I stayed at the townhouse longer than intended."

Nickie continued the story, her mother laughing at times so hard tears ran down her face. The part about the garishly painted carriage brought even more tears to their eyes. She told her about the gamble skipping rocks that she lost. Win or lose she would have agreed to leave with Collin.

She left out all the parts about the intimacy she shared with Collin, about the scarves and the way he slowly pulled them from her gown. By the expression on Allura's face as the tale neared its end, Nickie was sure her mother put the raw facts all together to form the only conclusion possible. A woman could not be with a man such as the McInnis for months on end and not share his bed.

"Does he want to wed you?" Allura's words took her by surprise, so much so she gasped in a strangled breath of air.

Feigning composure, Nickie lifted her shoulders slightly. Fought the tears that seemed to rise. "He says he does now that...that..." She caught herself before the words she was trying desperately not to say condemned her in her mother's eyes.

"Allow me to finish for you. Now that you've given yourself to him, you understand there is no other man for you." Allura held her hands within hers. Her mother's touch was reassuring. "Waiting until something like that happens is never the best way to proceed in a relationship. He should have made sure you were not a virgin when all this began. I *ken* he did not."

Warmth flowed into her, heated her cheeks. Nickie didn't feel the condemnation she half expected. Her mother wasn't like that. Allura's concern would be for her wellbeing as well as Collin's demise. In that respect she would act like her father. "He says he cares about me. Says he has never felt that way about another woman."

"You want more than the word care."

"Doesn't every woman. Want to be loved not just cared about. I can't let him take the blame for any of this. I was eager to share myself with him. Told him too many times to count that I wasn't ever intending on taking a husband. Even told Collin I wanted him to be my lover. At the time we agreed marriage was out of the question. The arrangement suited both of us."

"You didn't?" Allura sounded surprised but not completely surprised. "If he didn't want to wed you, why didn't he assure you he would take care of you no matter what happened?"

Nickie inhaled long and deep wishing she had a better way to put this. Wished her mother's words didn't make so much sense to her. None of this should be set at her mother's feet. However...however, Allura brought her up to be an independent as well as an honest woman in all her dealings.

"At the time it was how I felt. Even though you and father's marriage set an example that couldn't be denied, I didn't think for a moment there was another man in this world as good and true as my father. Was afraid I would never find such a man. Wanted to experience...lovemaking. Listened to Colby so many times expound on the thrill and the pleasure of bedding a woman. Thought what was good for him, would actually be good for me too."

Those words brought a small chuckle from Allura. "You will find there are many men with those virtues as well many who lack any virtue at all. Is Collin good and true? Is he an honest man? It sounds as if the two of you spoke openly about what you want." she asked, her smile growing as she focused on her daughter.

"I believe he is. He asked me more than once if I wanted to return to London. That was before we left the Thames behind. If I asked him, he would have taken me anywhere I wanted to go, even here." She breathed in deeply, once more looking over her room. "I also told him I've no regrets."

"Even for the babe you carry?" Allura asked. She looked away for a moment as if she wanted to give her time to gather her thoughts. "Why didn't he take precautions to keep this from happening or does he just not care? Does he have other children?"

Nickie covered her gasp of surprise with her hand. Several seconds ticked by before she asked, "You know about my child and you're not angry."

Allura shook her head, wispy strands of hair swirling around her face. "Guessed that you were carrying a *wee bairn* after so many months with a man you fell in love with at first sight. Your gasp of surprised resignation confirmed the guess. How far along are you?"

Nickie heard a change in her mother's tone. "You're angry."

Nickie didn't want to have this dialogue with her mother. It was too soon, the knowledge of the pregnancy too new. She was just coming to terms with the realization herself.

"About my first grandchild? Never." She too forced in a deep breath of air. "I wager some of this is my fault. I should have prepared you better. Our talks should have revolved around the way a man, the right man, can make you feel when he kisses you. When he touches you in certain ways. They are all seducers at heart. A mother doesn't like to think about a man turning her daughter into liquid heat."

"None of this is on your shoulders. I'm glad you aren't angry. Father was livid when he discovered the truth."

"Why would the two of you tell him?" Allura's expression seemed puzzled.

In truth at the time, she'd felt more than puzzled and confused. "Collin told him, bated him with certain things we did. Not in so many words but by everything he implied. I could have hit Collin I was so angry with him for his blind audacity, his inbred arrogance. He was too afraid to own up to his newfound feelings and ask me to marry him that he wanted father to force a marriage. What he didn't count on was that they, Drake along with my father, wanted to watch him swing from the gibbet for what we did together."

"Your father is in need of a good talking to if he actually thought to deprive a child of a father." Allura's color blossomed. "How dare he presume so much authority!"

Allura was now obviously angry with Hunter. Her cheeks developed a heated shade of pink. Her hands were now tightly fisted. "He will pay. In my way, I'll make him understand how far off the mark he strayed with you as well as your intended."

Nickie was learning slowly that women, despite their smaller stature, held immeasurable power over their husbands. Ella, Aidan and now her mother implied they could make their husbands sorry for their actions. If they so choose, could bend them to their way of thinking. Nickie didn't doubt for a moment after hearing some of the conversations the point was made by withholding their sexual favors.

Did she have power over Collin in that manner? That fact didn't seem too likely. To Nickie, it appeared to her that Collin controlled just about everything they did. The slightest caress with a fingertip would melt her. She was his to mold into whatever he desired. She didn't think she could ever remain unmoved by his attentions. Blade was afraid Aidan would make him sleep elsewhere than his bed. Could she do that to Collin if he didn't please her? Probably not, all the man had to do was kiss her to make her give him anything he wanted.

She would have to be stronger. Would have to keep her distance if that was to be the case. Perhaps if she could dodge his long arms, she could keep the caresses at a minimum. "Do you think Father will bring Collin here in one piece?"

"What I believe is the man is more bluster than anything else. The two of you made him angry, caused him to doubt his ability to protect his daughter. He discovered he no longer held the control, also came to realize his daughter loves another man. He didn't like that. By the tale you've expounded, he's been encouraged by your Uncle Drake to take backhanded shots at the man you love. Not for one second do I believe they would have gone through with a hanging."

Nickie breathed in a small breath of relief. "Maybe Collin will be safe."

"They only wish to put the fear of God into him," Allura said.

Although Nickie heard the slight hesitation in her words. Knew even now, her mother wasn't all that certain about what she told her.

"When do you think they will be here?"

She wanted to go to bed. Needed to think in private tonight. What her mother told her, as well as her thoughts about this man, changed direction one more time. Oh, she still loved him. Still wanted to wed him. Wished for the type of life her mother and father enjoyed.

Now, she needed to find a way around his easy swagger, his arrogance that he could dictate his whims. Of course, she always seemed to agree with those impulses simply because so far, she wanted what he wanted.

She would have to test this theory of her mother's.

However, it might be a while before she was given the opportunity to be alone with him. Using the tunnel would not be beyond her resources. Laughing softly, she bid her mother good night, her exhaustion so very overpowering once she closed her eyes, she slept soundly.

~ * ~

When she woke, all that happened in the last few days, catapulted into her head. Her hair fell over her face. Her mind ached from all the worry. Before she fully woke, steaming bath water was brought to her. Warm bread and honey followed coupled with a pot of hot tea. Her thoughts were for Collin. She missed waking up to his arms around her. Missed the brick wall of his chest to snuggle against.

What was happening to him?

Would she see him today, talk to him?

The bath was heavenly. The food warmed her insides. Dressing carefully, ready to meet her father to explain her wishes, she proceeded to the main room. She hoped Collin would also be in attendance. When she entered the room, she held her breath while she searched for the man she loved.

Nothing.

With a defeated sigh, she sat by her father understanding he was the only person who could give her the information she sought. Hunter appeared relaxed as well as unconcerned that he imprisoned an innocent man. His long legs stretched out in front of him as he spoke to one of his men. Nickie even had fears that she might find Collin in the antiquated dungeon that had yet to be renovated to use as rooms for their more curious and adventuresome guests.

"Where is he? Where is Collin?"

Nickie couldn't wait for her father to spill the truth to her. She thought she had the patience to play her father's game. She did not. She had the sneaking suspicion her father meant to keep news of Collin from her for as long as he could.

"Don't worry over the bounder. He's fine. Sleeping on the boat. I'm sure if he wanted to see you, he'd be here in the room. He must not care very much. Perhaps he values his sleep more than you."

Sleeping? She sucked air at her father's pompous word. Though they did put doubt in her mind. Which was most likely exactly what her father intended. "He's not a prisoner?"

She knew Collin well enough to understand there was more to this than what her father was telling her. She wasn't going to take anything her Uncle Drake or her father told her at face value.

"The door is not locked. He can come and go as he pleases. It should delight you that he has not been harmed."

He ate as if nothing happened. He drank his tea as if her life was not in danger of unraveling.

"Does Collin understand that? Does he *ken* he is not a prisoner? The lot of you probably left him feeling if he left the cabin you put him in, you all would pounce. You do recall that you threatened his life more than once?"

"Probably not."

"So, no one told him he could leave the ship. No one mentioned an unlocked door." Her fists were tight. She was barely able to contain her burgeoning temper. This was not what she expected. "I can go see him."

"I would advise against something like that. While his door is not locked, I might take it upon myself to lock your door." His voice was too calm, too condescending. "I failed to protect you once. I won't make that mistake again."

Nickie wanted to scream at him. She felt close to pulling out her hair in frustration. He didn't have the right to lock her in her room.

"Mother would take issue with your actions. Don't suppose you want to sleep alone tonight," she blurted the newly discovered information about ways to control someone who was bigger and stronger.

Hunter's glare shot his fury at her. "What would you know about that?" He didn't elaborate.

Nickie guessed that was territory he didn't want to venture into. Her father did shoot her mother the same type of glare, only it wasn't fury. It was something else entirely. She recognized the unrestrained passion in the way he stared at her mother. Only, there was something else in that gaze she didn't understand.

Allura smiled flirtatiously at him, lowered her lashes as she swished her unbound hair behind her. Nickie had seen that between the two of them before. Now, after her sojourn with Collin, she understood what drove both of them. Passion, what she witnessed was raw passion, desire flaring, if she didn't miss her guess. If her father left now, she would understand why.

Colby sat beside her and poured himself a cup of tea as he leaned against the back of his chair. "Why do you look as if you could kill?" he asked pleasantly.

There was nothing pleasant about the way she felt. Her stomach churned, flipped over. If she had to wait a moment longer, she was certain she would lose the minimal control she was achieving. "Where is Collin? Is it true he was not locked in his cabin?"

Colby grinned at her, chuckling at her concern. "Try to stay calm, little sister."

"Don't placate me," she shot at him even though she understood his good intentions.

In this instant she was tired of all men, not just her father and Drake who topped the list.

Her brother cleared his throat to continue in the wake of her anger. Colby held up his hands, "As far as I know, last evening the cabin door was definitely secured. However, I wouldn't be surprised if our notoriously devious Uncle Drake, including our father, unlocked said door this morning so they could tell you he was free to do whatever he wanted, which he is not. Collin knows that for a fact and will act accordingly, which means not ruffling anyone's feathers, especially the duke's."

She turned on her father who turned a heated shade of red at his son's words. Her father never got embarrassed. "Is that true? How dare you try to make Collin out to be a cad who doesn't care about me? He's not. You know it. I know it. Even Uncle Drake knows that for a fact. Drake Montgomerie is more a cad than Collin will ever be. Still, the two of you carry on as if you've every right to make both of us miserable. Is that any way to treat a daughter you profess to love? The worst part about all of this fiction is that you lied to me."

Colby, seeming to take umbrage at the deception wrought upon her, stood then said, "I'll get the McInnis." With that said, he turned on his heel attempting to leave the room.

"I'll go with you."

She was on her feet, rushing forward. Her heart raced at the thought of seeing him. She needed to make sure her uncles didn't harm him.

"No!"

The hand that stopped her was her father's. Easily, he brought her back to sit in the chair beside him. "You will obey my wishes in this little matter. When the man gets here, we'll talk about the terms as well as the conditions for the young man to court you. He will court you. He will not take you to his bed until you are wed. Is that understood?"

At her father's words she paled, felt the blood drain from her face. As if she thought it could happen again and at the age of twenty, she felt as if she was still the little girl chastised by her father for doing something stupid.

Perhaps she did do something stupid, though she was no longer a little girl who needed his protection.

He thought she was.

She had a mind of her own. She used it often.

Perhaps with good reason, no, she wasn't going to let his decision or his orders stop her from doing what she wanted.

Colby seemed to pick up his step as he disappeared from view.

With her father's word that she could wait in the courtyard, Nickie strode out the door, intending to give a regal impression to anyone who watched.

~ * ~

"You were too hard on Nickie." Allura sat down beside Hunter, watching her daughter leave the room with more dignity than Allura would have expected under this situation. "It's going to be difficult to keep those two apart if that's your intention. We should let them have time to speak together. I'm sure they have a great deal to sort out."

"We have men who will guard doors, who will make sure they never have alone time. Be advised, Colby won't be a chaperone. Where his sister's wellbeing is concerned, he's shown his true colors."

"Our Colby understands his sister's feelings better than the father. He knows the two of them will make a fine outstanding couple. Everyone knows rakes make the best husbands once they've found the woman they want. Nickie is the woman Collin wants. You can't keep the two of them apart."

Allura wanted to laugh at the look on her dear husband's face. She realized by the fierce scowl he suspected the two loved each other.

"He might understand one thing, that they want each other. What he doesn't understand is the fear that has rolled around in my belly since we were first informed Nickie was missing. He had no right to do such a thing. Still, he did and gave no consideration to the consequences." Hunter let out a snort of derision. "Nothing has changed my mind. McInnis has to prove to me he loves her. If he doesn't, there will be no wedding."

"How will that happen, Hunter? What will he do that will prove to you he loves her? She is in love with him. If I don't miss my guess, the pair are deeply in love. You cannot mean to keep them apart. The ploy will not work, as well you know. I understand my daughter. She will do whatever she has to do in order to be with the man she's in love with. We both brought her up to think independently. By denying them, all you will do is send her away. Is that what you want?"

Hunter rapped his fisted hand on the table in front of him. "I have to try. In fact, I know he's in love with her. I've seen the way he looks at her. The way he follows her with his gaze. That doesn't change anything. He has to court her to my satisfaction."

"Even more reason to make sure she gets what she wants. It will be as if you beat your head against brick if you try to keep them from even speaking to each other. Step back. Take a deep breath. Give the two of them some breathing room," she said while she watched him closely for any sign her words were getting to him. "You wanted him to court her properly. They cannot do that from behind locked doors."

"You want me to let the man bed my daughter right under my nose!" Hunter seemed to brim with anger.

"I didn't say that," Allura admonished, looking at him with narrowed eyes. "Give the man breathing room. If you do, he will show his true colors. Allow them to spend time together with supervision."

"If you insist," he said sounding as if he begrudged the giving in to her request.

"You won't regret this concession." She smiled now, as she understood she was winning him over to her way of thinking.

"Already do," he muttered while he picked up her hand to place a kiss on her palm. His eyes darkened.

She understood what he asked for. He thought a quick dalliance upstairs would win her over to his side. By now he should know her better than that. "Ah, I see...you fear your bed will be removed tonight if you don't give in to my wishes."

"Correct." He pulled her onto his lap. "Nonetheless, I've my ways to encourage you to think otherwise."

Softly he placed a kiss on her lips then another, his hands moving provocatively on sensuous spots. Places he knew aroused her most thoroughly.

She allowed him this simple pleasure because it wasn't bedtime, far from the hour. If she was careful today, she could stay away from him. He would expect that ploy though. This game she would win. Her daughter's future was on the line. She would never allow him to become autocratic over her daughter's happiness. He would see things her way.

Yes, he would give in to her.

Dropping her lashes again, she finished the ploy by smiling sweetly, "I'm going to send invitations to all the relatives. By my calculation the wedding should be in two weeks. That will give everyone enough time to get here. Her wedding dress will be ready by then. The cake and feast planned as well."

"You're going to do what?"

She was surprised she got one sentence out before he reacted. But then...with expert finesse honed by years of practice, he was busy exploring her neck with his lips. Not that he didn't intimately know every part of her. She sighed softly leaning into him.

"We," she paused as she gazed at him sliding her tongue daringly along her lip leaving a dewy trail of temptation, "We will plan the wedding, the flowers, the cake, the feast. Also, his clan should be advised when and where they should show up. Don't you think?"

She understood he would object. Hunter wouldn't want Collin to have allies he could depend on nearby.

He choked, "Don't want his clan here."

"Of course you do. He has three brothers who would want to attend the wedding of the oldest sibling as well as celebrate the joyous occasion. They might even arrive before the invitations are sent. Today, I'll send for the modiste. Her wedding dress should be beautiful; satin, tiny beaded pearls, Belgium lace. After all, one only marries once in her life."

Hunter snorted, seemingly resigned. "She will still be chaperoned. He won't bed her again until the nuptials have been said."

"In that we agree. When you decide to do so, you can be a darling."

She kissed his cheek. His surprise allowed her to wiggle off his lap. It was the last contact he was going to receive today as well as tonight. If he didn't behave himself where their daughter's welfare and future were concerned, he would do without her for longer than he would wish. Allura had in mind, the two weeks until the wedding just as he insisted for his daughter and Collin.

With hands clasped together, she watched the play of emotions across his face, noticed his brows were still drawn tightly. With that deed accomplished to her satisfaction, she whirled, her dress rising far enough that if he was looking, he would see her ankles as well as a bit higher.

Allura planned that too.

In the courtyard she spotted Nickie running to meet the man she loved. Collin opened his arms for her. After they embraced, he whirled her around and around in circles. As he slowly came to a stop, his lips found hers in a tender kiss that was immediately stopped by one of Hunter's men.

The smile that started with the sight of her daughter with Collin turned to a frown. There would be another talk, as well as another if the last talk was not heeded to her satisfaction

Chapter Seven

"This last week without being with you has been hell," Collin grumbled while he walked with Nick, his arm wrapped across her shoulder.

It seemed to him he'd been aroused the entire time with no possible relief in sight for another week. He didn't have to close his eyes to recall every vivid exotic part of Nick. The way she tasted along with the scent of her.

She was exquisite.

She smiled at him, her eyes shimmering with animation. "For me too."

She squeezed his hand that just encompassed hers, their fingers now interlocking.

They were walking outside the castle. Overhead the sun shone brightly. Thin layers of white clouds lined the horizon. If he'd been allowed some alone time, he wouldn't now feel so testy. One of their ever-present chaperones followed behind. He didn't care if he stole a kiss or two. By now he knew which ones would interrupt them the very moment it seemed they might kiss along with the men who would allow for a short interlude.

Stepping behind a tree, he pulled her into his arms. Never before he met Nick had a woman fit so perfectly to his body. They were made for each other. She was his. His hands cupped her adorably rounded bottom as he drew her closer. Her lips opened slightly as her breath seemed to rush from her lungs. He covered her mouth with his, his tongue delving inside the secret warmth that was Nick. He wanted to howl his delight as she returned the kisses.

The devil, she tasted of warm sunshine and sweet berry tarts. Her womanly scent filled him so thoroughly he couldn't deny the pulse of his body as she wriggled against him. With his legs braced apart he cradled her between his thighs.

She understood what she did to him. Just as he knew how his kisses generated the raw passion that left her spineless in his arms. They tempted and tantalized each other as they sought the ecstasy that waited for them.

He needed her.

Had to find a way to make love to her before he exploded in his need.

The clearing of the voice behind him left him complaining silently.

"Sorry, mate, got my orders." The man clearly sounded as if he regretted the job he'd been handed. "Would look the other way if I thought the act wouldn't lose me my job. Lord Montgomerie, now that man is a harsh task master."

Collin set her on the ground then waved a hand in the air, "I could pay you to look the other way. You could join..."

The man was shaking his head, his smile wide. The man's warm chuckle coupled with the way he looked at Nick told Collin he wasn't going to get anywhere with this employee of the duke's. "Not a chance. Known the little lady since she was toddling around, getting into trouble. Lord Montgomerie has sent me here on more than one occasion to help when the need arose. Wouldn't change this position for any bribe you might be offering."

"Course you wouldn't. We're going to..." He pointed to a large boulder, "sit over there. Will you give us time to talk? We haven't had much opportunity for that. We're getting wed in a week. Need to talk over our future. Make some plans."

"Seems, at least from what I've heard, you had more than three months to figure everything out." The man seemed to give in as he pointed toward the boulder. "Go on. I'll just make myself comfortable here. You two talk all you like. Nothing more though." He stretched out on a mossy piece of land, his hands behind his head. Chuckling again, "Don't do anything I'll regret."

"What are you up to?" Nickie asked as he tugged her along. She stumbled slightly. Impatiently, he scooped her up striding quickly to the rock as if he couldn't wait.

"We, my sweet Nick, are going to figure out how we will find some alone time besides the few minutes here and there we can steal. I want to make love to my soon-to-be-wife. Don't intend to wait another week for the wedding night."

He placed a chaste kiss on one cheek then the other. Knew if he kept it up, he wouldn't stop until the order from their chaperone blasted through his senses loud and clear.

"If you start kissing me, he'll be stopping you."

She sighed softly as his hands roamed across her breasts. Even through the fabric of her shirt, the crests hardened, tempting him further. His mouth watered with the need to thoroughly taste.

"Not now. I *dinna* fancy an audience to your lovemaking." She pushed at him, her attempts weak and ineffectual. "The man might have his eyes closed, however..." her breath wavered.

"Can that man see what we are about?" he asked as his nimble fingers found their way along her leg then higher to delve more intimately. "I don't believe so. Except for my back, we are hidden from his view. I doubt if he'll rouse himself to come over and look to see what we are doing."

She peeked over his shoulder, "No. Oh, you cannot mean to do this. Do that...Collin. Please...you cannot mean..."

He nibbled her ear then looked to see the chaperone was resting, his hands still behind his head, giving them carte blanche at least for a few minutes to cuddle and talk. The problem was this much of Nick just wasn't enough of her. He wanted to do more than cuddle, needed to taste every delectable spot on her body.

"Assuredly, I can."

"What do you want to talk about? You understand while I've known you for a few months, there is very little I know about you. Don't you think we should...Collin..." His lips brushed delicately across the back of her neck while his hands roamed and sought erotic places where the chaperone would definitely call a halt to if the man discovered.

He wouldn't though. He was snoring.

"I could probably make love to you right now," Collin murmured while he nibbled on her ear, his fingers finding very delicate swollen flesh slick, hot and tempting with her desire.

"You wouldn't dare," she spoke softly, the words tumbling from her lips in a long-drawn-out sigh that told him he was pleasing her. She arched against him, twisted and curled. Her breath lurched as he explored her more methodically.

"Are you challenging me?" he queried while he unfastened the top of her blouse. Her purr of pleasure while he caressed the hardened pinnacles of her breasts gave him reason to grin. Unable to resist he rolled the tips, tasted them before he explored other delicious areas.

"No..."

He turned her so his lips could find her mouth. Her now bared breasts pushed against his chest. "Good. Can you find a time to meet me tomorrow afternoon? Alone?" He travelled his way across her collarbone.

"Don't see how."

She tipped her head back as his questing mouth stopped at the pulse point on her neck. He kissed and bit then returned his attention to her mouth. He kissed her again and again deeper, more intimately probing and tasting.

"You can. Think of me. Just slip away. You'll be in a fitting in the morning. Plead a headache."

She laughed, "No one will believe that ridiculous excuse, least of all mother."

"Tell her you want to see me alone. She might let you go. You said she is on our side." He bent to suck a nipple into his mouth then turned to the other then back again to his first encounter. It seemed he didn't know which one he wanted more.

"Mother is not that much on our side. She wants us to be happy. Needless to say, she pointed out that she agreed with father in the fact we should not be left alone until after the wedding. She doesn't want us to have another wedding night until after the ceremony." Her fingers wound into his hair.

The scrape of her nails on his scalp along with the broken noises in the back of her throat told him she was coming very close to a climax.

Collin knew women's bodies. He understood how to please them. She would find satisfaction today even if he wouldn't. His fingers slid inside her. Her core pulsed against his flesh, squeezed and tugged beckoning to him. The passion rose higher, higher still until she shuddered.

He covered her mouth with his, stifling the cry of ecstasy that would have surely woken the sleeping chaperone. He groaned in the back of his throat. One hand ran along her back, soothing the trembling of her body in the aftermath of the climax. It had been too long since he touched her like this, since he held her so intimately he could feel each exquisite heartbeat.

"You are so passionate," he murmured so close to her lips he felt each whisper of breath, knew when she finally calmed.

Her head was set against his chest. Reluctantly, he fastened her shirt, smoothed her skirt over her legs.

"I want you inside me." She looked at him with passion-dazed eyes, her lips swollen from the caress of his mouth against hers.

"If you can get away tomorrow, I'll take you to the island."

The devil, even if they couldn't misplace the chaperone, they would have an afternoon together. He would take his time returning. He might find the time to kiss her by moonlight. It seemed to be an eternity since they were aboard the Promise, since they were able to share themselves with each other.

He was pleased when her eyes lit with the idea of the island. The girls were never allowed to go without a chaperone. Nothing would be different other than the fact she would have two chaperones. He wanted to understand firsthand the draw of the island. Why she spoke of that isolated piece of land so passionately. He did agree with her father, she should never go there without a man.

"I'll try."

"You've got to do more than try. Your mother will let you go after the fitting. Tell her it's a late afternoon picnic. I'm sure our chaperone will follow, although I've every intention of evading whoever is assigned to us."

He hoped Allura would do that, give Nick a chance for time with him.

"My mother will want to go over the details for the wedding. We've so little time. Everyone is on their way or making plans to attend. Guests will be arriving. Food will need to be prepared. There will be musicians and trades people selling everything imaginable. We will have the morning feast then the one after the wedding as well as the one the night before. I'm sure my Scottish uncles will play the pipes."

"Haven't you done that a thousand times? Gone over all the details? What more could there be to accomplish?" He was laughing yet the smile refused to meet his eyes. "Don't understand any of this. If your Uncle Blade had the foresight to leave Daniel in Lybster, we would be wed now. Their interference is annoying as well as frustrating."

She looked away from him. He sensed she would disagree. Women wanted weddings, the dress as well as everything that went with it. She probably thought about this day since she was a *wee lass*.

"If you must know the truth, I'm pleased Father interfered. Glad I'm having a wedding that includes my family along with my friends. Is that so bad? Would you have been happy with the vows beings said with only Hayes to hear them?" she asked while she traced the crease lines on his forehead, found a path along his jaw then down his neck. She followed the path with her lips and tongue.

"You wanted all this pageantry? The attention? I'm shocked. Never would have guessed that from my Nick. I don't mind. Whatever will make you happy will do the same for me," he told her, having trouble believing her words along with the location of her questing hands.

His shirt was pulled from his trousers, her hands beneath the fine lawn fabric. She explored his chest using her nails to entice and charm. Still, she used her teeth to tempt and beguile.

He gritted his teeth tight. His blood pulsed rampantly while his member became emboldened beneath his trousers. His hands gripped her arms. "Bloody hell, Nick, don't stop."

She was shaking her head, the motion soon turning to a nod, seeming to think only of his question while her nimble fingers drifted lower then lower still. She was straddling him. Through the fabric of his pants, he felt her slick dampness. She seemed immune to the feelings swelling through him as she answered. "Yes and no. Once we decided marriage was what we wanted, I didn't want to be wed with no one in my family to witness the vows."

"That matters to you?"

The question growled in a low moan when her fingers wrapped around the hard steel that wanted to be inside her sultry heat. His hips bucked, seeking her warmth.

"It does matter." She moved her hand along his length, slowly at first then faster until he could hold back no longer.

He would have shouted his release, caught himself as he swallowed the yell behind his teeth. "Nick..." her name on his lips generated an impish smile from her precious face.

She appeared delighted with her actions, immensely pleased with herself.

"Did you like that?"

She beamed at him. His body still ached for her. "Didn't want you to feel ignored."

"Little devil, you know I did."

Quickly, she touched the tip of his rod with her mouth, licked then fastened his trousers. "I did too."

Minutes ticked by before he could form more coherent words. He needed to make certain she understood what he expected to happen tomorrow afternoon. He would set a time. Nonetheless, he would also wait for her in case something delayed her. "Meet me at three tomorrow where the sailboats are moored. If you aren't there, I'll go to the island by myself. I do have a need to discover why it entices you so."

Amused, pleased with this woman he chose to become his wife, he moved silken strands of her hair from her eyes, kissed her cheeks then her nose. Brushed his lips across hers knowing they'd taken as much pleasure today as possible. He hoped this man who was asleep nearby would be assigned to them on the morrow.

"What if I'm delayed?"

She was toying with the dark hair on his chest, running her fingers through it. "You should probably tuck your shirt into your trousers unless you would like me to have the pleasure."

He loved when her smile took over her face.

"Ah, you would like your fingers to linger in certain places teasing me once more. No, while I would love more playtime, I'll do it. As for tomorrow, I'll give you some time as a just in case something happens that keeps you from getting there as expected."

A commotion coming from the front of the castle caught his attention. He assumed it was just the arrival of more people paying money to sleep in a real castle. Nick did say guests would begin arriving. Instead, he caught the sound of pipes. Saw the flash of clan tartan, his clan. He was amazed as well as pleased having not expected to see his family until they were finally free of the restraints Hunter put on them. Had not expected his family to receive an invitation.

"Your mother invited my family?"

Collin felt as amazed as she appeared. It was time to greet his family and men, his brothers...his allies.

"I'm sure my father didn't give his approval. Mother would understand good feelings between us would be beneficial in more ways than one. After all, this marriage is for a lifetime."

She laughed seeming to find his disbelief amusing. "He must have given in with the threat of losing his bed."

"Of what?" Collin asked, a blank look on his face purely confused. "What are you saying?"

She lifted those slim delicate looking shoulders he loved, her pert little breasts swaying endearingly with the movement, "Nothing, it's something my mother told me. I'd just as soon keep it to myself until the information is needed."

"Shouldn't keep things from your husband," he growled beginning to guess what Nick meant.

He didn't like the idea of her keeping him from loving her because of some disagreement. It was unnatural.

She tossed him a saucy smile. "You're not my husband yet. I don't have to explain anything."

With a coquettish wink she pushed off his lap. Without looking back, Nickie started toward the castle. "Should we wake our chaperone?"

"Since I admire this one immensely, do believe waking him would be a good idea." He spoke loudly.

The man moved then sat up, grinning from ear to ear. "Did the two of you find time to talk? By the sounds I heard, you two got sidetracked."

"Don't think he was asleep, do you?" Nick asked as she stared at the man who was a witness to their intimacy but did nothing to stop them.

Collin assured her he could not see anything. Heat flooded her face.

He bent low, "You've nothing to be embarrassed over."

"Easy for you to say. You're a man."

"I like the man even better," Collin chuckled then swatted her on her adorable backside. He supposed, if necessary, he could wait one more week to sample her delectable charms.

He would meet her tomorrow. They would go to the island. If he had any luck, they would manage both sailboats. In the process leave the chaperone behind on dry land searching for a means to follow them. There would be no water transport available. He was sure of that, just as sure as the undeniable fact they would have one dalliance before the nuptials.

Hand in hand they strode down the hill toward the castle. She had to skip from time-to-time to keep up with his longer strides. He was in a hurry to see who arrived assuming his brothers would be among the first of his clan. They would have come as soon as the invitation arrived. Bloody eyes, they were most likely on their way before that happened. All three of them would have taken umbrage with the fact he'd been taken captive, threatened with death. When his first mate arrived in Dornoch minus him, Hayes would have regaled them with all the details. Would have included the threat of the hanging and keelhauling.

They might be here to seek revenge not attend a wedding. He needed to intercept them before his brothers would do something they might come to regret.

His long-legged pace grew faster until Nick could not keep up with him. Sweeping her into his arms he continued as quickly as possible. His heart pounded with the hope that perhaps this decree that had been made about them that they have no time alone would be dropped in the presence of his family. He would have to make sure the clan also understood he was no longer a hostage, just a groom who was denied privacy with his soon-to-be wife.

When he reached the courtyard, he set her down in front of his three brothers. Hunter and Allura were headed outside. He hoped to greet the men of his family before threats that would have difficulty being undone were uttered.

"Introductions are in order," Doughall spoke, his gaze seeming to feast on his intended. Doughall would understand who she was.

Would also understand he was doing something he would not like.

When Allura and Hunter reached them, Collin proceeded to introduce all his brothers, Doughall, Gordon and Keith. "Are you here by invitation to our wedding?"

He'd set Nick down and now held her hand. Slowly he pulled her close, wrapping his arm around her waist, telling everyone who looked, she was his.

"Your first mate apprised us of what was done to you. No invitation was received," Doughall said as his gaze seemed to join and lock with Hunters. "We came to bring you home along with your intended. Say the word and..."

Collin waved his free hand in the air. He smiled broadly hoping to diffuse the tenuous situation between the clans. "Put your anger aside. The threats were meant as intimidation, naught else. At least I have to assume as much. Lord Montgomerie wields a wicked sense of humor along with more power and resources any man should command. These last few days he's used his subtle wit on me in order to provoke me. At least it is what I believe. While I've more reason than the family knows about to seek revenge, I also want peace between the clans. I intend to wed his niece. Anger between us would accomplish nothing."

"In that light, we are here to stay until the wedding," Keith said, his hand resting on his sword. "Care to introduce us to your fiancée? See why you were attracted to the *lass*."

His brother had no idea. So far Nick didn't smile fully on anyone here. When she did...well, his brothers would understand more completely. "This is Nick Gray." Collin didn't bother to look at Hunter for his reaction to the use of his nickname for her. He heard the grunt of disapproval from the man. "She is soon to be the next McInnis, Mrs. McInnis."

Suddenly he realized how proud he was of the announcement of his intended. She was a woman to be reckoned with. Once again, he heard the clearing of Hunter's throat as he took umbrage at the use of his name for his soon-to-be wife. He grinned satisfied now, feeling as if he was slowly gaining equal footing. It was nice to have his clan at his back.

"Nickie," Hunter said with a husky growl. "Call her Nicole or Nickie."

He grinned. Now that his family and crew surrounded him with more to follow, he felt ever more in control. "Unless my future bride objects, I'll call her Nick."

He gazed pointedly at her, silently asking the question.

She shook her head. For a moment she appeared hesitant, as she looked at her father then him. Collective breaths around the courtyard were held. He prayed she would not give in to her father's arrogant wishes in this matter. While the issue was pointless in the scope of their future together, he hoped she would at least for the moment agree with him, would stand beside him in the process gifting him with her loyalty.

He watched the rise and fall of her beautiful breasts as she swallowed air. Her nerves didn't surprise him. It would take getting used to, accepting the wishes of a husband rather than the father she'd known for twenty years. He supposed it was easier to go against a man's wishes when he wasn't present. With this strange situation there were too many factors involved to credit just one.

"I don't object..."

Her words whispered into the tense air surrounding the two clans. She looked at her father, the blue of her eyes deepening to midnight. When she leaned into him, relief swept through Collin. They would do well together. His pet name for her was hardly a reason to come to blows with her father. Nonetheless, the man seemed to want to make the name a priority. As far as he was concerned, Nick suited her perfectly.

He hoped to be sailing back from the island with her at midnight tomorrow or ensconced on the little piece of land he heard so much about. If all went the way he planned, he would sleep with her tomorrow night on the small portion of paradise. One more time, he would defy her father's wishes. He was beginning to have second thoughts about that.

Perhaps he could wait the remaining week.

Maybe he didn't want to.

Hunter growled low, the sound emanating from the back of his throat. Allura placed her hand on her husband's chest. It seemed to Collin she stopped him from making more of Nick's choice. Truthfully, the man should understand by now she would not be under this thumb much longer. He had less than a week.

"Come," Allura beckoned to the men, her smile wide. She seemed pleased his family arrived. "You must be thirsty as well as hungry after the long days of travel. You are welcome here. Hunter can be a bit gruff when it comes to the welfare of his daughter. Don't mind him. Once you have daughters of your own, you will understand."

Doughall chuckled at Allura's comment, his grin broad.

Allura tugged on Hunter until he reluctantly followed her into the main hall. She called out for food and drink to be served to her guests. Servants bustled around the room to do her bidding.

Collin linked Nick's arm in his, resting his hand on top of hers. His pleasure increased as he watched his brothers swagger into the McClellan domain then sit at the tables. They came for him. He never had a doubt in his mind. For his peace of mind, the only question had been when. The ever-loyal Hayes made sure they arrived in a timely manner.

He sat at a table, Nick to his right, Doughall to his left. Hayes along with his other brothers sat across from them. Allura played hostess. The food and drink arrived swiftly. The twenty men who traveled with his brothers surrounded him. It was a nice cocoon of security. Her uncles were not present. Hunter sat at the head of the main hall with Allura. In a matter of minutes, they were served. Lively chatter sprung up around the tables. Toasts to the bride and groom were made from both clans.

"So, you found a beautiful bride. When did this happen?" Gordon downed a long drink of the ale set in front of him while he eyed the surroundings. "It's the first we've heard about this. Thought you wouldn't wed for another ten years or so."

His brother's comment had merit since he never expected to meet a woman so uniquely different from the stereotype. Never expected to fall in love.

Collin wasn't about to regale them with the tale of their inopportune meeting. It wasn't their business any more than it was Hunter's. Nevertheless, he was quite positive Hayes told them some of the story, at least the parts Hayes knew.

"Three months ago. We met unexpectedly." Beneath the table he squeezed Nick's hand hoping to give her confidence. "We were infatuated with each other from first sight. At least I was infatuated with her beguiling smile along with the impish twinkle in her eyes. She's a saucy little piece who fascinates me."

He grinned at Nick who seemed to be listening to everyone except him. If she was distracted, he could deal with that. "Nick? Did you hear me?"

. "What?" Her chin tilted upward to meet his gaze with her own. "No, I," she moistened her lips sending him into exquisite longing.

He looked into sultry blue eyes. "We were infatuated with each other," he repeated for her benefit. "Is that the way you felt about me?"

He hoped for an affirmative answer. Didn't want to deal with anything less since he laid out his heart to his brothers.

Her laughter warmed him through and through, giving him reason to think of more pleasurable activities than sitting in a huge room speaking with his brothers surrounded by McClellan men along with her outrageous uncles. "You might have been. I thought you were insufferably arrogant," she paused for a moment. "A brick wall who was also the handsomest man I'd ever set eyes on."

Doughall roared, his laughter loud. Hayes cleared his throat. Keith slanted him a pointed look that asked more silent questions than he was willing to answer. Heat suffused Collin's face. He'd not expected that answer. The only brother who didn't seem to question how she answered was Gordon. Gordon didn't usually care about his exploits with women.

"So, you found a wench you couldn't take to your bed without answering to her family. At the first meeting is that what you believed?" Doughall said blandly. "Suppose in the next few years that might happen to all of us."

"Guess I did," Collin answered while he watched the woman he was just coming to terms with his emotions concerning her.

He'd fallen in love with Nick, head-over-heels in love with her. When that happened, he couldn't be sure. Now his life turned topsy-turvy.

Her gaze focused on his mouth. Once more she swept her tongue across her lower lip as she tempted and cajoled. What the devil, is she trying to get another rise from him? If she was, her ploy was working quite well as his arousal swelled beneath his trousers. He bent near to whisper close to her ear; sip tender flesh with the tip of his tongue felt the shudder whip through her when his breath teased the tender lobe. Two could dance to the same tune she started. "You're playing with fire. I hope you know what that means."

The smile she flashed him might have sent him to his knees if he wasn't sitting. Just when he believed he had his unruly body under control, she played with him. He found he wanted more of the same.

"I do know. I'm hoping with an escort to your room, we won't have to wait until tomorrow for some time to ourselves."

Beneath the table her hand rested on his thigh, massaged before traveling up then down. She came so close to his expanding rod, he almost stopped her hand to bring her fingers higher.

He was thinking this was no longer a game he wished to play in the hall. The end was too close if she didn't let up. Her father would know what she was about. Bloody hell, even her mother would *ken* it by the expression he couldn't hold back. Still, when and if they did get that escort, he hoped it wouldn't be that obvious how he felt.

Suddenly, Hunter along with Allura stood behind them. He stiffened, understanding he overstepped himself. Even with his clan here, he had little to nothing to say about what the two of them did. It seemed Allura assumed the initiative. They would not spend time together this afternoon.

"We have wedding plans to attend to. Nickie, will you come with me? If we are to have a splendid wedding, we must take advantage of every moment." Allura's request was so soft spoken, so innocent sounding.

Nick's mother understood the game he attempted. Allura's

strategy was impeccable. They still had tomorrow as well as the rest of the day to escape the watchful eyes of their guardians. He watched the gentle sway of her charming backside, her ever-sassy ass, as mother and daughter left the room.

"Wedding plans?" Keith lifted an eyebrow grinning at his older brother. "Not bedding plans?"

With a heavy lift to his shoulders, understanding he lost this one, "I tried. What's a man gotta do to get his way? Seems I've been out foxed...by a woman at that."

"Tell us more about this woman who seems to have stolen your heart," Gordon said, an all-knowing smile crossing his lips. "I'm sure you didn't want to embarrass her earlier. What you tell us now won't go beyond this table."

"I abducted her thinking she was my mistress who I intended to dismiss that night at the Montgomerie ball. After that...well...we ended up here. I'm sure Hayes has told you most of the story."

His mood turned sour. He didn't want to repeat their story even for his brothers. He felt as if the discussion was an invasion of his and Nick's privacy.

"We want to hear the tale from your view point," Doughall said, his eyes twinkling. "A forced marriage is not to my liking. The *lass dinna* sounds willing to me, not after what Hayes overheard coming from your cabin. Seems all the two of you did was fight. Now, along with a death threat, your wedding, a woman we've never heard about."

His eyes lit while he recalled how he smoothed his way into her good graces when her anger erupted. "She wasn't. Now she is. That's all you need to know. There is something amazing between us when her temper erupts."

With the ensuing inquisition, doubts surfaced. He understood all she wanted was a legitimate father for the baby. More than anything he didn't want the *wee bairn* to be the only reason she agreed to wed him. If they didn't wed, there were ways to make the boy his legal heir. If the babe were a girl, it wouldn't matter. The thought of any child of his being labeled a bastard, ate at his soul.

She wasn't being forced. Was she?

~ * ~

"You've only six days after tonight before the two of you will have a lifetime together. I know the last week went slowly for you. Think though, the two of you will have a lifetime together."

Allura reminded her daughter as she led the way to her solar. When the two entered, all the tables and chairs were covered with notes or stacked high with various fabrics. "Is it truly that hard to sleep without him?" Allura's hands were folded in front of her, a soft smile on her face.

The look in her eyes tore at Nickie's heart. Everything her mother said possessed the ring of truth. Even then, she wanted to put forth her assessment. "I don't understand why we have to wait to be together. Yes, falling into bed alone is hard. Makes going to sleep at night without Collin beside me, holding me, dreadful. Got used to his arms around me, feeling his warmth pour into me." Nickie let out a long-drawn-out sigh as if that dramatic affect would change her mother's mind. "Could you sleep well without Father by your side?"

Allura's face paled for a moment. She stiffened her shoulders before she spoke again. It seemed she hardened her heart as well. "A few nights without the man in your bed will make the wedding night better. Now, what kind of flowers would you like in your bouquet? You can pick just about anything because we have many different varieties in the greenhouse. If you want something exotic, we can send a special message to Uncle Logan. He is in residence. Has sent word he will attend the nuptials along with Eveleen. So, you must decide on that today if I'm to make the necessary arrangements. Do you have anything in mind?"

Nickie was angry at all the underhanded ploys by both families, especially hers. She was looking forward to a night with Collin. His most recent plan failed to materialize obviously because Hunter was two steps in front of him. Her father must have known what they were about. At that thought her cheeks flushed with heat. She didn't like the notion her father knew what she did in bed with Collin. Every thought of her father's invaded her privacy.

How could he not understand?

He was a man after all.

She was furious now. When her anger got the better of her temper, she didn't act well. This time it was no different. "I want orchids. The entire church should be covered in orchids."

She crossed her arms over her chest breathing heavily, adamant she have her way as unreasonable as her demand was. Collin always appeased her anger, gave her relief, soothed the inner turmoil with his lovemaking. This time as well as all the other times since she'd been home that sweet appeasement wasn't going to happen for her.

"Orchids? The entire church? Suppose you demand the hall be decorated with orchids too?" Allura questioned, brows slanted upward in speculation along with disdain before she gentled the expression with her words. "Wouldn't you like some other flowers as well? It will be difficult for Logan to grant you your wish. If your anger is with your father as well as me, don't take your pique out on your uncle, at least not this one who has done nothing untoward. He does not have the means to fill the church with orchids although I'm positive he would try for you. Your uncle Logan does adore you."

Feeling sufficiently chastised, she sent a tiny puff of air through her lips. For a moment she turned her head so she wouldn't see the scorn on her mother's face. She was not usually this difficult to get along with. "You've made a valid point. My apologies for my testiness. White orchids for my bouquet along with some tiny red roses if that is not too much to ask for. We have ample roses in the garden for the bouquet as well as to decorate the church. I've seen the miniature ones. What would you suggest for flowers on either side of the altar?"

For quite a few minutes the two discussed flowers as if nothing was unusual. That list was set on the folder marked completed. Their discussion continued. Slowly Nickie's anger changed from a simmer to nearly nonexistent. Unfortunately, during these hours she realized her parent's wishes would be fulfilled. She didn't have the heart to go against them.

"What would you like for the feast in the morning before the wedding?" Allura was taking notes as they spoke.

For her mother's sake, she tried not to let her despondency show.

"I don't actually care. Most likely I won't be there, now will I? Why don't you ask Father to speak with my fiancé? He should have some say in the wedding plans. Perhaps Collin does have a preference. The men will surely take part in the breakfast."

Nickie understood she would have wine in her chamber along with an assortment of finger foods while all the aunts would be there to help her dress. They would all be maids of honor she expected. "I don't have a bridesmaid. Is there anyone you might suggest?"

Allura was shaking her head, while her lips puckered thoughtfully. Something Nickie's mother always did when she didn't have an answer. "No, the only one I could suggest is Lyssa Andrews. She is closest to your age. Would you like that? I believe she arrived in London shortly after you left."

"Will we have time to have a dress made for her?" To Nickie that didn't matter although she was sure Lyssa would care.

"We'll have to see. Ella and Drake are not returning to London. I've no idea how she will travel here without a chaperone."

Allura tapped long slender fingers on her chin, as thoughts seemed to whirl in her head.

"I'm positive Lyssa Andrews can travel that distance by herself with her eyes closed," Nickie said sarcastically. "She's capable and intelligent. Why would she require a chaperone? That's ridiculous. This isn't the wild west where she is from. There is little to no danger on the roads. I'm sure Uncle Drake would supply ample footmen."

"The west where she lives is hardly wild. It might have been more so when Amorica and Damian moved there. Now, however, I'm told it is quite civilized. In any case, her father would never allow something such as that to occur. For that matter, who is chaperoning her right now with Drake and Ella here?"

The puzzled concern on Allura's face gave Nickie a reason to laugh. "I will have to ask."

"Don't believe Ella is cut out to be a reincarnation of The Duchess. Seems she leaves her charges in situations they will all take advantage of. Lyssa, without someone to tell her where she should be, could be quite amusing. I would assume she would spend the day riding.

I doubt if the balls and recitals are to her liking any more than they were to me. She is used to the open range surrounding her. Also, she has spent nights alone in the line shacks where the hired hands stayed when working." Tapping her finger on her chin before continuing, "Without a chaperone."

"I would not want to wear Ella's shoes for the next few years while she supervises all her nieces, fifteen at last count. Looking after one daughter is taxing enough. Needless to say, I'm certain the duke and duchess will improve in the years to come. They certainly cannot do worse than they have with you."

Heat rushed to Nickie's face. "Are you angry? What I did would not have been avoided by stricter supervision," Nickie said even though she knew the truth was different.

She thought of the sunrise she went to see. She asked Collin to accompany her to that lake. Ella had no idea what would happen. For that matter she'd did not expect to fall so easily into his arms as well as his bed.

Nickie simply acted on her feelings.

"You need to ask Ella if it's even possible for Lyssa to attend. If not, I'd like Aidan to do the honors. I'm very close with her. She has always been an intelligent voice in my head. I could confide in Aunty Aidan when I was afraid to speak with you."

Nickie wasn't at all certain that was something she should say to her mother. She told Aunt Aidan things she could not tell Colby either.

Allura's face paled with her words. "I...I..."

Nickie was right about her assessment. Her mother was hurt by what she said. She sipped in a slight breath of air before she continued. "Yes, you were my mother. There are things one has to run by someone who doesn't have absolute authority over them. You must understand. I always got around to telling you. Aunty would always tell me that I needed to speak with my mother. So, I did."

"In that case, there is nothing you haven't told me?" Allura questioned, a blond brow slanted upward.

"Not since I left for London. If you are asking me to divulge the intimacy I had with Collin, you will be disappointed. What happened between us is only for the two of us to know."

Allura laughed then, holding up her hands. "No, a mother should never be told such things. As you well know, I didn't have a mother to confide in, needless to say I did have my sisters along with the cousins. For most of our lives we kept no secrets from each other. We spent so much time on the island. That was our secret until Hunter arrived to snatch that one bit of joy from all of us."

"You kept secrets from father though. That's how Hunter won your hand in marriage. Did you love him before you wed?"

Nickie had never asked that question of her mother. She knew their courtship was fraught with troubles since her mother expected to run the castle by herself. Grandfather McClellan had other plans. He didn't want her left without a husband if anything happened to him. Hunter pursued her relentlessly until he had the answer to the one question Grandfather sought. "Where did the girls go at night?"

Allura cleared her throat while she looked away for a moment. To Nickie it didn't seem she wanted to answer that question. "Moving on, the breakfast feast, I'll plan that since you won't be there. One thing less for you to do. I will also, as you asked, speak with Hunter and Collin. What would you like to eat in your chamber where we will be getting you ready to walk down the aisle?"

Her sweet tooth spoke up for her. "Croissants, the chocolate kind. Cheese along with some of our cook's fresh baked bread. Tea and wine as well." Nickie knew she would need something to calm her nerves, nerves that already raced when she thought about the wedding. She would be giving herself to this man for the rest of her life.

Did she truly want to do that?

She loved him.

Did he love her?

"We will have Logan bring some of his fine Bordeaux from the winery in France along with his Chianti from the one he owns in Italy. Will that suit?"

Allura beamed. She appeared pleased. So much was accomplished in so short a time.

With that taken care of they continued planning the feast for after the wedding. The plans continued in much the same vein. With Nickie telling her she wanted chocolate cake with butter cream icing. If anyone in the McInnis clan played the pipes, she wanted them to play at the celebration.

"All the men in the wedding party will wear their clan tartans, velvet jackets and white shirts with lace down the front."

She'd never seen Collin in a kilt. The thought of how dashing he would appear left her mouth-watering in pleasure. Perhaps her parents were correct. If she didn't spend the next few nights in his arms, the wedding night would be the best ever.

"Aidan will be here in the morning. We received word from Blade as to their arrival. When she shows up, we can speak of a dress for her. I'm sure your aunt will be pleased you chose her."

Nickie's mind wandered to this afternoon then possibilities of the night and tomorrow on the island. She must have given her thoughts away.

Allura was quick to jump in with her opinion on that topic. "Nickie," Allura's hands held hers, "I would like you to promise me something."

Nickie's attention was now riveted on her mother. She swallowed a huge lump of air. She had this horrible feeling as to what her mother meant to ask. Under the circumstances along with the way Collin played her body so sweetly, she didn't think she would be able to give any assurances. She'd never told him no. Never wanted to stop him.

"What?" she asked, wary of the upcoming statement.

"You don't need to look so horrified. It's nothing we didn't expect from you the moment you and Collin were together."

"I *ken* what you're going to say. If you must know, I *dinna* have the ability to refuse the *mon*. He makes me weak in the knees with his smile. If he..."

"Just promise me you will try to tell Collin no when he pursues you. He will do his best to confuse you, to make sure you want him. With his clan in residence all has changed. He will become bolder as well as more brazen in his attempts to have his way. They will be able to waylay all your chaperones. I *ken* the private moments the pair of you have been seeking will undoubtedly be yours."

Nickie stared at her hands folded tightly in her lap, her body humming at the thought of his kisses. "I can't...can't promise something that is so impossible. He knows just how to touch me, to make me want him, desperate for what only he can give. Once he kisses me, I'll never tell him, stop."

"I'm not asking for miracles, Nickie, just a promise to try. I understand how difficult it is to tell a man who is intent on having his way with you, no. Perhaps if the next time you see him, tell him you promised me, promised me, not your father. Maybe he will not try to persuade you to break your vow."

"Don't know how that will help. He's not a man who is used to bending to another man's wishes...or woman's. He won't like the mandate."

Nickie didn't want to ask Collin. Didn't want to deny herself the pleasure of his sensuous lips and delicious caresses or culmination that left her dizzy with ecstasy.

"That's the point, Nickie. He won't be bending to a man's dictates but to a mother's wish for her daughter. My one request before the wedding is not too much to ask of the man who had my daughter all to himself for months. It's only a few days until he has you for a lifetime."

She let out the breath burning in her lungs before she inhaled quickly. Heard the sour note to her mother's words. "I promise to explain to him what you asked. For you, mother, I will try. Trying, I can promise."

~ * ~

Nickie didn't think she'd ever felt so forlorn in her life. When Collin knocked on the door that exited to the tunnel, she was afraid to open the barrier. After she did, he swept her into his arms. His warmth touched every part of her body and soul. Liquid fire swept through her.

"It's just as I hoped. My men have been able to intercept all the guards posted in the tunnel. They are all sleeping soundly. Won't wake up until morning. We don't need to worry about the ones in the hall. We've the night to ourselves."

His lips found hers in a long drugging kiss. He sipped and tasted, explored and tempted until she purred softly in the back of her throat. The tempest he generated left stardust in her eyes.

Unable to help herself, she wound her arms around him, tugging him ever closer needing and wanting more. Despite her best efforts, her mother's face kept intruding. His hands found her backside, squeezing filling his fingers with her. Against him her body squirmed. It seemed she had no control, didn't want to exercise restraint. All Nickie wished for was to keep these seconds going for as long as possible.

For a moment, she gained her battered senses, brought them back to the present with her mother's entreaty. Her promise sat as a lump in her throat she couldn't rid herself of. Nickie pushed on his chest. Always the thought he was solid as a brick wall came to mind. Most every part of him was hard as rocks. He was so big. Until he fought her father and uncles, she never actually realized he would tower over them. His shoulders were broader, his legs thicker.

"Collin..." Nickie managed a tiny amount of distance between them though in her heart she didn't want anything, not even a slim barrier of air separating their bodies. "We cannot. We have to wait for the wedding night."

She felt breathless. Could barely manage those words to pass her lips.

"Whatever for?"

His eyes held a wealth of questions. Ignoring the answer that would be forthcoming, he pulled her close, captured her lips beneath his. His tongue slipped inside as she willingly opened for him.

Once again, she was caught up in his tender assault on her body. Magical heat engulfed her as her mind tossed away the promise she made. Her heart thundered desperately. Her breasts were tender with longing. She wanted this more than ever before, needed him to find release inside her, to fill her as if they were one. Slowly, he moved her toward the bed. The backs of her knees touched gently upon the mattress. Expertly, he tumbled her to the softness, twisting in the air so she came down upon his massive chest. His legs were spread to cradle her. She plummeted on top, feeling the desperate heat of his arousal.

Before he could react, taking him by surprise she pushed off his body. Scrambling away from him, she put as much distance as she could between them. Her breath rasped from her lungs in desperate pants. Perched on her knees, she concentrated her attention on his eyes, a feature of his that always projected his feelings. The focus of her attention, his eyes were dark, shimmering with fire. She didn't think she'd ever seen him angry.

If she didn't miss her guess, he was now, furiously so. He expected her easy compliance. She didn't give that to him. For the first time, she rejected his advances. She forced a deep breath of air into her lungs.

True, they argued many times. She never told him no. Never denied him anything he asked of her until now. Had always melted in his arms. This was different.

He sat, his back resting on a large pillow. His hands were placed behind his head. His long legs stretched out and crossed in front of him. He gave every indication of a relaxed man, one who had no cares in the world.

Except his eyes.

She expected words, anticipated something other than what she saw and heard. He smiled but the gesture didn't reach his eyes. *His eyes*. One dark brow arched upward. He guessed at the reasons. She could tell him. Sooner would be better.

"I'm usually the angry one," she said as she plucked at her skirt unable to look his way for the time being. "You always, well...I don't mean to make you furious. Though I understood you would feel that way."

He nodded while his lips thinned. His silence shredded her nerves, stole every bit of confidence she possessed. The muscle in his jaw ticked menacingly. She heaved a breath of air then another. Didn't know if she had the courage to proceed.

"You're not going to talk to me."

Her words shivered from her lips. He would understand she was terrified.

Perhaps she should explain what was going on at this moment, explain what would be happening the days until the wedding. He did spend a considerable amount of energy to accomplish the daunting task of evading her chaperones. His men helped. She placed her hand on her heart thinking it was going to beat out of her chest.

"I can explain."

"The first noteworthy bit of words I've heard so far." Sarcasm coated each word, seeming to stick in the air. "Why, Nick? This does not make sense to me. Just this afternoon we spoke of this assignation along with the pleasure we would give and receive."

Truly, she had no idea what to say to ease his anger, which seemed to be pulsing in the most disconcerting manner beneath a calm facade. For this night with him, she had wine brought to her room. Cook made tiny sandwiches. Iced lavender cakes sat with the other food. She wished she were as calm as her fiancé. Moving from the bed to the table where the food was set, she poured them both a glass of wine. Handed him one.

He sipped. His gaze bore into her. She heaved a deep breath of air.

"The Bordeaux is from the last few cases of wine Logan sent."

He sipped. His gaze focused on her eyes. No other part of her. "Nice."

"I spent the afternoon with my mother." Her hands were wrapped around each other. Before this she never understood the concept of wringing one's hands. That was what she did. "We...we talked. We planned some of the wedding...I want orchids for the bouquet. Do you like orchids?" The devil she rambled nonsense.

He nodded. The look he slanted her, one brow raised in disdain terrified her. Would he call off the wedding because she refused him tonight? No, the babe would keep him from doing so. He didn't want a bastard. Only a cad and a bounder would do something so dastardly. That sudden thought didn't sit well with her. She never thought of him in that light.

Nonetheless, Collin was a self-proclaimed bounder. He never denied that fact. If not for the baby, she would most likely be his mistress simply by her actions. He would give her gifts. He would take care of her needs despite her refusals. She never understood that lover and mistress were synonymous in the eyes of men. When she requested that he become her lover, she played into his hands.

She ran her tongue across her lips leaving wetness behind, thinking of words, finding not one. After all she told him she would explain. The gaze he shot her way told her he didn't appreciate the obvious flirtation in the face of the rejection she handed him. From his expert teachings, she learned how to flirt, learned what aroused him.

Trying to swallow the apprehension along with the anxiety this situation between them created, "I promised her, m-mother." She pushed down the lump in her throat. Beginning again, "I promised my mother I would not make love with you until the wedding night?"

She tried. It was done. Now she supposed it was up to him to honor her promise.

His grin was lopsided, eyes sparkling with amusement. "Did you tell her you cannot resist my hands, my lips, my...penis deep inside you?"

Shock widened her eyes. He was being deliberately crude. Heat of embarrassment stole to her cheeks. "Of course I didn't say that. I could not...my mother."

Nonetheless, she told her mother she couldn't resist him. Told her she melted in his arms.

"Then you told her you asked me to be your lover. You might have told her that when you get angry having sex is what—"

She threw a pillow at him. He laughed. Threw it back at her. The laughter didn't sound amusing.

He was being purposely obscene. She fought back the small laughter that tried to bubble nervously to her lips. "I would never be so explicit with my mother." Indeed, she would never say something like that expect with Collin.

"Perhaps you should be. Your mother deserves the truth, especially if she expects your promise to withhold sexual delights with your intended. I fail to see how a few days could possibly make a difference. You are increasing with my child." His masculine, arrogant grin widened. "Come here, Nick."

He held out his hands to her. He believed she would do his bidding.

She shook her head. She had to stay as far away from him as he allowed. This time she had no words. Moisture pooled in her eyes. Silence seemed to be preferable to talking. Competing with his expert sensuality was not something she could do. Collin could turn an innocent phrase into something bawdy, subtle implications she didn't understand.

"Are you afraid of your mother? Now, after all we have shared together? Thought you were made of tougher stuff. Thought you could think for yourself. Believed you to be an independent woman."

He tossed that out to make her angry. He knew the truth as did she. They both understood what would happen when she was furious with him. "No, yes, I can usually. This is different."

"Come..." he said again then with a sigh while he patted the mattress beside him, "As long as you didn't promise your father, I'm fine with withholding my attentions until the night of our wedding. Well, not entirely fine. I've gone longer without a woman. I won't charm you so you cannot refuse me. Although we both know I can. I will respect your vow of chastity."

She shook her head again, long strands of her hair fell lose from the pins, the pieces tickling her face. She pushed them away. She drank deeply. The wine was delicious. Of course, it was. The Bordeaux came from Uncle Logan's winery. She poured them both more.

"I didn't promise my father. Would not do so after how he threatened you. Collin? His treatment of you was despicable," she paused wishing this wasn't so hard. "Are you still angry?"

"Not with you, never you but with your parents who seem to think they can take over your life and in the process mine as well." He smiled at her. "Will you let me hold you? There is a place right here for you on the bed next to me." He patted a spot beside him before he fluffed the pillows. "This is not all a waste of time. We can talk about whatever might be on your mind."

"Tomorrow? Do you still want to see me in the afternoon?"

She prayed he wasn't so angry that he would refuse that outing. Years had passed since she was able to go to the island. She wanted to show the sanctuary to him.

"At three?" she questioned not wanting to leave anything to

chance.

"I will wait for you."

"Where the boats are moored."

"*Aye.*"

~ * ~

Hunter paced. He stabbed his hands into his pockets then his hair. Curse words flew from his lips. Frustration and fear had been a part of his life for nearly three months. Still, he was exasperated. His fear for his daughter was eclipsed by the knowledge she was about to make the most serious mistake of her young life. How could he allow her to wed that bounder even though he understood the cad loved her?

His wife sat calmly in the solar with her cousin Ella plying her needle. Collin's family and crew tricked Nickie's guards. He was sure the two of them were together as they spoke. Allura would have his head if he barged into either room to discover the truth. At one time he even believed the rake loved Nickie. Now, he wasn't so certain. Now all Hunter thought Collin wanted was free sex.

He vented his thoughts hoping his wife would give him cart blanch with his wishes even though he understood she would never agree. "I should go into her room. Drag that bounder away from my daughter. Keelhaul him on his ship." Hunter swiveled on a heel to search Allura's face for some expression other than the calm serenity she presented him with.

She looked up. Her smile was purely angelic. "You won't do that as the embarrassment might not endear you to Nickie. Through all this you do not wish to make her despise you. Somehow, you are going to have to come to terms with the fact you are no longer the most important man in her life."

He pointed his thumb at his chest. "I'm the most important man in her life!"

"Keelhauling would be a good way to kill him. Worse than hanging," Allura said politely as she set her project on her lap to study the man, her husband. "His men would be infuriated if you even attempted such a dastardly deed. We are nearly on the eve of her wedding. By venting your anger, you could start a feud."

"The bounder calls her, Nick!"

He hit the door with his fist only to shake the harried fingers to ease the pain he inflicted on himself. It was what he wanted to do to the McInnis. Hit him square in the nose. He wouldn't be so pretty for the wedding. He still sported bruises from the beating he took at the hands of his uncles. By the wedding they would have faded to nonexistent.

"Nick is a man's name." Drake added his opinion thoughtfully. "Let it go, old man. Accept what you cannot change. I for one have had quite enough of the chaos as well as the threats. The fun and games with the man are over. The McInnis will become your son-in-law."

"The name fits her. I do believe you take issue with something of no consequence. Why don't you sit down? Help yourself to a glass of wine or perhaps more. It might ease your disposition. Possibly we could speak rationally about your daughter," Allura pointed out.

"I can speak sensibly about my daughter. It's that bounder I cannot abide."

His fury reverberated around the small chamber. Hunter didn't like how his wife's face paled. Couldn't abide causing her worry or unhappiness. He knew he'd be out one bed tonight if he continued his ravings.

He sensed her presence before her hand lightly touched his back. She smoothed her hand along his muscles. The caress across his back was gentle. "This isn't something you can alter to something more appealing to you. You must come to trust in Nickie's decisions. She loves this bounder you despise with all your heart. Nickie chose to travel with him to lie with him in his bed. She is bearing his child."

"He doesn't deserve Nickie," Hunter grit out as she wrapped her arm around his waist. "I don't want..."

"You do want her wedding to go off without a hitch. However, there are things we have to say to each other before you do something foolish. Despite everything that has happened, do you think you would like any man who was about to steal your daughter away from you?"

"Such as what?" he growled ignoring the last question which was too close to the truth for him to admit.

Still, he accepted the proffered glass of wine. Drank deeply before he set it on the table.

"Barge into Nickie's bedchamber. You would not do that now, would you?" She put the question to him.

"No, doesn't mean I'm not thinking seriously about doing just that."

He sat down then pulled her onto his lap.

Drake put his hand out to Ella, "Believe it's time for the two of us to leave. Our bedchamber awaits."

"Don't do something stupid," Ella said to Hunter as the duke and duchess departed.

Allura touched his chin lightly, moistened her lips leaving a dewy trail of moisture. "Nickie and I spoke of your wishes this afternoon. She made me a solemn promise. Would you like to hear what that is?"

Her eyes widened as he stroked a fingertip down Allura's neck. Delighted in her ever-changing response. Traveled along the top of her gown, dipping slightly into the valley between her charming breasts. He felt an urgent need to taste and suckle.

"Only if it has something to do with her not bedding the bounder."

He continued the exploration with his lips, flirtatious with his tongue, tweaking gently with his teeth over erotically sensitive parts of her.

A soft, seductive purr rose from the back of his wife's throat. "You will have to stop seducing me to discover the promise."

"When we are through here."

"*Nay!*" She pushed away her eyes flashing retribution. "While I do want you to make love to me, I will not be a vessel to appease your anger. It is not well done of you, Hunter Gray, to treat me as such."

He let his hands fall to her waist, holding her, still teasing her with the passion that rose between them so quickly. She was right on every count. He was using her.

"Tell me then we can continue with your seduction."

He grinned. His wife seemed pleased with herself. Her news must be good news or she wouldn't be smiling so sweetly at him.

"Part of it will please you, the other portion not so much."

He growled low in his throat realizing what she had to say was not everything he wanted to hear. Nickie would never make a promise she couldn't keep. "Tell me the measure that will please me."

"When you touch me, kiss me...well, I'm hard pressed to tell you no. You stopped now because of respect, not because I truly would be able to say no to you. We must hope Collin holds the same type of respect for our daughter."

"I *ken* what you say. That's why I adore you. You fall into my hands with very little provocation." He kissed the pulse at the base of her neck. "Your heart is beating hard and fast for me, only me. You want me inside you now."

"I do. Conversely, you are going to listen to me first."

Her fingers sifted through his hair, toyed with a lock that had fallen from its place.

Raked down the back of his neck. She aroused him just as easily as he did her. He smiled. Silence clung to the heated air. "Allura?"

"Nickie promised me she would try not to fall victim to his charms. It is all we can tangibly ask of her. She loves him."

"She would try?" Anger simmered once more beginning to bubble over. "Why doesn't she just tell him no?"

"Have you not been listening to me?"

"I did listen. I just want a different outcome."

"Yes, now, a father most likely doesn't want to hear how his daughter melts in a man's arms. I'm sure my father felt the same way about us. The less he knew about what went on in our bedchamber was what he wished for."

"He wants her to melt?" he ground out. "She melts?" His stomach coiled with retribution.

"Just as I melt in your arms." She laughed softly as she brought his face close so she could kiss him. "What more could you ask for? You don't want her to hate his attentions."

"I can't allow that."

"Hunter, no!"

He started to put her aside, more determined than ever to interrupt whatever was going on in Nickie's bedchamber or Collin's. He couldn't be sure which one they were in, making love. His daughter was melting. His fists tightened.

"Hold on! Stop before you do something you'll regret to your dying day. She will try to tell him no. As you and I both know, there are no guarantees. I have faith in her though. I even have faith in Collin simply because I also believe he loves her as well as respects her wishes. She will do what is necessary to appease me. If he is the man our daughter believes him to be, he will bow down to her wishes. Will not force the issue."

"I can't barge in on them?"

"You can try."

"If I do, then I'll have to sleep on the couch?" Hunter understood his wife's tactics to keep him in line. This would not be the first time he found restless sleep away from his wife.

"You read my mind."

Chapter Eight

Collin stood where the sailboats were moored staring out to sea. The waves were rougher than usual. The wind gusts harder than expected. He changed his thoughts on taking two boats while leaving one here. He was sure he would have visitors on the island if he left the boat. He could take the sails though or perhaps the tiller. He didn't want Nick sailing by herself in this weather.

He chuckled while he lifted the tarp from the boats. His laughter departed when he realized only one boat was moored here. He turned his attention back to the ocean. His gaze raked the swells. This was probably not a good day for anyone to take such a small boat across the seething water.

He spotted her. An instant later the boat vanished in a swell. There it was again. Curses passed his lips while his heart lodged in his throat. When she topped another wave, he saw that she struggled with the lines, the sail useless as she tried to use the tiller to bring the boat around. She was getting nowhere, spinning in circles in the churning sea.

Why the devil didn't she wait for him? What possible reason could she have for setting out alone? For some reason, maybe it was something she spoke of earlier or just a gut feeling, Collin didn't think she knew how to sail. He shielded his eyes with one hand while he wondered why he didn't see the boat when he first looked. Because the swells were too large, fool.

"Bloody eyes!" The boat wobbled and swayed. She stood, waving at him. Again, the small vessel disappeared in a swell before cresting the top of another wave. He sensed more than saw she was in trouble.

No sails were filled with air.

His heart lurched.

Her arms waved in the air.

The splash of water had him scrambling to set his boat in motion. She was in the ocean. Every nerve ending in his body tensed. His muscles flexed. Minutes turned into eternity while he prepared the sailboat to take on this part of the North Sea. The water would be freezing. She would be chilled to the bone. His heart raced, thrummed painfully. In slow motion, the boat slid into the water. Slowly, the sail rose on the mast. The wind blew in the right direction straight and true. He wouldn't have to tack. He set sail to pick up the best wind. The sheet worked as a spinnaker.

The bow rose and fell with the waves. Her boat bobbed in the water without direction. She tried to clamor into the boat. He was certain her skirts dragged her down. Was continually thwarted by the rocking of the vessel. Nature worked against her in this foolish endeavor of hers.

"Hang on!" he shouted. Knew his words would be absorbed by the wind. Still, he shouted again and again. "I'm coming!" he continued to scream.

Silently he pleaded with God. He forced this. Wanted so dreadfully to have her to himself. Should have made sure he obeyed her father's wishes and stayed away from her. She wasn't in his bed last night, simply because her mother asked. They should have put this expedition off until he could be with her in the boat. Until they could utilize the island the way he would wish.

Why the devil didn't she wait for him? He wasn't too late. Had told her he would wait for her in case she lost track of the time. Was sure less than ten minutes separated their arrival at the mooring.

Her hand slipped from the boat. It seemed she didn't have the strength to haul herself over the side. Her head bobbed beneath the water. Dear God, he didn't know if she could swim. Her head was above the water line then below. He didn't know if she went under or vanished because of the cresting waves or if her sodden skirts pulled her down. His breath caught when he sighted her. Once again, she reached for the boat. Once again, she tried to pull herself over the side. Her attempts were futile. Nick didn't have the strength, her arms too thin. He was struck by her fragility. Hadn't seen it before. He should have understood what she might do when he was late. Made a point to be there promptly, yet for some reason she didn't stay at the mooring.

He was almost beside her. Only a few cresting waves separated them. His boat pulled alongside hers. She went under again. Slowly, she disappeared from view. In the seconds it took him to remove his boots, she didn't surface.

The water was icy when he dove. He saw her hair, her skirts billowing out around her, sucking her beneath. This wasn't supposed to happen. She was supposed to be safe with him. In the future, her independent nature would have to be curbed somewhat.

Not all of it.

Just the part that pushed her to be foolish.

Finally, he reached her, tucked his hands beneath her arms. A violent kick propelled them to the surface. Frantic for air he gulped. In his arms, she didn't fight, didn't stir. Cradled by him, she was deathly still. Moisture formed in his eyes while he searched for either boat. His was close. One arm draped across her chest. He swam with her until he could hold on to the side. She was heavy, her soggy clothes attempting to drag her to the depths below. After a couple of tries he was able to shove her into the vessel.

Awkwardly, he followed pushing himself over on his stomach. He landed on the bottom beside her. She was unconscious, unmoving. For too many seconds he felt as if his heart stopped. He had to do something. Had to breathe life into her. He gulped a large mass of air.

Breathe for her.

He'd heard tales of such a thing.

When he looked at her, she was pale. A fingertip on her pulse told him her heart still beat. She wasn't breathing though. Breathe air into her since she couldn't do it for herself. He fit his mouth across hers, blew his air into her. When he felt his life-giving air across his cheek, he closed her nose. After that he tilted her back to straighten her neck hoping the path to her lungs would not be obstructed. Again and again, he did the same. After what seemed an eternity, he watched her breasts move up then down.

Another breath.

More movement.

His body shuddered.

She coughed. Sputtered water while he quickly turned her head to the side. He pulled her up so she sat, her back against his chest. He placed his hands on her belly, thinking that he almost lost the woman he loved along with his unborn child. In the future, he would have to do more to protect her.

Today, however, his prayers were answered. Now he needed to shake her to discover why she did something so foolish. Why didn't she wait for him? What could have possibly driven her to some action that went beyond intelligent?

His Nick was not a stupid woman.

Her eyes opened. She turned her head to look at him. He saw into the clear blue depths that for too many minutes he thought he might never see again. She was shivering. Goosebumps lined every part of her body, he could see that too. He pulled her into his arms to warm her. The devil, he was freezing. They needed to get to the island where there was shelter as well as a fire.

"I thought you left me behind."

Her breath whispered softly from lungs that a few minutes ago ceased to work.

He brushed dripping hair from her face. Trailed his finger down her neck to test the beat of her heart. This was not the moment to chastise her for not thinking clearly. "Never."

Yet he understood that perhaps he should do just that. He wasn't good enough for her. When she met him, his Nick was a virgin with no experience. For the time being, he needed to distance himself from her along with her family. There weren't too many days left before the wedding.

Bloody eyes, her family made him crazy.

He would have to think on this. He had the night. Had a few hours alone with her before dawn. "It's closer to the island. We'll have to go there to get you warmed up. Can you make it that far?"

She nodded while she wrapped her arms around herself, her violent shivering unmistakable. He could not warm her until they had blankets along with heat. A warm bath would help also. "You are cold too." Her teeth rattled as she spoke.

"I didn't almost drown. You realize you were almost food for the fish," he bit out, angry with himself and this ridiculous plan of his making to find a few seconds of privacy when they would have their entire lives together in a matter of days.

They should now be sitting in the warm hall, eating a filling meal, drinking until sated, laughing as well as chatting with their kin. They would be warm. She would sit next to him, despite her father's scowls.

"Neither did I...almost drown." She stiffened her eyes seeming to cross with indignation. "I would have made it back to the surface. Didn't need rescuing," she muttered softly refusing to look his way.

If she did look at him, she would witness first hand his disdain at the absurd notion she would have been able to pull herself from the seething water.

Collin wasn't in the mood to argue over a moot point. As far as he was concerned, Nick could believe what she wanted. He prayed there would be a means to warm her when they reached land. If not, he was making another horrible mistake in sailing the wrong direction. He knew there was a building where many times her mother passed the night with her father. It was a summer retreat. There would have to be blankets for bedding. Wood cut for the fireplace. Pails to heat water for a bath.

Once they reached land, he secured the boat. Collin scooped her into his arms, striding quickly up the path leading to the center of the island. The trail was narrow yet easy to walk. Every so often he had to turn sideways so overhanging branches wouldn't scratch her. While the sky threatened to send down a deluge, the rain was not forthcoming.

"I can walk." She pounded on his chest. "Put me down."

"You're too cold," he muttered not wishing to let her go.

As long as she was in his arms, he knew she was alive as well as safe.

"That's ridiculous." Her scorn reached him loud and clear, her anger growing "There is no earthly reason for you to carry me."

Until they reached a warm room, he wasn't going to let her out of his arms. He had more than one earthly reason to keep her sheltered as well as close to him, as close as he could get her. She would have to live with that. He wasn't going to explain.

She squirmed against his strength.

He had a change of mind.

"Perhaps I want to keep you close. We can warm each other. You're right about one thing. I'm also freezing. The North Sea is not a place to take a swim any time of the year, even summer."

The devil take him, he didn't have a right to think about warming her, holding her naked in his arms. A promise obligated both of them to hold back the raw passion they generated so easily between them. Nonetheless, he understood he might have to do something drastic to overcome the heavy shuddering of her body. Restraining himself would take all his willpower.

At the top of the trail, he found a house that seemed to have taken on additional rooms over the years. Kicking the door in, he stepped inside. Next to a stone fireplace he set her down on a fur rug. This place was everything he hoped for.

"You need to take off those wet clothes. Are there blankets?"

He scanned the room, noting an entrance to a kitchen. They would also appreciate food, as it seemed they were not going to make it back to land for a meal.

She nodded in the direction of another room. Minutes later he returned with several blankets along with two gowns she might be able to wear after he heated water for a bath. Already the salt water itched on his skin.

"You're still dressed."

He busied himself at the fireplace. Within minutes the wood began to crackle as the flames took hold. Warmth slowly emanated from the fire to the interior.

"As are you," she murmured softly. "You are just as cold. We could share the bath."

Not if she was going to keep her promise to her mother. "Go in the other room. Get those clothes off. I'm going to make sure the fire is going strong then I intend to heat water for your bath. It will not be comfortable to spend time with all the saltwater on you."

Even to his ears he sounded harsh. He didn't like the feelings coursing through him. The control he was going to have to have tonight

226

despite the fact there should be no need for it.

For control he had to have distance.

A decision would have to be made soon.

Thankfully, she did as he said. He didn't understand why she was suddenly shy. Until this moment she'd never been embarrassed to be naked in front of him. Horrid thoughts that perhaps it wasn't her mother who wanted a promise from her sped through him. Maybe she agreed because she no longer wanted him.

Damn, he never felt insecure before. Why did this woman make him so vulnerable? His arrogance always rallied within him to protect. He didn't know what to think. Women adored him. Confusion ate at his confidence.

By the time they both bathed and found warm dry clothing to don, his insecurities beat a resounding staccato in his head. His stomach growled, as did Nick's. The distance between them seemed palpable. He couldn't comfort her without taking more than she wished to give.

"I had a lavish picnic basket in my boat. You didn't happen to bring food, did you?" She laughed. "It might be at the bottom of the sea, food for the fish as you enjoy saying."

Her boat most likely still bobbed in the ocean drifting in a southerly direction. Soon the vessel along with the precious food would be fodder for the North Sea. She was right. Eventually what was meant for them would be at the bottom of the ocean.

"Don't suppose we'll starve tonight."

While he didn't like the notion of going without food, he'd done it for longer than this. Perhaps if she packed food, she wasn't averse to his attention. No, Nick wasn't adverse. Her parents opposed their relationship. It was a foolish thought. With that notion at the forefront of his mind, he understood better than ever if she was to keep that promise he would have to leave.

"We could return to the mainland," she sounded disappointed. "Although, we will obviously have this night together."

"Not in the dark, we can't return."

Another night without her in his arms while he watched her sleep would be another night of hell. It wasn't easy to hold her. In the interim do nothing else. Her scent stimulated every sense he possessed. The moisture on her lips generated the urge to taste. Looking at her soft skin with a blush of desire created the compulsion to feel the silken texture. She was this man's fantasy.

He paced the room in an attempt to calm himself. When he felt a small measure of control, he made his way into a tiny kitchen where he found two bottles of Chianti. With two glasses between his fingers, he strode back to the room and the fireplace. At least their thirst would be quenched. He poured.

With the glasses filled, he sat beside her on a divan. After all the self-doubt, he needed to feel reassured. "Do you still want to marry me, *Lass?*"

The question seemed to take her by surprise. Her lashes lowered to rest softly on her cheeks. When she gazed at him again, he saw confusion in the brilliantly blue depths. She shifted. Drank a goodly amount of the wine.

After a few moments she spoke, "Why do you ask? Are you having second thoughts?"

By the tremor in her voice, she might have doubts also. They needed to encourage each other, confirm that the wedding was what they both desired.

Yes, was the desired word. It was what he needed to hear from her lips. The hesitancy in her voice unnerved him more than the questions. He was no longer positive if she could say anything to bolster his floundering insecurities. She carried his child. That didn't mean she wanted to wed him. Her parents would shield her from unwanted taunts as well as rumors if she chose to remain single. If she said no, boy or girl, he would make sure they were legally his.

No bastards.

The question now was if she would agree to something like that. It would give him authority over the child. Could she release her part in the child's life to him? That was another problem. He didn't believe she could do that. Nor, did he wish for that scenario to occur. He was no better off than before his doubts surfaced.

Which was why she agreed to the marriage. He didn't know what he should do.

The answer to his problems came to him a few minutes later. It reaffirmed his earlier supposition. He debated again. Nothing was strengthened in his mind.

He grimaced, far from satisfied.

The wind howled around the eaves. Eerie silence enveloped the gloomy room. Silence between them unraveled his nerves. He lit several lanterns while she sipped the Chianti. With all these events, he struggled further with his decision only because of how this choice of his would affect her. He didn't want her to misconstrue his need for distance.

What he did come to realize was that he could not be part of a forced marriage. As to the child if they chose not to go through with the wedding, they could work out the details at a later date. If it became necessary, he would get hold of his solicitor as soon as possible.

"I'm going outside for a few minutes. Have to make certain the boat is secured so we can return on the morrow."

She nodded, seeming to have nothing to say. Grabbing one of the newly lit lanterns, he stepped outside to make his way to the beach. To walk, he had to lean into the wind. Even then gusts threatened to topple him.

On the beach, he pulled the sailboat farther inland before settling the vessel into a semi-secluded spot. He turned the dinghy over, securing the sails as well as the rigging. He stared to the mainland. Lights twinkled in the castle. He wondered if anyone missed them. His brothers knew where they were. In the morning there would be search parties. He hoped to find the way back before the rescuers reached the island.

A whisper of a sigh left his lips.

Most likely that particular wish was not going to happen simply because he didn't intend to wake Nick at some ungodly hour just to get her home before they were found out, one more damming act to give her father another reason to despise him.

A fat drop of rain hit his forehead. The storm would be upon them soon. This had been an eventful day. The choice he made was a good one. If and when he married Nick, he wanted the marriage to be real in all aspects. He wanted her love.

By the time he reached the rustic cottage, rain sluiced off the cape he donned before leaving. When he reached the door, he slipped from the coat then shook the moisture from it. He stepped inside. She sat by the fire on the fur rug. Her legs were curled beneath her. Golden hair tumbled down her back and around her shoulders.

She smiled at him.

His gut clenched, churned while his breath caught in the back of his throat. She was so damn beautiful. That was the same smile he saw the day he met her. It was the smile that tore at his heart. She was ravishing. To describe her differently would do her an injustice.

He wanted her now.

Was that enough?

Only love would do for Nick. Was what he felt enough? He knew over the next hours he would ask himself that question again and again. He would debate his future actions more than he should. Her father was a thorn in his side. Learning to deal with the man would not be easy if he chose to do so. Her mother had a way of twisting Nick's emotions into what she thought was right, not what was best for Nick.

"Sit, have some wine. I found some cheese that isn't spoiled. The bread is as hard as your brick wall of a stomach." She giggled.

Nick never giggled. Brick wall of a stomach?

"I see you've had some wine." He thought he surely liked her this way. This was a side of her he'd never seen.

She nodded, her eyes wide. She held up the bottle. A sizeable amount was gone. He could take advantage of her condition if he so chose. No, if he did something like that he'd be riddled with guilt. Hell, he never before felt guilt when he seduced a woman. It was a new emotion for him.

She poured her own wine, filled her glass more than once. It wasn't as if he plied her with the alcohol so he could take what she didn't want to give him until the wedding night.

"You should too."

She sipped, the sparkle in her eyes dancing mischievously. She looked at him flirtatiously over the edge of the glass. Her lashes lowered demurely. When she looked at him, dewy drops of wine dabbed her lips.

He gritted his teeth in an attempt to stop himself from tasting the wine drops on her mouth instead of the liquid in his glass.

He settled on the fur rug with a pillow behind him, his back rested against the hearth. "We can continue this here or take our discussion into the bedroom."

Nick giggled again. "You promise not to kiss me," she spoke softly, her eyes gazing at her feet. "If you kiss me, well..."

"Promise."

He felt adamant about his vow even though he understood how easily they could have a night of pleasure. Her mother would not need to know, to hell with her father. If Nick wouldn't be hurt, he'd have every intention to ram what they did here down her father's throat. Only they weren't going to do anything except talk then sleep.

"We should go to the bedroom. The bed is much more comfortable than the floor."

She stumbled slightly when she rose. A few drops of wine bounced from her glass. Her giggle generated a roguish grin. Once they were married as well as miles from the McClellan keep, he would see what could be done about recreating this scene.

"Go on."

He wasn't sure how much wine she drank. Perhaps it didn't take much to render her tipsy.

She twirled, her glass held tightly in one hand. When she walked to him, she rose on her bare toes to kiss him. Her fingertip smoothed its way across his bottom lip. He swallowed hard combatting his swelling rod. He would have to be a saint to resist his little vixen. This was so like her yet different. She was always bold and vivacious. She drank wine with him before. Evidently, not to this extent.

"Hurry." Her voice purred her demand.

Collin thought it best to take his time. Wouldn't Black and Drew, Jeremy too, laugh at this if they saw him now? In his bed, he had a willing woman who tempted him beyond reason. He was about to deny the surging lust, deny his enflamed manhood its satisfaction because of a promise to a mother.

Together, they settled on the bed. Amusingly, he realized most of the first bottle of Chianti was gone, vanished through her lips. He had one glass. He held her glass while she plumped pillows, her adorable backside high in the air enticing him in so many ways.

Once they were settled, he didn't know what topic to broach first. Suddenly, she was on her knees, taking his glass from him. She unfastened his shirt. The backs of her fingers flirted dangerously against bare skin, flicking invitingly across his nipples. His husky groan of pleasure surprised him. He'd not intended to seduce. Had not expected Nick to take the initiative.

"I'm hot. You must be too." Her hands ran across his chest, slowly with tantalizing purpose. "I want you, Collin. Do you want me?"

He closed his eyes against the mad rush of enjoyment her words gave him. Then regretted her vow to her mother to abstain until the wedding night. "Remember your promise."

By the look in her eyes, he felt as if he must have splashed ice water on her. "You have a way of ruining everything."

She turned, distancing herself from him. Leaned against the headboard. Her arms were crossed in front of her, a healthy pout on her saucy lips. One he would like to kiss away.

He didn't dare.

"Don't be angry. I *ken* how much you wanted to keep that promise. I respect you, Nick. Respect the vow you made to your mother."

He tried to soothe her jagged nerves. Saw the rapid beat of her pulse. Blessed hell if she was feeling as he did, no wonder she wanted him.

"I'm not," she huffed. "I did forget. Don't want to remember." After a long pause and a deep whoosh of air, "What's your favorite color?"

"What? What the devil does that matter?"

Perhaps he was foxed too. Did he have a favorite color? He never thought about something insignificant as that. Why would she ask such an innocuous question?

"Nothing. Doesn't matter. Forget I asked."

It seemed she sobered rather quickly. Instead of stopping though, she continued, "I told you my bouquet is going to made from orchids. I'm also going to have tiny miniature roses in it. Red, I do believe red is my favorite color. What about you? Since you won't make love to me, seems we should accomplish something."

"Oh..."

He was beyond understanding what she was trying to say? Did she want him to tell her red was his favorite also? Cautiously, "I like red."

"Good, that is settled. When we're married do you expect me to cook? You should be forewarned I don't know how to do anything in the kitchen except boil water. Cook says I burn that also." Her eyes were wide with what had to be confusion when she turned his way. "How does one burn water?"

"Cook?" He stifled the laughter bubbling up in his throat. In his household she didn't have to lift a finger to do anything if she didn't want to do so. "I've the means to keep an excellent chef at all my residences. I do believe your talent lies elsewhere."

He was tempted to show her exactly where said talents were.

"Where would that be?" Her eyes widened in question. Her tongue swept across her bottom lip. Left a path of wetness behind.

He could do naught but stifle a groan. His effort didn't pay off.

Was she twisting for an answer such as 'the bedroom' or would she be offended if he told her that her talents lie in pleasing him? Nick did please him, immensely so. At the moment without knowledge of it, she seduced him. Her tiny pink tongue seemed to be the root of everything tempting. Perhaps she did know what the sight of her tongue moving across lush pink lips did to him.

"Don't believe I'm brave enough to answer that," he mumbled wondering what ludicrous question would come next.

He was ready to douse the lanterns then attempt to sleep. Lying next to her tonight, he understood there would be no sleep forthcoming, at least not for him.

"Not brave? Hmm...don't see you that way, no, not at all. Well...when you swim do you swim naked? I do. It's the most luscious feeling to have water wash across bare skin, nothing but skin along with the titillating sluice of water. We could make love in the water. Would you like that? What would you feel like with only a slim breath of water between us? Do you think that would be delicious?"

Titillating?

Delicious?

The sip of wine he had in his mouth spilled out, drops sputtering everywhere. While he would love to swim naked with her, make love in the water with her as well, he truly didn't see where this line of questioning was coming from. Ah, but it had to be the wine. She was still tipsy. He should get her foxed more often. She was actually quite delightful that way. It was a side of her he enjoyed very much. It seemed before this they always fell into each other's arms before too much wine could be imbibed. This was worth remembering for another time.

Perhaps on their wedding night, tiny bit tipsy would do the job. After all, he wanted her to remember what they did. He had ideas to seduce. Ways to arouse to a fever-pitch.

"Nick, look at me." He touched her chin with the tip of his finger turning her so she had no alternative except to do his bidding.

When she did, her eyes were large pools of desire. Her smile changed to a frown. Suddenly, she was no longer tipsy. "I'm not going to like this. Am I?"

His heart caught in his throat. That was good. If she were too foxed, she wouldn't remember what he was going to tell her. "No," he sighed, "Probably not."

"You don't want to get married." The tremor in her voice shook him to the core. "It's the promise, isn't it? Because you had to promise not to touch me, you no longer want me."

His sigh of frustration left a shiver deep in his bones. She misconstrued everything. "I do want to marry you, more than you can imagine. You remember that. Nick, I have to leave. Have to get away from your father before I do something I'll regret. First, I'll make certain you are safe at home tomorrow."

"You're leaving me."

"Until the wedding, yes."

~ * ~

When Nickie woke in the morning, it was to a small breakfast of hot cereal and warm bread smeared with honey. Her mother hovered around her, humming while she seemed to fuss with everything. She rearranged the pillow then did so again. She dusted countertops that didn't need attention. The glasses from last night were washed. Allura put them away. She put water on to heat. Nickie didn't want a bath. She wanted to see Collin. She tried to remember what he told her last night before they slept. For that matter why was she here and not on the island?

From the window in the bedroom, beams of sunlight bathed the floor. Early rising birds chirped their unique melodies. A squirrel sat on the edge of the windowsill chattering at her. The storm outside was quietly passing on to the east.

The tempest inside Nickie grew.

Where was Collin? She didn't want to ask her mother. Why did she think he was no longer at the castle? Had he told her something? Her head pounded. More than anything she needed to recollect what he told her.

There was much about yesterday she remembered, more she wanted to forget. Other parts seemed hazy. She recalled the near drowning. A shudder ripped through her. Remembered Collin's strong arms carrying her to the small house. He rescued her. She wouldn't admit she needed his strength. It seemed every muscle in her body ached.

They had wine, some crusty bread and old cheese.

They talked.

He liked red.

That was it. Collin was leaving.

Suddenly, her head cleared, the muddled sawdust there vanishing. "No!"

She sat up. Her mother turned quickly at her word. It couldn't be. He decided not to marry her. He told her he couldn't stay here with her father. Had he been serious? She fell back with a groan, her head suddenly pounding harder than before.

What about her?

"What is it?" Her mother sat on the bed beside her. Allura placed her hand on her forehead. "No fever."

"My promise. He didn't like to be denied. Collin doesn't want to marry me. Father drove him off. I agreed to try to keep the vow." Frantic she pushed back the tears with the backs of her hand. "Where is he? I can stop him if I hurry. I'll tell him I love him."

"He's gone." Allura's voice was gentle but did nothing to soothe Nickie's frayed nerves. "Collin will be back though. When he left me here to take care of you, he told me everything. He needs to be away where he won't be tempted to make you break your promise. He's a good man, Nickie. He respects you."

"No, he doesn't want me. I remember now. He told me he was leaving." Her hands at her temples, she moaned softly. "I should have let him make love to me. Wanted him to do so. Instead, I tossed that promise in his face. I tried to seduce him."

Her mother's hands were on her shoulders holding her still. Allura gave her a tiny shake. "Look at me!"

Nickie didn't want to look. She wanted to bury herself in her covers and cry. Tears welled in her eyes, some of shame along with some of a lost love. It was a love she would never know again. "Mother," the one word was a thin wail of despair.

"Collin will be here the day before the wedding, perhaps even the afternoon before. Actually, he said he would be in the main hall at noon in case you asked. You've nothing to worry over. We will finish our plans. I think your man couldn't be near you without making love to you. That's a good sign. Don't you think?"

A good sign, Nickie didn't think so. It was an excuse. One he could use to escape a marriage he didn't want. He told her as much. She didn't like all the doubts bombarding her yet, they were there bold and offensive.

"Do you know where he is?" She sat straighter hoping her backbone would stiffen so she could get through this.

"I believe he went to his ship. Your man didn't tell me much though. All he wanted before he walked up the gangplank was to make certain you understood he meant to marry you in five days now."

Insecurities blossomed. Collin was the first and only man she knew intimately. For over three months, he'd been her rock. He made her laugh, with her ridiculous assumptions. Generated anger she had little control over when he risked his life. He soothed the rage with his sexual prowess. She didn't think she could live without him.

"Are you positive he will return?"

Trying to take her mind off her fears, she sipped the hot tea. The warmth sliding down her throat washed some of her tears away.

"Most certain. Don't believe the man would lie about something so important as a wedding. If he didn't mean to return, he would have told you. He's not the type of man who would simply run away."

Allura busied herself around the room. The bath was steaming hot. A clean dress was draped over a nearby chair along with petticoats and matching shoes. She tried for an air of calm. Failed miserably. Her fingers trembled so hard she could not unfasten the dress she wore through the night. It had been a protection of sort.

"Did he tell you what he wanted for the breakfast before the wedding?" Nickie asked as she slipped into the water.

The heat was delicious. She was glad her mother filled the tub for her even though when she first saw her heating the water, she didn't want a bath. That was before she realized how sore her muscles were. Nickie soaked until the water grew tepid, allowing the ache of her muscles to absorb the heat. She felt relaxed. More so than when she woke this morning.

"We didn't have time to speak of that," Allura said as she walked from the room, slowly closing the door behind her. "Think about what he likes for breakfast. You must have some idea."

It didn't seem they ever ate breakfast. It was usually the noon hour before they rose. No, there was a lot she didn't have time to speak with Collin about. Thoughts of her near drowning bothered her immensely. She always thought of herself a good swimmer. In the water yesterday, she floundered helplessly. Panic must have set in to render her so powerless. For several moments, she closed her eyes. If not for Collin's swift thinking, she would not be here now.

She owed Collin her life.

If he chose not to wed her after all, so be it. Though he would not claim the child. If he tried to do so, he would have to take her also. She didn't think she could live with that, not after the prospect of marriage. If Nickie could, she would reverse time. With the knowledge she now possessed, her decisions might have taken on a different angle.

Once she told him no regrets. So what if she had qualms now.

After she was bathed and dressed, she walked into the main room feeling better with her decisions. Weathering this storm would be most important. Nonetheless, she could not help the depression filling her from the inside out. Looking up, she gave a silent prayer that he would return.

She loved him more than her life.

~ * ~

One day slowly turned into the next. Uncle Logan arrived with the orchids for her bouquet. She stared at the lovely flowers while she wondered if she would get to carry them down the aisle. The church was gradually being decorated. Flowers adorned most every inch of the sanctuary.

Aunt Aidan and Uncle Blade arrived first. Aidan's dress was crafted from an intricately worked blue velvet with silver threads running throughout then trimmed in dark blue Belgium lace. All the other aunts wore blue gowns not quite so fine as Aunt Aidan's. If Blade was not already desperately in love with Aidan, one sight of her would cause him to fall at her feet.

Nickie met with her mother every afternoon to pour over her lists until every folder was marked complete. One afternoon after they finished, she stepped inside the room that had been assigned to Collin. The space was empty. The valise he took from the Promise was gone. Nothing that was her fiancé's remained. Her heart gave a tiny lurch. It seemed he didn't mean to return after all. No, she inhaled a deep breath of air, all it meant was that he needed his possessions wherever he was.

She spent too much time reminding herself that he told her he would return the day before the wedding. He would be there for all the festivities. She wanted him now. Needed the reassurance of watching him stride through the hall. Even if they couldn't make love, she needed his strong arms around her. Wanted her brick wall.

Her nerves were so rattled she jumped when Christel placed a hand on her shoulder, Eveleen behind her. Allura's sisters, they were here to give confidence where there was none. Their love stories had not been easy. Why should hers be?

In the beginning all seemed so carefree and wonderful. Collin was a wonderful lover. Nothing would happen to change that. At least that was what she told herself.

"He will be here," Eveleen whispered while it seemed she tried to give hope. "He promised. His brothers tell me he is a man of his word."

No, Collin never promised. Never gave his word. Nonetheless, he said the words. Was that the same as a promise given? She didn't know.

"Shall we go downstairs to eat? You have only one more day to get through before he returns. The time will pass by so quickly," Christel told her. "Collin will arrive back here tomorrow at noon. You will see."

Eveleen led the way to the main hall. Aidan and Christel flanked her as arm and arm they descended. They chatted about nonsensical things. When the threesome entered, Doughall and Blade were engaged in what seemed to be a dance competition. Everyone shouted and yelled while the music from the pipes grew louder and livelier. Their feet did the same. Sweat poured from both men as neither one wanted to cry defeat.

Aidan pointed to Doughall then Gordon along with Keith. "See, his brothers would not be here if Collin did not intend to return. Surely, they would know his intentions and would have left."

Keith and Ryder, Christel's husband, took up the challenge when the other men faltered. The two sat down with no winner declared. Mugs of Guinness were served. Challenges brokered.

"It could be a ruse to throw me off, to make me believe there might not be hope." Nickie didn't seem to be able to rid herself of her pique. She'd been wallowing in it for days now. Why should she change?

"Now, why would they do something like that? They would never do something so dastardly," Eveleen asked, her hands on her hips.

Logan appeared behind her, circling his arms around his wife's waist as he tugged her close.

"They would not," Logan agreed with Eveleen while he nipped a trail of kisses down her neck.

The man she wanted to see was Hayes. He was nowhere to be found. If Collin's first mate was in the room, that would tell her the Promise was moored somewhere close. He was not.

Without warning, her father was beside her. He placed her hand in his before tugging her toward a large table where her mother sat. "Come, we will have some food and wine together. Enjoy the night. You have this one as well as the next left to be a free woman. You should celebrate this too."

With the tug of her hand, he let her go. She bristled while she stood her ground. She didn't trust her father. Still, she blamed him for being the sole reason Collin left. "Don't want to dine with you. Why should I after what you've done as well as threatened? At least Uncle Drake has the decency to keep his distance. He's even eased back on his feelings for Collin. Told me yesterday he was a fine man."

Visibly her father bristled. "I'm sorry now for what I put the two you through. Nickie, it is but one more night before you see him again. He kept the promise you made to your mother. You do comprehend I had no part of that."

"No part of that, yes. Though you applauded it. Didn't you? Made his life miserable before he left." Stiff backed, she walked in front of him toward the table, fighting the rising moisture in her eyes, willing the tears to disappear. She didn't cry. She would do what her aunt's suggested and put some faith in Collin. It had to be enough.

For the days he'd been gone, she ate next to nothing. Her stomach continued to churn with nervous emotion. It wasn't the baby. She was long past morning sickness. Indeed, felt very little discomfort. It was nervous fear that caused her distress coupled with sleepless nights worrying about what was to come. She desperately wished they'd been able to wed earlier.

Weddings were supposed to be joyous celebrations of two lives coming together. Hers, except for tonight, seemed more like a funeral was taking place. She sat down between her mother and Aidan, refusing to look at or acknowledge her father.

She would give Collin until noon tomorrow to show his face. If he wasn't in the hall by luncheon, she would go after him. He'd set sail when he left. If the Promise was moored at the dock, she would find him on board. If not, she would ride to Dornoch. He would either reject her or marry her there. All the preparations for the wedding would be for naught. Nickie no longer cared.

The wine Uncle Logan brought was a new vintage from his winery in Bordeaux. Logan was experimenting with a different type of grape. Uncle Logan was like that. When he was home, he spent hours in his greenhouse experimenting with his orchids along with other varieties of flowers. He liked to see what new variations and colors he could create.

The wine was delicious as was the food. She searched the room for Colby. If any of her family would travel with her, she could convince Colby to go with her with little incentive. He would go simply to keep her safe. Her brother would see just how determined she was to discover the truth about her fiancé. She was bone-weary of waiting. It was time she took this into her hands. The moment was hers.

She downed the glass of wine. Found her brother dancing with one of the girls from the nearby village. His lips next to ear whispering sweet nothings, she supposed. She tapped him on the shoulder.

Colby stared at her before one brow arched upward. Possessively, he wrapped an arm around the girl's waist drawing her close. "I'm not going to like this. Am I?"

"Wouldn't know," she told him stiffly while she tried to calm the racing of her heart. "You can still have your dalliance tonight. Bed whoever pleases you. Tomorrow though..."

"Tomorrow is fine. Whatever you need, Nickie."

He laughed, scooped her into his arms before twirling her around the hall. The pair joined in the lively dance until she was breathless. What Nickie knew was that she'd much rather dance with the supposed bridegroom instead of her brother.

"Let's get something to drink."

Nickie pulled him off the dance floor to the table where she'd been sitting. Each with a glass of wine, she led him to the balcony. Fresh summer breezes, the scent of flowers on the wind, she sipped the air. "I'm sorry to interrupt you. Are you angry?"

"No, she'll wait for me."

"Good, that's good."

"What do you want, Nick?"

He laughed at his use of Collin's pet name for her then her ensuing expression afterward.

The lines in her forehead creased together. Her lips thinned. She poked him in the chest. "That was not well done of you, big brother. I don't need reminding of his absence. He's the only one who can call me Nick."

"What you need to do is stop being such an ass and enjoy your last days of freedom. If it was me getting married in two days, I'd be doing everything I wouldn't be able to do after the marriage."

With his unthinking words, all the blood drained from her face. Her stomach churned as her thoughts plummeted to the women he kept as mistresses. "Is that what he's doing? What he won't be able to do after we wed?"

She could barely breathe. Thoughts of him in bed with another woman blindsided her, left her gasping and her heart pounding so hard she was sure the beast would jump from her chest.

Colby seemed to notice her distress. His face changed color. "I'm sorry. Didn't mean to put thoughts such as that in your head. I know you're nervous about the possibility of his not showing up tomorrow. It's a well-known fact he had a multitude of mistresses before he met you."

"If he's seeing other women, I'll kill him," she gritted her teeth as anger built inside. Her hands fisted while her heart cried. "I won't stand for it. Won't marry him if that's the case. I'll side with my father and Uncle Drake. They can hang him from the yardarm of his ship."

"Where your man is concerned, you're a vindictive little thing. No, I'm sure he's just staying away from father. Yes, I'm sure that is what is happening," Colby tried to placate her as he attempted to add a soothing touch to his voice.

Truth of the matter, Nickie didn't think her brother knew any more than the rest of the people waiting for him.

Colby's ploy wasn't working.

"You're coming with me tomorrow. If he is not in this room, this castle, by noon, I'm going to see if his ship is moored at the dock. If the

Promise is not where it's supposed to be, we are going to Dornoch to bring him back for the wedding."

"That's not a good idea, Nickie. It will take more than a day to ride to Dornoch. We will have to sleep. If he didn't go anywhere, it will be you who is missing at the wedding ceremony not your fiancé." He sounded testy. "It simply won't do to leave. What if he shows up later? You'll be gone. Collin will believe you deserted him."

Letting Colby convince her to stay and wait wasn't going to work. "You will do this for me. You will go with me. I cannot venture the roads to Collin's home alone."

Nickie didn't like what her brother implied. What if he was simply delayed and she left before he could appear. She didn't think she would sleep tonight. Didn't want to in any case. She was too furious with Collin to do so along with the position he placed her in by his absence. She paced the small balcony where the two of them stood.

"Father will not allow you to ride all the way to Dornoch without an escort. The highlands are too dangerous for a woman alone or escorted by one man."

Colby's voice was hushed. It appeared he was hoping for a way out.

"Too bad," she grit out as she whirled to confront her brother. "He has no say in what I do. Hunter should understand that by now."

She refused the man who was second by second unraveling her life. As far as she was concerned, he was no longer her father.

Colby winced. Uncle Blade stood beside him. "I will go with you, Nickie. Two guards will be better than just one. As Colby believes, I'm also sure this is premature. Collin will do as he told you. He will be here tomorrow if not at noon, in time for the wedding feast."

"He said by noon. I'm holding him to that. The man cannot think to disappear as well as get away with the act."

She sank down on the nearest chair, her face in her hands. Silent sobs of despair wracked her body.

"Drink some air," her brother said a wry smile on his handsome face. "You need to get more color into your face. Everything will be fine."

"Would you like more wine," Blade asked from behind.

Her uncles seemed to rally around her. Tried to ease some of her nerves. If only they'd done that sooner instead of ganging up on them.

She did. She wanted to be tipsy tonight. Wanted to giggle again as she had that last night she was with Collin. What would it take...she drank deeply? Giggles didn't materialize. If anything, the wine depressed her more. She wanted the anger to surface. Anger she could deal with. Could direct toward Collin.

"I'll walk you to your room," Colby said, his eyes telling her once more he was sorry for his callous words that he couldn't retrieve. "I'm sure he misses you."

The night lasted what seemed like an eternity. Every creak and groan had her sitting up hoping it was Collin sneaking into her bedroom. If he did, she would give herself to him again. She no longer cared about the promise given to her mother. Nothing and no one save Collin mattered. As far as she was concerned, she tried, did her best. That had to be good enough. By the time morning finally came, she was exhausted with worry. Her nerves snapped with every dreadful thought that crossed her too agile mind. Despite her attempts not to see Collin in the arms of another woman, the images kept seeping into her mind.

Sabrina laughed at her. Her voice pounded in her head. "You thought he wouldn't grow tired of you. You were such an innocent to fall for that man. I'm surprised he stayed with you as long as he did. It was just the baby who kept him bound to you."

No, she never thought that. At first, she took precautions with her heart for just that sort of happenstance. She told him she would never marry him. She tried to hold to that notion. She loved the bounder. Her feelings were for naught since he didn't return the love.

"You weren't a good enough lover to keep a man such as Collin in your bed. You were an innocent little virgin." Sabrina continued to taunt her. "Why would he want you when he could have me? That's why he left you, to come back to me."

Most the night she tossed and turned. Hit her pillow too many times to count. Found her legs wrapped into knots with the sheets. Sleep wasn't to be. Once, in the middle of the night, she rose from the bed to pour more wine. That got her perhaps thirty minutes more of sleep.

When she looked at herself in the mirror the next morning, her eyes sported dark circles. She looked a mess. Well, today was the day. The day before the wedding. The day of reckoning. Now, if he did show up, she looked dreadful. At the sight of her, he would undoubtedly turn around then flee in the opposite direction.

By the time she walked down the stairs to the main hall, she'd had a long bath, had spent time with cold compresses on her eyes. She didn't look as dreadful as she did when the day began. Holding her breath, she searched the hall. Found every empty nook and cranny. It was just as she feared.

Collin wasn't in the hall. He wasn't anywhere to be seen. His brothers were. She wasn't marrying his brothers. Her hands fisted, she walked up to the oldest of the three. With her finger, she pushed on his chest. Doughall's broad smile grew. He was almost as charming as his older brother.

"What would you like, *lass*?" Doughall flashed even white teeth while he waited for the answer.

"I want you to tell me where your brother is hiding. He was supposed to be here in this hall at noon today. So far, he is two minutes late."

Anger bubbled, simmered explosively as she sucked a gulp of air.

"If the McInnis told you he would be here then he will be," Doughall said, his eyes twinkling merrily as if he knew some truth she didn't. He waved one broad hand in the air. "Two minutes is nothing. Give him a bit more time in case something happened to delay him. My brother has never been overly prompt. Tardiness is more in his nature."

"He did. He is not here." She wanted to take nothing more from these loutish brutes who were most likely taking after the oldest brother's footsteps. Thoughts of women who might delay him sent her anger seething higher. "Where is he? If you know…"

Doughall threw up his hands as if exasperated with the entire ordeal. "If I knew, I would tell you, *lass*. The fact of the matter is that he told no one except Hayes where he would be spending the days before the wedding. I'm sure Hayes is on board the Promise. He will tell you if he knows. However, as far as we know, the Promise is out to sea. So, there is that."

She turned her anger to the other brothers who both held up their hands in supplication while they laughed seemingly amused. "He left. Didn't bother to tell us where he meant to go. As Doughall told you Hayes went with him to keep him from doing something foolish. Perhaps the ship is now moored at the dock. If that is the truth of the matter, Collin would be on his way here. Sometimes the tides don't cooperate with time. He will be here."

"Something foolish? Something stupid like bedding one of his mistresses. I'll kill the man."

Her fury vented she had nothing more to say. She turned on a heel stomping from the room, Colby behind her.

She was determined to find the man. Colby reached out to touch her shoulder then turn her to face him.

"We will go to the docks before you do anything rash such as leave for Dornoch. Agreed?"

She sipped the air she needed before she nodded. "Agreed."

Blade along with James fell in line behind her. She would have three escorts.

~ * ~

Collin wasn't pleased that Hayes did not make it to the island soon enough for him to dress then sail to the mainland in time to meet Nick. He told her noon. It was now an hour past that time. If he knew his Nick, she would be furious. He grinned. She was even more ravishing in her fury. He could never get enough of her adorable temper.

Ah, but he could not soothe that blazing irritation the way he would like until after the wedding. The days away from her were hellish. Five days away from a woman never bothered him before. With Nick one day was twenty-four hours too long. He missed her ravishing smile along with the sweet curves of her adorable backside. As far as he was concerned this wedding couldn't come fast enough. His body ached for her. Thinking about her brought his manly parts to attention hard and swollen with need. The more he thought the harder they became until he was sure they were solid as steel.

Hayes made sure his valise was with him. He dressed in his best today, hoping to impress the lady he loved. Collin prayed Nick missed him as much as he did her. Thought of the wedding on the morrow then the wedding night filled him with delight. He thought of a means to make her angry. Grinned again. She was too easy to manipulate. He would capitalize on her overwhelming temper. She would turn to liquid heat in his arms.

Forced to adjust the fit of his trousers, he swore softly.

The trip to the mainland took more time than he wished. The currents were strong. Hayes needed to tack every few minutes or find himself blown off course. Collin couldn't help but shake his head at the thought the girls sailed these waters by themselves. Even without the wind, the currents were treacherous. By the time they reached land, the time was well past the appointed hour of his appearance.

Collin jumped from the boat before Hayes brought it onto the beach. Quickly, he strode around the refurbished castle to the front gates. When he stepped through the courtyard, merchants were already lined up around the exterior selling their wares. Entertainers sang and danced with open cases for coins. A carriage pulled into the main yard to be greeted by one of the castle's employees.

Striding into the main hall he was shocked to feel a condemning silence. Before he could find Nick, her father stood beside him. "Where have you been?" His voice was gruff, accusation ripe.

Collin felt the confrontational tone of Hunter. This was the reason he stayed away for days. He didn't want to strangle the man with his bare hands. Allura suddenly stood beside them becoming a buffer in a tense situation.

"Let him explain, Hunter. I'm sure Collin has a good reason for his tardiness. We both know if our daughter was not so impulsive, she would be here now waiting for him. Unfortunately, she assumed something I doubt is true."

"Nick is not here?" Collin felt a rush of fear to his gut. His hands fisted as the need to hit something overpowered common sense. His anger directed at Hunter. "Where is she?"

"Looking for you," came the sneering reply from the other man who had a way of stretching all his nerves to the snapping point.

"Drake, so pleasant to see you. Will someone kindly tell me where my fiancée is?" Collin's fists tightened further.

"Hunter," Allura spoke softly, "Collin deserves an answer."

"You said you would be here at noon." Hunter said his voice filled with unspoken yet subtle accusations.

Collin didn't understand yet what he did wrong except his tardiness. "Actually, I told her I would be here before the wedding feast. She wanted me here at noon. Told her I would try. Complications with the ocean currents along with strong winds made it impossible for me to arrive on time."

Collin was trying his best to be polite. Hunter was his future father-in-law.

"You're a sailor with a large vessel at your disposal. What complications could arise?" her father asked as if he didn't believe what he said.

"I was on the island waiting out the time. Didn't want to be confined to the small area inside my cabin."

No, sleeping in the cabin alone brought images he could never dismiss from his mind. For one night he attempted that feat. Thinking of Nick, he would wake in a hard sweat, his body aching for release only Nick could give him.

"Needed to roam the land, did you?" Logan asked.

As he frowned, he stared at Eveleen who's face paled.

Collin heard the story of her rape on the island. Heard how Logan rescued her. How the violence terrified her when Logan thought nothing of killing the men who attacked her. Because of that day, for the longest time she was too afraid of men to accept her husband's overtures.

"True, the tides and the currents were not in Hayes' favor while he maneuvered the small sailboat to pick me up. Nor did the return trip go well. Now..." He searched the large room once more. "You said Nick was looking for me. Where is she?"

Hunter's grimace every time he used his pet name for her did not go unnoticed. Inside he grinned with each of the man's scowls. It didn't seem Hunter wanted to tell him. Seemed to hold something back.

Finally, "At the moment, we don't know exactly. All I know is that with Colby along with James and Blade they were going to try your ship. After that, if you weren't in residence or on your way to the castle, they meant to ride to Dornoch."

"Why?" She didn't trust him, didn't trust his word. His mind raced with anger then fear for her. "You let her go! What kind of father are you? You should have done something."

He paced. His hands clenched then unclenched. He jammed his fingers into the pockets of his trousers then his hair.

"I'm sure you can catch up to her if you leave now," Ryder spoke softly as he seemed to think about the trials he endured in order to hold onto Christel. "Would you like company? I'm tired of sitting with not much to do."

Collin swiveled on his heel as he stared at the man. "Company would be accepted gratefully. At least I know where she is headed."

"It's late," Allura now stood beside them. "You will have to sleep at one of the inns along the route. Don't wish to have the two of you riding these roads at night."

His anger burst forth again. "Do not worry about me. I'll keep my promise," his words were sharp.

He hoped they stung even though he liked Nick's mother. In this instance, she deserved his ire. He knew part of Nick's insecurities were because they were not allowed to be together before the wedding.

Briefly, she looked at the floor then met his gaze. "Perhaps I deserved that."

Collin could not let it go. "You did. Not as much as your husband. I'm not going to dwell on that fact."

Chapter Nine

Collin and Ryder rode in silence. Collin didn't feel as if anything needed to be said between them. They both wanted to see Colby and Nick in the distance. Didn't truly care if he saw James though he had to be thankful the man guarded her so well. At least this time the protection she needed wasn't from the duke. He prayed for the reassurance she would not meet with anyone who might do her harm. What he didn't understand was why her father let her go on this wild, impulsive quest to find him?

Hunter must have guessed he was on the ship. Must have thought Nick would find him there. In that case, she would be safe in her home. He was shaking his head in disbelief. The man, who put new definitions of possessiveness to test, allowed his daughter go on a fool's mission. He should have reined her in. How to do that? In the future he would have to do better than her father.

Two hours passed. There was no sign of anyone in front of them. Bloody, bloody hell, she had almost three hours head start on him. They would have to rest. The three men traveling with her must certainly realize someone would follow. He hoped the men would use some of that aristocratic ingenuity they were known for to slow her down.

They stopped at two inns to change horses as well as check to see if Nick along with her entourage stopped for the night. At the third inn they picked up a sack of food and were told the party they were looking for did the same two hours before.

"We've only picked up one hour," Ryder grumbled clearly as displeased as he was. "Why the devil are her companions allowing her to ride so quickly? They should be doing everything possible to slow her down."

"Couldn't Colby or Blade figure out a way to stop Nickie's mad dash to find you?" Ryder asked clearly baffled.

Collin tightened his fist on the reins then spurred the horse forward. He debated what to do when he finally caught her. Truthfully, what he wanted was to drag her to the first church he found. He would wed her, bed her in the process forget about the wedding day tomorrow. They should have been wed by now, none of this necessary. All her insecurities would no longer plague her.

"You can't do that and you know it," Ryder told him with a soft chuckle following the words.

"What? You a mind reader now?"

Collin was curious about the man who was known for chasing sunrises. In his youth, he traveled all over the world, seeking new lands. Rumor was he was so fast with his hands and feet, no one saw the lethal weapons coming until it was too late. He supposed he was glad Ryder wasn't one of the men who tried to beat sense into him.

"Hardly. In your shoes, it's what I would be thinking too. This wedding stuff is overrated, just a great deal of commotion in order for a marriage to take place. In my mind, simple is better," Ryder laughed again. "Glad I'm not in your shoes."

"Wish I wasn't either. Just want to find her safe so I can hold her again."

"So, what are you going to do when she's staring you in the face? Her powder blue eyes soft and beguiling?" Ryder asked with a chuckle as he pulled up beside him.

Collin snorted as he thought of any number of things he would like to do. Perhaps he should make a list. "Shake some sense into her. Convince her she has to stop thinking she's a man. Possibly talk to her backside with venom." Collin could never do such a thing. He might hurt her. "Make love to her until she can't get out of bed."

Ryder tossed his head back to laugh. "Her brother will make them stop soon. Won't let her risk herself riding in the dark. The sun is just now beginning to go down. If he tries his hand too often or too soon, she will be on to his ploy."

"One can only pray."

"Colby might be a more practical source of reason where Nickie is concerned. He feels partially responsible for her flight. Seems they had a conversation the night before that gave her enough unease she didn't sleep well."

"What could the young pup say that would affect her so soundly? The conversation gave her grave concern about your intentions?"

Collin mused having understood for several months now the only woman he ever wanted to sleep with was his Nick. "She didn't sleep well last night? Because she was afraid I wouldn't marry her? Hell, I fought her uncles so I would have to marry her."

Collin felt shocked by the words. He didn't think he'd put doubt in her mind. He thought he made sure she understood he would be there for her before the wedding. Was certain she knew it was because of her father he had to remove himself from the confines of the castle walls.

Well, hell.

Ryder lifted his shoulders in an attempt to convey his thoughts. "Something like that. Seems Christel found her this morning, her eyes so red from crying along with dark circles underneath, she asked a few pertinent questions."

"Why?"

"Appears her brother said something that upset her." Ryder was staring at him as if he wondered about him. It seemed all the uncles doubted his attentions.

"What was that?"

"Colby told her if he left his fiancée in a similar situation, he would be doing what he was going to miss the rest of his life, sleeping with any willing woman he could find. He apologized for the words almost as soon as they were out of his mouth. Didn't do much for Nickie's disposition. Believe she started thinking about the other women in your life."

"What did she think I would do?"

"Need you ask?" One eyebrow quirked upward in conjecture.

"The devil, she didn't sincerely believe I would seek out another woman?" He was astounded, incredulous after all they shared, "She was jealous."

That made him grin. Where the emotion concerned Nick, he liked the idea she was jealous. He never felt that way about another woman.

"Believe she said she'd kill you." Ryder hooted.

He beamed. "She did, did she?"

He wanted to tackle that particular notion with a good deep kiss.

Ryder nodded as he caught the smile on his lips. "Also told Christel about a woman named Sabrina. The lady wasn't one of your mistresses, was she?"

A lopsided smile formed on Collin's lips. "Yes, she was the reason we met."

Fondly, he thought back on that first meeting, the dance then the sunrise after. Beyond a doubt he thought himself the luckiest man on earth to find such a passionate caring woman. One who wasn't afraid to tell him what she thought along with how she felt. His Nick was so damn sweet.

By the time the two men reached the fourth inn on their quest for Nickie, a slipper of a moon shone in the sky barely lighting the road they travelled. Collin prayed they would find Nick and her companions here. He didn't much like the idea that her uncles and brother would allow her to continue on in the dark.

Even so, they were at least a half-day ride from McClellan land and the castle. She would be exhausted, late to the wedding as well. Perhaps he should have had more resolve where it came to Hunter Gray. If...if, he had so many ifs' traveling through his exhausted brain, he couldn't think straight.

Relief flooded him when Collin discovered Nick stopped here. Blade lingered in the main room, seeming to be waiting for them. He rose when they entered. Extended a hand in greeting.

"What took you so long?" Were the first words out of his mouth. "Thought you would have caught up to us sooner."

"You had nearly a three-hour head start. The ocean tides were not suitable for a quick sail from the island to the mainland."

Collin didn't want to argue with anyone. He just wanted to find his soon to be wife to let her know he didn't abandon her.

"So you say."

"Of course I say. What room is she in?"

Collin started for the stairs hoping he wouldn't have to stop and wait for her bodyguards to tell him. Colby was nowhere to be seen. Blade seemed to have vanished into the woodwork. He supposed they all had rooms.

Stealing into her room then waking Nick with a solid kiss was in his mind. He wanted to hold her. The devil he wanted to do more than hold. Didn't know if he could restrain himself.

James stood in front of the stairs to the second floor, his feet braced apart. "You're not sleeping with Nickie tonight. Get the frivolous notion out of your head. You might as well retire to your room. No one here will allow you into hers. I made the promise to her father before we left."

"So you say."

Collin was ready for a fight. It might as well be with Nick's uncles. He knew he could best them one at a time. It was when they joined forces to better him that he faltered. Hell, the way he felt at this moment, he could most likely take them on two at a time.

The man smirked. "If you want to make it to your wedding before the preacher leaves, we'll have to get up before dawn. He pulled out his pocket watch. That gives you about five hours to sleep."

Realizing everything the self-appointed bodyguard was telling him was prudent and liking the facts were two entirely different notions. Collin didn't need five hours of sleep. What he needed was Nick in his arms. Intending to ignore the warnings, he strode to the desk to inquire as to her room. There he was met with stony silence. The clerk had the audacity to look down his long nose. His gaze never left the pages of the register.

"Paid him off." Her uncle stood beside him, his smirk turning into a leer. "You could try opening every door in order to find her. That wouldn't be wise though."

Collin was tempted to knock the smirk off his smug face. "The devil take you. Can't say I won't be pleased to be out of your life for good. Dornoch is a long way from London."

Collin was now counting the minutes to that time. If Nick were acceptable, they would leave the day after the wedding. It wouldn't be soon enough.

"Not so far as you might think. I'm sure on special occasions Nickie will wish to see her uncles then there are her cousins she will want to visit. Family gatherings she will want to attend, especially when her family from America has come across the ocean for just such an occasion. Since the brood is so large there will be many events you won't be able to shy away from. Indubitably, we will see each other quite often."

Collin could do little but groan. He stomped to the second floor. Walked down the rows of doors swearing softly. He didn't expect anyone to hear him. Didn't expect to see Nick. Her uncle was right, it wouldn't be well done of him to disturb her or anyone else.

Ryder strode behind him. "Don't do it. You'll most likely regret the deed."

Collin spun on his heel. "What? You're reading my mind again? Don't see why I shouldn't." Purposefully, he spoke loudly, his voice carrying down the long hallway.

Ryder watched, a smirk not too unlike the dukes on his face. "You truly mean to wake the entire building just to see her. You'll have that chance in the morning. Have patience."

"I do. Don't you think it would do the other uncles good to see her father's plans quashed? Not placing you in the same category, at least not yet. I've a mind to yell at the top of my lungs for her to come out to see me, her intended. Yell that I'm here for her. I want her to understand that fact sooner than later."

He put his hands on both sides of his mouth expecting to do that very thing.

A door swung open. "Collin!"

Nick rushed into his arms, nearly knocking him over with the impact. Without further thought, his mouth slanted across hers. The tension he felt since early afternoon vanished. His body thrummed with the delight he always found within her tiny female arms. His tongue pressed against her softness willing her to open for him.

He pulled away, her lips dewy from the moisture he left there. "Bloody eyes, Nick, what were you thinking leaving the castle, taking to the road? Did you have so little confidence in my word? I told you I would be there for you."

She lowered her lashes before she looked at him again. "I was thinking." Her tongue swept across her lips. "Come." She drew him into her room, the door slamming shut behind them. "This is not for anyone else to hear or see."

He heard Ryder's laughter booming through the door. "Sleep well, my friend. It will be an early rising tomorrow if you don't want to miss your wedding." There was silence for a second or two, "Don't forget your promise to your mother, Nickie."

"That was horrible for my uncle to remind me. I haven't forgotten the vow." She rested her head against his chest. "Have you?" The question held a wealth of hope. "I don't want to remember a single word."

How the devil could he forget a promise such as that one? A vow that created this very circumstance they found themselves in. Caused the tension radiating from his body. If he hadn't found the agreement impossible to keep, he would have never left the castle. He would have been on schedule to meet Nick in the hall at noon. He wouldn't have been up against unruly seas in a tiny sailboat just to make it back on time.

Unwisely, between the agreement and her father, he didn't have the fortitude not to stay where he was so tempted to give in to his wishes in the interim do as he pleased.

"I've not forgotten a promise that has sent our lives into shambles. While I can understand the intention behind it, I no longer agree to the vow. I'm letting both of us off the hook. There are no more pledges that will keep us apart unless that is what we want," Nick said, nearly breathless as his hands roamed over her, touching and exploring sensitive territory.

"What is it you want, Nick? I will honor your wishes."

No matter how difficult. His gaze drifted to the bed. The sheets along with the quilt were rumpled. She'd been asleep, or trying to get there. Her hair was tussled delightfully.

"I want you, Collin, only you." Her hands wound around his neck pulling her closer to him. Suddenly, she stopped. "Did you sleep with other women?"

"No, the only woman I want in my arms is you. Do you believe me? Colby was..."

"Yes."

Relieved she didn't intend to send him out the door, the heat of his lips brushed across hers again then again. His heart sped with the inferno generated. Slowly, he backed her toward the bed. When they reached the mattress, he picked her up before settling her there.

On top, he braced his arms on either side of her head. The devil, second even third thoughts assailed him, raced through his head with lightning speed. He spent five days away from her to protect the deal she made with her mother. Now, the two of them would toss that sacred promise a side for one night of pleasure when they could look forward to a lifetime. Deep in the back of his throat, he groaned.

Gently, he rubbed his thumbs on her cheeks. Her soft breasts rose and fell enticingly against his chest. He nibbled across her lips, wishing he wasn't about to say the words that would stop the lovemaking for the night. The dejection at his decision left him in a quandary. He didn't want to let her down.

"Are you sure this is what you want?"

Her powder blue eyes opened. The smile she gifted him with was hesitant. A moment ago, she'd been so sure of herself that she leapt into his arms. Now, he saw doubt in her eyes. Tender emotions rushed through him. He could have the physical release, except at what cost to the woman he loved. She would never deny him if he seduced.

"No, though I don't want you to sleep in another bed. We should reconsider. I'd like to be able to look at your mother and know I kept my word." Slowly, she traced the line of his jaw. Her touch was mercuric.

He didn't want that either. What he didn't know was if he could sleep next to her and refrain from loving her. He drank in a thick breath of air. He would have to be able to do just that or he would have to leave. Leaving her at this moment was impossible. Resting his head on her forehead, he closed his eyes searching for the words she wouldn't take offense at hearing.

Her hands ran across his shoulders before fiddling with the fastenings on his shirt. "Can we sleep in the same bed? Still honor the bargain made in good faith? Do you think that is conceivable?"

"It would be so very easy to lie." He chortled thinking this all could be so different. "We could have been lying for the past five days, you know, sharing a bed, making love. My men had everything well in hand."

"It wasn't as if I didn't think along those lines more than once," she spoke softly. "I'm not used to lying to my parents."

He sighed heavily before rolling off her to the other side of the bed, his arm across his eyes "I can't look your mother in the face and tell her I didn't sleep with her daughter if I did." That was the truth. While he wouldn't have any reluctance about lying to Hunter, her mother was a different story. He didn't have one doubt that every single male relative of Nick's would take one look at his face and know they slept together. For the last five days, even he could see the tole this was taking on him.

It was beyond the pale to think different.

"You sincerely want to wait?" She was on her back, her gown for the night pulled tightly across small pert breasts where he'd like nothing more than to bury his face. He wanted to suck and nibble until he heard her evocative purr of delight.

"No, however, for the last five days we've had the patience of saints. Don't you think? For pleasure found in one night of passion, do you want to undo five horrible nights in hell?"

He wondered if he lied to himself. His body was hard, desperate in its need.

"I ask again, can you sleep in this bed with me and not make love?"

The alternative was to leave her now so he could find his bed in another room. The alternative was not one at all. Honest with himself, he understood that at least tonight he would not sleep no matter whose bed he found himself lying in.

"I'll sleep in my trousers," he told her while he wanted to rip her nightdress from her slender shoulders then submerge himself inside her magical warmth. It was not to be. Not tonight. He could wait.

"We can put pillows between us," she beamed at him the smile mischievous as if she knew the truth. "A good idea, no?"

"No, if I wanted you, pillows would do nothing to keep me away, as you well know." He found himself shaking his head in disbelief.

"Pillows?" He thought amusement would help ease the pain in his groin, which seemed to grow with expanding speed.

"You can hold me. I promise I won't touch you anywhere you don't want me to." It seemed she was laughing at him.

"You're teasing me, right? If you touch me anywhere, I'll either have you beneath me or I'll explode."

"Explode?" She ran her fingertip along his jaw. "Like this?"

"Nick." He grabbed her hand, placing it on his chest. "I'm serious."

"This is decided then." She sounded disappointed. With her eyes closed, she ran her finger along his lips. "Very well." She lay on her back now. "You should..."

"Get undressed?"

"All but your trousers," she murmured sounding a bit disheartened.

With partial undressing accomplished, Collin settled next to her. He pulled her into his arms. She was soft, curves in all the best places. Tomorrow night she would be his again. His hand settled tenderly on her belly.

"How is my heir?" he asked with a soft chuckle.

As far as he knew, so far, she didn't have one day of morning sickness. Her cheeks were aglow with color. Pregnancy seemed to agree with her. They had about six months to wait. Less if she conceived during one of their first encounters.

"She is doing just fine. I'm doing fine also if you are asking." She sounded petulant. "Actually, I could be doing much better."

In hindsight, he should have asked about her first. Ah, well, he would learn. "Are you overly tired?"

"No, just been overly peeved at you. Mother told me the second trimester might be harder in some ways than the first. I hope not." She ran a hand along his chest, across his nipples. "Do you want this child?"

"What kind of question is that?"

"The kind a woman who is not yet wed to the baby's father needs to know." Her lips followed the path of her hands.

He shuddered realizing this would be more difficult than he

previously thought and he understood sleeping beside her would be arduous, a challenge he wasn't at all certain he was up to. He held her hand, keeping her exploration from drifting lower.

"Go to sleep, Nick," he murmured while he understood all too well sleep for him would be difficult at best. "We've an early rising tomorrow. Tomorrow night will be ours to discover new secrets."

He must have dozed. When he opened his eyes, one leg was sprawled across her. The fabric of her nightdress pooled above her waist. His hand was between her legs. He groaned then rolled away from her.

Tonight.

Booted footsteps stopped at his door. Quickly, he rose from the bed then traveled the distance before a knock could wake Nick.

In front of the open door, Ryder's hand was held high. "It's time to go." He peered around Collin to gaze into the room. He would most likely notice she was still dressed in her nightwear. "You did know we were leaving early?"

"Nick and I will be behind the rest of you by about two hours. Want her to get some more sleep."

Actually, he wanted her to sleep then eat a good breakfast before they rode home. Yesterday was taxing for her, as it also was for him. The tension had been unbearable until he finally saw her, held her.

Ryder smirked, "The two of you held to your agreement with Allura, I see." He wasn't looking at Nick but at him.

"You can tell."

"Been there myself. You've the look of a man who is in need of some gentle handling."

Ryder left to join the others whistling a bawdy tune. Before he reached the end of the hall, "I'll tell the others about your condition."

Well, hell, just what he needed was the uncles as well as Hunter lording it over him. Their smirks would lead to a fight. The devil, he needed to hit something. When he reached the castle, Montgomerie or her father would be the best targets. They would tease, shout out a few taunts. Still, this was what the man wanted for his daughter. Collin smiled then fully aware he proved the man wrong about his character. While a few months ago he was a notorious rake.

No longer.

Now he was in love. Never thought love would happen for him. Sincerely believed when he needed to finish with his escapades, he would wed some woman totally wrong for him just so he could breed his heir.

Gently, he closed the door. He leaned against the hard wood for several seconds while he gazed lovingly at his soon-to-be wife. Collin dressed then left to order breakfast to be delivered in two hours. The morning would still be early when they left this inn behind.

Back in the room, he slipped out of his shirt and boots before he pulled her into his arms again. She was so small, fragile too. Her passionate loving nature was what intrigued him from the start. When he kissed her, she turned to mush, while she gifted him with the enchanting passion that was hers.

Collin knew the moment she woke. As always, she traced the line of the hair on his chest to his waistband, usually further. When she met the barrier, she sat up, eyes wide, pushed hair from her eyes.

He chuckled softly, her expression so very endearing. "What were you planning?"

He beamed knowing full well that if he had not been dressed, her fingers would now be wrapped around his most manly parts, parts that were swollen, needing her tender administrations.

When she pressed herself over him, her hair fluttered across his chest. "Wouldn't be wise of me to tell you."

"Oh?"

Now, he was curious.

"I'll be doing it tomorrow morning. Wouldn't you rather be surprised?"

"Surprises are always nice."

It was then she seemed to realize beams of sunlight filled the room. "Weren't we supposed to leave before dawn?"

"Yes."

"Bounder! Why didn't you wake me?" She started to get up.

He pulled her down for a long drugging kiss. She didn't resist his advances. Her body yielded sweetly. "Ah, you still turn to liquid sunshine when I kiss you."

"I usually melt at your feet. Quite willing to give you whatever you ask for." She hit him on the chest. "Now, why did you let me sleep?"

He gave the requisite grunt. "We will be two hours behind them. Told your uncles to let your mother be apprised of the time. So for now, we have breakfast waiting. It will arrive," he pulled out his pocket watch, "in five minutes. I'll wait outside so you can dress for the ride home."

After he kissed her on the nose, he sauntered from the room. The door closed behind him. His eyes shut for a moment. He would be a married man in a few hours.

Damn, he liked the sound of that.

~ * ~

When the door shut, Nick brushed the hair from her face then twirled it around to make a bun on the top of her head. It wouldn't stay. She would have to add a few pins. Last night, well, all of yesterday for sure, seemed to be a muddled mess in her brain. She'd acted impulsively. Ruined the night before the wedding feast for both of them. Collin should have been angry with her. He didn't seem to be irritated, just amused.

When she discovered he was not in the hall, her temper ruled her. Nickie let out a long slow breath of air. In the future, she would have to try to curb that temper of hers. The fury could get her into a wealth of trouble. Now, she still felt a bit of annoyance at the arrogant man. Despite the mad dash across Scotland, he didn't tell her where he had been for the five horrible days. They were most likely the worst days of her short life. No, that night when she thought her father and uncles meant to hang Collin. That was the single worst day of her life. There was no comparison.

When she didn't find the ship moored at the dock, she was sure he sailed for Dornoch. Certain he left her to find a new mistress. In hindsight she should have stayed on McClellan land. Foolish pride set her on a ride that was for naught as well as delayed some of the festivities planned.

While she was pleased he rode after her, she was irritated that it came to this. There was no one to blame except herself. She should be waking up on her wedding day, expecting her aunts to greet her. A scented bath would be hers, steaming and waiting. They would all pamper her.

She supposed she would miss all the pre-wedding chats because of her willfulness. No, it wasn't just perverseness, it was the fact she failed to trust Collin. With that thought foremost in her mind, she didn't like herself. For a moment, disappointment fluttered in her chest. He had a lot to explain, a lot to make up for as did she. She gasped as she realized time slipped away. Breakfast would be delivered. She would still be dressed in her nightclothes.

Quickly, she bolted from her bed then rummaged through the clothing on the floor. In her haste she didn't pack anything. Of course not, there had been no logical or rational decision making on her part. She'd not thought past the first night. Had she actually considered they would see him? Haul him back? No, what she assumed was that she would find herself riding to Dornoch.

Just fastening the buttons on her shirt, a soft knock sounded on the door. "Are you ready?"

"Is it breakfast?" she queried as her stomach rumbled hungrily.

She placed her hands on her belly. "Easy their little lady, mama's going to put some food inside you."

Her laughter brought Collin's head up when he stepped inside the room, the food carried behind him by a lady she recognized from last night. Despite the fact she wanted to rake him over the coals for putting her through this pregnancy, she grinned at him.

"Breakfast then we're off. Should take us less time on the return trip. Won't be stopping at every inn to see if you are there. I figure four hours if you're up to it. We can stop to change horses once."

The woman set the tray on a table. "If there's anything else, let me know."

The pause was significant before she turned and left.

Nickie waited for Collin to say something. Instead of speaking, he strode to her. When he reached her, he wrapped his arms around her. His kiss was gentle, tender. She wanted more. He chuckled, backing away from her as if he knew what she was feeling.

"There will be time for more of that later tonight. I plan on making up for missed hours with you. For now, let's get you and our baby fed then we can be on our way. Need to arrive in time for the wedding."

Her face heated. He must have heard her talking to the baby. She didn't know if that was normal or not. "You heard me."

"Endearing is what it is. I'd also enjoy talking to my heir. Can start teaching the *bairn* all he needs to know. Want to feel him kick inside you."

"Don't you dare teach him those things! Not until he's a man..."

Collin beamed. "So, the child is a boy."

"Of course she isn't. It was just a warning for the future." She sipped the tea he poured then smothered the hot bread with butter along with the preserves that were brought on the tray. Nickie didn't truly care if the child was male or female. She didn't think Collin did either. It just seemed to be a conversation they would share until the child was born.

When she was satisfied, she set her fork down. She needed some answers. "Where were you?" The question was pointed and direct.

Frown lines formed across his forehead. "I was not with another woman or a past mistress if that's what you're beatin' around a bush about. I would have hoped you trusted me a bit more. Seems..." He stabbed his hands through his hair before rocking back on the chair. "Won't have mistresses while I've a wife. Don't want one. You're more than enough woman for the likes of me."

The jealousy she felt when that first notion occurred to her vanished. Nickie wasn't sure what he meant by more than enough woman for him. She guessed it had something to do with her temper. "I trust you, Collin. It was just at that moment, when Colby said what he'd be doing if he were about to find himself tied to a wife, well, I was terrified."

Did she trust him? Was she just saying the words to appease him?

"So, you still need guarantees. Not surprised after your father and Montgomerie gave you every reason to suspect me of ulterior motives. You've changed as well as challenged me in so many ways." He was sitting back in his chair, arms crossed in front of his chest. "Don't know how many times I'm going to have to tell you..."

"I." She caught the corner of her bottom lip between her teeth. "I do trust you."

She just wished he would tell her he loved her. That would be nice. If she knew he loved her, she wouldn't be having nearly the problems she was having now.

"Good, I'm pleased that is settled."

He pushed back from his chair, the look on his face unreadable, "We should go. Don't want to be late for our wedding, now, do we?"

She didn't move. Didn't intend to budge until he answered her question. Her eyes narrowed, "Where were you?"

"If you trust me, you don't need to ask."

"Bloody hell, Collin! This question has nothing to do with trust. If you don't have anything to hide, you'll tell me." Her temper rose. He was avoiding her on purpose. "This is not funny."

"Seems the question does speak of trust. As with you, I see nothing amusing here." He let out a long slow breath of air. "Very well, if you insist. I decided to stay on the island. Now, to tell you even more. I couldn't stand to be confined in a cabin where we spent three months together, nearly all of it on the bed where I was sleeping. You understand why I couldn't return to the castle. The island was the only location I could think of where I wouldn't spend every waking as well as every sleeping minute dreaming of you without recalling how you feel beneath me. That's not exactly true. Nonetheless it was easier."

She beamed. Knew she grinned from ear to ear. His words weren't a confession of love, however, they did tell her he'd been thinking of her just as she'd been dreaming of him.

"Shall we go then?" She stood extending her hand, smiling pleasantly while she thought about all he revealed. "You do understand I want to know more about what you did."

On the ride home, it wasn't her questions that amounted to most of the discussion between them. The queries were his.

It seemed he was curious too when he asked the next question. "So, tell me, where you went first and why you decided to head after me. I did give you my word. Thank God, you didn't go by yourself."

She agreed with Collin about that. He deserved to know all that transpired on the road yesterday. She was quite lucky three men accompanied her. Her welfare might have been in jeopardy if she'd gone off alone. She knew better. Had been raised in this part of Scotland. While it wasn't as dangerous as the highlands there were still thieves who roamed.

"I was too furious to wait at the castle any longer. Colby agreed to go with me then it seemed James along with Blade decided I needed them also."

"Wise men," he said softly. "Perhaps I should have asked Ryder to stay. He could have ridden with us."

She heard him but just barely. Explaining herself had not been something she expected. Didn't know why though. He deserved to understand what drove her to this point. She'd had every intention of riding to his home. When he wasn't at the dock, she'd been devastated. Clearly, she recalled the moisture seeping into her eyes, clogging the back of her throat. At the time she couldn't speak. Devastation combined with despair sent her momentarily to her knees. Colby helped her stand. Spoke a few encouraging words. She couldn't tell Collin any of this.

"Didn't think you'd ever say anything like that about my uncles." For a moment she almost laughed at his look of chagrin. It was apparent by his scowl he didn't think through his spontaneous praise of the man.

"Where you are concerned, all your uncles have your best interest at heart. I do take my hat off to the men as well as thank them for their consideration. I would not have been pleased if anything untoward happened to you."

She quirked a half-smile trying once more not to laugh, "Believe he does know me well. We went to the dock where the Promise should have been. Thought for sure your ship would be moored there. It wasn't."

She turned to him puzzled, tilted her head sideways as if thinking, "Where was the Promise?"

"Where do you think?"

She bristled at his cryptic reply. "This isn't a guessing game, Collin McInnis. Just tell me." He sparked her anger once again. She gnashed her teeth in an attempt to remain calm. It wasn't working too well when he turned his attention to her with a huge grin. His smirk sent more heat coursing through her.

He rode beside her for a while before answering. The silence left her nerves stretched to the snapping point.

"This isn't about me, Nick. The questions should be about your trip to the inn we just left. If you must know, I was moored off the island. Hayes made sure one of the sailboats from the mainland was at the island for the trip I would take for the festivities before we wed. Actually, I planned on returning that night to the island. Again, I didn't want to stay so close to you and not be able to touch you."

"You did?"

She felt her eyes widen at the disclosure. Felt her heart speed with each breath she possessed.

"Yes, couldn't spend..." He drew in a deep breath of air, reaching toward her then bringing his hand back to his side. "Fortunately, we did endure this last night together quite well if I do say so myself."

"We did?" She was mired in her thoughts. "I certainly didn't."

"What happened when you saw the Promise wasn't in its slip?" His question held a hard edge to it.

"What do you think?" She tossed the question back to him. With a soft sigh, "I was furious. Was positive Colby was right. You were off with some woman. You're not known for keeping your lovers for long. Three months, according to the rumors Colby heard, was probably three times the norm."

"It was." He smirked. "You're different. Never asked any of my lovers to wed me either."

"Thought you had to have another woman before you could make that choice to leave me."

She said the words even though she knew a lot of men weren't loyal to their wives. All her uncles were notorious rakes before they wed. They were all faithful afterward. Didn't believe even one strayed after they wed. If they did, no one would have told her.

In truth, if their wives knew of an affair, they would no longer be married. Divorce would be eminent, scandal or not. She laughed softly, "If any of my uncles or my father took a lover, they wouldn't still be wed. They would most likely have lost their most manly parts." It seemed she spoke her thoughts.

"You announced in front of everyone who could hear that you

would unman me if I left. Is that true?"

Her grin wouldn't leave her. She liked the fact he was wary of her. "Yes, did you think I might not have said it?"

"Not for one second. What else happened along the way? Blade alluded to something, however, he didn't get into specifics." He searched, probed for more than she would like to reveal.

Lifting her shoulders slightly, "Nothing truly."

She knew what occurred was far from nothing. The men were thieves, coarse in their dress. Disheveled and ragged. They would have taken that which was not theirs. Might have attacked her. The shudder coursing through her gave rise to goose bumps.

"Nick." He spoke harshly.

The way he said her name gave her good reason to believe he didn't mean to let her leave the subject without explaining to him.

She knew that look along with the tone quite well. He was going to insist she answer. "As soon as the uncles and brother saw the three men, they formed a protective circle around me. Nothing happened."

"If you'd been alone, things would have been different."

She didn't want to admit as much, intended for a moment to drop the subject. The slow burn in his eyes changed her mind. "The outcome might not have been something I liked. The uncles all swore and cursed a blue streak at me when the men vanished down the road, reminding me I had no reason to be searching for you."

"Anything else I should learn about?"

She was shaking her head, acknowledging the truth. "The rest of the journey went smoothly. We stopped everywhere along the way to see if you were there. Seemed to take an eternity. Why they thought you might have been riding when your ship was gone, I can't imagine. At times I just thought they were trying to slow me down. If you took your ship home, you wouldn't be in one of the damn inns."

Her eyes widened with the realization slowing her down was exactly what they intended.

As if he read her thoughts, his soft laughter had her wishing she had something she could throw at him. "They were trying to slow you down, Nick. At least your brother and I believe both James and Blade understood, I would never renege on the promise to wed you. As well as being known as a rake, I'm also known for my honesty and integrity."

"Where men are concerned," she agreed reluctantly. "Women on the other hand..." she lifted her shoulders slightly.

"Also, where women are involved, I've never lied to any woman."

"Sabrina thought you lied." She shot the words at him before she took the time to think.

His brows shot up. "What did she say?"

"Actually, not much."

Nickie wasn't certain why she brought up one of his mistresses. She never liked thinking about him with another woman.

"Is it what she didn't say? It must have been," he sighed.

His expression told her nothing. "I never lied to that woman."

"She didn't say you were going to find someone else. She was absolutely positive you would show up at the ball. Sabrina spoke of an engagement to come. At the time she was upset you didn't escort her."

"I did show up at that damn ball. Never told her I would escort her. In fact, I told her the exact opposite," he gritted out then grinned, his shimmering gaze focused on her. "Had a wonderful time with a newly introduced debutante. We danced too many times for etiquette, watched the sunrise over her uncle's lake. I was going to cry off with Sabrina at the end of the ball. However, I met a beauty who quite stole my breath along with my heart. Forgot all about crying off. Forgot about Sabrina completely. After the sunrise, I lost all rational thought. My only intention was to figure out if I could get this bewitchingly beautiful debutante on the Promise since I was leaving London. Didn't know one of your uncles was the duke. Someone didn't bother to inform me who her chaperones were."

Inside Nickie beamed. She almost giggled. He lost his heart? Did that mean he loved her?

The two of them rode in relative silence for the last hour. Nickie kept wondering if he did love her. She couldn't get those words 'stole my heart' from resonating in her head. Both seemed immersed in private thoughts. She didn't see the men until Collin commented.

"Stay close, Nick. Get behind me. If these are the men who you saw yesterday, best you plan on racing back to the inn we just passed. I'll hold them off as long as possible."

Shivers rushed down her spine. The fine hairs on the back of her neck stood on end. She pulled in a deep breath of air. "They are the same."

She didn't like the idea he would have to fight them. He was by himself.

She saw the stiffening of Collin's muscles. He appeared ready for a fight. Actually seemed pleased with the situation. His grin surprised her. The men approached. "Are you ready, Nick? Want you to ride as hard as you can to the inn. Wait there for me. This shouldn't take long."

When she nodded, she was looking down the road. Ryder and Blade were ahead of them. They must have doubled back. She let out the breath she'd been holding, fear for Collin driving her emotions. The blasted man must have seen her uncles. That was why he was all nonchalant and grinning.

Grinning!

Quickly, she reined in as Blade and Ryder passed her. They both nodded their heads in her direction. She was going to wait right here. After all was finished, she was going to vent her anger and fear on Collin. Her body shook with the emotions that swamped her.

The meeting was over before it started. The men, seeing the odds were no longer in their favor left down the road.

She pulled up beside Collin. Nickie found she couldn't say anything, couldn't swallow the fear that clogged her throat. It seemed the blasted man angered her more this last twenty-four hours than ever before. He wanted to fight.

Damn it all, he wanted to fight!

"We saw them when we rode by a few hours ago. Knew the two of you would be along shortly. Thought our presence would deter any mischievous thoughts."

Collin snorted, obviously in disbelief. "Mischievous thoughts? Is that what you call thievery now days? I was more than willing to tangle with them. It would not have taken long to dispatch them."

"Thought you might need a hand or two," Ryder said his grin widening. "I'm a bit disappointed though. Been hoping for a fight. Knew you were too."

"So, you waited." Collin chuckled softly when he saw the expression on her face. "You aren't angry are you, Nick?"

He leaned over to chuck her under the chin, knowing the insolent action would enrage her even more.

"What do you think? I was terrified. Now, I'm furious with you. Men!"

What he was thinking was apparent to her. If they weren't alone, if there wasn't a promise standing between them, she'd be in his arms. The desire in his eyes raged. She caught her breath as Ryder looked from Collin to her then back again.

"Well, bloody eyes...time we started back before something happens right now that we've been trying to avoid. Seems there's a wedding along with a wedding night that might happen before the wedding after all." Ryder hooted. "Better get those horses moving."

When she turned away from her uncles, it was to see Collin again. It seemed his emotions were under more control than hers. He schooled his features as soon as Ryder made the connection. She still wanted to throw something at him.

When they rode into the courtyard, the stable boys who seemed to be on the lookout for them greeted them. She was hustled by one of her mother's maids into the huge solar, which was next to her parent's room. When she stepped through the door, all the women smiled as if they knew what she thought. Perhaps they did. She was eager to get through the day. Understood it would be taxing. Thoughts of Collin paired with the wedding night filled her dreams. She was thankful she wasn't a virgin with a virgin's fears.

An assortment of food was set on trays. Glasses filled with wine adorned the tables. A bath of steaming water scented with jasmine waited for her just beyond in the bathing room. She was ushered to the small room. Chatter along with laughter filled the area. All her aunts were there. The flower girl sat on a bench beside Aidan, fiddling with her hands. Nick's dress hung next to a mirror beside a dressing table. It was beautiful, just as she imagined. Today, for the first time, she would wear the McInnis colors.

"We aren't going to rush to the chapel?" Nickie asked as she walked toward the tub. It looked delicious. "It is late. We should already be arriving."

"Hush. The minister was informed we would be at least an hour late if not more. He agreed the marriage must go forth in a timely manner, however, for you, sweetheart, he didn't mind the slight delay so you could look your best," her mother told her. "You've a lot of explaining to do. No one expected you to rush off the way you did. No one knew. We've been so worried all night. We didn't rest easy until your brother and James rode through the courtyard this morning to tell us what happened also that you and Collin would be along shortly. When that happened, we got everything ready finishing the flowers in the church just as if you didn't run off."

"I'm sorry you were all worried. That wasn't my intention. All I wanted..."

Heat rose to her face. When she set her hands upon her cheeks they cooled somewhat. The warmth was not from the nearby steaming water but from what she almost told everyone. In any case they most likely guessed as much.

Nickie was handed a glass of wine. There was a small stool by the tub where she set the crystal. Her mother helped her with the fasteners on her dress. She did want to rush to the wedding. Even though Collin's words had been sweet, she still feared he might change his mind. The 'I dos' wouldn't come soon enough for her.

"Take as long as you wish. No, we are not rushing to the chapel," Allura said again as if she saw the look in her eyes. "Even though you might wish for that very thing. The ceremony as well as the feast has been delayed until we send word that you are ready. Which of course, means your wedding night will also be delayed. I want this to be perfect for you."

Nickie didn't want her wedding or the night after to be delayed. She didn't care if anything was perfect. What she wanted was the vows to be said and the papers signed. She wanted to be held in Collin's arms. She wanted to lose her temper with him so he could soothe the anger with his kisses and soft beguiling words.

Her riding clothes were piled on the floor. She stepped into the tub. The water was hot and heavenly, the scent delicious. For a few moments she closed her eyes. This was happening. In an hour or so she was going to wed Collin McInnis. There was a moment, yesterday in fact, she actually didn't think the wedding would take place. Though, there was also a time she didn't think she wanted to marry anyone. Her hands rested possessively on her belly. For her everything changed.

Her child needed a father. Not one doubt entered her mind that Collin wouldn't be a marvelous father. After all and despite what her uncles thought, he was a wonderful man. She soaked until the water turned tepid.

After she rose from the bath, her towel wrapped around her as well as her hair, she stepped into the main part of the room. It seemed her aunts hustled here and there. Laughter and chatter still dominated the celebratory atmosphere. With her undergarments donned, her dress was slipped over her head. The gown's skirt and bodice were white embellished with tiny seed pearls. Around her waist a sash made from the McInnis dress plaid was tied. The dress was fastened in the back with hard-to-maneuver buttons. She wondered how she was going to get out of the gown tonight. Wondered too, if Collin with his large hands could unfasten those tiny buttons that were set there just to bedevil the groom.

Her hair finished, their lively chatter gave her reason to smile. They were all so dear to her. She was gifted with something blue as well as a new sapphire necklace from Collin. Her mother placed it around her neck. Her earrings were sapphires borrowed from her mother. Aiden gave her garters to hold up her stockings that were also blue. Ella sent her a negligée and robe that one could see through. For the groom as well as the bride, the message read. Yes, Collin would like this. Once more heat rushed to her face. Her thoughts so private, she didn't want anyone reading anything into the blush.

Her heart pounding, she realized she was ready. She steadied herself with her hands on the dresser while she looked at herself one more time. Her nerves wrapped around each other until she thought she'd burst.

"Nervous?" her mother asked. "You've no reason for nerves. You're beautiful. The McInnis is a lucky man. He knows it too."

"Very nervous."

She downed the remainder of her wine. It seemed she forgot to eat. Breakfast had been the last meal of her day. Too much wine, she felt a bit dizzy. Closed her eyes for a moment to keep the room from spinning. She wondered if she could walk down the aisle. Her father would either help her or decide she shouldn't be wed. With a deep need for fortitude, she drug in a long hard breath of air.

"Should we let your father know it's time?" Allura asked as she strode to the door. Before she opened it, she looked back to her.

She'd forgotten her father would be there to give her away. Would he do so? "Father?" she queried, her voice whisper thin vibrating with surging emotions.

Her nerves spiraled. Why did she think he might do something untoward, something to stop the ceremony? Would he object to the marriage? As her father he had every right to do so.

"He won't do anything to your bridegroom nor will he object if that's what has led to all color draining from your face. I believe Hunter has come to realize the McInnis is a good man. He loves you. You know that."

He loves me?

Well, that might be too much to ask. How would her father know that? Was it something men knew about other men? She fought back the retort, kept her fears close to her chest. Tried to keep her knees from knocking together. No one would let Hunter ruin her wedding day, least of all her mother. If necessary, she would take him from the church.

"I'll get him," Christel said as she left the room, leaving Allura to continue to soothe her sensibilities.

This was it. She hugged her mother then her aunts as they all assembled in the order they would walk down the aisle. Aidan's little girl was ready too. The girl held her basket of rose petals high. The little boy, the ring bearer, would be with the groomsmen until time to hand him over to the bridesmaids.

"You'll be happy with your man. I'm certain of it." It seemed her mother was thinking of another time, as her eyes grew dreamy a bit of moisture filling them. "You love him already. I barely knew Hunter when we wed."

Her mother seemed to be speaking from the heart. Nickie heard this tale before. It was heartwarming and tender. Mother fought his attentions until she had no choice. She discovered soon enough he was not as he seemed.

"You loved him from the moment you saw him," Aiden said laughing. "Just as I loved Blade. In your case, you were too stubborn to admit the truth. In my case, I pestered him until he had no alternative than to fall in love with me."

"That is not what Blade will tell you. If Hunter is to be believed, Blade had a devil of a time staying away from you especially as you grew older. He was enamored of you so thoroughly he thought he had to fight those feelings. When he first met you, he thought you to be an incorrigible little pest," Allura said, laughing as the two of them reminisced.

"Perhaps I was unable to look at Hunter realistically. Thought I was losing myself to a man who only cared for the estate. Didn't understand that wasn't all that drove him. Nonetheless, more than anything I needed his love."

The knock on the door sent another round of jitters catapulting through her. She knew the person on the other side of the door had to be her father. She supposed someone would have to open it. Also guessed if he was ready to escort her then he didn't intend to cause trouble. Allura opened the door. She saw her father standing in the opening. He was dressed in McClellan dress plaid. He wore the kilt well. Her father was tall, broad of shoulder and still incredibly handsome. Even though he was English by birth, Hunter adopted the ways of the Scots when he became laird.

He held out his hand for her while the aunts left the room. "You're incredibly lovely." He closed his larger hand over hers.

"You're thinking he doesn't deserve me."

Her voice wobbled. She didn't want to give in to the fear. Nevertheless, she had to know.

Her father's grin grew broad. "True, the man doesn't deserve you. Don't know if any man would fit that bill. If you love him, well, then, I'll not stand in the way. The moment I first saw him looking at you, his gaze following you wherever you walked, I knew he loved you. When you fainted at the sight of his bloodied face and he came down beside you more concerned for you than for his injuries, I knew he loved you. A man doesn't act like that if it isn't love driving him."

Relief rushed through her. She smiled. "I do love him."

"That's all I need to know."

Chapter Ten

All the uncles were standing in the room beside the chapel waiting for Allura to let them know Nickie was ready. Collin looked at his watch then set it back in the pocket of his velvet jacket. The uncles weren't all groomsman because his three brothers took the place of James and the duke as well as Jarrett Kingsly who was aunt Fayth's husband.

"Everything is ready," Allura spoke through the back door. Her smile beamed. "Hunter is escorting Nickie down from the room as we speak. Just give me a few minutes to take my seat. After that you can go into the church." She turned to leave, seemed to think better of it. "Hunter won't cause you problems if you're worried. Nickie was afraid he would object. I promise you, he won't."

She was gone, the door closing softly behind her.

The nerves that had been plaguing Collin since he left Nick with her mother escalated. Even Allura's softly spoken words did nothing to help. Hands behind his back, he rocked on his heels. His fingers clenched around each other. He didn't want to think about Hunter Gray. Unable to control the direction his mind was taking; the image was solid. The man wanted to hang him from the yardarm of his ship.

When he looked at his brothers' grinning faces, he understood what they were thinking. If he weren't the groom, his mind would undoubtedly travel in the same direction. He was the groom. What he knew was that to be with Nick for the rest of his life would be heaven. Now, he prayed nothing would happen that would delay the ceremony again. If not for his tardiness yesterday, they would be wed, sharing a glass or two of wine and headed to his ship for the honeymoon.

"You can leave now. I'll make whatever excuse you like as to your disappearance. Isn't that what a best man is supposed to do?" Doughall laughed, hitting his brother on the back. "I'll help you. Of course, your woman will dog your footsteps. So, fleeing won't do you a bit of good. As we saw yesterday, she'll follow you all the way to Dornoch, possibly beyond."

Logan laughed. "The best man is supposed to keep the bride from running away. Believe you've got your duties turned around."

The slap on his back took Collin by surprise. He stumbled. Caught himself. "Not leaving this place without a wife," he muttered.

That was so much the truth he chuckled softly. Suddenly, his nerves vanished. This was the moment he wished for from the moment she smiled at him. When she laughed at the fact, he kidnapped her. She even wanted him to kiss her. The dress she wore was filled with scarves to fill out her miniscule bosom. For him, a mouthful was enough.

She was like no other woman he'd ever met. There had been quite a few. Many he liked. Some he didn't. Some he bedded. Some he chose not to do so. None of them could hold a candle to his Nick.

"Want her that bad, do you?" Blade asked his smirk growing across his face. "Makes me remember when I needed Aidan more than my life. When I finally decided to wed her, I couldn't find her. Had to chase all over Scotland until one of the cousins gave me a clue as to her whereabouts. To reach her, I had to sail across the Atlantic. Though no one held any sympathy for my plight."

"Want her more than you would ever know."

Having tasted her, known her intimately, there wasn't another woman he would ever want. She was his. Almost his. By the time this hour finished she would be all his. Her father would have no legal standing. He smirked. Hayes and his crew would be aboard the Promise. In the morning they would set sail for Dornoch. She would have their child on the McInnis estate.

He would be hers. He grinned. That was always the way his Nick thought. He was her lover first, not the other way around. More than anything she seemed to long for equality. He would give her as much as the law would allow. Possibly more if he could find a way to do so. He would give her whatever she asked for.

"That's a good sign," Logan said giving him a slap on his back just as his brother did. "Can remember the exact same thing. Only my wedding night did not go smoothly at all. Hope yours is fraught with no difficulties."

"There's a story in that somewhere, just not sure I want to hear it." Collin watched as the men prepared to walk into the church.

"Eveleen would not let it be told. The moments we shared for the next year were far too private. It took us a while to mend our differences even though I loved her. At least both of you are walking willingly into this marriage."

The minister strode through the door. "Everyone is in position. It's time," the man said, smiling. "These are my favorite days. Glad you two waited for a proper wedding. Heard you thought to wed in Lybster with no family and friends in attendance. That would not have been a proper way to begin a new life."

Collin groaned softly at the reminder. Nearby Blade chuckled. If the duke were in the room, he would have further words, none to Collin's liking. The men walked into the chapel. Collin led the way. He stopped at the altar; his gaze now focused on the first woman in line. He couldn't recall all the names and faces of her aunts. He could match a few wives with the husbands. Of course he knew Ella went with Drake, Blade with Aidan. After that his mind was a befuddled mess.

Each woman walked slowly down the aisle. So many beautiful women. His heart raced while his fists tightened at his sides. His breath burned in his chest. He wiped his sweaty palms on his kilt. More than anything, he wanted this ceremony to end. Wanted to dance with his wife, feed her a piece of cake, smear a bit on her face, taste the cool, sweet icing then make his way to the ship rocking in the harbor. Would he be allowed to leave?

Perhaps he would have to go to the chamber granted him when he came. He wouldn't go to her room. It was a virgin's room. There were other possibilities. If it wasn't going to be dark when all was finished, he would take her to the island. No, his first thought was the right one. He should take her to the Promise. Just as he planned in his head a few minutes previous, together they would sail for Dornoch in the morning or perhaps hoist the anchor beginning their journey home tonight. The more he thought on that idea, the more he realized it was the solution.

The anticipation planted a grin on his face.

Hayes was in the church. When he found a free moment, he would instruct him to bring the ship to the dock as soon as the wedding finished. Collin wanted his Nick in his cabin where he first made love to her. The night would be perfect. Before the feast ended, he would make certain Allura knew where he wanted the wine along with the additional wedding night food to be delivered.

The ring bearer made his way down the aisle then a flower girl, tossing rose petals as she made her way. They were so young. Which aunt and uncle were the proud parents? Had to be Aidan's and Blade's. She was the youngest of all the sisters and cousins. Allura collected them as soon as they finished their jobs. They sat beside their Grandmother Allura as if they were little cherubs. Collin knew different. Before he left to find Nick, the pair along with many other children, ran wild in the main hall as well as the courtyard. There was nothing cherubic about any of the youngsters of this clan, none from his clan either.

He tucked the ring into his pocket. The gold band, circled in sapphires had been his mother's. He was glad his brother remembered to bring the ring when he traveled to the castle even though none knew if there would be a wedding or not. He would have to send Doughall to London to carry on the family business. He didn't want to return to the city until after the child was born. Maybe no return would be necessary if Doughall enjoyed the entertainment that could be found in the city.

His breath caught in the back of his throat when he saw her.

Even while the maid of honor, Aidan, walked down the aisle, his gaze remained focused on Nick. He couldn't tear his attention away. A veil covered her face. She wore the McInnis plaid. He stood tall and proud while he waited. The pipes began to play a haunting love song. It told of two people who fell in love, who couldn't live without each other. He knew Nick picked the music to be played.

Three months ago, he would not have believed this possible. Three months ago, he fell in love with a woman the first time he saw her. He needed to tell her. How and when does a man say those special words? He wasn't at all sure. What he did understand was the fact that the sooner he told her the better for their life together.

When Nick reached the altar, she waited for the minister to begin. Her smile was huge, her eyes a bit glazed over. Her father agreed to give her to him. Nick handed her bouquet of orchids and red roses to Aidan. She wavered on her feet then seemed to breathe in a deep breath of air to steady herself.

That was a relief. He let out the air he'd been holding. He held her small hands in his. The ceremony passed in a blur of words. They both seemed to respond at the appropriate time.

"Do either of you have anything you would like to say?" the minister asked as he looked from one to the other.

Collin nodded. "I do."

He smiled. It was a bit early for the words. He squeezed her hands in his when she looked at him her eyes wide. He cleared his throat. "Don't worry, Nick, I won't say anything that will make you angry or embarrass you too much."

Although he did intend to riffle her temper before the night ended. Making love to her when she was angry was always magically enchanting, simply because her passion would overflow. He would make certain he was the recipient.

He cleared his throat. He looked at her, only her. Her eyes shimmered. He saw the desire. "When I first met you, I was sure you would be angry with me, furiously so. I kidnapped you, believing you to be someone else. To make matters worse, I locked you in a bedroom undeniably tarnishing your reputation. After all, who would believe that you stayed for hours in a notorious rake's bedroom and not be touched by him."

He distinctly heard, Hunter's groan of displeasure. Was infinitely happy he wouldn't have to live near the man. The distance separating their homes would make visiting a semi-rare encounter. "I left her there. Attended a ball where she was expected to be only to discover the woman I believed to be in my third-story room was at the ball." Chuckles followed the statement. "I was shocked. Intrigued came next. After that curiosity as to who exactly the woman was.

"Needless to say, I rushed back to my townhouse, curiosity driving me. When I opened the door, I expected a furious woman to face me. Was sure there might be hard objects directed at my head. Instead, Nick laughed and gave me a smile that knocked my socks off. To me, she was ravishing. The most beautiful woman I ever encountered. I didn't know it then but I was half way in love with her." There were a few sighs in the room. "I took her to the ball. We danced too many times for protocol. When she hinted that she meant to watch the sunrise at the nearby lake and that she would like me to come with her, I couldn't refuse the invitation. Besides just watching, I had other ideas in mind."

Knowing laughter rippled around the room. After all, at the time, he was a notorious rake.

He touched her chin, gently lifted. Her eyes were smoldering pools of blue. "It was then she told me something I will never forget. Every time I watch the sun poke its head over the mountains or an ocean, I'll recall her words. They somehow touched my heart. Nick told me that unlike a sunset, which speaks to the end of the day, a sunrise is the beginning of a new one. Even if the day before was horrid, one could change that with a new beginning. She also told me she loved sunrises more than any other time of day. Nick is my sunrise."

He saw moisture pool in her eyes. Gently, he touched a silver teardrop, brought it to his lips, tasted the sweet salt. "Nick, you are my new beginning. We will do well together, you and I. You will bring joy to my life every day."

He stopped, turned to the minister then back to Nick.

"Nicole, do you have anything you would like to tell this man?"

"I suppose after that I should say something."

She began to sway. He tightened his grip, hoping her knees would not give out.

"It's alright if you..."

"Hush, I..."

She ran her tongue along her bottom lip. It was a normal gesture for her. He didn't think she knew what the slow glide of her tongue did to him. He squeezed her hands.

"I want to say that when you opened the door, I couldn't help but smile. For me there was no anger, only curiosity as to who you were. When you looked at me, you appeared so confused and seemed utterly frustrated, possibly even annoyed. I didn't understand why, although I was certainly willing to discover the truth. At that time, all I wanted was to come home, here to McClellan land. When I saw Collin all that changed. We danced. We watched the sunrise over the lake. That same day he asked me if I would travel with him. In my mind, the only possible answer was yes. I knew I needed to follow my heart no matter where it took me. Now, I will travel with him wherever our lives take us. He is my rock, my brick wall. He owns my heart."

Collin had never been so touched by words as he was now. In the congregation, he noticed there were very few dry eyes. Tears slid down her mother's cheeks. The minister continued. More words were exchanged. He slipped the gold band on her finger.

"If you like Collin McInnis, you may kiss your bride."

With the veil lifted, he brushed his lips across hers, thinking he'd like to do so much more. The devil, they were in a church. He didn't dare do what he was thinking. Yet, the heated tip of her tongue touched on his lip. Unconsciously, he opened for her. Tasted the sweetness that was always hers to share. His hands tightened on her waist. Intense arousal shot through him to pool in his groin.

The minister cleared his throat.

Regretfully, he pulled away, touching her lips with the calloused pad of his thumb. "There will be more of that later, Mrs. McInnis."

"I certainly hope so."

She smiled, appearing as relieved as he felt.

Once again, the minister cleared his throat. "Seems these two think the ceremony is over. However, there is one more thing. To all of you in attendance to witness the joining of Nicole Gray to Collin McInnis, I now introduce these two lovely Scots as husband and wife." The minister beamed, thoroughly enjoying his role.

The pipes played a tune. Aidan handed her the bouquet. To the sound of much applause the couple started down the aisle. When they reached the foyer of the church, they stopped. The attendants followed, the guests after that. They met each one with hugs and kisses along with a few exchanged words. When the line of well-wishers disappeared, Collin drew her into his arms.

He kissed her. Ran his hands down her back to cup her backside then tug her against his arousal. "How long do we have to stay at the feast?"

"I'm famished." She smiled then touched his lips. "You will have to wait until I sample every different dish that is served. You do recall we missed last night's wedding feast. I want to know if everything is as tasty as I hoped."

"We can take some to the ship. Hopefully your mother has seen to our post wedding feast."

"The ship? We are going to spend the night on the ship? Did you run that by mother?"

She was smiling. That was a good sign as far as he was concerned.

He nibbled on her ear, touched the lobe with the tip of his tongue. Heard the soft purr of pleasure escape her throat. "Don't have to run my plans by anyone except you now that you're my wife. Would you like to go to the ship?"

"Oh. Yes..."

"Do you want to retire to the ship now? Or after the feast and dancing?"

"As soon as possible," was her whispered reply. "I do have to eat something. Haven't put any food in my stomach since this morning. Too nervous. Didn't think it would stay where I put it."

"Is that why you were swaying on your feet during the ceremony?" he asked, suddenly concerned for her.

The need to scoop her into his arms then carry her to the celebration overwhelmed him. He did so.

"Collin, put me down. I can walk."

She was laughing, pounding on his shoulder, tears of joy in her eyes.

"Well, Nick, of course you can walk. Why should you, when I'd rather carry you?"

Nickie pressed her face into his shoulder when they entered the hall. Cheers went up all around them welcoming them as a newly married couple. He walked with her to the table meant for the bride and groom. After he set her on the chair, he handed her a sparkling glass of champagne.

"To my wife."

The toast was short. Collin understood his brothers would not be short. Knew the speech his sibling would give would not be in his best interest. He might even have to explain a few things to Nick.

Hopefully, not tonight.

He heaped her plate. She slanted him a look telling him she couldn't eat that much. He didn't expect her to do so.

"Shall we share?" He handed her a fork, set a napkin on her lap before sitting down next to her.

"If that's what you would like?"

He nodded. For a few minutes they ate in silence. He didn't know what to say to her. Doughall rose, extending his glass in salute to the new couple.

"Believe my brother's toast was way too short for the likes of me. Nonetheless, I'm hard pressed to say things that will serve to embarrass the man I call brother on this special day. Would you all like me to embarrass him or just to wish him well?" He handed the option to the guests.

The answers came in both varieties. His brothers along with her uncles wanted to watch his face turn red while the aunts just wanted the well wishes.

"Guess I'm going to cater to the fairest of us. If I don't do so, if I ever find the woman I wish to settle down with, the ribbing will be far more embarrassing if I give into temptation this evening. Wouldn't want that now, would I? Prudence is the name of the game tonight. I have to look to my future."

Collin's breath of relief caused Nick to giggle. "Have you had too much champagne?"

She was shaking her head. "I am satisfied though. Perhaps in another hour or so I'll want to eat more."

Collin did remember her delightful giggles when she was foxed the night they stayed on the island. He wasn't averse to recreating the scene.

~ * ~

"In another hour or so we will be on board the Promise. Now that Aidan is here and seems to want to talk with you, I'll go make arrangements for the ship."

Aidan sat. "Our home is close to Dornoch if you need anything."

"I doubt if we will. The same goes for you two however."

Nickie wasn't too sure where the line of conversation was headed. All the aunts gathered around her, chatting, sipping wine. Time slipped by while she waited for her new husband. Thoughts of the night to come shimmered in her mind. She was content. She didn't have a virgin's fears.

The pipes began to play. Collin returned. She beamed at him. "That didn't take long."

"That's the smile I fell in love with, Nick. Dance with me? Believe this one is for us." He held out his hand, whirled her around the floor until she was breathless. The music slowed. They waltzed. He pulled her close, closer than appropriate. No one cared. His hand rested where it shouldn't. She didn't care.

Nickie loved the way his body felt pressed against hers. Loved the play of his muscles while he moved around the dance floor. Now his hand rested on the small of her back guiding her. They danced to a private alcove. His lips brushed softly against hers. She understood the promise of the night to come.

"How long do we have to stay?"

He nibbled gently on the lobe of her ear, swirled his tongue inside. "Didn't you ask that before? Are you impatient"?

"You know I am. It seems as if I've waited forever."

She shuddered against him wishing they were alone. Her breasts pushed against the hard planes of his chest. His mouth moved from her earlobe to the column of her neck. Beside him, she coiled and arched. He brought her closer to him. She felt his arousal, hard against her belly.

"We can't leave yet. It's too soon. Still have to dance with father."

He groaned, his hand moving slowly down to her bottom then upward to cup a breast. Languidly, his thumb roamed across the tip. There was little fabric separating the two, his thumb and crest. She moaned softly. The groan in the back of his throat thrilled her. It had been so long. Well, five days was not actually that long. However, she found it to be an eternity.

"After that we can go?"

His kisses feathered across the scooped neckline. Her body coiled against him.

"Collin, stop, stop for now. I can't breathe, can't think either. You're going to embarrass me."

She moaned again as his hands teased the back of her neck and his kisses nibbled along her lips. Her hands on his chest, she pushed.

He didn't move.

"Collin..." her voice sounded a thin wail.

He stepped back, appearing to be delighted with the last few moments. "Your lips are swollen from my kisses. The color on your cheeks, a soft pink, makes me wonder what your beautiful jewels with the tight tips look like beneath your dress. Will your breasts also be this gorgeous shade of pink too?"

Collin did let her go. Her legs trembled though. "I'm beginning to rethink my wish not to see your face turn red, with the telling of your exploits by your brother."

He laughed. Nickie tried to straighten her dress. Nothing she did seemed to work. The gown felt cockeyed.

"Let me help." Collin pushed her hands away. He straitened the top of the gown so it once more fit across her shoulders. "Is that better?"

Slowly, she lowered her lashes, before she looked at him again. She smiled. He groaned. "Behave yourself now. You will have all night for other pleasures of the flesh."

With that said she flounced away. He would stay in the alcove for a while if her guess was right.

She intended to find her father. The dance then the cutting of the cake would end their entanglement at the celebration. They would be free to leave. His kisses joined with the sweetest caresses of his nimble fingers created the need for privacy for the wedding night to begin.

Nickie found her father sipping champagne with her mother. He looked up, a dark brow arched in question. His smile held a challenge she didn't understand as of yet. Perhaps he would enlighten her.

"Father, daughter dance?" he asked as he stepped forward to take her into his arms.

She nodded. They whirled around the room to another waltz. This time she wasn't held close. Hunter smiled at her. "You are happy? This is the man you wanted."

"Fine way to talk now after what you put Collin through." She hit him on the shoulder knowing full well he barely felt the punch.

"He should have courted you properly, Nickie. He had no right to treat you the way he did." Hunter still looked at her as if he searched for answers.

"I didn't give him a choice."

"He didn't give you one either. From what I am understanding he was leaving London. He had no intention of making you anything but his next mistress at the time."

"He didn't know who I was."

"That's no excuse."

She wasn't sure how to answer now. There was a wealth of truth in his words. "You know I was willing. He offered me something I couldn't refuse. The attraction between us was so strong..."

"Do you still hate me?" he asked as he whirled her in a tight circle.

"No, can never hate you. We don't need to talk about this or about the threats. Shall we put them all in the past? I'm afraid it's going to be a long time before he forgives you as well as Uncle Drake. Now, if you don't mind, why don't you take me back to my husband?"

Collin seemed to be holding up one of the columns in the room, his arms crossed in front of him. He watched her. His eyes blazed with desire, passion simmering. If they didn't leave the party soon, he might haul her off to the guest room he'd been given for his short stay so he could consummate the marriage. She felt the same.

"Take good care of my little girl. Don't ever hurt her," Hunter said as he handed her over to Collin.

If she heard the poorly veiled threat in her father's tone, she was sure Collin would too.

Allura seemed to sense the time for them to leave was at hand.

She stood at the bride and grooms table, tapping a crystal glass to get everyone's attention. The cake sat on the cleared table along with small plates and forks.

Collin held her elbow as they approached. He grinned at her, his thoughts clear in the depth of his vivid green eyes. "Shall we? I for one can't wait until this is finished." His hand resting on top of hers, the first slice was cut. "I'll feed you first."

Delicately, she placed a piece on his lips. He opened, accepting the piece of cake along with her fingers. He caressed her, his tongue quickly exploring the proffered tips. She stepped back. Surprised by the smirk on his face. It was at that moment she understood what he planned.

"No, Collin." She held her hands out.

"Yes, Nick. I've been waiting to taste more of you all night. That one tiny kiss in the alcove was not nearly enough to hold me until we're on board the Promise."

The piece of cake he broke off was not small or delicate. It seemed he found the part of the cake with the most icing. At the back of her neck, his hand held her in place. She tried to take the piece into her mouth. He would have none of it. By the time he finished, icing covered her lips as well as her nose. There were pieces on her cheeks.

Slowly, he licked and nibbled the icing and cake from her face. The erotic touch of his soft lips so tender against her sent all her senses reeling. He took his time. Seduced. Charmed. Enticed. Finally, he moved away, his smile broad. He seemed pleased with himself. Her mother handed him a damp cloth. Tenderly, he washed the stickiness away. When finished, he held up her hand.

"We are leaving now."

Pulling her along they ran from the room until she stumbled. He scooped her into his arms.

Before she had time to blink, they were in a carriage for the short distance to the dock. He carried her up the gangplank then into the cabin where he whirled her around and around in tight circles until they were both dizzy.

"Here we are again, wife."

He kissed her, backing her to the bed before gently lowering her to the mattress. His weight covered her. In little time, there clothing was scattered haphazardly on the floor.

Throughout the night they made love, ate and drank. They slept some then started again. Near dawn, she found him staring at her.

"I love you, Nick. Should have told you that, months ago. The feeling was all so new to me. I wasn't at all sure of myself."

Nickie touched him gently on the cheek. "My tender rogue, I love you too. So much so I was willing to do anything to keep you. You are Nickie's tender rogue. Don't ever forget that."

"Nick's tender rogue," he corrected as he proceeded to make love to her again.

Epilogue

Three years later.

Nick and Collin sat on a grassy hill near the McInnis estate. Nick did give him his heir. A fine son who would grow up strong as well as willful he was certain. The lad already exhibited many of his father's traits. Collin could not wait to teach him all he would need to learn to survive in this world. He would proceed as his father did with him.

The boy was three now. His little girl was born three months ago. He wanted more children. They both agreed after the boy was born, they wanted one more child. He wasn't sure what Nick wanted now. The pregnancies as well as the birth had not been overly taxing.

In the end it was up to her.

Now she was nursing the wee one who had the same blond hair as her mother. Though, there wasn't a lot of it. It was so blond the hair appeared white barely covering her head. He was certain the color would darken. Her eyes were the same powder blue. When he thought of her growing up, the men she would attract, he groaned deep in the back of his throat.

Suddenly, he held a new respect for Hunter. Somehow, he would have to figure out a way to keep her away from men like him. Perhaps that's how Hunter felt about Nick.

"What? You look so far away?" Nick asked, her hand resting on his arm. "What are you thinking about?"

"This conversation I suppose will be more relevant in another eighteen or so years. Just wondering if we'll do a better job when it comes to this courting business than your father. One notion of mine that this is for certain, we won't send our daughter to the Montgomeries for chaperoning."

She grinned provokingly at him. "The duke and duchess are doing a much better job nowadays. No one has run off with their lover. There have been several legitimate weddings before the beddings. Well, we wouldn't know which came first."

"That's supposed to make me feel better?"

"What I'm worried about is your heir. Are you going to teach him to be a notorious rake, a bounder? I have serious words to say about something like that." She was laughing, watching him with that smile of hers he could never resist.

He smirked. When she set the baby down, he pulled her into his arms for a long drugging open-mouthed kiss. "Don't think anyone taught me. My ways with women just came naturally."

"Well then, we'll have to make sure when the right *lass* comes along, he treats her with the respect she deserves."

Collin stilled for a moment, watching his boy chasing butterflies. He was a handsome lad with the same dark hair as his and vivid green eyes. "He will be taught all you say. It still won't change the fact he will most likely chase after the ladies until he catches the woman of his dreams."

"So be it. All a mother and father can do is their best then hope as well as pray life will proceed smoothly for their children."

"I love you Mrs. McInnis. Now should we start working on another heir? Everyone needs an heir plus one."

"Not today, Mr. McInnis, my tender rogue. That will have to wait for at least another year, perhaps more. Can you wait that long?"

"Suppose I'll have to. What choice does a man have?"

Dream About Lyssa
Naughty Book Two

Chapter One

London 1837

"It's the duchess, Ella Montgomerie, to see you."

The Earl of Blackmore, Black to his friends, set his pen in its holder before leaning back in his chair. In front of him he clasped his hands. His brows drew together while he digested the fact the woman was here to see him. He couldn't think of one reason for her appearance at his country estate, since the location was not amenable to visits. It must be important. He owned ten square miles a considerable distance from London. The land was his home away from Lakota territory in the states. Here he could act as he pleased. He could strip to his breechclout then ride the countryside; his war cry would be heard only by the nearby animals. The scents didn't remind him of the prairie. Though they were distinctive in their own way. He felt comfortable in the country, much more so than in the city.

A long slow breath of air sifted through his lips. The sixth sense he always relied on kicked in as the fine hairs on the back of his neck bristled. Ella was up to something. He'd just have to wait a few minutes to discover her ruse. "Show her in. Bring some refreshments as well. I'm certain she will be in need of something tasty to eat after such a long trip. If not hungry, she'll undoubtedly be thirsty. I want my finest Bordeaux to tempt her pallet."

"She has a young lady with her."

Sitting up straight, his interest grew. What the devil was she doing bringing a young woman to his home? *The humble abode of a notorious rake?* He certainly was not husband material, never would be.

"Perhaps lemonade with the snacks would be appropriate. How old is she?" Curiosity multiplied.

"You will have to ask the ladies." Abernathy clucked his tongue as if he had asked something ridiculous. "Don't you understand it is not fashionable to ask a woman her age?"

Ah, Abernathy was correct, one didn't ask a lady how old she was. Not if a man wanted to keep his head attached to his shoulders. No, the asking of age would be far too delicate a question for him. His butler was spot on in his assessment of the situation.

"No courage, eh?" Black asked as he straightened the papers and folders littered on his desk. He didn't have the fortitude either. A guess of his own would have to suffice.

"Courage with the ladies is your department, Sir. I would never do half the things that seem to occupy your free time." A smirk on his thin lips, Abernathy left the room, backing away and closing the doors as he disappeared.

Seconds later the door opened. Ella Montgomerie entered with a young woman behind her. Extending his hand in greeting, Black walked around his desk. When the woman stepped to Ella's side, his heart stopped. Slowly, the startled organ began to beat again. He placed a kiss on the back of Ella's hand before looking back to the ravishing young woman.

Except for the curves of her sumptuous bosom, she was rail thin, her eyes a deep dark blue reminding him of the color of sapphires, her hair the darkest brown. She possessed a pert nose. Her neck was long, alabaster in color. While he stared at her, the pulse at the base throbbed invitingly. He wondered if she thought about a man's touch, a man kissing her in that spot. He wondered then of the intelligence of Ella for introducing him to the most exquisite creature he ever set eyes upon.

She smiled at him, the gesture reaching clearly to her eyes. This woman was no coquette. The smile was honest while the slow curve of her plump bottom lip stole thoughts from his head. This time his breath caught in the back of his throat, which he cleared. Those eyes twinkled merrily as if the joke was on him. Boldly, she tilted her head a bit to the side as if perusing him from the top of his head to the tips of his toes if she could have seen them. Somehow, he understood her intent. Indeed, the way Ella stared at him, the jest might be on him. He didn't mind if her visit concerned the girl. He would step up to the job.

"What brings you here?" Black had the decided feeling he wasn't going to like her answer. Possibly, he might like it too much. In the deepest recesses of his mind, he understood his life was about to be turned topsy-turvy. If he told her no, she would remind him that he owed her. Also, he wondered how long she would capitalize on that fact. She used that ploy once before. She was solely responsible for his position here in London. She used her influence to secure his title. He was the only son of the previous earl. Sometimes, however, he missed his days on the prairie. Missed the hunting of buffalo along with the freedom, the sun on his bare torso.

The freedom he had here was different. He had to work at it, build it from scratch. Nothing was spontaneous as it was on the prairie.

"I've a favor."

He'd come around to stand in front of his desk, now he leaned against the wooden structure, one leg swinging. His thoughts muddled as he tried to keep his gaze from the young lady who had all the markings of a debutante. It was the season. "That seems to be when you visit. Isn't it?" Black watched her stiffen, her displeasure clearly written in her expressive features. "My apology. Didn't mean anything by that comment. You know I would do anything for you. Except perhaps murder. Just a bit testy this afternoon."

She laughed at his statement. "Actually, that statement is not factual. Though we both understand I would never ask you to kill anyone for me. Murder is so messy." Her chin lifted just as one would expect of a duchess. Admirably, she fit the role. She had years to fine-tune the characteristics.

"You do have to admit though…" He didn't think it too prudent to belabor the point. He motioned to the girl at her side. "Do have a seat, both of you. After Abernathy brings the refreshments, we can get on with this favor you're requesting. I would like to learn what is expected of me."

"You needn't act so put out. This will take little effort on your part." Ella straightened her skirts before smoothing the fabric. "You might even enjoy the task."

"Perhaps you've forgotten the introduction. Leaving something so important out is not like you, Duchess. Besides I've the distinct feeling this unannounced visit of yours has something to do with this young lady. Is she another one of your charges? I do pray you do better with this girl than you did with the last one."

Ella looked away for a moment, her cheeks suddenly sporting a delightful shade of pink. So, this was something she was having trouble asking. In that case the task must certainly be not to his liking. Must have something to do with the young lady sitting not so demurely at her side. The duchess understood that fact too. The girl was part of the favor. He supposed he would have to take her to one of those infuriatingly boring balls the debutantes flaunted in search of a husband. He could handle a ball or a recital for Ella, nothing else.

Before Ella could proceed, he stood, his hand outstretched. He wasn't about to get hoodwinked into escorting a debutante without putting up a bit of a fight. What the devil was the duchess thinking? His reputation alone would end her season, which was just beginning in the worst way. "No, Ella. My answer is an emphatic no. You do understand I would not be in her best interest. She can't possibly be seen with the likes of me. This beautiful young lady would find herself ostracized."

"This is Lyssa Andrews, my niece, my sister's daughter. She is very important to me, you see. I wouldn't ask this of anyone I could not trust with my life or hers. You would never do harm to a young lady who is so very important to me. As you are thinking, she is here for the season."

"No."

"You owe me, Black. It will only be for a few days, a few weeks at the most." Ella looked away for a second. The tone of voice she gifted him with brooked no argument from him.

His stomach clenched, as he understood all too clearly he would eventually give into this the duchess' request. The young lady grinned. Ella shifted in her chair. His answer remained the same. "No."

"Please."

How could he refuse when she asked him so sweetly? "A few weeks of my life, you say. I won't be saddled watching over a debutante. Good God, woman, you know who I am. Better than most you understand my reputation. This is the most ridiculous notion I've ever heard."

"You're right. I understand exactly who you are as does the duke, my husband. Indeed, this was his suggestion. I agreed. Despite your reputation you would protect Lyssa with your life. You would make sure no one would take advantage of her as Collin McInnis did with Nickie. You are the only man for the job. She must have a protector we can trust."

Well, hell, a protector? Her definition sounded as if she asked him to be something besides a chaperone. "I cannot be a chaperone to a debutante. That in and of itself will tarnish Miss Andrews' reputation. It is a ridiculous notion. I'm never seen at affairs she will be expected to attend. I don't go to balls or recitals. Don't travel in those circles. Won't receive invitations."

"I will have the invitations forwarded to you as they come in."

"It seems you have an answer for everything." He grimaced as his gaze rested once more on Lyssa Andrews then on her lush curves.

"Good," Lyssa spoke up, a devilish smirk on her face. "I'd rather be outside riding. Do you ride, Mr. Black? I promise you the man who wins my heart will have to ride and shoot as good as my daddy. Do you shoot, Mr. Black? Can you hit anything except the broadside of a barn? Can you ride a horse as if you are one with the animal? There is no one in London who can accomplish what I've described. There will be no reason for you to put yourself out by taking me to a boring ball. As to recitals, I cannot sing or play any instrument."

Ella smiled, dropping her lashes. Black was positive she was trying to hold back laughter that by the look of her threatened to erupt from behind her teeth. Hells bells, he was half Lakota Sioux. He lived the first fifteen years of his life doing little except ride and hunt. He knew he could outride as well as outshoot her daddy.

"I ride, as well as shoot admirably. Rather doubt though if I can do anything as good as your daddy. Rumors abound about Damian Andrews' abilities of that nature." Yes, Damian was a smuggler in his younger days. Rumor had it he kidnapped Amorica. Amorica shot him because of his profession. Seems he also heard it was only a flesh wound. That was over twenty years ago. Now he was about to be saddled with their daughter.

"You're too modest by far," Ella murmured thoughtfully as she gazed at her niece then back to him. "Suppose she will make you prove your statement. Lyssa doesn't believe an English dandy can do anything of that nature. I'm sure you will manage to surprise her."

Black moved to sit behind his desk. Tapping his fingers on the top, he wondered what the little minx was actually thinking in tossing out that challenge. Ella must not have told her about his background. No, she would leave all that to unfold naturally. The duchess still didn't refute the fact he was the farthest thing from an English dandy a man could get.

"So, if I agree…"

"Which you have," Ella interrupted. "There was no question in my mind." She paused for a few seconds. "Since you owe me."

"What are my duties? When do they begin?" He was resigned. The little lady seemed to be a challenging bit of frippery.

"Now, this moment. Her trunks are even now being unloaded. Abernathy has directed your servants to take them to a suitable room. For propriety she should be ensconced in the wing opposite your chambers."

"Why?" he gritted out all the while still wishing he dared say no to the duchess. He couldn't. Never could. When Ella smiled at him, all his resolve vanished. By looking at Lyssa, her smiles might have the same effect. He would have to harden his determination to stand by his dictates. Debutantes were out of bounds to him.

"About time you asked." She rose, walking to the window that overlooked the back of his estate. He didn't have perfectly manicured gardens or a gazebo. His land was natural, extended several miles to the east and north. A large stream meandered through the middle. There was a small pool at the border where he swam. Even in the summer the water was ice-cold.

"This situation you're in is all because of your friend, Collin McInnis. You can put this directly on his doorstep. He absconded with my niece, right under my nose. I had no idea. Thought she went back to the McClellan keep. By the time we figured it all out, well, it's been several weeks since she left with the bounder."

He tried to recall if he heard gossip about his friend in the last few days or even weeks as the duchess implied. Rumor had it he kidnapped a young woman thinking the lady was his mistress. That was all he heard. "Another notorious rake who I'm positive you would not entrust with one of your charges. Am I right? Now tell me, what has he done?"

"You understand exactly why I trust you with Lyssa."

He grimaced thinking about the hardened lesions on his back. Because of his audacity to court a white girl, he was whipped nearly to death. Ella along with Drake saved him. Brought him to England to claim his inheritance as well as his title. "Unfortunately, I do. Now tell me what Collin has to do with this."

"He absconded with Nickie Gray, another one of my charges. Drake is determined to make him pay, as is her father. They mean to chase him down. I have to go with them to make sure they don't do something they will regret."

"Collin left for home over a week ago. No, it's drawing closer to two weeks, maybe more. You say he took your niece with him? He wouldn't do that."

"He did," she shot out angrily, her lips tightening into a thin line. "He took her on his ship. We didn't learn of this until her brother returned from McClellan land to tell us she wasn't there."

"I assume you know this for a fact. It's a serious charge."

"You doubt the ability of my husband, the former spy, to ferret out all the facts. He still has numerous contacts in the bureau as well as out. Collin took her."

"She went willingly. You can't blame this situation all on Collin."

"Probably. She is willful. We all are."

"Neither will appreciate interference," Black reminded her.

"Nickie didn't want a season. Collin McInnis might just be taking her home," Lyssa spoke up, gracing him with another smile, "Although it's apparent neither of you believe that scenario. I do agree with Mr. Black. Nickie won't want interference from her family. I'm certain she is pleasing herself. Just as I plan on doing the same, as soon as I find the man I want for the rest of my life. I won't stick to social rules."

The Earl of Blackmore couldn't stifle the groan rumbling from his gut.

"Her wishes don't make a difference," Ella said. She leaned against the window frame. Her gaze centered on him. "You do see why we have to go. I'm traveling with the men to make sure nothing gets out of hand when they find the two lovers."

"You don't know they are lovers."

No, but I assume the worst in hopes of discovering a different scenario."

"Guess that's prudent."

"You do still own that hunting lodge in the farthest reaches of Scotland. Do you think he would take her there?"

Black leaned against the back of his chair, his legs crossed in front of him, watching Lyssa. She seemed to be studying him. Brazen chit. She was blatant about what she did. Once more, her gaze roamed the length of him. He might be able to deal well with her for a few days; a few weeks, never. Hell, it would take more than that amount of time to sail to his lodge then back. More than a month would pass before he saw any sign of the duchess.

"Collin understands he will always be welcome there. He knows I've no plans to travel that far north until the fall."

"I don't understand why you are in such a rush to find her. She won't be a virgin when you catch up to her," Lyssa said as her gaze raked over him, centered on his mouth before dipping lower. Fortunately, once again the desk hid the direction of her gaze from her view.

Brazen chit. He fought the tightening of his body. Bloody eyes, she wasn't for him. She was white. Would never presume to court a woman of her caliber. He learned his lesson. Once was enough for a lifetime. He was now this white girl's chaperone. It would be despicable of him to take advantage of the situation. If this one acted the same as the other one, perhaps Collin was the victim instead of Ella's niece.

Second along with third thoughts assailed him. He scowled at Lyssa when once again her gaze roamed his body. The young lady had the audacity to smirk. She knew exactly what she did. His scowl deepened.

"What do I have to look forward to?" he asked once more as he tried to focus his attention on Ella who seemed oblivious of her niece's blatant actions.

"You are stuffy now, aren't you?" Lyssa asked. Her stare riveted once more on his mouth. She moistened her lips, leaving an inviting dewy trail.

"Stodgy," Ella corrected her. "He is known as the stodgy Earl of Blackmore, not stuffy."

Black directed his attention to Ella this time. "Perhaps we should get on with my duties."

"You're committing. I knew you would."

He nodded, his gaze moving back to Lyssa, determined to keep a strong hand where she was concerned. Letting her out of his site for even one second was out of the question. This girl, as immature as she is, will not run away with a man under his watch. He meant to stay close.

"Guess I am. So, what is the first debutante affair she will attend? Do hope she has a wardrobe ready." Black chuckled. He didn't think Lyssa would like him to help pick out her gowns. He would make sure she was covered to her chin if he could manage the task. With her bosom, she needed fabric between her and the prying eyes of the lords seeking a young wife.

"Lyssa has more than enough to suffice for the next few weeks. You will not have to help her with her clothing."

"If you're gone longer?" he queried lifting a dark brow skyward in deep speculation. Bloody hell, he hoped this trip they were taking would end up being shorter than longer.

"Then of course you will have to accompany her to the dress shop. The modiste we most often use has her measurements. There will be little for you to do except make sure what she purchases is appropriate."

His frown lines deepened before he turned his attention to Lyssa with a smirk. "It will of course be my pleasure to accompany her. Anything for you, Duchess."

Coquettishly, Lyssa lowered her lashes before she stared at him again. His gut tightened. Her upper lip slipped beneath her teeth. He thought she needed discipline. Perhaps she understood life would not be quite the same with him, as it would have been living at Montgomerie Hall.

"Tomorrow night is her first ball. The invitation is here." Ella fished the gold engraved paper from her reticule before handing it over to

Black.

He swallowed a deep breath of air as he studied the invitation. His gut tightened. This was his worst nightmare coming to fruition. "We will stay in my townhouse for the night. First thing in the morning we will travel to London so she can prepare herself."

"I'd rather go riding," Lyssa said sweetly before adding a saucy smile for more affect.

What affect she was trying for, he wasn't positive. What he knew was that this spicy girl was trouble of the worst sort. This kind of behavior would have her increasing sooner than later. His breath left him in a slow whistle. She would be a handful.

So were her breasts. Possibly two handfuls.

This wasn't at all what he should be thinking. Ella would have his head if she understood the drift of his thoughts. With his eyes closed, he could almost taste her sweetness. She wasn't sweet. His scowl deepened further, if that was at all possible. This lady wasn't for him.

Bloody eyes, she was a debutante, innocent, a virgin. He meant to remind himself every day that he was her chaperone. She wanted to ride instead of dance. The deal was, he wouldn't mind a good hard ride with her. He groaned again. What the devil was Ella thinking leaving her with him? His thoughts were drowning him.

"Would you like to stay for dinner? Black asked as he rose from his chair meaning to summon Abernathy.

"No, Drake and I are leaving first thing in the morning. The ship sails with the tide. Don't believe Drake would be pleased if I detain the sailing. He's in a bloody hurry. Drake sent a guard in case it gets dark before I reach London. So, no worries in that regard."

Ella placed a kiss on Lyssa's cheek. "You behave yourself." She turned to Black. "Don't let her do something she'll regret. I trust you." Lyssa walked out with Ella. He chose to stay in his office until he heard the door close.

A few minutes later, Lyssa stood in the doorway. She was beautiful. "Can we ride?" Pink rose to her cheeks. "Can I pick out a horse? Aunty Ella told me you have about ten horses. She also said there is an Appaloosa." She whirled as if she was certain he would follow.

When he didn't trail along behind her, she was back in his office.

"Don't you think you should dress for dinner?" he asked.

"Thought we were riding. Doesn't take me only a few minutes to change my dress. Dinner won't be for another couple of hours. We have time." She grabbed his arm, attempting to tug him to her.

"You actually believe I would let you go now? Before we get a few things straight between us? There are rules for you to know, to learn as well as to obey. Consequences, too, if you misbehave. Don't want anything to happen to you on my watch."

He tried not to smirk at her expression, which turned from an arrogant grin to a scowl. Bemused, he waited for a comment or two. He didn't doubt there would be more than one remark coming from her saucy mouth. As long as he was putting his life on hold, she would do things his way.

"I don't misbehave unless I'm living with a tyrant," she shot out as she turned to flounce from the room, seemed to think better of her actions as she reappeared. "Not that I think that's what you are. Just stuffy!"

"Stodgy," he corrected with a chuckle then motioned to a chair near his desk. "Have a seat."

"Don't care for lemonade." She poured herself a glass of brandy. Smirked at him as if she wanted him to comment on her faux pas. "Cheers." She downed a healthy portion.

"By all means help yourself."

She placed herself on a wing chair in front of his desk. It was where she sat earlier. "Get on with it then." She sipped watching him with her vibrant blue eyes over the rim of the crystal she held to her lips.

"You will have gentlemen callers. They will meet with my approval before you go anywhere with them. There will be no rakes. I won't tolerate that."

"No notorious rakes for me." She grinned. "Well one, I guess one is meant to be in my future." She winked at him. Had the mettle to beam shamelessly. She shifted her position in the chair, her bosom making its debut more prominently than before. "You needn't worry overmuch. Already know the notorious rake I want to court me."

"Care to enlighten me? Give me a heads up so I can prepare myself. If need be, I will chase him off." He lifted an eyebrow mockingly.

This would be easier to keep her away from an unsuitable man if he knew who that man was. Any rake notorious or otherwise was unsuitable.

"You'll have to discover that for yourself," she taunted. "I've made up my mind though. Nothing you can do or say will discourage me."

"Good God, Lyssa, you've been in the city for a week. This is going to be your first ball. How could you have met someone so soon?"

"Just met the man today." Her smile widened. Behind her lips her straight teeth were pearly white her cheeks flushed a light shade of pink.

He ran that over in his head until the thought had nowhere to travel. Ah, he would discover who it was she favored soon he supposed. Perhaps the ball tomorrow night would tell him what he needed to learn. He could wait for the opportunity. He was a patient man. Whoever this man turned out to be, he would never get the opportunity to be alone with Lyssa Andrews. No, he would make sure this debutante remained a virgin until she wed.

"How can you know he's the one?" This sensation she was feeling couldn't possibly be grounded in fact. It had to be infatuation or perhaps lust. "You can't have known him for more than a minute.

"Love at first sight is how I see it." She lifted delicate shoulders, her grin giving away all that lustful fascination she must feel. "He checks off all the characteristics I want in a man."

He found himself to be too curious about these features she was going to describe. Was feeling as if he wanted to know what she thought. The devil…he had to ask. A half smile on his face, "What are those characteristics?"

"You want to know?" She sipped the brandy while her gaze roamed the length of him one too many times, finally resting on his eyes. Good God, at least she didn't stare at his mouth this time.

"I asked. Didn't I?"

She had the boldness to toss him a cheeky grin. "Well…to begin with…tall, he is very tall. I always wanted a man with black hair as well as sky blue eyes although those characteristics aren't as important as broad shoulders and stomach muscles that are hard as rocks. Don't like men who harbor paunches. Means they overindulge. Don't appreciate debauchery of any sort."

Shifting uncomfortably, he walked to the window. If he turned now, she would see the growing bulge beneath his trousers. "That's quite the list. You say you met this man today? What about his personality? That's important too." He rocked back on his heels, beginning to get his body under control.

"Oh, there is more. Would you like me to go on?" She sounded far too eager for his comfort.

Quickly, he strode to his desk to sit down behind it. Hide might be the more appropriate term. "I believe it's rather obvious what you want in a man. What you are thinking will not last a lifetime. There is more to a man than a hard stomach along with broad shoulders."

"I haven't even begun to elaborate." She shifted in her chair, one finger touching her chin as if in thought.

"Perhaps you should go dress for dinner." The need for distance from this little piece of baggage prompted the statement. He was uncomfortable with this description, which sounded far too close to him.

Finding someone suitable to court her would be his mission the next few weeks. He would have to find a way to take her mind from the mystery man. The sooner she was spoken for the better for him. The sooner she was out of his home he could breathe.

"You always dress for dinner? At my home we don't, simply because we're usually coming in from chores. We wash up. Mother won't let anyone into the house unless they've washed. Father always complains. His complaints are to tease mother"

"Suit yourself," he muttered wishing she would leave for a few minutes. "Dress or don't dress, I don't care."

"Well…" she set the empty brandy glass on his desk. "It might be fun to try out some of the new wardrobe Aunt Ella spent a fortune on for me. If I dress for you, can we see the horses after dinner?"

~ * ~

Lyssa was pleased. The moment she saw the man, she was in love with him. More than anything else she wanted to see him smile. She supposed being an earl he had a lot of duties that would keep him serious. Uncle Drake had a lot to do. He always found time to smile. Of course, his smiles were most always directed toward Aunt Ella as well as his children. She wanted Black to smile at her the way Uncle Drake grinned wickedly at Aunt Ella. Wished his gaze would lovingly follow her around the room just as her father watched her mother. The two of them were still madly in love with each other. She wanted a man who would be irrevocably in love with her in twenty or thirty years, longer if possible, if life looked on them favorably.

Lyssa stepped back from the mirror in her room. She turned sideways to examine herself, shoved her face close to the mirror to pinch her cheeks. She applied a small amount of makeup to highlight her eyes as well as her lips. It was not overdone still she wondered what he would think. Jess complained about makeup.

Now, she stood back. She wanted him to see more of her. Needed to find a means to tempt him. Jess, her brother, told her inadvertently all the ways to drive a man crazy with lust. Lyssa was certain it would take all that and more to entice the stuffy earl. She sensed he was a man of inordinate control. Known as a rake around town meant he would know women.

Damn and blast his power.

For now, she understood that he liked her breasts. He stared at them often enough. This gown was too modest by far. All she need do would be to remove the modesty piece. Quickly, she did just that.

She smiled. Her corset thrust her breasts upward. The valley between them was quite visible. Flaunting herself might not get the desired result. No, she meant to play coy as if she didn't understand what the sight would do to all his male sensibilities. He wouldn't know that aunty Ella made sure at the dressmakers all her gowns were suitable for a young debutante. This gown with the lacy piece removed was anything but appropriate.

Lyssa didn't care. Not when the man she meant to be her husband was the only male seeing more of her than was deemed proper. She shivered suddenly understanding implicitly there was a fine line that would separate her from a naïve debutante solely relying on her elders' opinions and the trollop he might believe her to be. No matter the cost though, she meant to be his. She could play the innocent with him. Never in her wildest thoughts would she do something so obvious when there would be other men seeing her.

With trepidation in her heart and mind, she walked down the long winding stairs to the drawing room. Her heart thundered beneath her chest pounding painfully. What little oxygen she could draw into her lungs did little to help her nerves. Negligently, he leaned against the mantel by the fireplace. Instinctively, she absorbed a deep breath of air that didn't seem to go past her throat.

Her wish came true.

As she prayed, his gaze rested on her breasts, specifically on the exposed valley between them.

The ever-present scowl that seemed to be always a part of his features deepened. It appeared he wrestled his gaze from her breasts to her face. Her smile was hesitant. She tilted her head demurely, innocently, while she fluttered her lashes.

"You look lovely tonight," he murmured as he stepped forward offering her his arm before proceeding to the dining room as if she wasn't showing him exactly what she shouldn't.

His comment was not what she expected. Damn and blast, she anticipated a comment of disapproval. His glower certainly spoke that way. Perhaps he was biding his time.

He always glowers.

What did she foresee? After the first sighting of her blatantly revealed charms, it appeared he ignored her. Found no interest in what she deliberately exhibited. He pulled out a chair for her to sit before walking to his own chair. All the while, his gaze remained fixed on her face. She ran her tongue along her bottom lip then repeated the performance. Jess told her men couldn't resist a woman who did so. She stared at his mouth.

"What are we having for dinner?" She set the tip of one finger on the moistened bottom lip imploring his gaze to rest there also.

It seemed to her, he looked as if he wanted to devour her as his gaze slipped from her mouth to her breasts then back to her mouth. His silver eyes darkened to pewter.

"Haven't the vaguest notion, nor do I care." His bland voice told her he was indeed seeing her in a different light. He wasn't immune to her charms.

"Oh. Aren't you hungry?" She positively hoped he was now hungry for her. Lyssa imagined the way his mouth would feel when his lips covered hers as well as when his tongue touched upon hers.

The dinner proceeded in stilted silence. As he ignored her, Lyssa's appetite dissolved. She picked at her food. Whatever thoughts he formed about her were going to remain in his head. She fidgeted with her silverware. Looked at him beneath lowered lashes for heart stopping seconds.

When he sat back seemingly finished, his hands folded and resting on his hard belly, he observed her. Finally, he spoke, "Would you like to pick out a horse? I'll have your mount brought into town for the duration of our visit. The duchess told me two days after the ball there is to be a recital. You will sing. You are supposedly very talented even though you deny the fact. Ella also pointed out you have the voice of an angel." He met her gaze with his own. "Do you? Do you have the voice of an angel? Perhaps your aunt is prejudice."

"I wouldn't know." She wanted to toss the glass of wine in his face. Needed to spark some emotion rather than the bland indifference he courted her with. Instead of his interest flaming, she received bored unresponsiveness looks for her efforts. Perhaps she needed to try something different, another ploy Jess spoke of.

Well, tomorrow would be another day. She would think on the measures she could employ tonight. There would be time for further thought during the carriage ride to the city. They headed to the stable. Outside, the night was warm. Before she left the house, she wrapped a shawl around her shoulders.

Inside the earl's stable, the sight of magnificent horseflesh greeted her. She ran her hand down the nose of every horse, sweet-talking her way down one side then the other.

"The Appaloosa, I want that one to ride while I'm here. The mare is gorgeous." She wanted that horse forever. The only way she would accomplish that was if she won the earl's heart. The stuffy man was proving more difficult than she thought.

What had she believed? That one look at her cleavage would leave him drooling for her. That he would bend his knee to the ground then propose she spend a lifetime with him.

Hah!

She now understood a bit of cleavage would not bend a notorious rake to her will. He probably saw cleavage most every day of his life. The only reason Ella picked him for the chaperone duties were because she knew he wouldn't cave to her wiles. Of course, Ella didn't know she fell in love with the man the moment she saw him. Her aunt also didn't know she would do absolutely anything to win his heart.

"I'll have the mare brought to the city tomorrow morning. Unless you would like to ride her there."

"You would allow that?" Lyssa didn't comprehend the underlying note of sarcasm in her question. What she did note was the lifting of his eyebrow.

"I'm not the ogre you seem to believe me to be or a tyrant as you implied earlier. If you wish to ride part of the way to the city, I've no objections. For myself, I do prefer a good horse beneath me instead of a closed in carriage where there is little to no air to breathe. That environment makes a man claustrophobic."

His comment about the ogre-tyrant stung. "It's just the rules you laid out for me. I don't like to think I have to ask every time I want to do something or go somewhere. That's not something that has been a part of my life. I rarely have to ask permission."

"The rules are for your protection, not to make you irritable. Since I've taken over this, I mean to do the chaperoning right. I'm assuming where you live, you've trusted ranch hands that oversee your quest around the range."

"Me? My protection. I don't need to be safe guarded." She placed a hand on her chest exactly where she wanted his gaze to travel. "Irritable? I'm not the least bit..." she broke off then realizing that was exactly what she was, although her burgeoning annoyance was his fault.

He let his head fall back as he roared with laughter. "Yes, you. Irritable as well as conniving. I know Ella well enough to know she wouldn't allow you to wear a dress that revealed so much of you. Where is the modesty piece? If you show up in something so skimpy tomorrow, I'll march you upstairs then dress you myself."

That was the best idea she'd ever heard. Lyssa beamed at his suggestion then thinking better of her smirk, dropped her hand, noting with satisfaction the direction of his gaze. She set her hands on her hips while she thrust out her large chest for his perusal. Perhaps she did interest him.

He turned away.

She smirked.

"You should retire for the night." His voice was gruff, didn't sound at all like him.

She recalled his father's voice when he wanted her mother in the bedroom. They were much the same. "We should ride. The moon is bright. It will make the jaunt enjoyable."

"Do you need help with your saddle?" he asked while he leaned against the stall, his pose giving none of his emotions away.

She was thrilled he wanted to ride tonight. Had not expected agreement to her proposal. "No, just point me to the saddle you'd like me to use. I've always saddled my horses. As long as it is not too heavy, I'm fine."

"Even in that gown? Never mind, I suppose you ride astride too." The tone could not be ignored censure seemed to coat every word as if he disapproved. His annoyance over this small issue surprised her.

Damn and blast, the earl was going to have to get used to her if they were to do well together. "Bottom line, if forced to ride sidesaddle, I'd fall off. I cannot ride in such a ridiculous manner. Have never done it. Have you?" Her sarcasm as well as her meaning was obvious even to a deaf ear.

One eyebrow rose. This was his turn to smirk. There was no other word for the expression. Well, she wanted to see a full-blown grin not a smirk at her position. He went on to say, "A woman should understand the complexities of riding both ways. The nobility here in London look down their long-pointed noses at a woman who chooses to be too unique. I would warn you, though, to be aware of that fact. As for me, don't see how a woman stays on a horse when she doesn't open her legs for the ride."

She comprehended his words held a double entendre. She just didn't understand the second meaning. Mayhap she should ask. No, another time might work better. "Do you?" Lyssa was creeping closer to losing her formidable temper at the man.

"Do I what?" he asked sounding totally unknowing as to the question at hand.

"Look down your long-pointed nose at women who...? Who don't open their legs to ride?" She couldn't repeat the words. If he answered yes to the question, she had a great deal of work cut out for her.

She was annoyed and irritated by his bark of laughter. He didn't answer her question.

Faced with the saddling, she grunted. Heaved. Grunted again while she tried to saddle the horse. Despite her best effort the damn saddle was too heavy for her. At home she had a saddle she could easily take on and off her horse. She let out a puffy breath of air thoroughly frustrated with her inability to prove herself competent to this man she wanted to adore even at this moment she was having difficulty doing so. In this she wanted to prove to the earl she was capable. He'd already told her she couldn't pick out a stallion because her arms were too scrawny to keep the animal under wraps. Now this. Giving up she finally admitted defeat. "It's too heavy."

His grin widened. He told her so, by his expression. If she couldn't presume to lift a saddle, she wouldn't have the muscle if the stallion decided he didn't like the direction she pointed him to keep the horse in line. She had strong legs, knew how to use her knees to guide a horse.

He didn't say anything. In a blink her Appaloosa was saddled. She could not complain over much. The mare was gorgeous. Her front was a blanket of dark brown. Her white flanks sported irregular shaped brown spots. After Lyssa mounted, she set off at a brisk canter, not caring if he wasn't ready.

Suddenly, he rode beside her. He rode bare back. His hair rakishly long flew in the breeze they created. The man was as majestic as the nearly pure gray stallion he rode. Black was one with his horse.

Magnificent.

Splendid.

At the sight of man and beast working so well together, her heart beat double time. Lyssa knew all along the man would ride splendidly. Every muscle in his body exuded primal masculinity. Before she could move her horse away, he grabbed the reins.

The earlier smirk vanished to become another deep scowl. "Never take off without me again," his words a low growl. "Not only is the night dark, you have no notion where you are going."

Taken aback momentarily, she rambled, "The moon." She looked upward to the black velvet of the night then back to him. "Is bright." It wasn't. However, she thought the suggestion might help him overlook her foolishness.

"Manages to conceal in shadows what one should be able to see. As I said, do not ever ride alone. I will be with you or you won't ride. I can just as easily have the mounts taken back to Blackmore estate if you choose to disregard my ruling."

Even though she knew he was right, indignation rose, fluttered in her chest before her furry erupted. She wasn't accustomed to be chastised so blatantly. "You cannot dictate to me! I'm not a little girl." At that moment she experienced a decided change of heart where the man was concerned. Damn and blast he hadn't bothered to saddle his stallion.

"Stop acting like a spoiled brat."

"How dare you?" She wanted to spur her horse forward, escape this humiliation.

After that, he had the boldness to remain silent. The man wasn't going to gift her with a retort. Well, he'd find out soon enough she was a liberated woman. She would come and go as she pleased with or without his consent. Telling him her every move would preclude her future with the man. She had to set him straight before doing so was too late.

First things first, before she could have a future, she needed him to see her as someone other than the helpless debutante he was supposed to chaperone.

"Do you understand?" He tossed the reins back at her. "Do I have to elaborate further?" He cocked an insipid eyebrow.

The tilted supercilious eyebrow was a gesture she positively wasn't enamored of. If she never saw him raise another eyebrow at her, the moment would be too soon. "I know what I think as well as want. No one has ever tried to be my watchdog. At home I was allowed to come and go as I pleased. That won't change here no matter your commands."

By his expression she comprehended her words would never sway him to allow the freedom she craved. There were other ways to get what she wanted as she understood she could turn the situation around to her favor.

"Very well, where are we going?"

"Your easy compliance doesn't ring true, Lys. It would behoove you to take my words seriously. If you don't, you won't enjoy the consequences of your disobedience."

Consequences of her disobedience?

He was just too damn calm. It seemed he thought he had the entire world under his thumb. She didn't intend to find herself under his thumb despite her mushrooming love for him. She paused in thought. Perhaps it would be nice to find herself under his big muscular body. Her imagination kept falling short of those feelings though she wished to discover more.

Prudently, Lyssa decided not to pursue the topic of consequences coupled with disobedience. "Where did you get this horse?" That question seemed to be a good diversion for her.

"Changing the subject, are we? Maybe that is a splendid idea. I did, however, expect you to ask about the punishments. I would expect you to be curious. Your overactive imagination must be doing tailspins."

She tossed her head back. Pins holding her hair in place flew. Strands of her long hair fell down her back. The feeling of her hair unbound always delighted her. It was also a means, as Jess told her, to catch a man's attention. A man liked to run his hands through a woman's hair he told her one day when he found her cursing the tangles.

"There won't be any consequences to my behavior." She literally loved the slant of his mouth, as he seemed to mull over her words.

"Why is that?"

She detected a note of laughter in his question. He was pursuing the topic. She liked that while she did want to learn what he would do if she disobeyed one of his rules, she wasn't going to push his hand tonight. She would be a model prisoner to the tyrant's ruling power; the very picture of decorum until she wasn't.

She flashed him a saucy grin. "Your rules won't be broken by me. Hence, there will be no punishment or consequences. Nonetheless, I don't believe you've the right to dictate as you seem wont to do." She meant to be constantly at his side asking permission for this or that. He wasn't going to find a single moment of peace for himself. By the time she finished with him, he would cave to her every wish.

"You are welcome to your belief. Come, let's return to the stable. The carriage will depart at six."

If he expected to get a reaction from the early hour, he wouldn't. Working on the ranch all her life, she woke up early. The hour of departure was nothing new to her. She wasn't enamored of lying around in bed. Although, she paused in thought, while she stared at his profile, lying in bed all morning with that man might indeed be something she would enjoy.

"So late," she asked while she lowered her lashes for a moment. "We could leave earlier. Didn't you tell me I could ride the Appaloosa?"

"You can, you might not…well, it's a long ride. You might want to take the carriage the latter part of the trip."

She bristled, her back rigid with the implication he slashed out to her. Truly, he had no idea. This man actually didn't know who she was. "I can sit a horse for hours on end. My father's ranch is a working ranch, you understand. Can you?" she challenged. Couldn't help the grin when she looked at his sour disposition.

"We shall see."

She pulled a sharp breath of air into her lungs before she sent it out in a rush of understanding. "You don't like me." Her blurted words got her another frown from him. If he didn't like her, she would have to change that before she could win him over. Maybe she shouldn't be so sarcastic. She did want him to like her before he loved her. She thought of her parents' love story. Her mother liked her father then she despised him for what he was, after that she turned an about-face when she fell in love.

"It isn't that," he began by hedging. "Your presence here has come as a shock. This is a bachelor abode as is my home in London. Never expected Ella to call in a favor such as this one. Don't know what to do with a young debutante."

"It's true. Ella did."

"Ella did," he repeated. "I'm sorely inept at chaperoning a young lady, a debutante."

"Can you please stop referring to me as a beginner. I'm not." The gallant earl did not miss her huffy tone.

"You are not a beginner? Then what pray tell are you?" Once more an eyebrow lifted. "You have vast knowledge as well as experience in the art of love? In what men and women do together?"

"Didn't say that," she muttered dispirited by the turn in conversation. It seemed every word she spoke made matters between them worse.

"Then you are a beginner."

"Told you I wasn't," she shot back, determined to make him understand.

"Are you purposely trying to confound me?"

"Well, no, of course not. I don't know anything about love, save what Jess tells me." Lyssa had not meant to blurt that. He would query her. She didn't want him to know things about her until she was ready.

"Who, pray tell, is Jess?

"My brother."

"Your brother talks to you about love?" His voice faltered for a moment. He seemed to come a bit unhinged.

Lyssa would love to know what he was actually thinking. "As I said before, he doesn't know he's telling me. He's either talking to his friends or he allows little things to slip. I've seen mother and father in bed. She's always hiding beneath the sheets. He's always laughing. They both tell me to leave. Since I've grown up, haven't ventured into their domain."

"Thank God!"

In her defense she felt as if an explanation was needed. "We were little. Sometimes I'd go in there because of a nightmare. Sometimes I just needed to cuddle."

"You never saw them…"

She laughed at his look of horror. "Never saw much. They were always underneath the covers. Heard some things though." She grinned at his look of displeasure. "Have a few thoughts. You could tell me or explain more thoroughly."

"This conversation needs an end."

"I was going to ask you what some of what I overheard meant. Most the time it was just masculine groans along with puffy little feminine sighs. I did hear father scream mother's name once."

"Lyssa." He waved his hand in the air. "This is something your new beau will want to speak of with you or teach you. It is not appropriate for me to commence explaining to you what any of this means." His voice turned husky. She had an idea what that might mean.

It was appropriate, she wanted to yell at him. You're my new beau. "Didn't think about that," she told him feeling subdued for the time being. It was far too soon to tell him he was the man she fell in love with. There were no thoughts in her head as to how to proceed with that information. To fight another day would be her mantra. Tomorrow would be soon enough. The ball would serve her purpose. Jealousy might be a good ploy to utilize. After tonight, she didn't think he would be jealous if he watched her dance with someone else. He told her in vivid terms that he wouldn't allow her to be in the presence of a known rake.

None except him. She beamed.

The thought did give her good reason to smile at least for a few seconds.

They were at the stable. The night ride seeming to be over before the jaunt began.

"Do any of your lady friends ever scream your name?" she asked while she watched him hang her saddle on a rail. Lyssa kept her face averted. She heard Jess speaking about just that very thing. "Jess told his friend that the woman of the night before screamed his name."

"Lyssa…" he growled. "Enough questions."

"Does it puff up your chest when that happens? Jess says it makes him feel really good because it means he gave his lover pleasure. Do you give your lovers pleasure? I know you have them. So, don't deny anything."

"Wouldn't dream of denial," he said his voice lacking emotion.

"Is that what it means?" she persisted while she understood she ventured into dangerous territory. "I'd like to feel pleasure, whatever that is, in my lover's arms."

"Lyssa!"

She looked at him. Well, her gaze riveted on him. Followed the line of his body to his crotch. He looked different. Immediately, as if he had something he wanted to hide, he moved to the other side of his stallion to give him food. She wondered at that.

"You can't blame me for my curiosity. While I told you I'm not a beginner, there are questions in my head I've no answer for. Do your ladies scream your name?" Courageously, or maybe foolishly, she asked again. She understood he wasn't at all pleased with the question.

Keeping her queries in her head was not something she was used to doing. "A girl should know. I do believe if you gave me pleasure, I'd scream out Blacky."

The tick in his jaw increased in speed. "It's time you went to bed. I'll finish up here."

"I can take a hint."

"Can you? I haven't noticed."

"You should look more closely. I didn't mean to make you angry. You're so easy to tease. If I wait for you, will you walk me to my bed? Will you tell me more about pleasure?"

"Lyssa!"

~ * ~

"Not at all certain paring Lyssa with the earl was a good idea," Drake Montgomerie leaned on the rail of the ship as they pulled up anchor.

In a few minutes they would leave London behind. Their search for Nickie would take them east then north onto the North Sea. Their first stop would be McClellan Castle. If Nickie wasn't there, they would continue to Dornoch, Collin's ancestral home. If not there, they would try the Earl of Blackmore's hunting lodge in the far reaches of northern Scotland.

"It's actually all wrong to allow Black to chaperone Lyssa Andrews. I do, however, believe with all my heart she is the breath of fresh air the man needs. I'm hoping a bit of matchmaking on my part will help the man. Do you realize the girl was so bold to tell Black she would make him smile? He's been a good friend. I want to see him happy. Truly believe Lyssa can do that for him," Ella said while she leaned against her husband, his strong arms surrounding her. Drake always, well, almost always made her happy. Once she got by that first rocky decision she made, she understood he was the only man for her. It wasn't easy though, putting her reputation on the line.

"What if she runs off with him?" Drake asked squeezing her closer to him. "We'll have two charges to search for."

"He will resist her until he can't do so any longer. If that happens, I believe he will marry her in the way of his people, the Sioux. That will suffice until she can wed him in the way of the English. I did see the way they looked at each other." Behind her Ella felt his hard arousal. It pleased her.

"He will compromise her. You know that. Is that what you want?" Drake said as he placed tiny kisses along the back of his wife's neck. His hand now cupping her breast beneath the shawl she wore.

She turned in his arms. His kiss stopped the words she planned to say from bubbling from her lips. When he finished the kiss, "Black will resist her until she has him firmly wrapped around her little finger. As I said, he will wed her in the way of Sioux."

"Think so?" One of his ducal eyebrows shot upward in a perfect arch.

"Know so," Ella told him feeling smug about her plan to find a wife for Black as well as a husband for Lyssa. The pair was made for each other. "Actually, don't care if he makes love to her before the wedding. We both know someone who did just that. All turned out for the best in their case, now, didn't it? I'm not a hypocrite where love is concerned. Will never judge, especially my nieces.

"You're making a damn bad chaperone for your charges. What did the first duchess say to you?"

Quickly she shot back, "Time will tell."

"For now, I'm going to accept what you've told me. Lyssa is your sister's daughter. She's been brought up in the west. I'm sure there will be no end to surprises for Black. She seems to have a way of saying what's on her mind without thinking."

"Like I said, a breath of fresh air for the stodgy man."

"Impulsiveness is not always the best."

"True, all that you say. I'm not implying their journey will be easy. It won't. I know Lyssa is in love with him."

"If she is anything like you, he will not be able to resist her persistence," Drake said as he ran his hands along Ella's arms.

She shivered with the passion he so easily created. "He will find himself blindsided by her innocent nature. She will be blatantly surprising. While she is nothing like the white women he is used to, he will fall victim to her honesty. He will want to touch her, make love to her. Eventually, he will give in to his needs."

"You believe he will keep his hands to himself."

"No, however the question is how long it will take him to give in to his passion for her. I saw that desire blossom the first time he looked at Lyssa. The passion shimmered in her eyes too."

"Just be advised this scheme of yours could all backfire."

Ella pulled in a large breath of air, thinking on all Drake said. "I will take that under advisement. Right now, however, our biggest concern is Nickie. I'm sure she also follows her heart. She might be increasing by the time we reach her. She will have a big decision to make."

"The McInnis lad has a great deal to account for. A man can't run off with a well-born lady. He's not above the law."

"I won't have you threatening the lad. Not when I'm sure the pair are in love and will eventually do the right thing. Just as we eventually did."

Drake turned her in his arms. His kiss was devastatingly sweet. Ella knew Drake would do as he damn well pleased in this matter. Damn the consequences. If Nickie loved the rake, she would fight for him.

"You know I will. I plan to put the fear of God in the young'un. He has to understand the family he is dealing with. When he does, their future together will go much easier for him. Shall we retire down stairs to discover further pleasures?"

"Thought you would never ask."

Other Books by Christine Young
Available at Rogue Phoenix Press

Connal's Eternal Love
Sweet McKenna Book One

A few days shy of All Hallows' Eve Connal McKenna, Laird of Clan Chattan stands on the parapets of his castle. Bonfires line the hillsides while his clan prepares for the upcoming festivities. Drawn by the whispering of the wind, Connal McKenna feels a strange restlessness in his soul. Setting out to discover the wickedness that is calling to him, he discovers his mate. With gentle words and sensuous kisses, the auburn-eyed highlander conquers his mate, the beautiful, defiant Wynnie Adair who he comes upon during an evening ride. She must ultimately put her trust in the only man who can save her from the ruthless plans of her father and succumb to his gentle coaxing.

In Brady's Arms
Sweet McKenna Book Two

Forced to run from the only home she knows, beautiful, headstrong Lillian Townsends seeks shelter in the wild highlands where the McKenna clan live. Trying to avoid a betrothal contract signed by her stepfather to an aging lord, she is desperate to find a means to sidestep the inevitable, including a marriage to the oldest son of the laird. Lilly is enamored of the young lord who pursues her with unrelenting determination flashing his devilishly handsome charms. She is hard pressed to resist.

Besotted from the first moment Brady McKenna sees Lilly, he is determined to find a means to coax her into his arms and bed. With only the promise of carnal pleasure as his mistress, Brady relentlessly pursues the woman who has unwittingly forged a place in his heart. She is like no other woman, proud, defiant and enchanting. Despite his father's advice to stay away from her, he cannot. He boldly seeks her out and makes her his own.

Nobody but Walker
Sweet McKenna Book Three

The Highland Lass...

She was brought up, adored and loved by a doting mother and father ardently protected by her brothers. She was everything sweet and innocent until she was faced with betrayal and an unexpected and out of wedlock pregnancy. When she gave her love to a man who couldn't return her passion and commitment, she was left devastated and furious. Faced with the loss of her child if she didn't comply to his demands, Crissie McKenna followed him to Belfast then on to his country home to discover he was already married.

...The Irishman

Stunned to find out his one and only encounter with the woman he wanted to love forever created a child, Walker Endicott, Earl of Briarwood, claimed his child as his only heir. Walker threatened all her previously held values even while he thrilled her senses. From the moment he first saw her to the second she ran after him begging him to make love to her, his captivating masculinity held her fascinated. In his arms she would know tempestuous passion, bitter despair, and a soaring joy that would humble them both before the power of love.

Roby's Moonlit Night
Sweet McKenna Book Four

Once she'd been a pampered child with high expectations for her future blessed with love. Then she became an innocent pawn in a terrible game of greed and power. Now, with a noose around her neck, Pippa was to hang before she had the chance to unveil the men who drove her from her home, before she had the chance to live.

Roby McKenna was a man blessed with endless charm and wit. While he searched for his eternal love across the Atlantic in a new land, he would have to come home to find her. His silver blue eyes could sparkle with amusement or harden to steel gray with displeasure. He had all the women a man could want or need. As he grew older, mistresses were not enough. A quirk of fate brought him to the gallows, a spark of destiny made him claim the condemned Pippa as his bride.

Made for Houston
Sweet McKenna Book Five

Leah Kennedy is as wary of people as she is strikingly beautiful. However, the shocking death of her father that forever changed her girlhood has left her terrified of the very love she desperately longs for. Only in the untamed splendor of the Scottish crags does she feel safe from the feelings she stirs in men and the cruel mockery of Selkirk's villagers.

Debonair, well-educated doctor Houston Stuart has turned his back on social privilege along with professional honors to set up a medical practice in the lowlands of Scotland. There, serving those who need him the most, he hopes to forget the bitter memories and disillusionment that disturb his days.

Coincidence brings the cultured doctor and this fey mountain girl together. Something as bizarre as destiny disrupts the obstacle of birth and breeding, stubborn pride and fear which has kept them apart...as each seeks to heal the other's wounds with a raw passion neither can deny and all the odds against them cannot defeat.

My Sweet Broc
Bad Boys Book One

He's a bad bad boy...

Broc Wallace is a fun-loving rake who never thought any beautiful woman could melt his heart. He lives life in the present enjoying the camaraderie of his friends and the pleasures of his mistress. When Bliss races into his life, he is ill prepared to deal with her secrets or give up the tenor of his life. When the truth is revealed, he finds himself unable to forgive and forget the betrayal.

...but she's sweet for him

Bliss MacTavish knows she's playing with fire when she refuses to tell this bad boy her name. He tempts her with sweet whispers of seduction knowing her innocent nature will be unable to refuse all he yearns to give her. Deciding to follow her heart, she finds the repercussions more than she bargains for when she gives herself to this bad boy.

Crazy for Cam
Bad Boys Book Two

He's a bad bad boy...

Lord Cam MacEwen, Viscount of Rosehill, tries his best to be proper and court the lady of his dreams in the acceptable way. The feat proves impossible when the lady in question uses every means at her disposal to tempt him. He fights his jealousy for another man as well as the need to make her his own, finally giving in to her irresistible passion.

...but she's crazy for him.

Chelsea MacTavish wants the bad boy she fell in love with and kissed just before her eighteenth birthday. With feminine wiles and irresistible allure, the sensuous lady plans to best Cam at his game of hearts and make him forget his need to court her properly.

Falling for Flynt
Bad Boys Book Three

He's a bad, bad boy...

Fascinated by Hope's loss of memory yet haunted by her sultry beauty, Flynt is irresistibly drawn to the stoic miss—and into her troubles with the sultan who wants her for himself. When he discovers she is the sister of his best friend, his pride keeps him from pursuing her and making her his.

...but she's falling for him.

Raised in a harem but now penniless, alone and without her memory, Hope must discover a way to remember all that she has lost. She finds a way to continue with her life as a servant in Flynt's home. The first sight of Flynt steals Hope's breath as well as her heart. Can she overcome her fears and give herself to the man she fell in love with.

Dancing With Donal
Bad Boys Book Four

He's a bad bad boy...

Once a bad boy always a bad boy, Donal Chamberlin's carefree ways come crashing down around him when he meets the ravishingly beautiful Daryl MacTavish, the innocent little sister of one of his best friends. He is determined to win her heart as he sets his sights on marriage and an heir. His past gets in the way of his quest when a woman he once loved threatens Daryl's life.

...but she's dancing with him.

Daryl has seen the control her sister's husbands hold over them. She yearns for a life where she makes decisions for herself. No man will have power over her. But no man kisses her the way Donal does. No man can make her forget all her goals leaving her helpless to give up her dreams. Yet Donal is determined to dance through all the barriers she thrust in front of him, pursuing her until she says yes.

Loving Leslie
Bad Boys Book Five

He's a bad bad boy...

Leslie Stewart, Duke of Southcliff is stoic, set in his ways, a spy who is used to having his life well ordered. He expects life to continue on in this perfectly conventional fashion. He assumes his bad boy status while keeping mamas and debutantes at arm's length. An heir is needed but Leslie has every intention of finding a woman who doesn't covet his wealth and tittle. He is irresistibly drawn to the headstrong young lady who becomes more beautiful as she develops into a woman.

...but she is loving him.

When Leslie kisses Lacie MacTavish, she knows even at the tender age of fifteen this is the man of her dreams. Forced to wait until she comes of age, Lacie withdraws into herself. Now she is eighteen and Leslie has returned from a mission for the British Government ready to claim her as his bride. She refuses him and he must find a way to seduce her and in the process create a burning passion within her, which she cannot deny.

Pleasing Arie
Bad Boys Book Six

He's a bad bad boy...

Arie Demir has never been denied anything in his life. He takes what he wants. What he undeniably yearns for is the beautiful redheaded spitfire he sees in a restaurant in Glasgow. At every turn, she confuses him by disputing his power over her. Alison refuses to accept the fact he owns her. While Arie tries desperately with patience and tenderness to drive her wild with new sensations, his scorching kisses ignite the fires of her very soul to make her understand he is all she will ever want.

...but is she pleasing him?

Alison Fletcher never expected to find herself kidnapped and sold to a whorehouse then bought by a Turkish sultan to become his slave. She vows to never surrender to the arrogant man who believes he owns her.

She is stunned by the magnificently handsome man who awaits her compliance. Unexpectedly, she finds Arie the lesser of all the evils. The hidden depths of his mesmerizing dark brown eyes hold her into their power; his muscular embrace makes her weak with desire. She is his to do with as he wishes.

Graham's Wicked Kiss
Bad Boys Book Seven

He's a bad bad boy...

Graham Chamberlin is stunned to find three young boys dangling from the trees lining the drive to Runningmead Manner. On further inspection, he is astonished at their obsession to protect a young woman who has been brutalized by her pimp. The woman he discovers hiding in a third-floor attic room is gravely injured. He takes the silver haired stowaway under his wing. Clearly, Graham's new guest is a lady with many secrets. He is determined to unlock all the mysteries surrounding her.

...But she can't resist his wicked kiss.

The years since Ria left the convent where she was raised have been a nightmare. Her secrets are dangerous—as is the powerful man determined to find her. Handsome Graham Chamberlin is clearly a gentleman with secrets of his own, but staying with him could mean the difference between life and death for Ria. With each passing day, her handsome host turns Ria's convalescence into an increasingly sensual escape. Now her greatest challenge may be imagining anything less than a future in his arms.

Feeling Etienne's Love
Bad Boys Book Eight

He's a bad bad boy...

Etienne Dubois is the son of a wealthy vineyard owner who craves the excitement of putting his life on the line. Working with the French government and as a confidant of King Charles X give him reasons for living. An encounter with a beautiful young woman in a plush bordello in Paris has him rethinking his roguish ways. Etienne never expects to become a father especially from one encounter with an innocent prostitute who whispers his name and has him rethinking his well-ordered life.

...But she can't help feeling his love.

Elisa Moreau, the only daughter of Angelique Moreau, the owner of an exclusive bordello in Bordeaux, France, has loved Etienne Dubois since she was six. Unfortunately, until an unexpected encounter at a brothel in Paris puts the two of them in the same room, Etienne doesn't even know she exists. Confused but wanting Etienne and this chance meeting to never end, Elisa gives herself to the man who has held her heart in hands for what seems like her entire life.

All I Want Is Link
Bad Boys Book Nine

He's a bad bad boy...

Merry Stewart is wildly unpredictable. Left alone to run wild over the Bordeaux and Scottish countryside she becomes impetuous and daringly bold. Over the years, she's found she can bedevil her softhearted brothers into allowing her exploits to go unnoticed. As a young woman she has learned she can do as she pleases when she pleases. Now, Merry has set her amorous sights on the Duke of Weston—a man she has never met but has every intention of marrying. No other suitor will satisfy her—

especially not the exceptionally striking, horse breeder, Devlin Mathews.

...she's the woman of his desires.

Posing as commoner Devlin Mathews to escape a potentially fatal confrontation, Devlin is enthralled and infuriated by the audacious, duke-hunting dark haired vixen. Bedeviled at every opportunity, he finds dealing with the tiny she-devil exasperating as well as intriguing. Without revealing his true identify, the infamous rogue pledges to thwart Merry's plans to wed the man of her dream-never imagining the bewitching strategist would turn out to be the only woman he would ever dream of marrying.

Devlin's Angel
Bad Boys Book Ten

He's a bad bad boy...

Merry Stewart is wildly unpredictable. Left alone to run wild over the Bordeaux and Scottish countryside she becomes impetuous and daringly bold. Over the years, she's found she can bedevil her softhearted brothers into allowing her exploits to go unnoticed. As a young woman she has learned she can do as she pleases when she pleases. Now, Merry has set her amorous sights on the Duke of Weston—a man she has never met but has every intention of marrying. No other suitor will satisfy her—especially not the exceptionally striking, horse breeder, Devlin Mathews.

...she's the woman of his desires.

Posing as commoner Devlin Mathews to escape a potentially fatal confrontation, Devlin is enthralled and infuriated by the audacious, duke-hunting dark haired vixen. Bedeviled at every opportunity, he finds dealing with the tiny she-devil exasperating as well as intriguing. Without revealing his true identify, the infamous rogue pledges to thwart Merry's plans to wed the man of her dream-never imagining the bewitching strategist would turn out to be the only woman he would ever dream of marrying.

Foolish for Piper

The pickpocket...

Piper has spent her life surviving the streets of St. Giles Parish in London, a den of iniquity and crime. Masquerading as a boy she escapes the whorehouses the young girls are sent to as they come of age. The day she encounters Brett MacLachlan begins the same as every other one. When she picks his pocket, she has no idea her life is going to change irreversibly.

...and the mark

Handsome aristocrat Brett MacLachlan has come to London for his amusement only to find his world turned upside down by a thief and her dog. From the moment he spots her, Brett knows there is something intrinsically wrong. In his arms, Piper discovers passion and joy. Yet secrets of her past haunt her, and a scar will tell the true tale as well as her identity.

Taylor's Destiny

She traveled to another time and place to change destiny...

Enjoying a day of sailing, Taylor Maxwell never expected after a suffering a concussion she would wake up in another century. A resilient independent woman in the twenty-first century, the blond beauty is ill prepared for life in the 1800s. Her first sight of the naval captain who rescues her makes her heart stop, giving her hope for her future.

His life is transformed by a woman who appears from nowhere...

Born to a life of ease, Reid Stewart defies the dictates of those born to aristocracy and chooses a life of adventure in the navy and as a spy for the crown. When he discovers a nearly naked woman on the bow of small sailing ship, his heart warms. His love for Taylor and his need to protect her from a man who pursues her might cost him his life as well as hers.

Caitlin's Duke

She played a fiddle in an Irish pub...

Caitlin O'Shea Is the most beautiful woman Roc Leighton has ever seen. With her blue violet eyes and long black hair she captivates him. In turn he mesmerizes Caitlin. Caught in the power of his gaze as he watches her, she is wise enough to know he desires her but will never give his heart to her. Caitlin has vowed to never be any man's mistress.

And fell in love with an English Lord...

Roc knows the first time he watches her play the fiddle and dance around the pub, she will be his next mistress. Despite her protest, he will find a way to convince her that her place is with him. While Caitlin's determination to keep her vows, fate takes a cruel turn and she is forced to seek refuge with Roc.

Catching Meara
Book One in the McKenna Clan Series

Meara Thorton was a feisty, world-class computer hacker—cornered by the FBI and shockingly given the chance to be their newly acquired technical analyst. Brilliant and intuitive, yet aching with the loss of everyone she has cared about, her restless heart led her to discover a love she fought and a world she didn't know could possibly exist.

Sweet Sexy Sadie
Book Two in the McKenna Clan Series

From the first time Sadie's eyes met those of Brody McKenna in the hot Sierra Madre Mountains, theirs was a potent attraction—not gentle, slow, and easy, but hot, hard, and all-consuming. The daughter of a dysfunctional family, Sadie had dreams no man could wrench from her with hot sex and an all-consuming passion. She'd challenge this alpha male with all the strength she possessed. But her red hair, fiery temperament, and indomitable spirit obsessed Brody...and he knew he had to find a way to show her he was more than he appeared and convince her to make a life with him.

Sweet Misbehavin'
Book Three in the McKenna Clan Series

Cast adrift after fleeing the home of Jokul, the ice demon, Atantsi, a firestarter, grew to womanhood as she moved through time to keep the demon from finding her. Though stubborn and courageous, she was ill prepared to use powers she had not been taught. Her first sight of the intoxicating Carr McKenna left her breathless, and her second encounter gave her hope for a future she never thought she had.

A playboy, a second son and a shifter, a man who thought his life would be carefree, Carr McKenna was shocked to discover the woman he'd paid as an escort is a firestarter who is running for her life. He is the leader of all the McKennas around the world and that he has multiple powers. His passion for Margo and the need to defend her might cost him his life as well as hers.

Sweet Talkin' Sugar
Book Four in the McKenna Clan Series

Lyonesse McKenna, was dreaming, or was she? From the instant Lyn saw Deacon McClain across a black jack table in a crowed Las Vegas casino the unmistakable attraction sent Lyn's senses flying into overdrive. Her family of shapeshifters believed in soul mates. She'd always been skeptical yet she couldn't help but question the way her heart sped when he looked at her.

When Deacon appeared in Las Vegas he knew his first job was to save Lyn from a Sea Demon, but the next order of business was to convince her he would someday mean more to her than she'd ever expected. But her stubborn nature and unbendable spirit consumed Deacon...and he had to chase away all the demons real and imagined in order to win her heart.

Sweet Surrender
Book Five in the McKenna Clan Series

Ripped from her family at the top of Infinity Cliff, Kimi McKenna finds herself thrust somewhere into the future. Dark elements threaten to destroy the earth unless Kimi can work together with the white witch to stop the destruction. Confused by her mate's role in the conspiracy, she refuses to acknowledge the connection. But amidst raging fire and attacks on the people she is coming to hold dear, she allows Maska O'keefe into her heart.

Maska O'keefe has loved the beautiful shapeshifter for years. Unable to save her life years ago, he vows to watch over her as he is given a second chance to convince her that even though he is a witch and not a shifter, they are indeed soul mates. Kimi's divided loyalties between her family and the cause she is now a part of will determine their relationship. Only the part she plays as the messiah can bring this to a conclusion in the final battle.

Dakota's Bride
The first book in the Lakota/Pinkerton Series

When Emma St. John received her brother's letter imploring her to escape her stepfather's vengeful scheme and to trust Dakota Barringer with her life, she was willing to chance it. But the handsome, brooding riverboat owner Emma found in Natchez a danger of another kind. For Emma soon found herself surrendering to an unrelenting desire.

Raised by the Sioux when his parents were killed, Dakota had been betrayed once before by a white woman. He wasn't about to trust another, especially one claiming that her stepfather, a powerful U.S. senator, had framed her as a murderess. But he couldn't let Emma's intoxicating effect on him. Now Dakota would risk his very life to protect the innocent beauty who had seduced him with her tender love.

My Angel
The second book in the Lakota/Pinkerton Series

A BEAUTY IN BUCKSKINS
When her father decided to send her to a finishing school back East, Angela Chamberlain refused to be confined to stuffy drawing rooms. Instead, the daring spitfire who could shoot like a man and ride like the wind longed for a life of adventure and romance—and she knew exactly who could give it to her. Devil Blackmoor was a hired gun with a dangerous reputation. But Angela was willing to go to the ends of the earth to capture the handsome devil's heart.

A DEVIL IN DISGUISE
He'd come to America looking for excitement, but Devil Blackmoor got more than he bargained for when he encountered a beautiful rebel who answered his kisses with a wild innocence that touched his very soul. Yet standing between them were more obstacles than either ever dreamed. For Devil had strapped on a gun for the wrong man. And that made Angela his enemy. Now he'll have to choose between his duty and the woman he loves more than life.

The Locket
The third book in the Lakota/Pinkerton Series

The year is 1894. Seeking revenge for crimes against his family, Misha Petrovich follows a path that leads straight to Ariel Cameron's boarding house in Mist Harbor, Oregon. A family heirloom in Ariel's possession leads Misha to believe she is guilty. The locket has been handed down to the oldest girl in the Petrovich family for generations. Ariel is innocent of wrong doing, but her father is not. Misha is torn by his feelings for Ariel and his need for restitution against her father.

Knowing that the relationship between them is fragile, Misha does everything in his power to protect Ariel's father. His efforts are to no avail when her father is shot. Ariel comes to realize Misha's steadfast courage and determination to protect her and her father despite what has happened to his family. Ariel's love and devotion heals Misha's heart.

The Talisman
The fourth book in the Lakota/Pinkerton Series

Running from a marriage that lasted one night, Dr. Moriah McKeown discovers the land she has settled on is coveted by determined and lawless men. Yet the proud young woman who once vowed never to abandon her home has second thoughts when her adopted children are threatened. Her only recourse is to enlist the aid of a dark, dangerous gun for hire.

Haunted by the past and a betrayal he will never forgive, Ian Civanovich uses his fast gun and his reckless courage to forget the faithlessness of a woman in his past. He will trust no female—nor will he rest until the threat hovering over Moriah McKeown is put to rest.

Forever His
The fifth book in the Lakota/Pinkerton Series

Struggling to come to terms with the part she played in Jacob St. John's death, Etta Barringer resigns from Pinkerton Agency and seeks peace and solace in a Rocky Mountain Cabin.

Jacob has vowed to discover the reason Etta has betrayed him, sold him out to his enemy and left him for dead.

Isolated in their cabin, they discover their love for each other and learn to trust. But the trust is shattered when Jacob learns she is married to his sworn enemy; the man who left him in the desert to die.

Allura's Secret
Twelve Dancing Princesses Book One

Allura McClellan is horrified by her father's decision to take out an ad in the Times awarding her to the man strong enough and smart enough to win her hand and uncover her secrets. She's an intelligent young woman who takes great delight in the freedom allotted to her by her father. She's well aware that marriage would effectively curtail the adventures she's shared with her sisters and cousins.

Hunter Gray is nothing like the other men who've arrived to vie for Allura's hand in marriage and everything that goes along with it. However, he is the first to refuse to concede defeat and pursue her despite her attempts to disguise her true appearance. It's her temperament that is of more concern to him than her looks. Hunter has worked all his life with the hope of someday owning his own land. Now that it looks like there's a very real possibility that everything he's ever wanted is within reach nothing is going to deter him – including Miss Allura's disagreeable disposition.

Amorica's Wager
Twelve Dancing Princesses Book Two

Amorica Hepburn was sent to London to find a husband. Finding a man was the last item on her agenda. With her two cousins, Amorica wagers she can dissuade her suitor before the others. Despite her efforts she discovers a chemistry that cannot be denied. Suddenly she is the arrogant man's wife, pledged to a marriage neither desire. But swept off to his ancestral home above the Dover cliffs and into his strong embrace, Amorica is soon possessed by a raging passion for the husband she had vowed to despise...

Damian Andrews couldn't afford to trust the emerald-eyed spitfire who happened upon his secret. Amorica's hatred of all men of his kind only inflames the war that rages between them. Still, he can not control the intense desire his stubborn bride inspires, or make her surrender to his will until he has conquered the headstrong beauty on the battlefield of love...

Ravyn's Marriage of Inconvenience
Twelve Dancing Princesses Book Three

A REGAL BEAUTY

When the duchess decides to wed her to a wastrel and a fop, Ravyn Grahm takes matters into her own hands and declares her engagement to another man. Instead of fessing up and telling her great aunt what she has done, she goes through with the pretense. Ariec Lakeland is the bastard son of an earl and has a dangerous reputation. But Ravyn is willing to do most anything to keep the duchess from discovering the lie.

A DEVIL-MAY-CARE SMUGGLER

He'd bought land in America, looking to put down roots and end his life of adventure, but Ariec Lakeland got more than he bargained for when he encountered a beautiful heiress who made a promise she didn't want to keep. But the promise could not be undone and standing between them were more obstacles than either ever dreamed. Ariec had made plans to spend the rest of his life in America and that was at odds with Ravyn's plan of living in England and running her father's estate. Now, he'll have to choose between his dreams and the woman he loves more than life.

Christel's Sunrise
Twelve Dancing Princesses Book Four

He Made Her An Offer...

Life has thrown Christel McClellan some experiences that could have devastated a less determined woman. Beautiful, self-assured and fiercely independent, she is trying to forget the loss of her stillborn child. But is the child alive?

She Couldn't Deny...

Life is carefree for Ryder MacLaren who loves to see what is on the other side of the sunrise. Laird of Clan MacLaren, he is wealthy, handsome and happily unencumbered...until stunning Christel McClellan enters his life. When he hears her story, he believes the child she thought dead has been sold to a wealthy buyer.

Storm's Passion
Twelve Dancing Princesses Book Five

SHE MADE A PROPOSAL...

Life strikes Storm Graham a shattering blow when she learns her father has bartered her to a man she detests. Storm is beautiful, self–assured and fiercely independent, and refuses to be a pawn in her father's schemes, yet she can find no way out of this bargain made in hell. Going on the offensive she asks the wealthiest man on the eastern coast of England to marry her, never believing she might fall in love.

HE TRIED TO REFUSE...

For Hadden Johnston life has provided everything he ever wanted, including a sanctuary for homeless children. He is wealthy, handsome and happily unencumbered...until stunning Storm Graham marches into his life and proposes a marriage of convenience. Yet this type of marriage to a woman who inflames his senses is far from acceptable. If he's going to be tied down, he will move heaven and earth to have this woman warming his bed.

Gotta Have Fayth
Twelve Dancing Princesses Book Six

A regal beauty with raven hair and piercing blue eyes, Fayth Graham is unwilling to parade herself in front of the wealthy Lords of England during the season. Seeking a means to dissuade any man wishing to wed her, she seeks a way to ruin herself for marriage. When she unexpectedly meets a man with sparkling gray eyes and an infectious grin, she decides this is the man who will keep her from agreeing to obey.

He returned from six months at sea, looking for a few nights of pleasure with a willing lass, but Jarret Kinsley got more than he bargained for when he met a beautiful debutant who responded to his kisses with a wild innocence that touched his heart. Yet the obstacles looming between them might rip them apart. Both had vowed never to marry, so when consequences of their dalliances got in the way, Jarret would have to choose between the life he's always desired and the woman he loves more than life.

Ella's Pleasure
Twelve Dancing Princesses Book Seven

A WHISPER OF PLEASURE

Ella Hepburn was an auburn haired debutant from the harsh Scottish coastline—a wild innocent to be seduced and tamed. A spirited beauty, she captivated Drake Montgomerie's jaded heart—while succumbing to the smoldering desire she felt for her unyielding suitor.

A WHISPER OF DANGER

In Drake Montgomerie's glittering world of money and privilege, young Ella discovered passion and desire could overcome everything she'd been taught to resist—entangling Drake, the heir apparent, in a lethal coil of aristocratic family intrigue. But grave peril would only nurse the sparks of a love that knew no limits and a magnificent ecstasy that would not be denied.

Eveleen's Seduction
Twelve Dancing Princesses Book Eight

A WHISPER OF SEDUCTION

A brutal attack on Eveleen Hepburn's cherished island off the Scottish coastline leaves her shattered and bewildered. Learning a man she once trusted can kill as easily as he can breathe even though the deed saves her life, creates questions that need answers. An innocent beauty, she enchants Logan Maxwell's cynical heart—giving in to the raging passion she feels for her mysterious suitor.

A WHISPER OF INTRIGUE

In Logan's Maxwell's world of espionage and privilege, young Eveleen discovers truths about herself she never expected, and a need for passion and love can overcome all her fears if she learns to accept certain truths. She finds herself entangled in a lethal battle for land that was once owned by French nobility, taken from them during the revolution and sold to Maxwell. But grave peril would unleash the flames of love that simmers, creating a magical union that cannot be refuted.

Tavia's Deception
Twelve Dancing Princesses Book Nine

WHISPERS OF DECEPTION

When her father decides to send her to London for her season, Tavia Hepburn resolves to see the world instead. The raven haired beauty decides to disguise herself as a lad and find employment on a ship bound for Barcelona as a cabin boy. But she never bargains on finding passion and love to a red haired sea captain who rescues her from certain death.

WHISPERS OF MURDER

For James Macmurra, the world is black and white until he meets a young debutante, who turns his world upside down. He's unable to deny Tavia's intoxicating effect on him. In a match tense with obstacles, unwillingness to divulge secrets, and unforeseen peril, irresistible desire and passion grows into undeniable love. James would risk his life to shelter and protect the innocent debutante who seduces him with her sweet love.

Larena's Fascination
Twelve Dancing Princesses Book Ten

WHISPERS OF FASCINATION

Fiery, free spirited Larena Graham never wanted to marry a duke. She is thrilled to be in love with the fourth son of an aristocrat, Gavin Broon. But when it seems Gavin ignores her, she set her sights on politics and bettering human life. Unsuspecting intrigue and a plot against her, she continues her dangerous plans despite Gavin's wishes.

WHISPERS OF TRUST

Gavin has every intention of properly courting the beautiful Larena until he must leave the city in order to put his affairs in order. Returning to London, he finds the woman he means to make his own is embroiled in political protests that could lead to a prison ship. Larena must learn to trust the handsome Scotsman whose most pressing mission is to protect her and keep her from harm.

Tira's Education
Twelve Dancing Princesses Book Eleven

WHISPERS OF EDUCATION

Learning how to build ships is Tira Hepburn's only dream until she meets Jamie Lundin and her world is turned upside down. With her raven black hair and vivid green eyes, she tempts Jamie and pushes him to defy his vows. She never bargains on finding an irrevocable love and a passion to a man who cannot fulfill her dreams despite his burning desire for her.

WHISPERS OF A BARGAIN

Arrogant and self-assured Jamie is brought up short when Tira captures his heart. All his carefully made plans are put to the test when he decides to teach her the art of ship building if she will spend a week with him alone on his ship. He is unable to deny Tira's intoxicating effect on him. When Tira leaves him behind unwilling to live with him without the benefit of marriage, he races after her. Jamie will risk everything to shelter and protect the innocent debutante who seduces him with her sweet love.

Aidan's Love
Twelve Dancing Princesses Book Twelve

Whispers of Love
Aidan McLellan has loved since she first set eyes on him as a young girl. Spontaneous, wild and eager to grow up, Aidan haunts his waking thoughts day and night, insinuating herself into his life. With her fiery red hair and sparkling sapphire eyes, she seizes Blade's heart even while he tries to resist the innocent child until she becomes a woman.

Whispers of Courage
Blade has waited what seems a lifetime to claim the woman who captures his heart as a little girl. Claiming his inheritance before his younger brother takes what is rightfully his, Blade must convince Aidan of his sincerity after years of avoidance and wed her before his father dies so he can return home, securing his rightful place. Everything is put to the test when his life as well as Aidan's is threatened by the man who once called him brother.

Don't Hustle Letty
Good Girls Book One

She's a good girl...

As tempted as Scarlett was, she had too many secrets to let someone enter her world—secrets that would send any reasonable man to the farthest ends of the earth. Bobby was far from reasonable and despite her desperate attempts to hold him at bay, he would not let her past destroy their future. With her escort service, Scarlett used men and their insatiable lust for women to capitalize on the means to survive and prosper. She vowed to never wed, to never put herself in the control of a man.

...nonetheless he has other ideas.

Lord Robert Munroe, with his newly acquired title of marquis goes to Scarlett's for training on how to comport himself. The marquis, better known as Bobby, knows how to pick a pocket as well as get into a bloke's home to steal them blind. What he doesn't know is how to be a gentleman. When he sets his sights on the prim Miss Scarlet, Letty, to his way of thinking, he decides she is the woman he wants to call his wife. He tempts all that she is with sweet words and tender coaxing until she is unable to refuse all he hopes to give her.

Only Caro's Baby
Good Girls Book Two

The Scheme

Genius botanist with theories of inherited traits, Caroline Kenworth desperately wants a baby. Finding a suitable father won't be easy. Caroline's super-intelligence makes her feel pushed aside, unwanted as a woman. As a bluestocking she is determined to spare her child the suffering that plagues her life. Which means she must find someone very special to father her child. A person very...well...ignorant.

The Target.

Duncan Murray, the Earl of Downsberry, well known for his lack of intelligence as well as his rakish ways with women, seems as if he is the flawless man to fulfill the role. His amazing good looks and Scottish brogue are misleading. Caro learns too late that this debonair earl is a lot smarter than she first thought—in addition he's not about to be used then abandoned by any woman who has schemed to steal his sperm.

The Detonation

A dazzling solitary woman whose desires to learn what it would be like to become a mother... A man who is in control of all he does never allowing anyone to usurp his role will settle for nothing less than surrender... Can lust coupled with physical attraction drive two strong-minded yet vulnerable people to a completely unforeseen love?

Twelve Days to Love

When Archer Steele shows up at Calanthe Durand's failing plantation with an alligator over his shoulder, Cali thinks she's never seen a more handsome man. During the war she had to defend herself and her servants from both union and confederate soldiers. Independent and self-sufficient, she vows to never marry.

But Archer Steele has different ideas. The first time Archer sees Cali in town, he feels an instant attraction. He decides he will do everything and anything to convince the beautiful Miss Durand he is worthy of her love. During the weeks leading up to Christmas, he gives her twelve gifts in hopes she will fall in love with him. Yet they are faced with challenges they must overcome before Cali can commit to a marriage.

Door to Heaven

Jessica Lawrence is the stepdaughter of a woman born in the twentieth century transported back in time to the year 1868. An acclaimed suffragette, she raises Jessica to believe in the equality of women. Jess Law believes everything she was taught, and when the time is right she becomes a private investigator. Courageous and impetuous, Jess finds danger in her quest to save all women from white slavery. Her passionate mission results in a wedding to Roc Newman, a man she knows can steal her heart...

Roc can't trust the sapphire-eyed spitfire who invades his home in search of secret papers and knocks him flat with her karate moves. Jessica's refusal to obey his wishes serves to inflame the war between them. Still, he cannot control the intense desire his reluctant bride inspires, or make her surrender her independence, until he has conquered the headstrong beauty on the battlefield of love...

Rebel Heart

HER REBEL SPIRIT DEFIED HIS OUTSIDERS SOUL...She was velvet and silk, eyes the color of a summer storm and amber hair. Victoria DeMontville, because of a promise and a codicil to her father's will, was forced to marry one man to protect her from another. She hated Cameron Savage with a fierce passion. But to hold on to her genetic research and find a cure for the deadly Signe virus, she must pretend to love the enemy at her door, come with weapons of fire to melt her icy heart...

HIS OUTSIDERS TOUCH IGNITED RAGING PASSIONS... He wore a mask, disguised as the Phantom, a true legend come to life. Even as war and debate over new genetic research engulfed them all, he would find his greatest adversary in the beauty who'd branded him an outsider and barbarian, the woman he was born to possess, his soul mate.

Safari Moon

Solo St. John, a wildlife photographer, is preparing for a trip to Alaska. Suddenly, Solo finds women of all sorts invading his privacy, his home and his office, all cooing nonsense words and blatantly throwing themselves at him. Solo doesn't know why, and he has no idea how to rid himself of the persistent women. He finally decides to beg a favor of his best buddy Nyssa Harrington.

In love with Solo for the past ten years and knowing he doesn't return her feelings Nyssa doesn't want to talk to Solo. She knows if she accepts his phone call, she will not be able to resist the temptation to hope again.

Straight to Heaven

Running from demons, Alexandra McMurdie stumbles into Forbidden Ground where up is down and elements of nature are contested. Though a strong independent woman in the twenty-first century' she is unprepared for life in the 1800s. Her first site of the formidable James Lawrence makes her heart skip a beat, giving her cause to reconsider her desperate need to find a way home.

Born with a silver spoon, James' life was torn apart during the War Between the States. Moving west he vows to put the life he once knew in the past. When he discovers a half-frozen woman near Gold Hill, his heart begins to thaw. His love for Alexandra and his need to keep her from a man who has pursued her through time might cost him his life as well as hers.

A Valentine's Anthology

The Lending Library-a fantasy by Christie L. Kraemer
Faeries try to fit into the human world when the forest where they make their home is destroyed by a mysterious enemy.

Chasing Rainbows-a contemporary romance by Genene Valleau
An eccentric aunt, an inventive uncle, a mother who wears poodle skirts, and a brother who wears pearls provide a hilarious backdrop for the courtship of a young woman who yearns for a "normal" family.

The Gift-an historical romance by Christine Young
A man and a woman on opposite sides of the Civil War get a second chance at love after one final battle returns soldiers to their war-torn homes to rebuild their lives.

A St. Patrick's Day Tale
Christine Young, C. L. Kraemer, Genene Valleau

Tumble through time...

...to Ireland in 1817, when tensions are high between Protestants and Catholics and fae people guide the fate of villagers. A lovely Catholic lass stumbles upon the weakly ritual fisticuffing between Irish lads. She falls into the lap of a handsome young Protestant. Family ties, grudges, and two conniving faeries threaten their budding love. But the faeries outsmart themselves when they hijack a time machine that has mysteriously appeared in their forest and are whisked to...

...Eugene, Oregon in the 20th century, amid a property feud between the local faeries and night elves. The conniving faeries from Olde Ireland try to stir up more mischief. However, a warrior gnome convinces the magic folk to control their own destiny, and forces the intruding faeries to take refuge in the time machine again, spinning their way toward...

...A modern day castle in western Oregon. An eccentric inventor is determined to reclaim his wayward time machine and save his beloved wife from her latest misadventure. If only they can travel safely past the black hole...

a May Day Anthology
Christine Young, C. L. Kraemer, Rosemary Indra, Genene Valleau

Highland Miracle — Christine Young
HURTLED THROUGH TIME, Sean Michael Sterling, landed in the midst of a May Day celebration he didn't understand, assuming the role of Laird Sterling.

ILLIGITAMATE CHILD OF NOBILITY, Reagan Douglas searches for a way out of her half brother's house.

Defying the Odds — C.L. Kraemer
The night elves on the hill aren't happy without their magic. They concoct a plan to punish those who were involved in the act that rendered

them almost human. Meanwhile, Uther, the rogue night elf, has returned to woo the Librarian to be his eternal mate.

Love in Bloom — Rosemary Indra
When childhood friends reunite it takes two fairies and a matchmaking daughter to help them admit their true love for each other.

No More Poodle Skirts — Genie Gabriel
After drifting for years in the innocent age of the 1950s, a woman struggles to join today's world by finding a career and a new love, with some help from her zany family.

Once Upon a Christmas Moon
Christine Young, C. L. Kraemer, Genene Valleau

TWELVE DAYS TO LOVE
When Archer Steele shows up at Calanthe Durand's failing plantation with an alligator over his shoulder, Cali thinks she's never seen a more handsome man. During the war she had to defend herself and her servants from both union and confederate soldiers. Independent and self-sufficient, she vows to never marry. But Archer Steele has different ideas. The first time Archer sees Cali in town, he feels an instant attraction. He decides he will do everything and anything to convince the beautiful Miss Durand he is worthy of her love. During the weeks leading up to Christmas, he gives her twelve gifts in hopes she will fall in love with him.

BOOTS AND BLADES
An ancient evil from the old country has arrived in the high desert of Oregon. Gnome children are vanishing then re-appearing, showing various stages of traumatization. Tiamoon, warrior gnome, will put her skills to use alongside Killian, a handsome warrior, also in need of a cause.

CHRISTMAS PAWSIBILITIES

With their world destroyed and their space ship malfunctioning, the dogizens of Planet Canid have little choice but to crash land on Earth. They face tortuous experiments at the hands of the Geeks in Green...or they can trust an eccentric inventor and his zany family to deliver the Canine Queen's puppies and help them celebrate new lives.

VISIT OUR WEBSITE
FOR THE FULL INVENTORY
OF QUALITY BOOKS:
http://www.roguephoenixpress.com

Rogue Phoenix Press

Representing Excellence in Publishing

Quality trade paperbacks and downloads
in multiple formats,
in genres ranging from historical to contemporary romance,
mystery and science fiction.